The Gilded Girl

ALSO BY LORNA COOK

The Forgotten Village

The Forbidden Promise

The Girl from the Island

The Dressmaker's Secret

The Hidden Letters

The Lost Memories

The Secrets of Trelenna House series

The Distant Daughter

The Gilded Girl

Lorna Cook

This is a work of fiction. Names, characters, organizations, places, events, and incidents are either products of the author's imagination or are used fictitiously. Any resemblance to actual persons, living or dead, or actual events is purely coincidental.

Published by Lake Union Publishing, Seattle

www.apub.com

EU Product Safety Contact:
Amazon Media EU S.à r.l.
38, avenue John F. Kennedy, L-1855 Luxembourg
amazonpublishing-gpsr@amazon.com

ISBN-13: 9781662539152
eISBN: 9781662524356

Cover design by The Brewster Project
Cover image: © Resul Muslu © faestock © MartiBstock © Artiste2d3d
© poprock3d © paradigmclub © Litvalifa
© Creative Travel Project / Shutterstock

Printed in the United States of America

For my daughter Alice, who is far too young to read this.
But one day you'll be old enough.
This one's for you.

Chapter 1

Trelenna House, Cornwall

Present Day

Zennor

Zennor walked through the house switching the lights off one by one at the end of the day. She had done it. She had brought two of her siblings home – though why her sister Veryan was still absent and uncommunicative was a worry. And if today's opening day was anything to go by, then Zennor was on the way to saving her family home. As long as nothing else broke or went *expensively* wrong, Trelenna House would be saved for future generations. As she turned down the long corridor leading from her kitchen to the main entry hall, Zennor reflected on how far she'd come in such a short amount of time. Who would have believed just a few months ago that Trelenna – the only place she could ever imagine calling home – would be so full of life and laughter again? But then why was something niggling at the back of her mind?

Portraits of nameless ancestors disappeared into darkness as she turned off the final lamps in the long corridor. Today had been just the start, Zennor reasoned as she paused. It was the first day of what she assumed would be the rest of her life. The first day she'd opened the doors of her beloved ancestral home and welcomed paying visitors. Like her sister Lamorna, nervously running the first tour groups, Zennor had put her *all* into today – into the food offering, into planning and cooking, baking and serving hungry customers. And she had loved every single second of it. It was days like today when Zennor knew this was what she was supposed to be doing. Days like this when she felt her very purpose in life was feeding people, making them happy. And they *had* been happy. It had sent pure joy into her heart watching people pick over the crumbs of cake on their plate, listening to excited youngsters take her handmade children's lunches out into the play area or off for a stomp in the woodland.

But today was only the beginning. After the first full day serving with her catering college friends in the tearoom, Zennor was ready to fall into bed after one final job. The task of closing up Trelenna House for the night fell to her, as it had done ever since her parents had left the UK a few months ago in order to tick off everything on their bucket lists now retirement had beckoned.

In their absence, Zennor had been left running the house – or, as she'd discovered, it was more a case of realising the house had been running *itself* slowly into the ground. Only she hadn't known how bad it was until she'd been left with piles of paperwork and unpaid bills, cracked windows and a house in a state of despair.

Seeing the house falling down around her, Zennor had come to a visceral understanding that the house needed *her* as much as she needed *it*. That it was her job to keep it alive. She was intertwined with this house – her house, her home – far more than any of her older siblings were, and evidently far more than her parents. At one point or another, they had all left. Every single one of them. Only she had stayed.

Her parents had given her permission to *try* to save it however she saw fit, or cut it loose to the highest bidder. For so long, generations of Trelennas had walked these corridors, slept in these rooms, wandered in the parkland. She had been given the opportunity to save it and it wouldn't be *her* – after hundreds of years of family ownership – who would allow the house to fall away, become a hotel or be converted into a block of flats. No, she had been more determined to save this house for future Trelennas than anything she'd ever wanted before.

A heavy responsibility at nearly twenty-two, and Zennor had never felt more grateful when her older sister Lamorna had returned home this summer. Lamorna might've had her own agenda – escaping her failed life on the other side of the world – but despite the decade that separated them, together they had found a way to both save the house and themselves.

Zennor didn't know what she'd have done without Lamorna here to help. And she was so grateful. Especially navigating a gentle refurbishment, followed by a whole host of cost-saving measures and tours set up, all thanks to her clever sister. When Lamorna found the archive room – long since neglected and in a jumble of nonsensical order going back to the early 1800s – the boxes of the house's history had been the answer to their prayers, drawing in a crowd of visitors excited to uncover the forgotten stories of the people who had lived in Trelenna House.

One story in particular had captivated not only Lamorna and her new boyfriend Zach, but social media. The wartime story of Issey Trelenna, a long-forgotten relative, who had been one of the many British women stationed in Singapore in the Second World War. Her desperate attempt to escape had come to a close with an ending no one had expected. Tackling the rest of the archives she hoped would fall to Merry – her brother was a writer and could do with a new project. Plus, if they wanted return visitors, then they'd need to keep things fresh, and there must be plenty of family history in those boxes.

Although Zennor's body was tired, her mind was too wired to sleep, too full of excitement at how well the first day had gone. But they had to do it all again tomorrow and the next day and the ones that followed after that. Before the siblings knew it, the summer season would be over but until then they had every intention of working flat out and making hay while the sun shone.

The house was quiet now, the enthusiastic chatter over the celebratory dinner table between Lamorna and Zach, Zennor and Merry was the rowdiest it had been in a long time. They'd been speaking over each other excitedly, comparing how the first day had gone, which tour had been the most engaged, and which of Zennor's creations had sold out first (scones). But now, at the midnight hour, after the familial buzz had trailed away, forcing everyone to bed, Trelenna was quiet again, exactly as it was when she'd been here, lonely, by herself for all those weeks when her parents were on their round-the-world tour, before Lamorna had drifted home from Singapore, before Zach had found his way into her sister's heart, before Merry had arrived in grief and seeking a new start. It was all so quiet, Zennor mused contentedly, as she finally finished checking that each sash window on the ground floor had the catches in place, that both the back door at the far side of the kitchen and the large wooden front door had all the bolts drawn across, that the lights were out, one by one. Only a table lamp remained lit in the hall at the bottom of the sweeping staircase to guide anyone in the night who was thirsty or peckish downstairs towards the kitchen – her kitchen, the heart of the home.

She stood at the top of the stairs, listening to the house – its creaks and draughts, the grandfather clock as it ticked away noisily. Zennor never normally noticed it when there were people in the house, but now she did and it gave her comfort. Having experienced loneliness, she knew the difference in silence. This quiet echoed back to her that everything was exactly as it should be as she climbed the stairs to bed.

Her room was in darkness and she yawned as she entered, working her way across the rug at the end of her bed towards the lamp on her bedside table. She knew the room's layout in pitch surroundings – but she didn't reach the table or the light. Instead, her foot hit something that wouldn't normally be there and she stumbled, tripping and unable to balance herself before she fell to the floor.

Crying out in pain, Zennor scrabbled for the bedside lamp on all fours, reaching up to flick the switch. The dim bulb brought itself slowly to life and she saw the oversized pile of family archive boxes – brought down from the attic and in need of sorting.

'Oh, for god's sake, Lamorna,' she chastised her sister, who, at the other end of the corridor was probably sleeping soundly, curled up with Zach, and could not possibly hear her. She'd forgotten Lamorna had told her the boxes were there, to keep them out of the way for the tour groups. But then again, Lamorna had mentioned she'd put them under the bed, not haphazardly piled them everywhere.

Surveying the damage she'd caused, she was confronted with a sea of papers, letters and documents spread in every direction.

She sighed and knelt on the floor. She was too tired for this. The possibility of going to bed was so close, but if she didn't pick all this up now, she'd only forget and slide on it when she got up in the morning. And then where would she be? Hospital, probably.

Zennor picked up paper after paper, document after document, letter after letter, intending to put it all back in the boxes. And then something caught her eye, something written in the contents of an old letter, ink faded through time and age, something that she didn't quite understand. She turned back to the start of the letter, sat back against the bed and, trying to make sense of it, Zennor began to read.

It was a handwritten note to a Mrs Davis from a Mrs Trelenna about two members of the household who had *vanished without trace in the middle of the night.* Zennor's curiosity was more than piqued but she also thought she recognised this letter. Hadn't she picked this note up only a few weeks ago when she'd been idly looking through one of the boxes while she and Lamorna had been chatting downstairs? Or was it something else she'd seen weeks ago? Something else about two people leaving? She couldn't remember now. What had it been? And would it be here? The chaos on the floor looked uninviting at this time of night, so Zennor bundled everything up, bar the letter in her hand, and placed it all back haphazardly in the boxes, hoping her sister and Zach hadn't boxed them up in any sort of order.

Unable to see some sections of the letter, Zennor sat on the edge of her bed, inching closer to the table lamp, holding the letter as close as she dared and trying to read the rest of the faded writing under the light. But a lot was nearly invisible after so much time since pen had touched paper. She read the date at the top, faint but present: the year 1869. And then glanced back to the end of the short note where the letter ended.

> *While we find ourselves in this unfortunate position, I should like to look at the advertisement for the new cook before it is sent off. Please make it clear when you compose it that we will correspond with the most recent employer with regard to character reference. That is of utmost importance given what has happened with Miss Pascoe. I do not want anyone young. Or pretty.*

Zennor scoffed. Mrs Trelenna had felt threatened by a young, pretty servant despite the huge divide in wealth and status that would have existed between them. Why was a cook a threat to her? What had happened here? She wished she had the original letter from whoever Mrs Davis was, so she could see exactly what this piecemeal reply related to. She yearned for more detail.

Mrs Trelenna's tone was no nonsense, her eyes on new servants with good references in light of the two who had vanished. Or maybe it wasn't two *servants* who had left suddenly? Two members of the household, it said. That *had* to be servants. Didn't it? What else could it be? Would it be family? No, of course not. But why had they fled and who were they? Why do people flee? And who was this Mrs Trelenna writing in 1869? Obviously an ancestor of Zennor's, but who? Zennor had so many questions from such a small snippet.

Her sister Lamorna had drawn a family tree, of sorts, when they'd been trying to establish who Issey had been to them. But it didn't go further back than Issey Trelenna and her brother Antony, both born in the early 1920s. That had seemed far back enough to be interesting, but this letter had been written by a Trelenna relation from the late 1800s about two other people who had lived in this house long ago. There was so much here but also so little.

'I'm sure I've seen something else about this in these boxes somewhere. I'm *sure* of it,' Zennor said aloud. She put the letter on her bedside table, moved over to the switch by the door and flicked it on, flooding the room with light. Despite her tiredness, her wired mind was committed to this task now. Who were these two people who'd lived in this house and what had they done back in 1869 to prompt them to flee so suddenly? Zennor picked up the first piece of paper from the box and scanned it, then the next and the next, building a pile around her of discarded documents that seemingly had nothing to do with anything. Then she found it, an entire copy of the newspaper *Western Morning News*, folded over so that the words *crime* and *Trelenna House* could be seen clearly stamped on the front-page headline written over a hundred and fifty years ago. As she scanned it, she knew exactly who had fled.

And more importantly, why.

Chapter 2

Trelenna House, Cornwall

Summer 1869

Grace

Grace watched him as he walked through the door to the kitchen. She tried to avoid looking directly at him whenever he visited the servants' hall or kitchen, pretending to immerse herself in the custard she was making. But Laurie Trelenna was too hard to miss with his golden hair and sun-kissed skin. He hadn't always caught her attention. He'd always just been there. First a child, as she had been when she'd joined the household staff. And then all of a sudden, when they'd both grown up, Laurie Trelenna had returned, finished with his education, and one of the most beautiful men she'd ever seen. Grace stood to attention now with the other staff, trying to avoid his gaze, trying not to be caught up in a moment where she smiled at him, he smiled in return, and her world caught flame.

'Sorry, *sorry,*' Laurie called affably, presumably aware that every time he entered the room everyone had to stop what they were doing, greeting him 'sir', attempting to help with his every request, of which he often only had the same one.

'Is my dog back in here again?' Laurie asked the room full of staff, knowing full well the Yorkshire terrier was always in here any chance he could get. Cleaning the floor of any scraps was the dog's chief reason to exist. He was always under Grace's feet, waiting for her to drop the odd morsel accidentally on purpose. 'Gladstone?' Laurie called, scrambling behind Grace's kitchen maid Ethel and the other staff who had long since learned to put up with the daily antics of dog and owner.

'Master Laurie.' Mrs Davis the housekeeper entered the kitchen at speed as she heard one of the family among the servants. 'You know by now, if Gladstone is not with you, he is in here,' she mock-chastised, hands on hips.

'I know, I know. I'm sorry. I really thought I had him by my heel upstairs while I was dressing for dinner but I turned around and he was gone. What's he stolen from the table this evening, Grace?'

'Nothing from me, sir,' Grace replied, forcing her eyes to meet his. 'But Arthur dropped a scrap of mutton for him.'

First footman Arthur paused from loading a dinner tray for the family and gave Grace a disbelieving look that she'd informed on him. But his face fell back into place as Laurie turned his attentions on him.

'I don't blame you, Arthur. It's those eyes. They tell a story of sadness and starvation, but between you all down here and me up there, Gladstone is really the most pampered of dogs.' The terrier was scooped up reluctantly into his owner's arms. 'I'd better take the stairs at the double if I'm to beat Arthur with your wonderful cooking, Grace. What is it tonight?'

'Beef fillet with a brandy sauce, sir,' Grace replied.

'Sounds marvellous.' Laurie walked behind Grace, close to her, stroking her back gently as he passed her. She tried not to draw in an audible breath at his touch. She didn't know how long she could keep doing this, keep pretending there was nothing happening between them, keep avoiding his gaze. Collecting the dog was an act. She knew that. She wondered how many of the other staff knew that too. This was becoming dangerous. Too dangerous.

Arthur resumed stacking the tray but his eyes were on Grace. She had to avoid his chastising glances. She knew he knew, but, so far, had said nothing.

It had been this way since the dog arrived as a stray puppy six months ago. It was Arthur who had found it while walking on his day off, had brought it to the kitchens and the family had come down to admire and examine it. But it was Laurie who showed compassion, hatching a plan with Arthur that it should become the house's dog – as much a part of the servants' life downstairs as the family's upstairs – although Laurie's claim had grown stronger with every passing day. He had named the dog after the new prime minister – saying something about the similarities in facial hair – and the dog slept by the fire in his room at night. But it was Arthur who fed it and watered it, and the dog's draw to the kind footman who gave him scraps in the kitchen equalled his draw to Laurie and the warm fire upstairs.

'The dog must be confused as to who owns it. Every time Gladstone comes down here, he gets carted back upstairs again,' Arthur grumbled when Laurie had gone.

'That's because he's not your dog anymore,' Mrs Davis said.

Arthur placed the last of the consommé dishes on his tray in sequence with the second footman, and they presented their trays to the butler Mr Rowe to inspect before they all followed the butler up the short steps to serve the family dinner. It went like clockwork, as it did every day since Grace had run this kitchen.

She stepped back, knowing there was a few minutes' respite before the main course needed her attention on the range. Ethel the kitchen maid knew to stop the custard from sticking for the Charlotte Russe pudding, and for a moment there was nothing

Grace needed to do. Soon another dinner would have been served to the appreciative Trelenna family, and her day once more would be complete. Until it all began again.

It was never meant to be this way, of course – a woman of her young age, only twenty, being privileged enough to cook for a family such as the Trelennas. Grace had been resolved to a life as a kitchen maid for another few years before she thought she'd try to find a job in a smaller property, perhaps in Truro to a middle-class family who required a plain cook. But when the Trelennas' aging cook Mrs Day had retired, taken her savings and opened a boarding house up-country with her sister, the position had opened. As advertisements were being drawn up for a new cook, Grace had found herself standing in front of Mrs Trelenna and her son Laurie, who had wandered in just after Grace had been summoned to her employer's ornate morning room, bravely making her case as to why she should be considered for the cook's role – a role she could do as easily as breathing. She *had* been doing it. Cooking came so naturally to her that Mrs Day had happily given Grace anything she could take on – glad to step back and let her younger apprentice learn on the job. That sort of training had been invaluable and Grace, with her natural flair for intuitive cooking, had excelled.

It was the son who had asked more questions than his mother – how had Grace found herself employed in their kitchens rather than as one of the many housemaids ('because I love feeding people, making them happy, sir. I always have'); where she was from ('Redruth, sir'); what she enjoyed cooking best ('Everything, sir'); and least ('Offal, sir').

Laurie had made a sickened face at that response. 'Oh my goodness. We don't eat that, do we? How has old Day got that past me? She must season it well. I feel quite sick at the thought.'

Grace had let a laugh escape. 'No, you don't eat it, sir. But we have it in the servants' hall from time to time.' She didn't know it, but it would be that laugh that captivated Laurie Trelenna, he had told her later, in the snatches of private moments.

'Grace, will you promise me faithfully that if my mother agrees to promote you to the position of cook that you will never, ever serve me offal, no matter how well it's seasoned? And I would also like to request that stewed prunes and creamed rice is halted too. I am twenty-one and cannot be expected to put up with nursery food any longer,' he said with a smile.

Grace had tried not to laugh again.

'For goodness' sake, Laurie,' Mrs Trelenna had reprimanded her son. 'Am I allowed to ask a question?' She turned back to Grace. 'Perhaps you might agree to a trial?'

Unwilling to let the chance slip through her fingers, Grace had answered in the affirmative. 'I'd like that very much, Mrs Trelenna. Thank you for the opportunity. I'll show you what I can do.'

Don't send me away. I have nowhere else to go.

'You are very young to be a cook.' The older woman tapped her fingers on the surface of her writing desk. 'But Mrs Day thinks you are able. And she should know. She's been with the family thirty years, but the years move forward. Perhaps, Grace, as my son has hinted, it might be nice if some of the dishes you served moved with the times too. If you understand my meaning. Is that something you can do?'

Grace nodded, smiled, tried not to let her enthusiasm run away with her. She had studied Mrs Beeton, Eliza Acton, Charles Elmé Francatelli, devoured their writings, analysed every step of every recipe they'd ever written. She'd been perfecting her own recipes in her mind's eye too. She just needed the chance to create, to prove herself. The chance was astonishingly within her reach.

'Very well,' Mrs Trelenna said decisively, interrupting her son who had piped up again. 'If only to stop your incessant questioning, Laurie. A trial. Let us see what you can do, Grace. Impress us.'

Her new wages had been agreed at forty pounds a year, a tremendous rise to her previous pay of twenty-four pounds, and she'd been dismissed, back to the kitchen.

Her kitchen now.

◆ ◆ ◆

It had started with a touch, as Laurie's hand accidentally brushed hers when they were stroking the terrier together. It happened that very day Arthur found the dog, bringing him to the kitchen – those two events forever linked in Grace's mind, lacing their way into the fabric of rare excitement of life downstairs. As Laurie's hand and hers had met on the dog's ragged fur, it was she who had sprung back, not him. But his dark eyes when they met hers said he'd felt it too, that *something* that dared not exist between a servant and a member of the family. He'd blinked, glanced away. And then a week later he'd turned in church and looked at her, just for a moment, and it had been she who'd dropped her gaze first.

Coming to see the dog each time was a ruse, she felt sure of it, accidentally obliging the few staff in the adjoining servants' hall to stand and greet him formally, forcing them from their work. 'I just came to see how the dog's getting on,' Laurie had said days later as he passed through into the kitchen. 'Has he a name yet?'

'I don't believe so, sir,' Grace had replied, rolling out shortcrust pastry. The dog was looking up at her hopefully from his position under the table. 'Arthur still thinks someone will be wanting him, sir, although it's been two weeks, so I have my doubts.'

'I have my doubts too. Don't you think he looks like the prime minister?'

'I don't think he does at all,' Grace had said thoughtfully, forgetting to add *sir* to the end of her comment. 'I think he looks like a dog.'

'Do you think Arthur would mind if we named him?'

'We, sir?'

'You and I. Let's name him. Shall we? Any ideas?'

'I don't know, sir. We've just been calling him *dog*.'

'You can't keep calling him *that*. It's . . . inhumane.'

'He's not human. He's a dog,' Grace insisted.

Laurie smiled. 'Let's call him William Gladstone . . . you and I, shall we? He looks just like him.'

Grace had laughed. 'If you like, sir.' What was this all about? She had no idea but she liked the way Laurie Trelenna brightened the place up.

'I want *you* to like the name, Grace. I assume you're the one finding him scraps to eat, so you should choose.'

'I feel Arthur should choose his name, if the dog is allowed to stay. He's the one who found him, rescued him.'

'Of course the dog must stay,' Laurie said. 'Mother and Father won't object. They're forever telling me to make my own decisions and recognise my status as *son and heir*. Well, here it is. First decision made since we had our little talk and it's that the dog can stay. Can't you?' He leaned down and scratched the terrier behind both ears. 'He's no trouble, is he, William Gladstone?'

'We're settled on that name, are we?' Grace said archly, wondering at her own daring.

'We are. You and I have named him.'

She felt a thrill run through her, and before she could stop herself said, 'Then can we drop the William? It's such a mouthful, all that. Just Gladstone.'

'As the lady wishes,' Laurie had said, eyes bright, and Grace felt herself colour. She wasn't a lady. She was a servant, but she knew what he meant.

'I must get on, sir.' She bustled about, flouring the rolling pin and starting on the next round of pastry dough, hoping he attributed her flush to the activity and not his words.

'Have I upset you? I'm sorry if so.'

'No, you haven't,' she said honestly. She'd upset herself. 'But I must get on. There's a cold ham in the larder if you want to feed Gladstone a little something before you go. I can fetch it.'

'I can fetch it. I remember where the larder is. Many a time Mrs Day let me raid it when I was a boy. I believe it stopped being endearing around the time I turned sixteen.'

Grace couldn't imagine a time when Laurie Trelenna would cease to be endearing.

'If I came to see you again,' Laurie said, dropping his voice, aware of the servants round the table in the adjoining room. 'Would you mind?'

Grace's mouth had fallen open, unable to answer for disbelief.

'Of course, you can hardly answer that question without concern, can you? Might I ask you a different question, in that case?' His eyes cast behind him quickly and then fixed on hers. 'Grace . . . might I walk with you one day?'

She was too surprised to answer anything, but nodded.

'Really?' he asked hopefully. 'Do you mean it? Would you like that as much as I would?'

'I . . . Yes.'

An elated smile lifted into place. 'When is your next afternoon off?'

'Sunday,' she said. 'After church.'

They both heard the tread outside the open door.

'Where can I meet you?' Laurie whispered quickly, moving a fraction closer. 'And when?'

She thought of her favourite spot on her favourite walk. 'By the first elms along the south wood path. One o'clock.'

'I'll be there,' he said. 'And, Grace, my intentions are honourable. You do know that, don't you?'

'Yes,' she whispered truthfully, just as Ethel entered the room with a heavy milk pail.

'Let me help you with that.' Laurie moved away swiftly, lifting the pail into place with a cheerful smile. Then he left them to it, leaving Grace wondering if what had happened could possibly be real.

Chapter 3

Nothing mattered to Grace more in this world than her job. Nothing. Without it, she'd be destitute. She'd found her first – and so far *only* – job as a servant in much the same way any young girl without hope or purpose, means or family did: through charity. Grace's mother had died of consumption when she was only two, and ten years later her father had followed. And so Grace credited the vicar of Trelenna with finding her a place at the house and had spent the best part of a decade in this kitchen, proving to herself and to the family that they had not made a mistake saving her from the workhouse. Her tiny servants' room at the top of the house that she'd shared with a housemaid had little touches she'd never have dreamed of: a nightstand and mirror, a rug to stave off the chill of the floor, cold even in summer. And as cook, no longer *Grace* but newly christened Miss Pascoe to show her elevation, she'd been given a room to herself. She was taken care of here, well fed. And so walking with Laurie Trelenna . . . didn't that threaten to overturn what she'd built? She toyed with the idea for hours as the time loomed closer. But with no way of sending a message to him that wouldn't draw attention, she had no choice but to go through with it after church, wandering through to her favourite spot in the woods, unsure if she wanted him to arrive or not.

When he appeared through the trees, she felt like she had swallowed the stars.

'I realise this must feel very unusual,' Laurie said, standing close enough she could almost feel the heat from his skin. They both knew it was more than just unusual. She felt sordid, meeting him like this. She was putting her reputation and her job on the line. But try as she might, since his return from university, she couldn't put him out of her mind. One walk, that's all it would be.

'I thought you might not be here,' Grace revealed.

'I thought you might not come,' he said at the same time. It prompted them both to smile awkwardly as she pulled her shawl around her. Despite the relatively balmy weather, the trees had forged a canopy of leaves, shielding the sun from the chilly woods.

'Are you cold? Would you like my jacket?' he offered.

'No,' she said hurriedly. 'No, thank you.' It was unimaginable that he would shed a layer for her. As if she wasn't taking the most outrageous risk being here, they couldn't add anything else into the mix. What if someone should see them?

Seeming to catch her concern, he said, 'We aren't doing anything wrong, meeting like this. We are just going for a walk and some conversation. But if you prefer, if you're worried about being alone with me, I won't be offended if you'd rather leave. I'll understand and no more will be said about the matter, I promise.'

The look of sadness on his face as he said it made her waver. 'I am worried. I'd be a fool not to be. But I'm not worried about being alone with you. I'm worried what others might think if they see us. I'm just a servant and . . .' She wasn't sure if it was worth continuing. He knew. He must know.

He seemed to think about this for so long that Grace didn't know if she should say something else to fill the silence until he said, 'I wonder if there will come a time when someone who lives in a house like this and someone who works in it will be able to be friends without judgement from others.'

'Not in our lifetime, I'm sure,' she replied.

'It seemed easier when I was a child, being in the kitchen. No one stood to attention then when I entered.'

'I don't really remember much about you as a child,' she confessed.

'I ate a lot between meals. Hence why I was in the kitchen a lot. Mrs Day's cakes . . .' He sighed.

She laughed. He was easy to like. 'She makes a better malt loaf than me.'

'You'll have to make one, so I can compare. But I'll bet yours are better. The meals coming out of the kitchen now are beyond anything I've eaten at Trelenna before. You're really an incredible cook, Grace. Sorry, Miss Pascoe,' he corrected.

'Thank you.' She glanced away, embarrassed.

'Mother didn't know what to do about that, you know. She had to seek advice from Mrs Davis about what she should call you. The norm is to address you as Mrs but you are so young. It made me wonder if ever an unmarried young woman had been a cook before. Are you the first in history, do you think?'

'Hardly,' Grace replied, trying not to laugh. 'But perhaps in a house like this it's a little unusual to have one so young.'

So far neither of them had moved, the promised walk long forgotten as they occupied the hinterland between saying goodbye out of propriety's sake or committing to a walk together. Neither direction felt like the right one. Standing still seemed much safer.

'How old are you, if I may ask?'

'Twenty,' Grace replied. 'How old are you?'

'A year older than you. The age to enter the world and find out where my calling is. Apparently.'

'And where is it?' she enquired.

'I'm afraid I don't know yet. Whatever my calling is, it has not called.' He smiled, looked at the ground, but the sadness in his eyes was evident as he looked back at her. 'I envy you, you know. You love what you do, no?'

'I do, yes.'

'I could tell when you were talking with my mother. I have nothing I love, nothing I can do well enough that makes me want to do it. I suppose I'll be heralded into trying to keep this house and all its land going and . . . who knows after that? Who knows if there will *be* an "after that"?'

'You're very lucky to have a house like this,' Grace pointed out gently.

'I know. I must sound very ungrateful.'

'Not ungrateful,' she said honestly. 'Perhaps a bit lost.'

His eyes met hers. 'Lost? Do you really think so?'

She panicked at her rudeness. 'Perhaps I meant *unsure.*'

'You might have been right the first time,' he said with a nod. 'I'm unsure what my parents want for me is what I want for myself.'

'And what is that, sir?'

He winced. 'You don't have to call me sir. Not here. Not like this.'

'I do,' she said sternly.

He nodded, sighed again but didn't answer the question. Perhaps he was lost after all.

'Grace . . . sorry, Miss Pascoe – I wonder if we might be able to be friends.'

She laughed at the absurdity of it. 'Friends?'

He looked taken aback. 'Yes, I enjoy your company and I hope you enjoy mine, although you look more startled I've asked to be your friend than you were when I asked you on a walk.'

Why did he keep making her laugh?

'And how do you think we might be able to be friends, sir? How do you think it's achievable? Are we going to form a friendship in the kitchen with everyone else watching and talking and wondering? Or are we to become friends here, in the woods on Sundays.'

'The Sunday suggestion feels least problematic.'

'Oh my word.' She oozed exasperation, which made him chuckle.

Behind her a branch cracked. Both of their heads whipped around to find the cause of the noise, but there was nothing there. 'It's probably a squirrel in the undergrowth,' he said.

'I've been gone too long,' she replied, her heart suddenly in her throat. 'I must go.'

'Already?' He stepped forward, a small smile that made her wish she could stay. 'I'm sorry to see you go. We didn't even walk anywhere.'

'Next time,' she said and then wished she hadn't.

'Next time? Do you mean it? Will there be a next time?'

'Against my better judgement, sir.'

Laurie looked elated. 'Next Sunday? Here? At the same time?'

'But not for long. Goodbye, sir,' she replied, feeling a bubble of something rise within her. She refused to feel ashamed, she wouldn't. As he had pointed out, they hadn't even had their walk and it wasn't as if one walk would change the direction of the rest of her life.

But it did, and so much for the better. Because over the next eight weeks, every Sunday afternoon Laurie met her at one o'clock in the south wood and they strolled for an hour.

Grace knew she was walking a dangerous line but she couldn't stop herself walking with him. She enjoyed his company, his easy demeanour, his openness. He seemed genuinely at ease with her, and after allowing herself to open up just a tiny bit to him she felt much more comfortable with him than she'd ever felt with anyone.

They had become enthralled by each other, the two of them walking in the wood, under a canopy of trees, a world all their own. It had taken three weeks before, at his earnest encouragement, she had completely dropped the 'sir' from the end of her sentences. Although she couldn't bring herself to call him Laurie. Until today, their eighth Sunday.

'Why do I feel so free when I'm with you?' he asked as they took their favourite path down towards the stream that ran through the woods and eventually led to the sea.

'I feel it too,' she said. She was falling in love, she knew she was, despite having never felt anything like this before.

'May I hold your hand?'

Her heart jumped ecstatically, and she let out an, 'Oh.'

'Is that a yes?' He spoke quietly, reverently, almost as if they were on a precipice of something.

Her lips became dry. 'Yes,' she replied quietly, allowing her gloved hand to be held in his.

'My mother expects a lot of me and she expects it soon. My father too. They want me to marry,' he said despondently as they walked hand in hand, her own feeling as if every nerve ending was on fire. 'And I don't know how to stop it. How to stop *them*.'

She glanced down at their entwined hands and then up at his forlorn expression.

'They don't see the world as I do,' he continued as they strolled. 'They don't see beauty in anything around them other than the possessions they have. Their life is for gathering things – houses, art, jewellery. Mine isn't like that. I've never wanted that. Never needed that. But I can't tell them. I can't tell them *that*. Yet, I can't help the way I feel. If I could throw this all off and hand it to someone else, I would.'

'The house?' Grace asked.

'And the responsibility too. I hate all of it. I think I was born in the wrong time.'

'When would suit you best, sir?' she asked, laughing softly.

He looked at her. 'Your laugh has quickly become my favourite sound, and it's Laurie, not sir.'

Grace closed her eyes for a moment then opened them slowly. 'I'm finding all this very difficult. It's so confusing.'

'I know,' he said. 'I didn't expect to feel this for . . .'

'For a servant?' she queried. Although he'd never expressed what the feeling was, she wondered if he was falling for her the way she was for him. They had not said it, not dared.

'I wasn't going to say that. I was going to say *for a girl like you.* You are perfection and you know I don't care about whether you're a cook or a kitchen maid, housekeeper or, or . . .' he said, grasping for a word, 'or chambermaid. Being a chambermaid might be easier for us though. To have you in my bedroom every morning making a fire would please me no end. Not the fire bit, just the . . .' He stopped.

'The bedroom bit?' she murmured in shock.

'Grace, I've said the wrong thing. My intentions are honourable. You must know that by now. I'm sorry. I don't want you in my bedroom. Not until we are married.'

'What?' she exclaimed louder than she'd intended, her mind feeling thick, as if it had been stuffed with cotton.

'My word, I'm suddenly saying all the wrong things.' And then he looked directly at her, his hand tightening. 'No, I'm not. I'm not saying the wrong things at all. Grace—'

'No,' she warned immediately.

'No? But you don't know what I'm going to ask.'

'I've got an idea,' she said. 'And you can't say it. You can't ask it. You can't even think it.'

'What?' It was his turn to show surprise. 'I can't even think it? Why not? And why can't I ask it? What do you think I intend to do? Get to know you, fall in love with you and then . . . what . . . forget about you?'

He had said it. He loved her. 'What else *can* we do? You are . . . *you*. You are Laurie Trelenna and I *cook* for you.'

'Being a servant isn't who you are,' he snapped as they walked further into the woods. 'You are Grace and you are magnificent and you have enchanted me. You have shown me a different sort of world.'

'One in which we stroll in the woods in secret every week because that's all we can do.'

'It's not enough,' he said in frustration. 'How can this ever be enough? I am a different sort of person when I'm with you. I'm more hopeful of what my life holds in store when I'm with you. Don't you feel the same about me?'

'I don't know,' she said, still holding herself back. No good would come of telling him how he made her feel, she knew it. Everyone in the world knew that this situation, servant and master, never ended well.

But he had been as good as his word. He hadn't tried to take advantage, press his position as her superior. He had held her hand. And it was – excruciatingly – not enough. None of it was enough.

'I love you,' he said again.

He took her breath away but she knew they had to stop this. 'Oh Laurie, you *can't*.'

He gave a surprised laugh. 'Of course I can. It's been two months of this. I can't make the feeling of wanting to be with you stop. I can't *force* it away. I thought it would, between our walks, but it has intensified into a burning feeling of desperate love. It's why I'm always in the kitchen during the week. I can't wait until

Sunday now. Sunday isn't enough. None of it's enough. I can't keep away from you. You must see that.'

'I do see it,' she cried. 'And I don't want you to keep away. But you can't be with me. Not really. This is just for now. It can only be here. And one day when you do as your parents ask, when you find someone of your class, and your engagement is announced, I'll be far from here because I'll have to be. Because I won't be able to see you, cook for you and your *wife.* I just won't. It will be too much for me.'

He pulled her towards him. 'Please, Grace, don't say that. None of that will happen because I won't let it. I *won't* fall in love with anyone else and I *won't* marry. Over these past few weeks it is you and only you.'

Tears formed in her eyes. Eight blissful afternoons with Laurie Trelenna and snatched moments in the kitchens had pushed them in a direction from which they had to find their way back.

'Laurie,' she said desperately, but she couldn't say any more as Laurie's lips touched hers for the first time, and she felt every single worry of the past eight weeks melt entirely away, swept up as she was in the intensity of his kiss.

'I love you,' he said when he pulled back, looked at her, stroked her face. 'Be with me.'

'How?' she wailed. 'We can't.'

'We can,' he said with determination. 'We can. I don't know how yet but we can. We can . . . leave this place, run away together.'

'Laurie, you're mad.'

'I'm not. I'm entirely sane, although perhaps driven a little *insane* by being in love with a woman I know my parents will never let me have. But I *can* have you and you can have me, if you want it. I can find a way for us. Just tell me you want it. Tell me you love me too.'

The feeling of love burned deeply in her heart. How could it not?

'I do,' she cried. 'I do love you and I do want it, but it's a dream. It can't be real.'

'It *can* be real,' he said, determination and joy radiating behind his eyes. He stopped, calming himself and thinking. 'We can go away together, build a new life, somewhere else, a different country where no one knows who either of us are.'

His eyes searched hers.

'No one knows who I am anywhere else but *here*,' Grace said, playing along with Laurie's plan that she knew could not possibly come to fruition.

'So you're not against this idea?' he asked seriously.

She took a breath and allowed herself to dream, just that little bit more. 'I'm not against the idea, Laurie. I love you.'

He sighed with relief. 'In which case, let's not rush things. I don't want to scare you off. But I will make this happen if you want it as much as I do. I love you and I *will* marry you, Grace. And we will have children and we will live in a warm, tropical, perfect climate, far from here and we will be together until the very end of our lives. And it will be the best decision either of us made. Say yes. Say you'll marry me if I can make this happen.'

Her eyes met his own desperately searching ones. 'Laurie Trelenna, you are mad.'

'I know. But I'm madly in love too.' He sank down on one knee in the damp woods, muddying his trousers, his eyes promising the world. 'Grace Pascoe, will you marry me?'

Was this real? Was this really happening? Any moment now she'd wake to realise none of it had been real. With wide eyes she nodded at him, unsure if she was asleep or awake, unsure if she'd really agreed to his proposal.

'Oh Grace,' he cried happily, picking her up and spinning her around in the woodland glade. 'You have made me the happiest man alive.'

'Happy until your family disown you,' she pointed out, breathlessly. Were they really doing this? It felt incomprehensible that she would be married to Laurie Trelenna.

'I won't care,' he said, beaming, setting her down. 'Honestly. I don't want this life here like this. No real sort of life awaits me here, marrying a woman for money. And being stuck in this monolith of a house for the rest of my days, wishing I'd married you instead of having someone forced upon me. I want to marry a woman for love. I want to marry *you*. And I am not going to live a life of regret by not acting on how I feel – how you feel too, yes?' he asked desperately, as if he needed confirmation from her that this could be their life, their love.

'Yes,' she said. 'But I want to be sensible about this. Let's please not rush.'

'Alright,' he said in a hurry, his eyes still glowing. 'Whatever you want. Whenever you want.'

She breathed in, exhaled slowly. She must be sensible. She *must* be. 'I want you to go away and think about this. And I want you to be sure. Then, next Sunday, I'll see you here as usual and if you really mean it, we'll talk about it again.'

'Then you'll let me plan our life together?'

She tried not to be wrapped up in his excitement, forced herself to slow everything down. 'Yes, alright,' she said in mock exhaustion, trying not to laugh with shared elation. 'Then and only then, when I know you're not acting on impulse. Then . . . I'll let you plan our life together. Do we have a deal?'

'It's a deal, Miss Pascoe,' he said formally, trying to keep a straight face. 'And until then, you can think about where you would like to go. Where you would like to see first. We can travel the world.' He dipped his head to kiss her, the second kiss he'd dared.

'Oh, Laurie.' It seemed to sigh out of her.

'Do you mind that I keep kissing you?'

'No,' she said, feeling as if she was floating. 'No, I don't mind.'

'May I kiss you again?'

She nodded, whispered, 'Yes.'

He did, and on the back of his proposal it felt otherworldly, unreal. She loved him. The man she loved was kissing her, proposing to her, talking to her of their combined futures. 'We can go anywhere' – a kiss – 'you' – another kiss – 'want.'

She looked into his dark eyes, so true, at the way they crinkled at the edges slightly as he smiled. She trusted him, believed him.

'I'll think about it while *you're* thinking about it,' she said eventually, touching his face, falling a bit more in love with him with every passing minute.

'And I'll see you next Sunday, here, at one o'clock, as usual,' he replied.

'Unless you sneak into the kitchen before that pretending to visit Gladstone.'

'Oh, I shall be doing that too. But it's not the same as this. Nothing could ever be the same as this,' he said as he gave her yet another addictive kiss, both of them eventually pulling away reluctantly. Laurie whispered goodbye and she watched him depart the glade in a different direction to the one he'd arrived from, leaving her behind him by a few minutes as usual, both attempting to avoid suspicion. So far, in all these weeks it had worked. She held her fingers to her lips, feeling his lips imprinted there. Then she too left, walking back in the direction of the kitchen door – emerging from the trodden path out of the wood, out of the shade of the trees, out of the darkness and into the light.

Chapter 4

Over the course of the following week, Grace tried to focus on her work but it was near impossible. Lovesickness was making her stupid, forcing her into silly mistakes – burning sauces or overcooking her usually perfect soft-boiled eggs. She needed to carry on as if nothing had altered, because if Laurie changed his mind, she had to continue in this job until she found another and there were precious few kitchens like this one. Now was not the time to let herself or the Trelenna family down. The thought of Laurie letting *her* down, however, filled her with fear. Because she believed him, that he wanted to live a different life with her. And she loved him. She had fallen the way he had. Although Grace liked to think she was a realist to her core, always holding a tiny piece of herself back from Laurie, not giving in to his immediate whim that they run away, making him think about it, not falling headlong into the plan the way he had. Impetuous, that's what he was, the kind of man who fell in love quickly and fell hard. She could tell that about him. And she hadn't thought she was that way inclined. But it turned out she was too. Perhaps they were perfectly matched.

If she gave him everything, all of her heart, and he let her down, she wouldn't be able to face it. It would be too hard for her to see him happy with someone else, someone more refined, more elegant than her, who didn't wear a cook's uniform, who didn't have short-clipped nails so pastry didn't get caught underneath them.

She was inferior to him in this house, and she felt it. But he had never once made her feel it. It was all of her own doing. That, and society. Of which Laurie said they need never be a part of.

She was making a cheese soufflé for the family's lunch, staring mindlessly at the pile of grated Parmesan, and adding it bit by bit as she stirred. She loved how any slightly more unusual recipe she suggested was immediately accepted by the family and she loved exploring flavours, working her way through a variety of cheeses and finding the only one that really made the soufflé light enough.

Arthur wandered into the kitchen with Gladstone at his heel. 'He's been following me around while I work upstairs,' he said, hovering over the pile of cheese. 'Can I give him some of this?'

Grace nodded. 'A bit.'

'I know what you're doing,' Arthur said.

'Cheese soufflé,' Grace replied absently, focusing on stirring the mixture in front of her.

'That's not what I meant. I know what you're doing with *him*.' He glanced to the ceiling and then back to her.

Grace stopped stirring. 'Don't be ridiculous.'

'You're not denying it. And I'm not going to tell you off. But I've seen the way he looks at you and I've seen the way you look at him. I want you to know I know. And if I've spotted it, it won't be long before others do too. You're playing a dangerous game, Grace. In all the years I've known you, you've never once done anything this stupid before.'

She wanted to burst out with anger, deny everything, chastise him for calling her stupid. But she'd known Arthur for years, too long for pretence. She glanced around to see the corridor was clear. 'I'm leaving,' she whispered.

He looked genuinely aghast. 'Are you being thrown out? Are you having a child?'

'Of course not. Neither of those things. He would never. He hasn't . . .'

'Then why are you leaving?'

'We're leaving together. He's asked me to marry him.'

Arthur's mouth dropped open.

'He's serious,' Grace continued, ducking her head to hide her smile. 'I've made him think about it. For a week. He can take back his offer of marriage and we go on as before, nothing to each other. Or if he still wants to give everything up for me, we're leaving.'

Arthur's shock was still written all over his face. 'Is that what he'd have to do? Give everything up?'

Grace glanced around again, to check they weren't being overheard. She spoke quietly. 'Yes, of course. His suggestion. Not mine. It's too much to ask of him so I would never make him do it. The decision is solely his.'

She watched Arthur swallow. 'When? When are you leaving?'

'I don't know. But I do know that Laurie wants—'

'Laurie,' Arthur mumbled as if it was incomprehensible she should be on first-name terms. It *was* incomprehensible. All of it was.

'Grace, be careful, won't you? None of this sits right with me.'

'I know. I am being careful, don't worry.'

'If he leaves you high and dry—'

'He won't,' Grace promised, her eyes meeting his.

'You don't know that,' Arthur replied. 'It happened to my mother and she didn't think it would happen to her.'

Grace blinked. 'What do you mean?'

'What do you think I mean? My mother was a servant at a big house in Devon. She didn't fight off the attention, believed the promises she was told, so my grandfather told me. Whatever those empty promises may have been, it's how I came to be here. Sent away to my grandparents through the shame, and then from there too. I was unwanted all round, it's how I ended up hall boy here so young. I was sent away.'

'I didn't know that,' Grace said.

'And why would you, but I'm living proof that young pretty girls who don't tell their betters to leave them alone end up bringing children into the world who no one wants. And then terrible things happen to the pretty girls too.'

Grace blinked in surprise.

'You'll be sent away. You'll end up in the workhouse. You don't have any parents. Where will you go?'

She shook her head. Nowhere. She had nowhere. Trelenna was her home. She'd been happy here.

'Don't be a fool, Grace. There's still time to stop this if it hasn't gone as far as all that.'

'It hasn't,' she muttered.

The butler, Mr Rowe, strode in through the kitchen door. 'Is the family's luncheon ready?'

Grace swallowed, her mouth so dry she could barely answer. 'Yes. The devilled eggs are ready and the . . .' What was she making? She'd forgotten. 'The . . . cheese soufflé is not far behind. Ethel is looking after both the salmon and the pudding today, and she's nearly there too.'

'Are you alright?' Mr Rowe asked her with narrowed eyes. He missed nothing.

Grace forced her mouth into a smile. 'Yes, perfectly, thank you.'

He nodded as if he didn't believe her and moved off while Grace put the soufflé in the range. She had twenty minutes while they ate their first course until the soufflé needed removing and serving immediately. Arthur was assembling the first course on to his tray and caught her eye with worry, but she looked away.

Ethel arrived with a cream sauce for the pudding about which she wanted Grace's approval. Grace tasted it. 'Well done, Ethel. We'll make a cook of you yet.' She tried to act as normally as possible, but couldn't stop herself feeling rattled by Arthur's words. She checked the clock. 'At a quarter to one you need to get the soufflés out, give the dishes a little wobble and decide if they're set or not.'

Ethel looked frightened.

'Don't give me that face,' Grace replied gently. 'You've watched me do it so often, I know I can trust you. But you can show me, if you're still worried.'

Ethel started tidying up Grace's detritus and Gladstone was fed a bit more leftover cheese. There was not a lot about being a kitchen maid Grace missed but she especially didn't miss the tidying up, the pan scrubbing, the range blacking first thing in the morning. Her life was easier now, more enjoyable. And she might just be about to give it all up for Laurie. Because she loved him.

'I didn't know any of that about your parentage,' Grace said later that evening when Arthur was standing outside the back door, smoking one of his rolled cigarettes.

He started to walk over the cobbles, towards the wall on the far side that shielded the comings and goings of the servants' entrance from the gardens.

'I don't go telling people but, Grace, I told you. Don't abuse my trust with that information. No one needs to know.'

'I would never.' The two of them had become as friendly as two people the same age in a house of mostly older staff could be over the years since Grace had ended up at Trelenna. Grace, who had learned to read and write with the reverend's wife at Sunday school before both her parents had died and her world had shattered, had taught Arthur over many late nights when the tallow candles burned down in the servants' hall. The chambermaids and kitchen maid were much younger than both of them and spent most of their time giggling over articles in old copies of Mrs Trelenna's periodicals that were sent down months after she'd finished with them. Despite Grace and Arthur being nearabout the same age, there had never been any hint of a romance between them. Instead, what bound them together was mutual respect, a shared camaraderie and gratefulness they had jobs with a family who treated them well.

Gladstone bounded out to find Arthur, who greeted the dog and bent down to scratch his ears. 'I am cross that he prefers being upstairs with them rather than down here with me.'

'He's here now,' Grace pointed out.

'I'm the one who found him. I'm the one who saved him. He's my dog, only he's been given a silly name and now he's not mine anymore. The man who's trying to take my only proper friend away is going to take my dog too.'

Grace was taken aback as sympathy flooded her. Poor Arthur. Until today she'd had no idea about Arthur's unfortunate start in life.

She dropped down and scratched Gladstone behind the other ear. Gladstone's deep-brown eyes closed in pleasure. 'He is still your dog,' Grace said as her gaze connected with Arthur's. 'And we won't take him when we go.'

'If you do, I'll have nothing again.'

'Arthur. The dog stays here with you. And please, when we eventually do go, keep our secret as long as you can?'

'When you've upped and gone, I'll feign ignorance. I cannot imagine what Mrs Trelenna will do when she finds out her only son has run away with the cook. She'll blame you, you know that, don't you? They think the sun shines out of his—'

Grace thwacked him on his arm.

'Ow,' he said, laughing, then stood, stubbed his cigarette out on the cobbles under his feet. 'I'll miss you,' he said simply.

'I'll miss you too.' Grace rose and threaded her arm through his, resting there so lightly, before the two of them returned to the kitchen.

Chapter 5

Laurie met her in the woods on Sunday afternoon. There had been a few glances between them in the kitchen when he continued to visit Gladstone, and she could tell the inability to touch each other, hold each other, pained him as much as it did her. She could see it in his eyes when he looked at her, never for too long. They were careful. Although not careful enough if Arthur had noticed.

'It's settled,' Laurie exclaimed excitedly. 'I've got enough to get us started with a new life abroad. And then after that I'll have to wait for my trust to release further funds in a year's time. But we'll have more than enough to live on until then. Tell me you still want this?' Laurie asked hopefully.

She looked into his dark eyes, all doubts that had crept in during those midnight hours over the last week finally removed, blown away by his words, his looks. He meant it. He truly meant it. 'I do still want this. And in answer to your question about where we should live, I rather like what I've read of Italy.'

He grasped her hands. 'Oh, Grace, you've made me even happier than ever before. I cannot wait to spend the rest of my life with you and call you my wife, Mrs Grace Trelenna.'

'Mrs Grace Trelenna,' she repeated, having not thought about that before. 'It sounds so strange.'

'It sounds beyond perfect to me,' Laurie replied. 'It sounds exactly right.'

She reached up and touched his golden hair, wondering at her daring, and then allowed herself to be scooped into his arms, kissed, held, touched.

'When?' she asked.

'Whenever,' he said. 'Why are we delaying? I've found a willing vicar who will be discreet.'

'You've already found a vicar?'

'I told you I was serious about marrying you. He'll find us witnesses. We can set off from here, marry and then begin the rest of our lives together. Tomorrow?'

'Tomorrow?' she echoed in surprise.

'The day after then?' He laughed, trailing a finger down her cheek, making her blush. 'I'm at your mercy. Tell me when and I will act.'

'You really mean it, don't you?'

'I am beyond besotted with you, Grace. I promise you, we are going into our dotage together, come what may.'

Every shred of doubt, uncertainty about this was being thrown to the wind with every passing second.

'I love you,' he said, holding her again, kissing her, stroking her face as she fell against him. She understood then what was enough and what wasn't. She loved him. This wasn't enough. He adored her and she him and she couldn't ignore the desperate need, the yearning for him that she'd felt every time he kissed her. His hands stroked her face and then travelled gently down, over her dress, cupping her breasts. She groaned gently at this first touch.

'Laurie,' she breathed his name in between kisses.

He pulled back and looked at her. 'Do you want me to stop?'

She shook her head. 'I love you.'

He rested his forehead against hers, chest heaving as she saw him try to pull himself under control. 'You're going to be my wife. We don't have to do this now. We have all the time in the world for this.'

'Yes,' she said as she found herself inexplicably touching his chest over his shirt. His stomach was hard and taut and she hadn't known what would meet her fingers when she touched him but she hadn't expected him to be so solid.

'I want to see what you look like,' she said.

'You want to see what *I* look like?' His eyes flashed, like a match catching. 'Can you imagine how desperate I am to see what *you* look like?'

'You can,' she said. 'You can see. If you want to.'

'Grace,' he warned, glancing around. They were hidden deep in the woods, far away from prying eyes, far away from anyone and anything that might disturb them.

Slowly she undid her bonnet, holding the ribbons in her hand. 'May I undo your hair?' he asked.

She pulled the braids out of their tight knot at the nape of her neck and Laurie pulled his hands through the strands so that her long fair hair fell in waves over her shoulders. He had a contented smile on his face.

'What?' she asked.

'This is what you'll look like when you wake next to me each morning. I've been trying to imagine it for weeks.'

She laughed. 'You'll only have to imagine some things from now on. Not *all* things.'

'I know,' he said. 'I don't want to imagine though. I am desperate to experience every part of being married to you. But I know I have to wait.'

She touched his hand as he continued slowly running his fingers through her hair. 'You don't have to,' she said, knowing he wouldn't hurt her, knowing she could trust him. 'You don't have to wait.'

He swallowed. 'Grace,' he whispered. 'You don't mean it.'

'I do,' she said. 'I do mean it. You're going to be my husband. Am I wrong to trust you?'

'No,' he said and she saw truth in his eyes.

'Then show me what it is to be a wife. Show me what you'll be like as a husband.'

He watched her with his lips parted in surprise and she touched his chest again, looking into his eyes. She wanted to know him entirely. Her fingers undid his buttons, exposing his chest, his stomach as he untucked his shirt, helping her along. She ran her hands down over his trousers and he groaned. She glanced up in surprise. She had a vague idea of what was about to happen, but not the full facts, and she suspected that now she'd felt him she understood a bit more. The desperate need in the pit of her stomach told her as much. He let his clothes drop to the ground and she cast her gaze on all of him.

'Oh,' she said.

'Alright?' he asked, with a shy smile.

She nodded. 'Yes, just surprised.'

He smiled nervously. 'Not unpleasantly so, I hope?'

'No,' she said.

'May I see you?' he asked and she turned her back to him so he could unlace her dress. He helped her out of it and she turned back to him in only her undergarments, her dress pooled by her feet.

Slowly she slipped off what remained, and stood in front of him.

He couldn't speak.

'You aren't unpleasantly surprised?' she asked, the cold of the shaded glade pricking her body, making her shiver in tandem with nervousness.

'Absolutely not. Quite the opposite in fact. You are beyond beautiful.'

He closed the gap between them, kissing her again, his hands in her hair, running over her breasts, down her body so she inhaled in heavenly surprise. She didn't know what to do, where she should put her hands in return, so he guided her towards him, the two of them exploring each other's bodies, until they were on the ground, his jacket underneath her and his eyes searching hers for permission as he knelt over her, touching her and caressing her and sending every one of her nerve endings into a delicious spiral.

'You're going to be my husband,' she said, her eyes telling him everything.

'Yes, I am,' he promised as he held her gaze and slowly, so slowly she thought she might die of anticipation, entered her. There was pain, initially, alongside such a strange feeling she couldn't identify. Laurie Trelenna was inside her, holding her, loving her. He didn't move, just watched her reaction.

'Are you al—'

'I'm alright. What happens now?'

He smiled. 'I'm no expert, I'm afraid, so we're learning together.'

She didn't think she could love him any more but her heart burst with joy all over again.

Slowly he moved and involuntarily she clasped his shoulder. She cried in further surprise as he moved again, and again, slowly, gently, watching her the entire time, his face deep in concentration. It was dizzying, what he was doing to her and how he was doing it. He sank so entirely into her, forcing her into a state she'd never felt before. What was this? What was he doing to her? Over and over again he moved, pulling back and then moving slowly until the dizzying feeling overwhelmed her entirely and she knew her body was about to do something unprecedented.

He looked at her in surprise but didn't stop, moving faster, encouraged on, hurtling her body towards an inevitable conclusion that made her mouth cry a sound unlike any she'd ever made before as both her hands gripped his shoulders tighter and tighter and her eyes widened in surprise. Whatever she felt, he felt it too and he fell into her, his body shuddering the way hers did, their limbs tangled together as their furious rhythm led to stillness, kissing, words of love, disbelief.

Grace looked at him anew as they lay together on his clothes, against the undergrowth. She'd not been aware of the ground beneath her but now she was as Laurie picked tiny pieces of bracken from her hair. They didn't speak, just watched each other in a mix of awe and surprise, love and closeness. 'I'll have to tidy you up before you go,' he said eventually, doing just that. 'I don't want to let you go, though.'

'I don't want you to let me go either. But I'm afraid you have to, for a while at least,' she whispered as he kissed her once again.

'Only until the day after tomorrow. I'll book boat passages for us and confirm with the vicar. The day after tomorrow,' he said again thoughtfully. 'You will be my wife.'

'And you will be my husband. I don't think I can wait.'

'Neither can I, Grace. I am counting down the hours.'

Grace left Laurie in the woods, the two of them walking in opposite directions. He'd picked pieces of bracken from her clothes and she had done the same to him. And he'd watched with interest as she'd braided her hair and wound it into a neat bun at the nape of her neck. She had only half the pins she'd started with, the rest lost somewhere in the undergrowth. Her dress was a little damp from the woodland ferns that helped carpet the floor but otherwise she hoped, rather than felt, as if she was the same as before.

But she wasn't. What had just happened had felt so entirely natural between them but it had changed everything. She knew what Arthur was referring to when he'd told her to be careful. But the day after tomorrow she would be Mrs Grace Trelenna. She felt this to her very core. She was so in love with Laurie it now hurt when she wasn't with him. She'd been careful until now, and he'd no intention of doing her any wrong. They were leaving. It felt incredible but she didn't doubt him and she didn't doubt herself now. She had to take this chance with him, this chance of happiness, of a home, a real home of her own, with the man she was never supposed to fall in love with.

Chapter 6

'Italy,' she whispered to herself the next day while she was in the servants' hall preparing a menu suggestion to show Mrs Trelenna for an upcoming society dinner – a dinner she wouldn't be there to cook. Tomorrow she would be gone. Tonight was the last dinner she'd ever make at Trelenna House.

'Pardon?' Arthur asked, looking up from a copy of the *Western Morning News* discarded by Laurie's father.

'I was thinking aloud,' she replied. 'Ignore me.'

'Italy? Is that what you said?'

'Yes.'

At the other end of the worktable Ethel was studying a recipe Grace had tasked her with as part of the family's dinner tonight.

'Is that where you fancy going?' Arthur questioned. 'On your next day off?' he teased, but he gave her a look that said he knew exactly what she was talking about.

'Yes, perhaps tomorrow I'll go,' she said, giving him a sad, meaningful look. She hadn't had a moment with Arthur alone to tell him her plan, to tell him goodbye. This would probably be as good as it got.

Ethel giggled, not understanding. 'You'll go to Italy tomorrow?'

'Of course not,' Arthur shot back good-naturedly. 'But that's where you'd like to end up one day?' he asked, turning back to Grace.

She nodded. The kitchen maid clearly had no idea what the conversation was about, or was entirely uninterested, and returned to her task.

Arthur swallowed. 'America for me.'

'Really?' Grace asked. 'Where? Why?'

Arthur blew air out of his cheeks, putting down the newspaper and committing himself to the conversation. 'My cousin John is there. The only family member who keeps in contact. If I take him at face value, he's having a grand time of it, making money and living better than he ever did here.'

'Doing what?' Grace asked, intrigued. 'Is he panning for gold?'

Arthur rolled his eyes, before answering. 'America's come a long way in a short space of time. He's in New York, doing well, working for an import company on the docks. He works hard. And gets paid well because of it.'

Grace's eyes widened. 'How well?'

'Very well, he tells me.'

'And that's why you want to go?'

Arthur shrugged. 'Maybe. Why not? I've no ties here. Perhaps it's time to do something else and be somewhere new. He's the only family I've got. The only one who remembers I'm alive. He can find me a job and a room to sleep. Or so he keeps saying. Plenty of jobs for hard-working immigrants. I'm saving enough for a boat passage and then I'm gone. I'm nearly there. Six months' wages and I think I can do it, if boat passage prices don't rise.'

'I didn't know any of that,' Ethel responded from the end of the table.

'Neither did I,' Grace said, smiling at Arthur's plans.

'Oh, I don't know,' he said dismissively. 'It'll probably never happen.'

'Why do you say that?'

'I've been planning it for so long it just seems so far away, so unlikely. A dream. But if I can, I'll do it. Maybe.'

'You *should* do it,' Grace encouraged.

'You should,' Ethel agreed. 'I can't imagine leaving my family and going to another country. Your dreams of Italy and America seem so strange to me when I'm so happy here with my family close by.'

'Then you're lucky,' Arthur said kindly. 'To have a family. I've got one cousin and he's been on the other side of the world so long I doubt we'd even recognise each other.'

Grace looked at Arthur and smiled knowingly. Neither of them had family, neither of them were going to be here much longer if they both had their way. Not seeing Arthur's face every day in the kitchen, along with all the other staff, was going to be so strange. She could hardly imagine it, hardly imagine what her new life had in store. A life no longer in servitude. What would that look like?

Later, when the family had dined and the house was being put to bed for the night, Arthur snuck outside to smoke a cigarette. Grace went to join him.

'This is goodbye, isn't it?' he said.

'Yes. Laurie and I are leaving tomorrow.'

'I can't believe you're actually going. I'll miss you,' he said.

'I'll miss you too.' She put her arms around him and hugged him, something she'd never done before because there had been no call for it. 'I'll miss you more than you could know. I think you might be my best friend.'

'I think you might be mine too. But you never know, maybe this isn't goodbye. Maybe I'll see you again, when you come back here eventually, when all's forgiven or when *he* inherits. I'll see you then. Although you'll be a cut above me, this might not be goodbye after all.'

'It is going to be goodbye. Because even if I end up back here again, you won't return. You'll end your days in America – happy, free, with a wife and family of your own, and having done so incredibly well for yourself.'

'You don't know that,' he said. 'But thank you for humouring me.'

'I'm not humouring you. It will happen because I have something for you that will help.' Grace pulled an envelope out of her apron pocket. 'It's every penny I've saved over the past few years. Barring what I've spent on a few hairpins and recipe books. Laurie and I are going to be just fine and so I'm giving you this. And I want to know you'll put it towards the rest of your boat passage and somewhere to live while your cousin finds you work.'

He held his cigarette halfway to his mouth as he listened. His eyes fell to the envelope and then back to her. 'No,' he said, 'I can't.'

'Of course you can. It's yours now. In this envelope is your new life. Let me do this for you.'

'Grace, I . . .' She saw tears in his eyes and he turned away, wiping them, throwing away his cigarette as he used both hands. 'No one's ever done anything like this for me. I don't deserve it.'

'You do, Arthur. You do. And this is a selfish act for me really because I need to go away being happy knowing *you're* happy too. So I'm doing this for me, really. Not you.'

He laughed.

'Please let me do this,' she said gently.

'I can't even talk for crying.'

'Then don't talk,' she said. 'You don't need to talk. You don't need to say anything.'

'Thank you,' he said, blinking away the rest of his tears. 'Thank you, from the bottom of my heart.'

'When will you go?' she asked.

He clutched the thick envelope tightly. 'Not long after you, now you've made it possible. I'll tell them after you've gone – let the dust settle and then I'll start planning.'

'Good,' she said. 'Don't let them talk you out of it.' She stepped up and kissed him on his cheek. 'I need to pack my few things. I'll be gone by the time you wake up.'

He touched his face where her lips had been and looked at her fondly. 'Goodbye, Grace. Good luck.'

'You too,' she said with tears in her own eyes, and then she left him standing by the wall, the envelope in his hands and a look of sadness in his eyes.

Chapter 7

Grace took a final look around the kitchen before going to her room. She wouldn't sleep here again, wouldn't dress here again, wouldn't surround herself with her books here, adapting recipes again. She wouldn't walk with Laurie in the woodlands again, or stand with Arthur against the wall and inhale his company as well as his smoke. It was all over. She reasoned it was a funny time for her and Arthur to confess they were each other's best friends. But then, they'd become friends through circumstance, a happy accident. Just as she and Laurie had found themselves falling for each other against the odds. And as the hour approached, she left her room silently and swiftly, and headed towards the edge of the wood, the agreed meeting place, holding her bag of clothes and the recipe books she valued most, bound together with string. As she waited for Laurie, she regretted that she'd never see Arthur again. She was bound for Italy and he for America, and on different sides of the world they would neither of them be able to find each other. She silently wished him luck again and waited, watching the moon lowering itself through the dark night sky. Watching as, one by one, the stars that had studded the heavens began to dull.

She put her carpet bag down as it grew heavy in her hands. He loved her. She knew he loved her. He was coming. She didn't dare doubt him. He'd been so true. So honest. Grace pulled her shawl tighter around her, grateful for its warmth as a cold breeze found her, heralding rain. As the moon disappeared behind a dark cloud, the promised drops began and she moved to shelter under a tree. Looking up towards the house through the canopy of trees, she noted there was no movement, no lights on this side of the house. It was so dark now the light of the moon had been extinguished.

Grace had no idea if Laurie was on the lawn walking towards her or . . . ? Or? The alternative didn't bear thinking about. She'd doubted him at first but that had been at the start. That had been before. He loved her, he did. Every action, every glance, every word, every effort to see her in the kitchen between their woodland walks, everything told her he loved her. So where was he?

Where *was* he?

Chapter 8

Present Day

Zennor

Zennor had every intention of showing her finds from the archive boxes to Zach and Lamorna, but the following day fell entirely out of her control. Day two of opening the house to visitors felt even more frenetic than day one and the new, expensive coffee machine, which had been threatening to go wrong all afternoon, had finally sputtered and fizzled itself into silence halfway through their final orders. Merry had promised he'd take a look at it after Zennor had tried and failed to identify what was wrong.

The steady stream of guests – families and pensioners, backpackers walking up to the house from the nearby coast path for a bite to eat and then deciding to tack on a quick tour before hitting the road again – never stopped.

'Do you think we should offer camping in one of the meadows?' Zennor surprised them all later that evening as they added up how much they'd made through ticket sales, food and gift shop items.

'You might need planning permission,' Zach said immediately.

'Easy enough to apply,' Zennor replied.

'And you'll need to provide a tap for running water. And facilities.'

'Hmm, I'll think about that. We had a few backpackers in the café today from the coast path. We've obviously started appearing on maps and online guides, so a few came up through the meadow to rest and eat. If we gave them somewhere to camp for the night, I think a few would pay a fee to pitch a tent quite happily in addition to stopping for the afternoon. I could also offer them an easy supper of wood-fired pizzas or something.'

'What a good idea,' her sister agreed, barely looking up from the day's takings. Lamorna really did love a spreadsheet, something that made Zennor break out in a sweat.

'Do we even own a wood-fired pizza oven?' Merry asked, glancing around the kitchen as if he'd missed an industrial-sized wood burner.

'I'd buy one,' Zennor said excitedly. 'I've always wanted one.'

'How much are they? We probably can't afford it, whatever it is. And haven't you got enough going on with the tearoom? You want to work at suppertime too?' Lamorna asked, finally glancing up and fixing her sister with a look of concern.

'It wouldn't be much extra work, and probably only for a few of the summer months. I doubt people pitch tents in November. And besides, I'm cooking at suppertime already for *us*,' she said, gesturing to the oven where she had a chicken roasting. 'I think we should capitalise on the walkers from the path. They're an unexpected bonus.'

'I think you're right,' Merry agreed. 'But it might be a bit of an outlay. And it won't be this year if we need planning permission, so it gives us a while to think about it.'

'I'll add it to my never-ending to-do list,' Lamorna sighed, reaching for her phone and typing. 'Speaking of to-do lists, aren't you supposed to be fixing the coffee machine? Zennor's had a look and can't work out what's wrong with it.'

'I thought catering was her department,' Merry retorted as if Zennor wasn't even in the room. 'And what if I can't fix it in time for tomorrow's visitors? What's your back-up plan?' He turned to Zennor. '*Do* you have a back-up plan?'

'Um . . . not really, no. I've only had it a few days so I wasn't expecting it to break so soon. Someone can come out and fix it, but it's not going to be immediate, is it?'

Merry sighed. 'I'll look after dinner.'

Zennor cast Lamorna a frustrated expression and Lamorna mouthed, 'Don't worry,' before saying, 'I also think we should take turns making dinner. Lighten the load for you now you're cooking lunches and serving food all day.'

'Hmmm, maybe.' Zennor turned her back on the family to remove the chicken happily sizzling away and began plating it up with a fresh salad and vinaigrette she'd prepared, trying to hide her reluctance to hand over her kitchen to her siblings. She much preferred it this way, her family sat around the table while she prepared meals she'd painstakingly planned a week in advance and shopped for regularly. She didn't want them microwaving something in a plastic tray and presenting it as a family dinner. She shuddered at the thought. No, it was just safer if she kept making supper too. That way no one would die of malnutrition.

'I have something to show you,' Zennor said after they'd eaten and cleared away. She knew this was the point she'd lose them to various corners of the house. Lamorna and Zach would curl up in the drawing room with the fire on despite it being summer, and then Zach might stay over or return to his own home – Port Carrack, further round the headland, where he was busy trying to host guided tours and run his house as a wedding venue. And Merry, only back a week or so, had already taken to wandering the ramshackle gardens until the sun went down or he disappeared up to his room where she could hear Netflix documentaries playing on his laptop. She hoped, rather than believed, that he'd started writing novels again, but she doubted it. He'd not been able to write in so long and she didn't like to push.

'I found some things in those boxes you left in my room,' Zennor continued. 'They kept me awake, thinking all night.' Then Zennor directed her next sentence at Lamorna. 'You left them sticking out, by the way. I tripped over them. Hard. Papers went flying. So did I.'

Lamorna looked sheepish. 'Sorry,' she said meaningfully. 'What did you find?'

Zennor opened the top drawer in the bureau where all the little items went that had no home. String, Post-it notes, chargers for mobiles that no one owned anymore. At the top, out of harm's way, she'd placed the two objects that had caused her to lie awake most of the night wondering. 'One is a letter,' she said, passing it to Merry first. 'And the other is a newspaper. It's folded over on to this page but it's from 1869, the same year as the letter, and it's reporting a crime at Trelenna.'

'A crime?' Lamorna asked, almost snatching the paper out of her hand.

'What kind of crime?' Zach's ears pricked up, leaning over Lamorna's shoulder.

Lamorna read aloud. '*Wanted, Arthur Lander, First Footman at Trelenna House, who is believed to have absconded without notice.*'

'That's the crime?' Lamorna looked up at Zennor, incredulous. 'He absconded without notice?'

'It was a breach of employment contract,' Zach explained, taking the paper out of her hands and smoothing it out over the table. 'Punishable by imprisonment sometimes, if the servant didn't give three months' notice.'

'Three months? That's ridiculous,' Lamorna said.

'The newspaper is from the same week this letter was written,' Zennor continued. 'And I think Mrs Trelenna – one of our ancestors, but I don't know who or where she fits on the family tree – has written about Arthur Lander here when she says two people have vanished without trace, but it's a bit vague, as she mentions only one name.'

Zach now read the rest of Mrs Trelenna's letter to the housekeeper.

> *While we find ourselves in this unfortunate position, I should like to look at the advertisement for the new cook before it is sent off. Please make it clear when you compose it that we will correspond with the most recent employer with regard to character reference. That is of utmost importance given what has happened with Miss Pascoe. I do not want anyone young. Or pretty.*

Zach whistled through his teeth. But it was Merry who spoke first.

'Oh, I get it. The cook's been trying it on with the husband.'

'Or,' Zennor said, with more than a tone of annoyance, '*the husband's* been trying it on *with the cook*. He probably felt he could because he's in a position of power.'

Lamorna glanced over at the page blankly. 'Where the heck are you two getting all that from?'

'Whatever it was, it does sound fishy,' Zach volunteered, scanning the page again. 'Typical Victorian stiff upper lip though, alluding to something but not flat out saying it. Alluding to something *untoward* somewhere along the lines with a young, pretty cook too. She's saying two people have gone, though, so it's the cook and someone.'

'How do we find out?' Zennor asked Zach. 'As our resident historian—'

'Amateur historian,' he cut in. 'And I definitely don't have time to take on yet another one of your house's ancestors, I'm afraid. But I can point you in the right direction and you could do some digging. It shouldn't be too difficult.'

'One sec.' Zennor went to fetch a notepad and pen.

'Now?' Zach asked in surprise and Merry smothered a laugh.

'Just some hints as to where to look to find out who lived in the house, who the cook was, who Mrs Trelenna was and if Arthur Lander ever got caught.' Zennor clicked the pen and looked expectantly at Zach.

Instead Zach wordlessly took the notepad and pen and began writing.

'They're advertising for a cook but not the footman's position,' Lamorna said thoughtfully. 'Why do you think that is?'

'Perhaps they'd had enough of absconding footmen,' Merry piped up.

'Or maybe,' Zach said distractedly as he tried to write and talk at the same time, 'they already had a second footman they could promote to first. And a hall boy they could promote up to second footman? They could have found a local, willing lad to appoint as a new hall boy.'

He handed the page back to Zennor – websites for census records, shipping records, prison records, a list of other websites to scan through. *Oh, this looks terribly boring,* she thought. Surely there was another way?

'You should keep going through the box too,' Zach said, clearly having seen Zennor's disappointed face. 'Your sister and I were lucky. We had Issey's diary, which painted a fairly complete picture of her time in Singapore.'

'And we had Molly, who knew Issey's best friend from the time to piece together most of the rest of it,' Lamorna joined in.

'But there will be no one alive now who knew any of these people,' Zennor lamented. 'And you two had each other. I don't fancy doing this on my own.' Zennor looked at Merry expectantly while he studiously avoided her gaze.

'Look at the census records first,' Zach said, obviously taking pity on her. 'I'll give you my login details. It's fairly straightforward. Who knows, you might even have fun finding out who lived in your house back then. I did.'

Zennor gave him a doubtful look. 'Maybe.' She might have a little play with the census website, if it was as easy as Zach said.

'I'm sure I can help,' Lamorna volunteered. 'After we close up tomorrow?'

'I can't do that time,' Zennor said. 'I'm interviewing a gardener then, remember?'

'Oh, yes. We only need a few hours every week,' Lamorna pointed out.

'We need much more than that,' Merry retorted.

'We can only *afford* a few hours every week,' Lamorna clarified. 'Don't be talked into more.'

'I know, I know,' Zennor said to Lamorna. 'I do remember what you tell me.'

'Sorry.' Lamorna flushed a little in apology. 'We just need to keep a tight grasp of the finances – we're a new business only days in . . .'

'I remember that too,' Zennor said. With a busy day tomorrow cooking for the tearoom while Merry and Lamorna ran tours, *and* interviewing a gardener, Zennor wasn't sure when she was going to be able to delve further into the history of the missing servants next, but she was intrigued by the idea of Trelenna's (presumably) young, pretty cook being one of those to disappear without a trace.

As Zennor closed down the kitchen for the night, she struggled to marry up the elegant, professional, functional new space she'd recently designed with what had been here long before. Even though years separated them and much of the original kitchen had been modified or ripped out, she wondered about that young woman. The woman who had bustled about in here all day, standing right where Zennor stood, day in day out, on exactly the same flagstone floor, doing the same job nearly. She would like to find out more about her. What had happened to this woman? The young and pretty Miss Pascoe? Why had she gone? And where?

Chapter 9

The gardener, when he arrived just after the house's closing time the next day, was not at all what Zennor had been expecting. The agency had told her they'd be sending someone who was happy with part-time hours because they were gently increasing their workload after an injury. Zennor had assumed a middle-aged person with a hip complaint would turn up, ready to plant the occasional bulb and generally potter about weeding for a few hours a week. She'd been quite happy imagining that scenario, imagining cutting a slice of cake for tea breaks, listening to their life stories. Instead the man standing before her made her do a double take when he knocked on the kitchen door.

The effect was catching, as Kayleigh – one of Zennor's catering college friends who'd been recruited to help at busy times – paused before saying hello in a voice not quite her own. The man almost filling the back door of the kitchen was in his mid-twenties, dressed in shorts and a t-shirt with cropped blond hair and a tan that made him look like some sort of model going to the gym – not a gardener.

'Hi, I'm looking for Zennor,' he said. 'Am I in the right place?'

Zennor swallowed. 'Charlie?' she asked doubtfully.

'Yeah. Hi.'

Kayleigh turned and discreetly mouthed to Zennor, 'Thank you, god.'

Zennor tried to ignore her as she swallowed a laugh, and stepped forward to shake Charlie's hand. 'I'm Zennor. Nice to meet you. Are you the gardener?' she had to ask.

'Yeah. Well, I'm training to be one. I've done quite a lot of courses and the agency said you just needed some small things doing and to pop along for a chat to see if I'd be suitable.'

'Oh, I'm absolutely positive you'll be suitable,' Kayleigh called from the other end of the kitchen.

'Ah, that's . . . great,' Charlie replied, missing the double-meaning.

'Let's go into the gardens and I can show you around,' Zennor suggested, eager to stop her friend hiring this man before she'd even had a chance to speak to him. She wiped her hands on a tea towel and left Kayleigh to finish up.

'I came past some of the garden on my way from where I parked my car,' Charlie said. 'I'll be honest, from what I saw, it could do with a little TLC.'

'It's completely neglected.' Zennor plumped for honesty. 'It needs more than tender loving care. It needs firebombing and starting again.'

Charlie laughed. 'Nothing needs firebombing. But it does need rotovating and, well . . . maybe you could tell me what it is your current gardener does and how many days a week I'll be working alongside them, what they want me to do . . .'

'We don't have a current gardener. It'll just be you.' Zennor winced as she waited for his reaction. 'We haven't had a proper gardener in . . . I don't know how many years.'

'It'll just be me?' He looked around.

Zennor's wince remained on her face. Oh well, she'd had three minutes in a very handsome man's company and now he was about to run a mile. It had been a nice three minutes, though.

'Right,' Charlie said, looking around at what had once been the kitchen garden, supplying vegetables to the house a very long time ago, and now was just a mish-mash of weeds and toughened earth. She could see his mind working. 'Okay,' he said slowly. She watched as he ran his hand through his short hair for no reason at all as it wasn't in his face. Was he stalling for time? Making a decision? What could she say that might make him stay?

'We don't need anyone full-time,' she tried.

'You *don't*?' he asked doubtfully. 'It looks like you need a whole bunch of gardeners, all working flat out. What is it you want doing?'

'Everything,' she said without thinking. 'But only in small doses.'

'Small doses of everything?' He gave her his full attention, his green-grey eyes sparkling with humour.

He had an infectious smile and Zennor had no choice but to smile back. 'Look . . .' She stopped. Her smiled dropped. She'd forgotten his name.

'Charlie,' he said, his smile turning into one of curiousness.

'Charlie.' She'd momentarily turned into an idiot. Why couldn't she be as commanding as Lamorna? 'I understand if this is too much. I understand if you feel you'd be taking on a ridiculous amount of work given your . . . injury.' She had no idea what his injury was but rather hoped he'd fill her in, given the agency had made a point of mentioning it. He didn't. He just waited for her to finish. 'But it would only be a few hours a week for now, so if you're looking for more hours or an easier gig, I get it. It's okay to say so. And it's best you say it now rather than settle me into a false sense of security feeling everything's okay, only to find that in two weeks' time the one job my sister Lamorna let me do has gone horribly wrong and you quit when you could have said so on day one.'

He blinked at her. 'That's quite a lot to, er . . . to think about. Shall we keep walking, maybe? It's probably not fair I judge just by looking at five hundred square foot of what, I imagine, was once a kitchen garden, and what I spotted on the walk from the car.'

'There's not too much more,' she said as they walked. 'There's the ornamental garden on the other side of the wall,' she explained while they headed in that direction.

'Which is now neither ornamental nor a garden,' Charlie pointed out with a grimace as they rounded the corner.

'I think the brambles have taken over. It's great in September for making crumbles when blackberries appear, but the rest of the year it's just overwhelming. Then there's the parkland.' Zennor gestured as they kept walking towards it. 'Which you drove past on the approach to the house. We used to have deer and then when they went we had sheep from the neighbouring farmer who kept it all looking neat, but I don't know what happened about that. My dad bought a sit-on mower and gave it a good go a while back, and Merry was looking forward to having a play on it this week, so you might not have to do anything about that.'

'Merry?' he quizzed.

'My brother.'

'Merry, Lamorna and Zennor,' he said with a knowing smile. 'Two of you have Cornish places as your names.'

'There's four of us and we all do. Merry is short for Merryn. And my oldest sister is Veryan.'

He smiled again. That smile. Zennor swallowed, trying to move on. 'So, what do you think?'

'It's going to be a challenge, is what I think. Especially if it's only going to be me. How many days a week do you need?'

'We were thinking more *hours* than days.' She forced her expression out of another automatic wince.

'Are you joking?' he asked affably. 'How many hours?'

Good question. Lamorna had said a few. How many was that?

'A few?' Zennor tried.

'How many's a few?'

'Yes, I was just wondering the same thing. Um . . .' She tried not to laugh at herself and watched as he smothered a similar grin. 'How many do you think a few is?'

'How many do *you* think a few is?' he countered, the smile revealing itself.

'Less than fifteen, more than . . . five?' Zennor attempted.

'Split the difference? Let's try ten, shall we? For now. Just to kickstart things?'

'So, you'll do it?' she questioned. 'Really?'

'Really,' he said, and then he winced the way she'd been doing as if immediately regretting his decision.

'I don't mind how you spread the hours out. You choose depending on your schedule when you can fit us in, but while you're here there's free tea and cake whenever you fancy. Just come and find me in the kitchen, which is where I'll always be.'

'Always?'

'Mostly.' She shrugged. 'It's my happy place.'

He nodded. 'Gardens are mine. Free tea and cake sounds great. Maybe I'll start with a couple of hours each weekday for now and see how I get on?'

'It's a deal,' she said, shaking his hand again to seal it. It was warm and the skin was soft, not remotely like a gardener's. Maybe he wore gloves. Her hand was still in his, contemplating this, and on realising, she removed it.

'See you tomorrow, then?'

'See you tomorrow,' she echoed and waited politely while he walked to his car – an old estate vehicle that she could see was loaded with garden tools. He climbed in and started the engine, waved his hand briefly, then drove away.

◆ ◆ ◆

Later that evening in bed, Zennor had her laptop propped up and a cup of tea next to her. Merry had fixed the coffee machine but it was still making the strangest noise, so she fired off an email to the manufacturer to confirm a time for someone to come out and look at it properly. If it did break, she needed a back-up that didn't cost the earth, and began looking at small units that might serve them in the interim. It wouldn't hurt to have something on standby even if Lamorna would moan about the cost for a second coffee machine sitting idly and, hopefully, unused.

Refusing to give up the only – and very limited – time to herself to any more work, Zennor decided to indulge in a bit of checking up on Miss Pascoe. She'd been putting off discovering more about the cook, who she liked to think of as her counterpart, but now was the time. So far she had a last name but no first name. Zach had told her to start with the census records; apparently lack of a first name might be less of a problem there. Navigating to the website's frontpage she discovered the census was brought in during 1801 and was mainly a means of gathering data about the population for food supply purposes. Then every ten years since there had been one – up until the Second World War when things went a little wonky. Within a few clicks and with Zach's login details, she was in and entering *Trelenna House, Cornwall* into the search bar with the date she wanted – 1861, the closest census record available before the two servants had left – and waited for the image and accompanying transcript to load.

Her eyes lit up with excitement, and she shuffled into a more upright position and scanned the document listing everyone who had been residing at Trelenna House in April 1861 when the census records had been gathered.

Within these very rooms on the upper floors were the Trelenna family. Mr and Mrs Herbert and Georgiana Trelenna. *Herbert?* She'd never heard of him. And the delightful Georgiana must be the

Mrs Trelenna who'd written to the housekeeper with strict instructions about proven respectability for the new cook's position.

Master Laurie Trelenna was listed. Aged fourteen. Scholar.

And that was it for the family, although Zach had said census records provided a snapshot in time of who was where and when. So all she knew now was that three members of the Trelenna family were in this house the night the census was taken.

'So many staff,' Zennor muttered as she scrolled, looking at the list of occupations next to each name. Housekeeper, butler, first footman, second footman, hall boy, valet, lady's maid, two grooms for the horses, three permanent gardeners (how she wished she had *any* now), two housemaids, kitchen maid, cook.

Cook. But at the time this census was taken, eight years before the date of the letter, Miss Pascoe was not the cook. Someone named Margaret Day was.

But there was Miss Pascoe, first name Grace, listed as kitchen maid, aged thirteen, place of birth Redruth, Cornwall.

'Grace,' Zennor said aloud without realising it. Her finger traced Grace's name on the screen, as if she'd made a real connection with this woman across the years. Although all she knew about her were the purest facts: her name, age and where she was born. It felt like enough, but it wasn't really. 'Grace Pascoe, you lived and breathed in my kitchen a hundred and fifty years ago. Although,' Zennor giggled to herself, 'perhaps it's really that I'm now in *your* kitchen.'

Writing down her full name, just in case she might forget, Zennor asked her, 'Where did you go to, Grace Pascoe?'

Chapter 10

1869

Grace

The hour moved on and the rain had trickled through the leaves and Grace's clothes, her bonnet and on to her skin. She was becoming drenched, her dress and cloak heavy with water as the rain continued. She had a choice to make and she didn't want to admit it to herself. She could stay and wait longer – just a bit longer because surely Laurie had been held up – or she could return to the house, to her room and accept the unthinkable – that Laurie Trelenna wasn't coming.

It was the only, devastating conclusion. But she couldn't accept it. She couldn't. He wouldn't do that to her. He loved her. *He loved her.* As she loved him. They had made a promise, they had made a plan. They had plotted the course of their lives together. But . . . he had duped her. He had left her standing in the rain, waiting for him, and he'd never been coming. He'd never planned to. He had hurt her on purpose. Why? Why would someone do that? Why would *he* do that? Was she just a plaything? Something for him to tease and then to abandon? Had she meant so little to him that he could do that? She went through every moment with him, every time they had been together, everything they'd said to each other, and she couldn't marry up the man she'd come to know with the horrible betrayal he'd just committed. But she had to. She had to accept it because that is what had happened.

The hours passed alone in her room and night turned to day. Grace went to the kitchen at the same time as she always did, met Ethel blacking the range and lighting it as she always did at this hour, greeting each other the way they always did – Grace hiding every emotion she felt. Her eyes were red through lack of sleep and crying, but she began assembling the servants' early breakfast of fresh eggs, buttered toast and porridge as she always did, then got to work on the family's more elaborate breakfast dishes. And everything looked as it always had. Grace glanced at the door, waiting. Soon Laurie would come to the kitchen to see the dog as he always did, and he'd slip her a note to explain.

Until then she worked through muscle memory, seeing but not seeing her tasks, noticing but not noticing anything she did until porridge was cooked, bread was toasted and Ethel had placed a bowl of fruit from the orchard on the table as usual. Pots of tea were made and the servants began emerging from their morning tasks of laying fires, delivering hot water upstairs and cleaning banisters.

Arthur walked into the kitchen looking glum and sat at the table. Then he looked up and saw her. He started and his eyes widened. He opened his mouth to exclaim at her presence and then clearly thought better of it. Grace wondered if her face betrayed her shame. Everyone ate speedily as usual, scraping butter on toast and pouring tea. Grace said barely a word while she waited and waited for any news, any explanation.

She would need to plan the family luncheon, the servants' too. She had no idea what she would cook. She hadn't planned to be here. How much longer would she be here? Where was Laurie? Why hadn't he come? Gladstone sat under the table looking for dropped scraps. Arthur broke a piece of toast off and discreetly fed the dog, all the while his eyes on Grace, trying to get her attention.

A bell rang in the adjoining corridor and the hall boy scrambled to see which room it was attached to.

'Mrs Trelenna's bedroom,' he returned saying. Dolly, the lady's maid, shoved a piece of toast into her mouth quickly and pushed her chair back, running into the kitchen to make a fresh pot of tea for her mistress while Ethel followed to assemble the breakfast tray. 'No rest for the wicked,' Dolly said through a mouthful of toast as she disappeared out of sight, carrying the tray.

Arthur's eyes were still on Grace and she wished they weren't. One by one, the servants finished their breakfast and Grace went to the kitchen to put together the dishes to be carried along to the dining room. While Mrs Trelenna always took breakfast in her room, her son and her husband ate in the dining room. She was making Laurie's breakfast and she had no idea where he was or what had happened.

The lady's maid arrived in the kitchen. 'She wants *you.*'

Grace looked up at Dolly and then behind her to check she wasn't gesturing to Ethel, washing up at the sink.

'Me?' Grace asked, confused. 'In her *bedroom*?'

'In the morning room in half an hour, she says. What do you think it's about?'

'Didn't she tell you?' Grace asked nervously.

Dolly shook her head. 'Maybe it's about your trial. Maybe it's over and you're safe? It's high time. Yours is the best cooking I've ever tasted.'

'Thank you,' Grace said absently, while her mind ran away with itself.

Half an hour later, Grace wiped her shaking hands on her apron and then took it off, neatening her appearance and heading towards Mrs Trelenna's morning room. When she'd last set foot in here it was to discover the most handsome man she'd ever met helping to secure her rise to the position of cook. His energy had been so palpable, he'd won her over and worn his mother out within only a few moments. And now Grace was standing here again and Mrs Georgiana Trelenna had the same weary expression.

'Grace,' she said. 'Please sit.'

She wasn't sure if this was normal or not. She'd not been invited to sit last time. She didn't know what was customary and what wasn't now she was a slightly more senior servant.

Mrs Trelenna spoke immediately, stunning Grace with her words. 'I'm very sorry to say that my son has led you a merry dance.'

Grace inhaled sharply. And then, collecting herself, said, 'I'm sorry. But what do you mean?'

'In the early hours of this morning, Laurie came to see me, confessed everything and I think, feeling rather guilty it had gone as far as it had, decided that it would be best if you left as soon as possible. It is an incredibly embarrassing incident for Laurie and for all of us. And we would not want news of this sort of dalliance running through Cornwall and beyond. For your sake and for Laurie's. He's a good man.' She looked exasperated. 'But sometimes good men make silly mistakes. You are his latest mistake.'

Grace's mouth opened and she felt sure her heart had stopped beating. No breath came. Mrs Trelenna paused, giving Grace time to talk, but no words came either. Her mouth was entirely dry, her mind spinning with uncomprehending turmoil as she tried but failed to take this news in. She couldn't. She just couldn't.

Mrs Trelenna continued. 'Grace, you are a good cook – the best we've had – and I'm sorry to see you go. I will give you a month's wages, a good character reference so you may find further employment, and you will have to leave today. You understand that, don't you? It's impossible for you to remain now. I have already written your reference, which you may take along with your wages in here.'

She leaned forward and handed an envelope to Grace, which she took automatically.

Grace's heart thudded. No. This couldn't be happening. This couldn't be true. He loved her. He did. And she loved him.

'Where is he, please?' Grace dared.

'He's not here,' Mrs Trelenna answered softly, almost kindly. 'He's embarrassed. He's gone.'

'Will you tell me where?'

'London,' she said. 'We are all fools in love every now and again. I hope you are able to find happiness. Once you are packed, please ask the coachman to bring the carriage round. He can take you to the railway station or home to your family.'

'I don't have any family,' Grace replied quietly.

Mrs Trelenna chose not to reply. 'That is all, Grace. You have been a marvellous cook. I am very sorry to see you go.'

Grace muttered her thanks, stood and, quite unsure how she would ever survive this, left the room.

Chapter 11

It was Arthur who saw her first as she entered the servants' hall, taking her to one side out of earshot of the others.

'He's gone,' Arthur whispered. 'The maids say his bed hasn't been slept in.'

Grace couldn't speak, couldn't think.

'What happened with Mrs Trelenna?'

'I've been dismissed. She knows. He told her.'

'And she blames you? How dare she—'

'She doesn't. She blames him. She blames Laurie.'

'I blame him too,' Arthur said, fury simmering in his words. 'And so should you.'

'Please,' Grace protested weakly. 'Please don't. I don't . . . I don't have anywhere to go. She wants me gone today.'

'Today?'

Grace's hand shook as she held the envelope. 'She's given me a month's wages. And I'm to leave now.'

Arthur's eyes widened. 'Where to?'

'I don't have anywhere or anyone,' Grace said, and then her strength left her and she felt herself fall. Arthur grabbed her and held her up.

'Come here. Let me think. What can we do? Where can you go? There must be somewhere. You can rent a room and begin looking for work on a month's wages. I'm not sure how long it'll last you though.'

'Not long at all,' she muttered.

'All that money you gave me. Let me fetch it for you so you have—'

She shook her head. 'No, that's your money. Yours to start your new life in America.'

'Grace, don't be ridiculous. I'm not taking the money now, am I? How can I start a new life with your money now? You must be mad if you think I'd do that to you.'

'I don't know what to think.' She was going to start crying. 'Arthur, what do I do? Where do I go? How do I start again after trying so hard to make something of myself? No one will give me a cook's position like this after only serving a few months in the role.'

Arthur pulled her towards him as she broke, sobbing into his chest.

'I'll be back to being a kitchen maid again, which is better than being in the workhouse, but I'll be starting all over again, I just know it. I should be grateful she gave me some money, grateful I can live.'

'This isn't living,' Arthur said with meaning. 'This, here, for these people. This isn't living. This is serving. We live a life of servitude. And you think you should be grateful they kicked you out with a few pennies in your pocket? Don't you want more than this, than how they treat you?'

Until Laurie Trelenna had turned her head, she had never wanted more, never really allowed herself to dream of more. Being a cook for those precious few months had been everything she'd ever wanted. It had been enough. More than enough. And now she had nothing.

'I want more,' Arthur said. 'I want more for you too.'

She shook her head slowly. 'I'll never have more. Not now. It'll take forever to get back to where I was only this morning.'

'Not if you come with me,' Arthur said passionately, his eyes lighting up.

Grace looked up at him, uncomprehending.

'Come with me to America – we can start a new life together. It won't be so frightening if we've got each other. You can be anything you want to be in America. If you don't want to come, I'll give your money back, of course I will. But if we pool everything we have, we can leave immediately, if we want.'

'I *have* to leave immediately,' she said, feeling wrong-footed, unable to follow.

'There you go then,' he replied with a wide, confident smile. 'Come to America, Grace. Come and make something of yourself in America. No more servitude. Riches as far as the eye can see.'

She smiled at him, half-heartedly. 'I'm not sure it's going to be quite like that, is it?'

'It will be for us. We can make it anything we want it to be. We're almost there. We've just got to get on a boat.'

She felt her heart quickening at the thought. If she did this, she'd never see Laurie Trelenna again. She'd never understand why he'd done this to her, why he'd left her in the middle of the wood before dawn broke, soaked to the skin, with promises of a marriage he'd never intended. Mrs Trelenna's words echoed, *'You are his latest mistake,'* and Grace's thudding heart broke in two.

'Arthur, are you serious? You've got to give your notice,' Grace pointed out. 'You'll be in so much trouble if you don't.'

He gripped her upper arms then. 'Damn them and their notice. They'll have to catch me first, and by the time they see I'm gone, we'll be on a ship in the middle of the Atlantic.'

'Arthur,' she warned lightly.

But he was serious. 'Let's go. Let's go tonight. Let's go to America.'

Chapter 12

Present Day

Zennor

Zennor found the 'criminal' Arthur Lander in the census too – he was listed as the hall boy in 1861. He'd come a long way between the census and the date he'd 'absconded'. Arthur Lander, aged fourteen, place of birth: Exeter.

Grace and Arthur were both children here. But fast forward a few years and they would've been adults, leaving Trelenna.

She let the cursor hover on the screen without much idea of what to do next. Zach hadn't prepped her past this point. But she finally understood why Zach was hooked on all this family-history research. This was quite fun. Zennor went further forward. She searched for Grace Pascoe in the 1871 census and then in the one following it in 1881. She wasn't at Trelenna on either of those dates, according to the results. There were a few likely candidates further afield, but none that matched the date of birth or even the place of birth, leading Zennor to conclude that *her* Grace Pascoe had not been anywhere in Britain at this time. She tried Arthur next and it was the same story. Was it so much of a leap to imagine they went together?

Zennor tapped her fingers on the laptop idly. She was so tired but addicted. She needed to know more, like her sister had, obsessed with tracking Issey Trelenna's story.

She sipped at her now very cold mug of tea, thinking, then grabbed the list of pointers Zach had written out for her. What else was on it? Passenger lists? Maybe they didn't leave just the house behind them, maybe they left the country altogether, although even with her rudimentary knowledge of boat tickets she knew most servants wouldn't have been able to afford that.

Shrugging, she typed Grace's name into the passenger list search bar and included the year of the letter, just on the off-chance, and then she sat straight up. 'Bingo!' Name, age, occupation, destination. It was all there. Grace Pascoe, the same age, the same occupation. Destination: New York. Then, on a hunch and because she didn't know what else to do, she did the same for Arthur and smiled as the same result appeared. There he was. Same boat. Same day. Adrenaline pumped through her and she did a little celebratory shimmy in bed. She really was obsessed now.

The next morning, she bounded into the kitchen to find Merry and Zach hunkered over their mugs.

'Where's Lamorna?' she asked, barely containing her excitement, but hoping for a full house – not that it happened often. They all seemed to move at different speeds in the mornings.

'Out for a run,' Zach supplied around a mouthful of toast.

'Well, you'll have to do,' she said, and excitedly shared what she had uncovered the night before.

'So they're both in New York together?' Zach asked. He had listened so attentively she had almost felt self-conscious. 'This might get tricky now. There are US records available, but I've never really had to look for them.'

'I wonder if they go off to be a cook and footman over in New York,' Merry said, with less enthusiasm than she had hoped.

'Maybe.' Zach chugged his mug of coffee and checked his watch with a wince. He had tours at his own house to get back for.

Lamorna burst through the door in her running gear and looked at Zennor with a wide smile on her face.

'What?' Zennor asked, a little bewildered.

'I've just met Charlie,' Lamorna said in a sing-song voice with a giant smile breaking out on her face as she stood, stretching in the doorway. 'Digging the vegetable garden in a *very* tight t-shirt. I can see why you hired him.'

'I didn't hire him because he's attractive,' Zennor defended herself automatically.

'*I* didn't say he was attractive.' Lamorna looked at Zach when she said this, then pointed at her sister. 'She said that.'

'*Is* he attractive then?' Zach asked good-naturedly.

'Yes,' both sisters replied in unison.

'How attractive are we talking?' Merry asked while scrolling absently on his phone.

'He looks like he should be modelling,' Zennor admitted. 'But he was the only person the agency said would be suitable given how little money we have and the level of work involved.'

'How many hours are we hiring him?' Lamorna's eyes narrowed as she stretched out, never one to miss an opportunity to count pennies.

'He's doing ten hours a week, and he's picking and choosing when and how he spends them. He seems to know what he's doing.'

'Well, he'll give the tourists something nice to look at in the garden this morning when they're having tea and cake,' Lamorna said with a laugh. 'Maybe we should add it to the website: Charlie the gardener is beyond gorgeous.'

'Charlie the gardener is standing right behind you,' Charlie said, and Zennor watched her sister's face turn the shade of a tomato as she spun round, startled.

Zennor couldn't even look at Charlie. The shame of having been caught discussing him like that. Her voice caught in her throat. 'Hi.'

'Alright?' Charlie greeted her. 'I've found the outdoor tap, but I was just looking for a hose, if you have one?'

'We've only got one and it's attached to the other tap round the side. I'll show you,' Zennor said in a voice not quite her own, eager to get him away from the kitchen where they'd been discussing him as if he was an object of desire, which – now she looked at him again – she was ashamed to admit he sort of was.

'How much of all of that did you hear?' She addressed the elephant in the room as soon as they stepped outside.

'I think, possibly, all of it.' He glanced at her and chuckled.

'At least you know my sister and I were saying nice things,' Zennor attempted nervously.

'You were saying *very* nice things. Thanks.'

'You're welcome,' she said stiffly. This was all beyond humiliating.

Charlie glanced over to a side wall where one of the taps was with a hose attached. 'Found it,' he said. 'I'll let you get back to your happy place.'

She was surprised he'd remembered that, and frowned all the way back to the kitchen, not quite sure what had just happened.

Chapter 13

Two hours later, tours were underway and Zennor had been back and forth from the kitchen to the tearoom to top up cakes and tiffins. She'd plated fresh sandwiches and covered them over ready to take when ordered. She'd worked out with Kayleigh that they were best having a few of each flavour made and ready to purchase from eleven o'clock onwards, when people started getting hungry. It lessened the manic rush in the kitchen. When they'd made a bit more profit, she'd have to find a better system, maybe by purchasing some open refrigerated units in the tearoom so she could stockpile and people could help themselves rather than her going back and forth ad-hoc. It needed thinking about.

Zennor was happy, working alone today, with Kayleigh upstairs serving and sending over orders. She sang along to the radio and was just about to plate up a few ploughman's lunches with the freshest Cheddar cheese from nearby Davidstow when Charlie knocked on the open kitchen door.

'I'm just going now,' he said. 'I've done a couple of hours, as promised.' He had mud on his face and she wondered if he knew.

'You didn't pop in for tea,' she commented, not quite sure if she should mention the mud.

'I didn't like to ask on my first day.'

'You must be gasping for a drink. Can I get you something? If you don't have to rush off?' She didn't wait for an answer and flicked on the kettle anyway.

'I don't have to rush off, no. I'd love a tea. Just milk, thanks.'

'Sit down,' Zennor said, gesturing to a chair on the other side of the table away from the food she was prepping. 'Cake? Or you're welcome to have a ploughman's. I've got plenty. Or a sandwich.'

Charlie gave her a curious look. 'You like feeding people.'

Zennor noticed it wasn't a question but she answered all the same. 'I love it. It's my favourite thing. I'm a trained chef.'

'Are you? That's incredible. In a restaurant?'

'Absolutely not in a restaurant, no. That's my worst nightmare. I like the pace of being a private chef – dinner parties. And now I'm here cooking for the tearoom. I like an easy life.'

'Don't we all.'

'You didn't answer the question about what you want to eat,' she prompted. 'I've got loads of everything. Choose what you'd like.'

'Ploughman's? Is that okay? Only if you're sure. I don't want to put you out.'

'You're not.' In truth she was happy to have the company. His company.

While she assembled a plate for him, his gaze fell on the old, aged newspaper on the sideboard. His head turned to an angle. 'That doesn't look like today's.'

'It's from 1869. I found it in some of our house archives.'

His eyebrows raised with interest. 'Can I take a look if I'm careful?'

Zennor nodded and then placed his plate near him, turning her attention to the freshly boiled kettle to make them both tea.

'This is about your house,' he said as he pointed to the notice about Arthur Lander having absconded.

'Yes,' Zennor said as she sat next to him with their teas. 'I'm trying to work out what happened but I'm at a bit of a dead end.' She relayed the story of Grace and Arthur and how she'd found them on a boat to New York only a few days after leaving the house.

'Was the footman found back then? Was he arrested?'

'If he was, it wasn't in England. He was long gone a few days after this article was written and I can't find him on any of the censuses going forward. The whole experience obviously left a sour taste in Mrs Trelenna's mouth because she was going through the process of hiring a new cook, but not a footman.'

'Strange times,' Charlie said absently as he placed it back on the sideboard gently and then sipped his tea. He looked around the room. 'Has this always been the kitchen?'

'It has,' she said. 'It's all got me thinking what this kitchen would have looked like when the footman and the cook were here, when the letter asking for a new cook was written by one of my ancestors from her bedroom or wherever. The bedrooms look much the same, only with en-suites in most cases carved out before the house was listed. But down here it would have been so different. It's hard to imagine, but someone before us got rid of the servants' hall next door, turned it into the pantry with lots of storage cupboards. Much more useful for me. But servants would have sat in there eating their meals. And this kitchen would have looked so different. A large range, the kitchen maid coming and going, copper pots gleaming. One of the outbuildings would have been a dairy, whereas now it just holds all the stuff we really should jumble sale, and the kitchen garden would have served the house with fruit and veg.'

'Whereas *now* most of the kitchen garden is sun-baked soil.'

'Some of it's on your face too,' Zennor said.

Charlie smiled, touched the wrong cheek. 'It is?'

'The other one,' she said.

Charlie rubbed self-consciously. 'Has it gone?'

'Yes.'

'Thanks. You let me sit there like that for, what, five minutes?'

She chuckled. 'I didn't like to say.'

'Fair enough,' he said affably, his green-grey eyes holding her gaze.

She was the first to break, clearing her throat nervously and rambling on. 'There was a stable out there too but it got turned into the garages, and then of course it just became yet another storage facility for all the old clutter no one wanted in the house anymore.'

'Is that where you found the newspaper?'

'No, I found it in a box in my room.'

Charlie's eyes narrowed. 'What, just sitting there?'

'No, I mean, my sister put it there when she was researching one of our ancestors . . .' Zennor explained the events of the past few months since Lamorna had returned. 'And then I kicked the box and a few things flew out and . . . here we are.'

'What else is in the box?'

'I'm not sure,' she said thoughtfully. 'I did a bit of delving but in addition to the paper and the letter, I didn't pay too much attention.'

'You should,' Charlie replied.

'I will. But I wonder if I'm going to find much about them in a box all about Trelenna House given they went to America.'

'Well, see if you can do a search for them in the US in some way. They must turn up somewhere. Presumably they got married?' Charlie continued. 'So look for a Mrs Grace Lander and see what you find.'

Zennor stared at him. It had never occurred to her that Arthur and Grace might have *married.*

'If they were running away together for romantic reasons, then I doubt very much back then society would have stood for them being together but not married,' Charlie reasoned.

'That does make sense. Okay, I'll give that a shot. Thanks.'

Charlie finished his lunch but Zennor was reluctant to let him go. 'Do you fancy a slice of cake?'

'I'm a bit full after your amazing ploughman's and I've got another job to get to – don't want to fall asleep while digging. But maybe I could take a piece with me, as I sense you really want me to eat some cake.'

Zennor smiled. 'Is it obvious? I've just perfected the recipe for blackberry vanilla meringue cake and would love to know what you think. While the berries are out it makes sense. Although I got cut to shreds trying to pick them. But . . . free fruit.'

'I was thinking about those brambles. How do you feel about goats?'

'Is this a trick question?'

'Goats will keep the brambles down. We can wait until the blackberries have finished and let the goats at them. My next job is helping out on a smallholding where there are a couple of goats. Madly enough, goats love eating brambles, thorns and all. I can ask if we can borrow them in winter?'

We. Lovely how he was already part of the team. 'Thanks. Good idea.' Zennor's phone dinged with orders from Kayleigh. 'I'd best get moving,' she said reluctantly.

'Thanks for lunch. I'll see you tomorrow.'

'Looking forward to it.' She groaned inwardly. *Looking forward to it. Who says that?* She recovered with a simple 'Bye' as he left. Now that was more normal.

Chapter 14

Over the next few weeks, Zennor couldn't face looking in the archive boxes after seven days a week of being on her feet. She just needed sleep. She was only twenty-one, why was she so tired all the time? Admittedly, she'd never worked this hard in her life, but still. She loved it, but perhaps seven days a week was unwise. Merry and Lamorna were doing the same, running tours on rotation every hour, but when they finished for the night, they finished. Zennor kept going, kept batch baking so they had a wide choice for the tearoom. Then she cooked everyone dinner. And got up as early as she could to unload the dishwasher and start again. Perhaps she did need to let go of cooking the family dinner a few nights a week. She wasn't a control freak about much, but over the quality of food and how things should be cooked, she was. It was all she knew, all she loved, and she didn't *want* to let go of it.

Stretching out her aching muscles, she hoped she wasn't coming down with something. In these first few weeks of opening she couldn't let everyone down. The archive boxes had to be put on the backburner as she tried each evening to get ahead of herself. But with it turning decidedly autumnal, September's weather being that strange mix of warm and chilly often all at once, and the school holidays being a thing of distant memory, it was going to get quiet very soon. They all knew this. That initial opening wave was going to die out and they'd braced themselves for impending disappointment when it came to turnover. Pensioners and mothers with small babies coming for coffee would now be the norm, hopefully. They needed as many customers as possible to keep the money coming in, and Lamorna was already making sounds about tidying up her CV and possibly going back to work to help fund things when the tourist numbers fell away.

'What do you think of this?' Zennor placed a freshly baked pumpkin spiced muffin, soft and plump, in front of Charlie one morning as he popped in to say his usual goodbye – although she'd finally convinced him to come and say hello when he arrived and collect a mug of tea before he started work too. But he didn't stay long, making a point of getting right to it. And she relished the twenty minutes or so he spent with her every Monday to Friday where she'd convinced him to eat lunch with her, even if it was at the very early time of eleven o'clock in the morning when he finished working in the garden. 'The pumpkin isn't fresh,' she said. 'It's from a can, but I just wanted to try it quickly before committing to roasting whole pumpkins for the real thing.'

'Is this for your new autumn menu?'

'Mm, what do you think?' She watched him eagerly.

'That's great. What's in it?'

'Pumpkin.'

'Yeah, and?'

'A special blend of sweet spices,' she said cryptically. 'Merry had an idea to put on a Halloween trail for the October half-term, so I'm seeing what I can do for adults and kids. I thought I might try chocolate lollies in shapes of cute ghosts and vampires.'

'Cute vampires?'

'It's a thing,' Zennor said.

'Is it? And kids are into that?'

'I have no idea what kids are into. I'm winging it.'

He smiled. 'I have no idea what kids are into either. But chocolate is always a winner, no matter what shape it's in.'

'That's what I thought,' she said as she put a mug of tea down in front of him. 'Still want lunch or just the muffin?'

'What was that quiche you forced me to eat yesterday, even though I said I hated quiche?'

Zennor put her hands on her hips and stared at him mock-accusingly. 'Um, excuse me? I did not *force* chorizo and Manchego quiche down your throat. You volunteered to try it and you loved it, you said.'

'I did love it. That's why I'm asking for it again.'

'See? I've converted you to quiche already. What else do you hate? I'll see if I can get you to love that too.'

'Marmite,' he said immediately. 'I always wanted to like it but I just hate it.'

'You're right about that one. Marmite's the devil in a jar. We're not having that in this kitchen, thank you.'

Charlie chuckled as Zennor found two thick slices of quiche from yesterday's batch in the fridge, assembled salad and added her own oven-roasted tomatoes to it. 'Want me to warm yours up?'

'Zennor,' he said and she looked at him. He hadn't used her name since that first day she'd met him. 'You do enough. Don't you ever sit down?'

'I sit down to eat lunch with you. And then, dinner later on.'

'And that's it all day?'

'Yeah. What about you?'

'Well . . . same, I guess, but a couple of tea breaks when I sit on an upturned plant pot. And I drive to and from jobs, so I'm sitting then.'

'We're even then, I'd say. In the unhappy competition of who's more tired than who, there's no clear winner.'

'But you look tired.'

Zennor's eyebrows shot up. 'Wow. Thanks.'

'That's not what I mean. I mean . . .'

'You mean . . . I look tired.'

'Er . . .'

'It's fine.' She slumped into a chair. 'I am tired, actually. I think I'm overdoing it. And it's a big deal for me to say that. But I know I just need to get past these few weeks, then it'll be quieter. Until October half-term, when it'll be non-stop again, so Lamorna seems to think. But it's all worth it.'

'Can I do anything to help?'

Zennor shook her head. 'No, but thank you. It's just nice to sit down and have lunch with you. If I didn't do this, I'd probably snaffle a sandwich in double-quick time over the sink so . . .'

'Do you ever take a day off?'

'I haven't taken one yet. But before we opened the house to the public, I'd had quite a lot of days off, quite a lot of time to myself, so this is . . . nice. Being busy, everyone being home. Well, not everyone. But most of them.'

'Then you'll be even busier? Cooking for how many more?'

'Mum and Dad – and Veryan, who may or may not come home at some point.'

'What's she doing?'

'She's an influencer.'

Charlie looked at her sheepishly. 'I'm not entirely sure what they actually do.'

'Neither am I, but she's travelling the world being funded by views on her YouTube videos apparently, so good luck to her. I wouldn't come home either if I was her,' Zennor said flippantly, and then immediately knew that wasn't true. Of course she would. She was built differently from Veryan. 'I don't mean that. I would never have left in the first place, let alone stayed away so long.'

'It's nice to feel that about your home. I don't really feel that way.'

'Don't you? Why not?' It was only now, in this moment, that she realised Charlie had been a closed book, hardly telling her anything about himself, whereas – at his invitation – she'd talked non-stop. Perhaps she needed to give him the space to speak. Perhaps she'd been talking too much. But he made her feel as if she could be herself.

'My mum and dad divorced when I was quite young,' he said. 'Then they both remarried. Then they both had children and I found myself quite on the outside, a bit homeless, or perhaps just a bit unwanted, maybe, in a way. I had two homes and so it never really felt like I had a *proper* one. I was a bit torn, floating between spare bedrooms. A bit in the *way* of things. I only went to uni so I could live somewhere different, somewhere new. And then I never went back to either of my parents' respective homes. I guess neither of them expected me to come back to them at that age, and they never questioned it when I got a flat down here.'

'Down here? Aren't you from Cornwall originally?'

'Surrey.'

'And you moved here by yourself? At how old?'

'Twenty-one. Straight after uni. My best friend at uni was from Newquay and we spent a lot of time surfing or doing not a lot at his during some of the holidays, so I got a thirst for this place. I love it here. I've finally found somewhere that I'm happy.'

'It's sad it took you this long to find somewhere to call home.'

'I'm not sure I've really found *home*. But it'll do for now. I'm happy renting a little flat in Tintagel. I had one with a sea view until it became an Airbnb.'

'Bloody tourists,' Zennor joked. 'Although I need them here, so let's not say it too loud. Twenty-one is so young to move by yourself, though. I'm twenty-one, and don't think I could do it.' She wanted to know if he was living on his own or if he had a girlfriend, but she couldn't work out if it would sound smooth or silly to ask.

'It was only four years ago,' he said. 'I didn't feel young at the time but I had a lot to learn – how to pay council tax and the TV licence. All those things no one tells you about. I work in a variety of gardens, have made some nice friends, through work mostly.' He nodded in her direction, as if they were friends. They *were* friends, Zennor realised. She liked his company and he must like hers if he spent every day popping in to spend time with her. Or maybe that was because she forced him. Like with the quiche.

'Our lives couldn't have been more different,' she said. 'I never wanted to leave home, this is my happy place.'

'I thought that was the kitchen.'

'It's all of it. I love it here. It's all I've ever really wanted.'

'I can see why you're happy. I'd imagine it's hard to be unhappy in a house as beautiful as Trelenna.'

'Oh, it has its moments, trust me. But I bounce back quickly. It probably helps that I'm quite a happy person generally. But it's the feeling I have when I walk through the door, the feeling I have knowing I'm nurturing the house, nurturing that feeling for us and for the generations that follow. Family is important to me. It's the most important thing in my world and I want them here, but I know not everyone will remain at Trelenna forever. They'll come and go. But knowing the house is safe for them to be *able* to come and go from it, because I started it all off, that's a feeling that can't be beaten.'

Charlie smiled, looked around the room thoughtfully.

'I'm sorry. I'm being insensitive.' She could have kicked herself given what he'd just told her.

'You're not. Not at all. Everyone's circumstances are different. I suppose I want what you have. I suppose I've always known it. But I have to make it.'

'A home?'

'Yeah. A home. A proper one. With a family too, or else what's the point?'

Zennor wished she could see into the future. A home and a family of her own, not just her parents and her siblings . . . that felt like something a long way away. 'See, I understand this completely, but I'm sure my brother and sisters think I'm mad, being such a homebody. Lamorna's forever checking how many air miles she's earning on her credit card. Everything I want is here, including the challenge of cooking for a *lot* of people every day. I didn't realise I wanted that, that I *needed* that challenge. But I love it. I'm fulfilled. You must feel the same way about gardening?'

'Yeah, I do. Perhaps not as strongly as you feel about food,' he joked.

'Hey.' She laughed. 'I'm just enthusiastic. And I don't believe that at all about you. I've seen you out there. You frown at the soil far more than I frown at the oven.'

He smiled. 'Maybe. Sometimes the earth just doesn't play ball and something won't grow and I have to go away and work out what's going on. Or perhaps something is just growing in the wrong place. I do love it, though – gardening and that sense of achievement it brings. And believe it or not, my dream is to take a really desolate piece of land and make it grow.'

'You've come to the right place then,' she joked. 'You've seen the grounds.'

'Trelenna's not that desolate. I've seen worse. It's salvageable.'

'That's exactly what I thought. What I still think. Hence why I'm trying so hard to save it. It's not a *completely* lost cause.'

'It's definitely not a lost cause at all. The visitors look happy enough, so you must be doing a great job. It certainly looks as if you are.'

'Thanks, I hope we are too.' She yawned. 'Sorry. I'm not bored,' she said hastily. 'I'm just really tired working flat out.'

'I haven't got to be anywhere for a bit. Can I do something to help?'

His eyes were kind, his smile genuine. 'Really?' she asked.

'Of course. For a start,' he said, rising with his dirty plate, 'I don't have a dishwasher but I could probably learn how to stack one.'

'Oh, thank you,' she said. 'You've been deprived. I couldn't cope without a dishwasher.'

'And then I can take the trolley of food along to the tearoom?' he volunteered.

'Kayleigh would *love* that. She might feast her eyes on you for a full minute instead of serving customers. Let me just grab some more plates from the fridge.'

Charlie laughed and looked away, embarrassed, as he loaded tea things into the dishwasher. 'You do know how to make someone feel good.'

Zennor wasn't sure how to reply to that, so she just looked away shyly; then she said, 'I'm really pleased it was you who was sent along, by the way. You're very easy to talk to. I've enjoyed spending time with you these past few weeks.'

'Thanks. Same.' He stopped stacking the dishwasher and looked at her. 'Zennor, this might be a bit presumptuous but . . . would you like to go out for a drink with me one evening?'

Her heart leaped about in her chest and she couldn't immediately answer.

'Do you have a boyfriend?' he asked, looking worried.

Zennor shook her head. 'No. No boyfriend. And I'd love to go out for a drink with you.' She stifled a yawn.

'Perhaps an early evening drink?' Charlie suggested jovially. 'So you can get to bed on time?'

‘That would be lovely.’

He gave her a happy look. ‘Great.’

‘Great,’ she repeated, sure she was giving him the same look.

‘I’ll just take this trolley along . . .’

‘Thanks,’ she replied as he went off down the corridor. And then when he was gone, she caught herself smiling like an idiot in the reflection of the window.

Chapter 15

It took another week before Zennor and Charlie saw each other again, and in that time it struck her that he might have regretted asking her on a date, seeing as he hadn't followed up on it. Perhaps it had been an impulse decision and he was backtracking silently.

Kayleigh and Zennor swapped places most afternoons, now that they'd forged a routine of what food needed making and when. They were working well as a team with ad-hoc help for a couple of hours every lunchtime when someone had to be on non-stop duty making hot drinks. Zennor found herself in the tearoom serving most mornings, and she was trying to work out if she preferred working silently in her kitchen doing what she loved, *or* being among people in the tearoom. She'd come to the conclusion that it was nice to mix things up, and keep things fresh, and see people enjoying her creations for herself.

Kayleigh was appreciating the change too, and loving putting suggestions for new bakes and savoury dishes forward, and then putting it into practice in the kitchen, stretching her wings. Zennor wanted her friend to feel a valued part of the team, and given it was the first time she'd ever had to manage someone, she hoped she wasn't doing too bad a job of it. And with Charlie too, who, Kayleigh reported, hadn't once popped in for tea and lunch since she'd been down in the kitchen. Although he had been coming to work because Zennor could see the vegetable garden taking shape with tall canes and old-fashioned metal frames installed that he must have found in the potting shed. The ornamental garden looked as if it had been given some attention too.

At eleven o'clock, Zennor was taking a tray of cream teas over to a table on the outside terrace when she spotted Charlie walking round. He raised his hand in greeting and waited for her to finish serving before approaching.

Zennor walked towards him, her heartbeat suddenly sounding a bit louder in her ears. 'Hello, stranger.'

'I could say the same. You've been let out of the kitchen, then? I was wondering where you were.'

'I've been here the whole time. Kayleigh says you haven't been popping in for lunch.'

Charlie glanced around as if not wanting to be overheard. 'I haven't. I go in to see you. And you haven't been there, so I've just gone off to my next job.'

Zennor wasn't sure what to make of that. Flattered, special, that's how he made her feel. 'I see. So you've gone off to your next job hungry. Kayleigh would have made you something to take away. She's under strict instructions to keep you fed.'

'Good to know. Thank you. Are you up here for the foreseeable? Because so far it's knocked my plan off course to ask you out.'

So he hadn't forgotten. 'What was your plan?' she asked in the calmest voice she could muster.

'I wanted to ask you face to face, rather than by text. I'm afraid I'm not very cool like that.'

'Neither am I.'

'Okay, great. We can be not very cool together. If you're free tonight, I thought, maybe a drink at a vineyard?' he questioned uncertainly. 'Would that work? I passed one that's opened a bar this summer, with a view over the vines, and while the weather's still bright I thought it would be a nice place to take you. If you're not busy?'

'I'm not busy,' she said quickly, although she was, but she could delay prep for tomorrow for a few hours and the others would have to make their own dinner for once. 'But which vineyard?' Because she had a sneaking suspicion she knew which one he meant and she didn't want to go there.

'The one near Lanhydrock?'

Zennor made a reluctant face.

'You don't like that one?'

'That is where my sort-of-ex loves to go. So I'd rather not, if that's okay?' She winced. 'Just in case we bump into him.'

'Of course. We can do something else. What's a *sort-of*-ex?'

'It's someone who says he really likes you, makes you like him, then ghosts you after sleeping with you.'

'Oh, shit. Okay, yeah, let's avoid that place. Where's safe?'

'It's a beautiful day. Do you fancy a picnic on the beach? It's just round the coast path a little way and then down, if you haven't seen it yet?'

'I haven't. I'd love that. I finish at five today, so I'll come straight back and meet you here?'

'I'll make the picnic,' she said. 'I've got time. That way you haven't got to stop and buy anything.'

'Not a fan of pre-packed things in plastic wrap from petrol stations?'

'Not hugely,' she admitted. 'I'd like to make dinner for you, if that's okay?' She felt nerves creeping into her voice.

'I'd love that. Thanks.'

'Okay,' she said, already mentally planning her menu.

'Okay,' he said too, lingering and smiling just as much as she was.

'Excuse me, do you have another pot of milk?' one of the customers called out.

'I'd better go,' Zennor said quietly.

'See you later,' Charlie replied as Zennor rushed off to serve.

All afternoon Zennor beamed, attending to the last trickle of customers with a spring in her step and a smile on her face as she thought about the evening that lay ahead of her. Normally she enjoyed every moment of her job, but she couldn't wait to rush through the afternoon and get to the highlight. Although she paused when she counted up the day's tearoom takings – deeming it a good day all round, and eagerly texted Lamorna and Merry the amount. Who knew where they were in the house?

Zennor felt a continued need to prove she knew what she was doing in this part of the business, if not in the other parts. She knew food. She loved it and felt grateful to think she was doing something she loved and continuing to save the house in this small but rather profitable way.

She had some freshly prepared pizza dough and got to work making supper for her and Charlie. She couldn't bring herself to force the others to make their own dinner after everyone had been working so hard – on their feet all day with the tours – so she made pizzas for them too and left a note for how long to reheat them. They wouldn't be as good reheated, but she doubted they'd even notice or care – just be grateful to be fed. Once she'd cooked a batch for her and Charlie, decorated with fresh torn buffalo mozzarella and scattered with some basil leaves, she considered it finished. After, she prepared a pudding of Eton mess with clotted cream and kept the berries in a separate pot so the colour wouldn't leach into the pristine white meringue until the very moment of serving.

Then, because time was against her, she pulled a pack of Lamorna's Kettle crisps down and some pre-made dip, which went against everything Zennor stood for, but she was hopeful the pizza and homemade pudding would make up for it.

She had been told many a time by Merry over the years that no one cared about food as much as she did, and that no one even noticed when she lovingly made crisps from excess vegetables versus ripping open a packet of Walkers. She'd been horrified and a little offended, but Merry hadn't meant to hurt – he'd been trying to lighten her load. None of them realised she didn't necessarily want her load lightened that way though.

Just after five o'clock, Charlie arrived, and Zennor's heart pumped a little quicker at the sight of him. She'd been ready for ages and had assembled a small cool-box of organic drinks she'd been meaning to taste-test to stock in the tearoom.

They talked about their days as they walked through the parkland towards the coast path. Charlie had taken on a few hours a week at a plant nursery and had been busy there this afternoon. As he carried the picnic hamper, Zennor quizzed him about what he loved growing and, more importantly, what he loved eating.

'There's a synergy with what you do all day and what I do all day,' she prompted. 'You grow it, and I cook it. I'm so excited for whatever you manage to grow in that forlorn-looking veg patch.'

'It's not forlorn anymore,' he replied. 'I've put in onion sets and garlic. We'll have to have a celebration of sorts when the first crop comes in.'

They walked close together along the coast path, which was thick either side with gorse and heather. The greenery was already showing an array of burnt oranges mixed in. At the final curve down to the cove, the path narrowed, forcing them into single file. Charlie was in front of her and he stopped, taking in the view. 'This is why I love Cornwall. This is why I moved here,' he said as a wide-open blue sea stretched endlessly in front of them, and a small patch of sand, where the tide was in, met them below. The sun, on its slow evening descent towards the horizon, gleamed and sent sparkles on to the sea.

'It looks tropical this evening,' Zennor commented as they moved down the steps, carved into the side of the cliffs from hundreds of years of past Trelennas stomping their way down. 'That's one of the reasons why *I* love Cornwall. Because every day the scenery is different, even when you're looking at exactly the same thing as yesterday. It's magical. I never want to leave.'

'Why would you leave?' he asked.

'I wouldn't. Not if I can help it. I'm not that brave.'

'Oh, I'll bet you are. You just haven't had to be, perhaps?'

'Maybe,' she replied, thinking about it. No, she hadn't had to be brave, not really. She wasn't sure if her parents leaving her to run the house counted as a situation where she'd had to be brave. Decisions had needed to be made but that wasn't bravery, surely? It had been thrust upon her and was the only course of action if she wanted to keep her home. She knew there'd been a time when everyone – her parents, her siblings – had wanted to let Trelenna go, sell, move out and take the money, until she'd convinced them not to. 'No, I haven't had to be brave really,' she said with a long sigh. 'On the face of it, I realise I've led a very charmed, easy life.'

'That's not a bad thing,' he said as they reached the sand. Zennor rolled the large tartan picnic mat out and Charlie put the hamper down before they sat next to each other, cross-legged, appreciating the view, watching the slow waves roll gently in.

'I don't think life should be about being brave. The ideal life is one where you don't *have* to be brave, but, I think, make the tough choices,' he continued. 'My family was a bit messy. I love hearing about your family, though, how solid it is.'

She coughed out a laugh. 'Hardly. We're all over the place, mentally and geographically. But we're there for each other when needed. And that's the important thing.'

'It is,' Charlie agreed as Zennor offered him a drink.

'These are sort of fruit spritzers,' she explained as he opened a can of orange fizz and she a lemon one.

'Like a non-alcoholic Aperol,' he said, grimacing after a sip.

Zennor tried hers. 'Limoncello?' They looked thoughtfully down at their cans for a beat.

'Want to swap?' she asked.

'Yes, please,' he said genially and took a swig of the new one. 'That's better.'

'I prefer this one too,' she said, making a hole in the sand with the can and pushing it in to keep it stable. Charlie did the same.

'This view is better than a vineyard,' Zennor said, hugging her knees towards her.

His face was unreadable, and she hoped she hadn't offended him. 'It is. Also less chance of running into your ex, perhaps?'

'*Much* less chance of running into Reece. He's not the outdoorsy type, unless he's looking at vineyards. A beach picnic wouldn't be on his agenda.'

'Reece sounds like a tool,' Charlie said, making Zennor laugh loudly.

'You might be right. And I love that expression,' she said as in front of them a series of waves rolled in to shore, the first never fully retreating before the one behind chased it in.

'Why did he let you go? Was he mad?'

'Quite possibly,' she said in a regal voice. She glanced at him, enjoying this flirtation, enjoying being with him on a date she never thought would happen. And here they were talking about her ex.

'How long did it last?'

'Only a couple of months, off and on. Just chatting, flirting and then a few dinners out and then . . .' She paused. *And then a dinner at his where he pulled out all the stops,* she thought. *Seduced me very artfully and then never messaged me again . . .* 'We were taking things slowly and then suddenly we weren't and then it ended. A bit abruptly, I guess.'

'He's obviously a loser,' Charlie said, shooting her a grin.

Zennor sighed, leaning back into the sand and stretching her legs in front of her. 'He's a very successful wine merchant, annoyingly.'

'He's a very successful loser, then,' Charlie conceded, leaning back on the sand to meet her gaze. 'And he'll probably never be very happy if he does things like that to incredible women like you.'

Zennor glanced out to sea bashfully. 'Amen to that. Although I don't want to see anyone *truly* miserable,' she said. Although she could probably be quite happy if Reece was alone forever, not doing *that* to other women. 'What about you? Anyone serious?'

'No one serious. Just a bit like you, I guess. Some off-and-on things. Mainly off,' he joked.

'I'm going to ask you an even more personal question now,' she said.

Charlie braced himself and put on a serious expression. 'Okay. Shoot.'

'What was your injury?' she asked from out of nowhere.

'Oh.' He looked relieved and then embarrassed. 'I fell off my bike.'

'A motorbike?' she asked, her face immediately adopting an expression of horror.

'No, I did tell you I'm not very cool. A pushbike. I was doing a trail one Sunday and absolutely stacked it. Very embarrassing. Broke my leg. Had to take a couple of months off work, and because I'm freelance I lost a few of my contracts. It's nice to be back to work again, though. Nice to have something regular to come to among the ad-hoc work.' He paused for a beat, holding her gaze. 'Nice to spend time with you every day. That's a bonus I didn't see coming.'

She looked away, blushed.

'Why do you do that?'

'What?'

'Look away every time I pay you a compliment.'

'I don't,' she said, focusing on the waves.

'You do.'

'You do it too,' she protested.

'No, I don't. And I can prove it. Pay me a compliment and I promise I'll hold your gaze.'

'You've trapped me,' she said, thumping him playfully on the arm.

'Ow, and no, I haven't. Okay, I'll go first, then, just to prove it. But you have to hold my gaze.'

'I won't be able to,' she whined.

'You'll have to. Ready?'

'No,' she said and put her head in her hands, laughing into her palms.

'I'm not saying it until you look at me.'

'Aaagh,' Zennor whined again and forced her gaze up to his.

Charlie started. 'Ready?'

'No.'

'Tough. When you told me Kayleigh would feast her eyes on me, I didn't want her to feast her eyes on me. I wanted you to.'

She breathed in suddenly, all the air from her lungs long gone while forcing her eyes to remain on his. That was a brave thing to say. She exhaled, then got brave in return. 'Oh, don't worry. I am.'

He threw back his head, laughing loudly, and she joined in.

'See that wasn't so bad, was it?' he asked, catching his breath.

'That was *torture*,' she exclaimed through giggles.

'It shouldn't be.'

'Is that why you haven't been in the kitchen recently? Kayleigh mentioned you don't come in for lunch or even a cup of tea.'

'I looked in the kitchen door as I went past on the mornings you weren't there and when I saw it wasn't you, I just kept walking.'

'Why?'

'Because I'd spent weeks getting to know you and I really like you and you weren't there. So I didn't go in. I wanted to wait until you were back before asking you out properly. But you never showed up. So today, I thought enough was enough and I went on the hunt.'

'And you found me.'

'And I found you,' he echoed. 'And I'm really pleased I did.'

'Me too,' she said as Charlie leaned a little closer to her on the mat. She looked into his eyes the way she'd not really been able to before, taking in the circles of green and light grey. Like the sea when a storm was brewing. And then she closed her eyes, letting herself be swept up into the softest, most gentle kiss. His lips grazed hers so lightly she thought she'd explode with urgency, and she heard a little whimper of frustration that she realised must have come from her. It was all the encouragement Charlie needed as the kiss deepened and her hands touched his face, pulling him closer and feeling as if she was falling from a great height, but without any of the fear she usually felt.

Chapter 16

Whenever Charlie was at Trelenna House over the coming weeks, he found Zennor either in the kitchen or the tearoom. He always looked so at home in the comfort of her kitchen and so nervous when he entered the grand ballroom where the tearoom was situated. As if he shouldn't be there. Zennor always beckoned him over, found him a space to sit and fed him. After work, they went for long rambling walks through the woodland or down to the cove, picnic in hand each time. But now the evening light was fading fast – autumnal October heading towards its chilly conclusion – and Zennor decided she wanted to cook a meal for Charlie in the comfort of a heated room.

It was such a novelty, Charlie returning after his afternoon work in the garden centre as planned, and then offering assistance, getting stuck in, helping Zennor make dinner. She enjoyed the feeling of having him near her, feeling him brush past her in the kitchen, reaching over her to the utensil pot to dig around for wooden spoons. It made cooking dinner a slow but enjoyable process, fielding his affections, pausing while stirring the sauce so she could be kissed. As if cooking wasn't enjoyable enough. Determined to take things slowly, that was as far as they had gone. But what kissing it was.

And when it was time to eat with Lamorna, Zach and Merry, she admired Charlie's ability to remain unfazed as they quizzed him about what he'd been doing in the garden, where he was from. He even remained calm when Lamorna asked if he really needed to be here ten hours per week, to which Zennor shot her sister a look that would have killed, making Zach snigger into his glass of water.

So far, Zennor had remained unusually tight-lipped with her siblings as to how she felt about Charlie, determined not to wear her heart on her sleeve and ruin a good thing. It had only been a matter of weeks since that first kiss on the beach. But this dinner must tell them Charlie had entered her life and her heart. She had to keep reminding herself not to fall too hard, too fast. But he was so easy to fall in love with. And she knew it was happening, which both worried her and spurred her on in equal measure. When she looked back, she didn't know what she'd done with Reece to make him cast her aside so quickly. Unless it was simply sleeping with him too fast. She'd given him everything and he'd taken it from her so freely. And then what was left? Nothing. No wonder he'd thrown her away. She'd been determined not to let the same thing happen with Charlie. And because she liked him so, *so* much more than she'd ever liked Reece, she was keeping as much back as possible until she couldn't hold it in any longer. It was hard-going. She wondered what it was doing to him.

'How's your hunt for Grace going?' Zach asked excitedly as they all ate together. 'What have you discovered about where she went and what she did since I last saw you?'

'Nothing,' Zennor replied guiltily. 'It's been slow. Non-existent. Sorry, I've been a bit distracted.' She glanced at Charlie conspiratorially.

'You don't need to apologise, it can be hard when doing all of this,' Zach said with a smile, gesturing at the house. 'Want a hand with the hunt?'

'No, thank you,' Zennor said politely, realising immediately that something about Grace, this hunt for her life, her story, felt personal, like a secret she wasn't ready to share. 'I'm very happy to do this on my own. But I do have one problem – I don't have access to US records through that login you gave me, so I think I'm just going to google her.'

Merry tried not to laugh at Zach's horrified expression.

'I'm not sure that will yield results,' Zach said stiffly. 'History can be a little complex and you probably need to really drill down into some established archives to find someone as random and everyday as Grace.'

'Why is she random and everyday?'

'Because she's a servant who went to America. She's essentially a bit of a . . .' Zach trailed off.

Zennor stared at him. 'Are you about to say a nobody?'

'I was going to say *a statistic*.'

'I'm not sure that's kinder,' Zennor said.

Zach laughed. 'I'm not sure it's kinder either, *but* I would be very cautious of just searching for a name on the internet. There will probably be a hundred women called Grace Pascoe who emigrated to America during the Victorian era. If you stumble on one Grace Pascoe, don't expect it to be her.'

'I thought,' Charlie said, smoothly covering Zennor's bristle of anger, 'that she and the footman might have married. They went overseas together, from what Zennor found. Unlikely they'd have been living together unmarried if they were trying to make a fresh start of things? Frowned upon back then, no?'

'More than just frowned upon, and yes, it's a strong possibility,' Zach agreed. 'So now you have to hunt for two Graces. One her maiden name and one Arthur's last name. God, I love this bit,' he enthused, melting Zennor's irritation immediately. 'I love the chase. It's the best bit.'

'It's the most frustrating bit,' Zennor retorted.

After the simple dinner of roasted sweet potatoes stuffed with lentils and sausages from Zennor's favourite butcher Philip Warren, Merry peeled off to his room as usual, and Zach said he needed to get home to Port Carrack House. 'If I roll in seconds before tours start one more time this week, my sister is going to kill me. I'm off to show my face before she locks up.'

Lamorna walked with him to his car, leaving Charlie and Zennor alone.

'So . . . that's my family,' she said, passing him plates for the dishwasher as if they did this every night. 'Or rather, a small portion of them, and Zach.'

Charlie grinned at her. 'I think they're great.'

'No doubt I'll hear what they think about you tomorrow. But I imagine they think you're great too.'

'I didn't say much.'

Zennor laughed and turned on the tap to wash the baking tray. 'No one new ever does. I'm amazed Zach gets a word in edgeways either. Dinners are usually a noisy affair when everyone's here: talking over one another, seven conversations going on at once.'

'It sounds perfect,' Charlie admitted. 'I never had that.'

'It is perfect, I suppose. It's also a bit frustrating.'

'As frustrating as trying to hunt down people from the past?'

'Not *that* frustrating, no,' she admitted with a laugh, feeling so comfortable she wondered why she was delaying anything, why she was holding back.

'*Would* you like some help with finding out more about Grace? I know you told Zach no—'

'Yes, please,' Zennor said before she'd even formulated the words in her mind.

Charlie's eyebrows lifted.

'I see Zach enough,' Zennor rushed in, to fill the awkward silence. 'If you want to help, I'd be okay with that.'

◆ ◆ ◆

They made themselves comfy later in the study at the large writing desk, Zennor's laptop open in front of them. The fire was lit and crackling, while steaming mugs of Earl Grey sat on the table alongside a plate of homemade lemon crunch biscuits Zennor was testing from an old recipe book.

'Where do we start?' Charlie asked, helping himself to a biscuit and making an appreciative noise as he munched.

Zennor typed *New York marriage certificates* into Google and it brought up the New York City Municipal Archives, which had the majority of historical records digitised and available for free from 1855 to 1949.

'Perfect,' she said and narrowed the search filter down so it only covered 1869 onwards, then typed in *Grace Pascoe,* clicked Enter and hoped for the best. A copy of an official-looking certificate loaded on the screen. They both sat forward and read:

> *I hereby certify that Arthur Lander and Grace Pascoe were joined in marriage by me, in accordance with the Laws of the State of New York in the city of New York, this twenty-second day of October 1869.*
>
> *WH Birkins, Minister, residence 327 W. 30th St.*
>
> *Witnesses to the marriage: John Lander and Mary Lander*

'They did marry!' Zennor exclaimed. Then she hunched closer to read the next page, scanned in as fresh as the day the ink was applied, listing Grace and Arthur's names respectively and places of birth noted as Cornwall and Devon, England.

'And two more Landers,' Charlie pointed out. 'John and Mary.'

'He must have had family there,' Zennor said. 'That's nice. They knew people when they arrived. It's my worst nightmare going somewhere new and knowing nobody.' She looked around the safety of the walls of Trelenna House – the place Grace had lived and then left, to find a home so far away. Zennor still couldn't fathom why her own siblings had all wanted to leave, let alone people from the past, when life and travel was harder to navigate.

'Let's keep looking. What else can we find?' Charlie asked, leaning forward enthusiastically. 'Maybe they had children?'

Zennor changed the search criteria and looked for birth certificates attached to Grace. Two entries were available. Daisy Lander born in 1870 and four years later, Rose in 1874.

'They had two daughters,' Zennor exclaimed excitedly. 'I'd love a daughter one day. What else can we look for?'

'This website only shows births, marriages and deaths.'

'I've just found her alive, I don't want to find her dead now.'

But Charlie was already typing. There was nothing for Grace. Zennor sat up and stared. 'Why isn't she here?'

'Maybe she didn't die in New York. She must have died somewhere else.'

'How do we find that out?' Zennor asked, the whiplash of marriage, children and death almost too much to handle.

'I have no idea.'

Shaking her head, Zennor took charge again. 'It doesn't matter. I'm not too bothered about her death. I want to know what she did when she was alive. I know Zach said not to do this because it was unreliable but . . .' Zennor turned the laptop a little towards her and typed into a search engine: *Grace Lander, Cook, New York City, 1869*. Then crossing her fingers, she hit Enter.

Chapter 17

New York City

1869

Grace

Grace and Arthur took a moment to pause near the six-storey brick tenement block where Arthur's cousin John lived. She'd never seen buildings this big. They had travelled so long and far from a home that wasn't theirs anymore that it felt as if they would never make it here at all. And they had no real idea what awaited them. The address was tucked away deep in Arthur's pocket, as if it was precious. It *was* precious. It represented the start of their new life together.

Arthur had grown into the best kind of friend anyone could wish for on the journey, fetching water for her when she'd been violently sick on the voyage, encouraging her on to the deck to look at the horizon when she'd been adamant she couldn't possibly move, holding her hand to keep her steady at all times. His hand within hers had become so natural that it took a moment for her to notice that her hand was within his even now.

As they stood on the other side of the street, horse-drawn carriages moving in and out of view, hawkers shouting from street corners, she soaked it all in. Almost anything was preferable to the voyage they'd just endured. It was the first time either of them had ever been on board a proper boat – a ship, really. The first time they had experienced rolling waves. The first time they'd ever been away from south-west England. When they had left the harbour, both had stood on deck, watching the port drift out of view as eight long weeks of turbulent surf took them away from land, everything they'd ever known and towards a new life in a strange and foreign climate. They had even made a pact on the boat to look after each other forever.

He had proposed when they were out at sea. It had been simple, no frills, like Arthur himself: an uncomplicated confession. 'I know you don't love me. But I love you. I've always loved you. You're my best friend.' His eyes had searched hers. 'Isn't that the perfect basis for marriage? Shouldn't you marry someone you already care so deeply about? I don't expect anything of you. But this is our chance to start something new together.'

His words promised a fresh start. And Grace had been in desperate need of one, fiercely needing to put all thoughts of Laurie Trelenna from her mind. She had fallen for Laurie too quickly and it had ended in disaster. She, with some trepidation, had agreed to marry Arthur somewhere between her past and her future, in a sea where no land was in sight. And now, weeks later, she never wanted to be without him.

Arthur was her rescuer, the only man she'd ever been able to trust. It was a pity she hadn't recognised it long ago, a pity she hadn't paid attention to the man right in front of her every morning, every evening; the man who'd always been good and kind. It was a pity she'd fallen for Laurie first. Arthur hadn't needed to leave

Trelenna with her, but he had left, put himself in harm's way by fleeing his job suddenly and taking her to New York.

Love had crept up so slowly, through circumstance, and a sense of inevitability of being each other's salvation. Love was the inevitable conclusion.

Each of their carpet bags was on the ground in front of them and Grace noticed a man on the other side of the street looking at the luggage.

She didn't know what felt right and what didn't in this new world. 'Do you think we should pick our bags up and hold on to them?'

Arthur's hand slipped from hers and he lifted both bags. What remained of her money, after they'd paid for their ship tickets, was clipped safely in her undergarments – a tip from a fellow female passenger who had been told New York had its fair share of pickpockets and thieves, advising they should keep their wits about them. As if the prospect of beginning again somewhere neither of them had been before wasn't daunting enough. In Cornwall, Bodmin Moor was wild and lawless, and highway robbery often happened at night, especially to lone travellers. But to be told an entire city they'd risked life and limb for might pose their greatest threat yet frightened Grace. She'd thought the worst had already happened to her. She couldn't bear the thought that the worst might be yet to come.

It was as if Arthur could read her mind. 'Whatever happens next, it's happening to us together. We'll be alright if we're together.'

Grace nodded and looked from the buildings stretching up so far above her to him. 'Yes,' she agreed. And she felt it. She really felt it, that everything would be alright as long as Arthur was by her side.

Arthur looked at her meaningfully. 'Shall we?' he asked.

'Yes,' she said, holding his arm as they prepared to dash between the carriages to reach the other side of the street. 'Let's find out what this new life looks like.'

1871

Grace lay in Arthur's arms in their own tiny, airless bedroom, their clothes discarded hurriedly in a heap on the floor. It was an unwritten rule that every Sunday, after church, one couple would take themselves out of the tenement block with the children for a few hours, giving the other couple time alone.

Arthur's chest was warm, his expression relaxed as his hand stroked the bare skin of her arm. They revelled in each other's embrace, the glow of a rare moment of showing one another how much they yearned for each other, and the silence to think and talk afterwards. Grace allowed her mind to wander, safe in Arthur's arms, safe with her best friend, her husband who she fell in love with a bit more every day. His skin was tanned from his work outdoors at the docks, whereas hers was white from hours cooking indoors. He looked healthy but his hands were roughened by manual labour, heaving wooden boxes on and off ships all day. She dreaded him being dock-side, dreaded his exposure to the dangers of falling crates. There had been enough accidents at the dock for Grace to feel a sense of dread if Arthur returned home even a few minutes past his usual time. And there were moments she wished he'd sought a butler's position in one of the newly built mansions on Fifth Avenue, or gone back to being a footman. But a life of servitude was not what Arthur wanted ever again. He'd escaped it once. He didn't want to go back, even if it meant he'd be safer.

Grace thought she'd achieved all her dreams at Trelenna by becoming the youngest cook in the house's history. All she'd ever wanted was to use her natural talent for cooking, but in this new country, with a few menial jobs here and there, she felt so much further away from cooking for employment than she'd ever been. She'd forgotten how much having her own sense of purpose meant to her. She needed to regain it.

'What are you thinking about?' Arthur asked her languidly.

She smiled into his neck, Arthur was always asking her what she was thinking; it made her feel loved, like she mattered. 'The other day, when you told me the stevedores at the docks enjoyed the pasties I made, were you telling me the truth?'

Arthur laughed at her abrupt question and looked at her curiously. 'Of course.'

'Hmm,' she murmured.

He kissed her hair and whispered into it, 'Tell me what you're thinking.'

Truth and honesty, that was what had always ruled their marriage, so she took a breath and confessed, 'I want to cook again, properly. I want to bring in some regular money.'

'Pasties?' he asked curiously.

'Why not?'

He was quiet, so Grace prompted him. 'Go on, why not?'

'Because you can cook the most delicate, beautiful dinners I've ever tasted.'

'But no one will buy those,' she pointed out. 'Dockworkers will buy pasties.'

'You want to sell pasties on the docks?' Arthur clarified.

'We're living in a new, vibrant city where anyone can become anything they want to be. Hard-working immigrants with dreams and ambitions are being rewarded. Except me, it seems.' She trailed off, not quite daring to meet his eye. 'I'm struggling to find a job. Your ambition and drive is—'

'It's hard, horrible, back-breaking work on the docks. Far harder than being a footman,' he interjected, trying to play down his own success.

'I know,' she said soothingly. The scars and scrapes of near misses told their tales on his body. 'But you're earning, and you and John and Mary are all saving together. If I can help contribute much more, think how quickly we'll be able to move out of here, how quickly we'll be able to change our circumstances.'

'To what?'

'I don't know. I don't know yet. But isn't that the joy of it, the hoping for something better? I never hoped for anything better after I became a cook. I thought that was it. But here . . .' She pulled away a little, looking at him fully now. 'Here, anyone can be anything they want to be. I have to try.'

He breathed in slowly and looked across the crumpled bedding at her with an expression of pride. 'You don't need my permission,' he pointed out.

'I know. But I might need your help,' she said with a knowing smile.

'Oh, you want to use my big strong arms to fetch and carry?' he teased.

'I do,' she confessed. 'I need your *big strong arms* to haul pasties to the docks each day. I'm sure I can be persuaded to pay you in some way though,' she said coyly.

He laughed, pulling her over to him. 'Alright, Mrs Lander,' he said, his full attention on her again. She giggled as her naked body willingly met his for the second time that morning. 'Begin negotiations.'

Chapter 18

1874

Grace

It had been three years of rolling dough, peeling vegetables, braising cheap cuts of meat for hours, making gravy, bundling the pies and pasties up, and heading to the docks to sell her wares when Arthur and John left each morning. The three of them walked with trays of pasties, watching the sun rise at the beginning of their day and set at the end. It had all felt so normal, so natural. Hard work, but it had put money in her pocket. The tiny stove and unreliable small range hadn't been enough for the demand she was experiencing at the docks as her inexpensive, hearty dinners grew in popularity. Through all seasons and all weathers she had made the very best of it. And for those first few years in a new city she had felt as if she'd gone back to a bygone age, to the kitchens of Trelenna.

'You are his latest mistake' . . . The words swam in her head at the strangest times, stopping her from her task and sending a jolt of pain into her heart as fresh now as it had been then.

'You are his latest mistake.' It implied there had been others. But she hadn't seen Laurie again, had never known why he'd treated her so badly. She'd been cast away because, as a servant, she was

disposable. It took her a long time to understand that. Too long, if she was honest with herself. But her life now in New York City was uncomprehendingly different from rural Cornwall. It was so loud, so large, and building work to expand the city was incessant. She and Arthur had helped each other, relied on each other, needed each other. And they still did. He loved her, and she loved him too. She had given Arthur her whole self and he had done the same in return. A loving, trusting relationship was something she'd never experienced before. She'd given him children. She had given him her love. And he had done the same.

'We need bigger rooms,' Grace said to Arthur, Mary and John as the four adults sat around their small table one evening when the children were in bed. 'We need *more* rooms. And we can just about afford them now. But I need a bigger kitchen, a bigger range. The docks are growing, the ships keep coming and the amount of mouths I can feed there are increasing. And you need a proper space to look after the children, Mary.'

'If I take on any more children to look after, I'm going to need someone *else* to help me,' Mary said, her Irish accent softening with every passing year. Grace and Arthur's accents had changed too, an American inflection peppering their words. Their Cornish accents were slowly disappearing, as if they were leaving fragments of their past behind, piece by piece.

'Exactly,' Grace replied excitedly. 'Exactly. If we move out to Brooklyn we can get something with more space and we can both carry on doing what we do. But on a bigger scale. I can get a proper oven, a proper kitchen. I can make so much more in the same amount of time and it'll bring in more money. And you can accommodate more children.'

Mary looked thoughtfully through the flames flickering in the temperamental stove. Over the years Grace and Mary's friendship had grown, firstly through family and circumstance, but had solidified when they realised they shared something important: the very essence of why they were all in New York. They wanted to make something of themselves. Over the years their fierceness of spirit and sharp minds had helped them make the best of every opportunity that came their way. The two families lived together simply, increasing their space when a bigger set of rooms in a newer tenement block had become available – giving each family a bedroom, use of an outside privy, and a sitting room and kitchen space all in one room. But it wasn't enough. They dreamed of more. It was time. Time for them to commit their savings, to take another risk. To prove to themselves and everyone else that crossing the Atlantic had been the right choice.

'Why would you want to keep selling just to the dockers?' John asked after a few moments of quiet contemplation. 'Arthur has been promoted to a foreman and me to a dock superintendent. We're getting there. It's taken years but it's working. You don't have to cook for dockworkers. You could do something else.'

'What else would I do if not cooking?' Grace sagged a little, the idea was unimaginable.

John smiled softly at her. 'I'm not talking about giving up cooking. We all want to better ourselves. You said it yourself though, you've gone backwards, hauling food down to the docks instead of cooking for a rich family. You really want to keep doing the same thing forever?'

'What else did you have in mind?'

'Rent a proper kitchen, rent a proper premises. You could serve people there and then. No more hauling. No more walking fifteen blocks. No more getting up at the crack of dawn to serve dockworkers.'

Grace looked between Arthur and his cousin. 'Have you been discussing this?'

'We have. We've been giving it some thought. Because we saw an advert in the *New York Herald*,' Arthur said.

'An advert for what?' Grace asked warily.

'Premises.'

Grace and Mary shared a look.

'A restaurant to be specific,' John finished with a flourish.

'*A restaurant?*' Grace spluttered. The banking crisis that had begun so suddenly last year was still having disastrous effects, its reach long lasting. 'Do we think a restaurant, a proper premises, is a good idea given everything—'

'Not everyone's poor,' John said. 'Some are doing well from others' misfortunes. There's money still being spent around this city. Trust me on that. And why is a restaurant so different from what you've been doing? You wouldn't just be serving pasties and rolls. You could cook breakfast, luncheons, suppers. For a lot of people. All day long.'

'That's more demanding than cooking for one family,' Grace pointed out, but her mind was whirring as she considered what it might be to dream that big.

'You cooked for all the staff at Trelenna too,' Arthur countered, and just hearing the name *Trelenna* brought a sharp, silent, invisible sting to the conversation that affected only her. 'And all those dinners and charity luncheons they held and made you cook for. They made you stand on your feet all day then.'

'They didn't *make* me. It was my job and I loved it.'

'Exactly,' John said, his point made. 'The city is being built up and out much quicker than when I first arrived ten years ago,' he continued. 'Even in the past few years since you got here – you must have seen it? All those new shops that have sprung up. They're even calling it *Ladies' Mile*. Women are going out by themselves now to buy things in those shops springing up around Macy's and A.T. Stewart's Marble Palace. That didn't happen before. Restaurants are already opening *inside* some shops. Fancy that? Shopping and eating all in one place? The restaurant available to rent is right in the thick of it. Think of all those rich women with nothing to do but shop and spend, then dine together after. It's rich pickings. If they shop with their friends they'll need somewhere to eat luncheon, take tea and cake. And if we don't snap it up, someone else will and we'll have missed our chance.'

'You're wasted on pasties,' Arthur took over, his eyes alight with the idea. 'As delicious as they are, your strength lies in intricate cakes, delicious and fancy meals. Imagine being able to do all that again for people who would *really* appreciate it and would pay handsomely in nice surroundings.'

'She can't cook and serve lots of people all by herself,' Mary pointed out.

'No, she can't,' Arthur confirmed. 'But this is what we've been working towards. We pool our money, rent the restaurant, make a go of it. Get a kitchen maid in to help cook and someone to serve. The city is teeming with people willing to work, to earn, and it will cost a fraction of what we're all earning if the three of us can keep working to help pay for it all in the early stages.' He paused, fixing Grace with his firm, trustworthy gaze she knew and loved. 'Look, why don't we take the lease on and see where the land lies? We need to try. We've *got* to. What else are we all here for? We're in the luckiest position,' he continued, almost without breath. 'We're a family. Until I came here, I didn't have a family. I had to travel an ocean to find it. And I brought you with me. And I'm so glad I did.'

Grace reached out and held Arthur's hand. She knew this decision rested with her. If she said no it would be because she was scared – which she was. If she said yes, she *hoped* their world would change. She just didn't know how.

'I didn't have a family either,' Grace said, looking around at the people who now felt so much more than family. 'And I'm so lucky I have one now. I'm so lucky I have you all.' They were all waiting for an answer. They had pooled their money once before, she and Arthur, and it had brought them a new life.

If she didn't say yes to this now, nothing would change. She'd said yes to Arthur once and her uneven world had righted itself. She had the power to change all their futures.

'Alright,' she said, and John punched the air with happiness.

Arthur closed his eyes and squeezed her hand. 'We're all in this together.'

'We'd better be.' Grace laughed. 'This isn't going to be just *my* restaurant. It's going to be *ours*. We're going to do this as a four. As a family. And between us, we're going to make this work. Because we have to.'

Chapter 19

1890

Grace

The scissors snipped through the large red ribbon as Grace opened the family's fourth restaurant. The feeling of disbelief that they'd ever got this far didn't grow old. The feeling of pride that she had achieved this – that *they* had achieved this – didn't grow old. With every restaurant they opened, it all felt like the most incredible dream. When would this end? How would this end? It felt as if after so long waiting for financial success to lift them from their dreary existence hand-selling at the docks and dwelling in tenement block after tenement block, finally – *finally* – their life now was one she would have never dared dream about back at Trelenna. From stepping off the boat until today, it was all the most incredible fantasy, but it had taken years and years of hard work for the four Landers.

This newest branch of Lander's was in the financial district. From the moment the first restaurant had opened – specialising in afternoon tea – the society women of New York hadn't been able to stop themselves making Grace's acquaintance. An English afternoon tea made by an Englishwoman had been the unique selling point that had catapulted Grace to fame and them all to fortune.

More at home in the kitchen, it had taken all her resolve to allow herself to be praised by the sort of women she'd never have been allowed to speak to back in Cornwall. But America was different, this new world was different, and it was incomprehensible to her that after so long struggling, now she was viewed by many of the new-monied women as equals.

This fourth restaurant was slightly different. Instead of attracting mainly women, or those on their way to or from the theatre looking for intricate fine-dining experiences, Grace had her sights set on the men of the city who were banking and investing on Wall Street. Not for them pastries and cakes. It was prime cuts, pies and hearty comforts. She'd never have served shepherd's pie to the Trelennas. She'd never have dreamed of it. That was nursery and servant-hall food. But here, at Lander's, on a cold winter's day when the air off the Hudson whipped through the streets cutting you to the bone, she was doing what she always did – trusting her gut. It was on the menu and they'd soon find out if it worked.

Grace stole a look across the floor at Arthur, who was showing one of the banking Lehman brothers to their table. The Landers had invited the great and the good of New York society, including journalists, and some of the top financiers who dominated nearby Wall Street. There were two lunch sittings, two dinner sittings, and tables were booked far into the weeks ahead.

'I love you,' Arthur mouthed to Grace, who smiled back just as if she was in the first flush of youth. She felt as if they were in their twenties again, discovering their love for each other for the first time. She had only grown more and more in love with him with each passing year. And while it was true money could not buy happiness, it had brought them financial freedom, had torn away the anxieties of day-to-day living and enabled them to relax into their life together – to grow together, to fall more in love with each passing moment as they put hardship behind them.

Arthur joined her a few moments later. 'John's going to try to speed the line up – they're queuing around the block. I'll go out, greet some of those waiting in carriages, let them know it won't be long until they're inside.'

'Good idea,' she said and felt the gentle squeeze of his hand on hers before he let go and moved out of view. They'd celebrate later. They'd sit together over delicious wine – wine that would never have been placed on their servants' dining table in Cornwall. But here, as she smoothed out a crisp, white tablecloth and adjusted the position of a wine goblet, Grace and Arthur were unrecognisable as the cook and first footman of Trelenna House; their dreams – now seeming so small – had all come true. Smiling as she watched her husband make his way through the restaurant's elegant dining room, through the front door, she knew they had made it.

'Mrs Lander! At last we meet.' A woman in an elegant black and white high-necked dress exclaimed as Grace stepped forward to keep the queue moving.

'Mrs Vanderbilt,' Grace replied with a dip of her head, because everyone knew who Alva Vanderbilt was. 'Thank you so much for coming to our opening.'

'I wouldn't have missed it for the world. I must thank you personally for lending us one of your restaurants for our charity gala next week.'

'I'm very pleased to help. Setting up nurseries for small children so their mothers can earn is a cause very close to my heart. It's important women feel they're able to work and contribute if that's what they want to do. Important they have choice and that their children are looked after so they can do it.'

'I quite agree,' Mrs Vanderbilt replied, her pale hooded eyes intense and sparkling with enthusiasm. 'I couldn't have put it better myself. It is too long to wait for a child to reach the age of eight and attend schooling. Mothers are forced to leave their children alone from far too young an age so they can contribute. I hope this will go some way to alleviating that circumstance and giving those children a chance at an early education.'

'I hope so also,' Grace replied smiling, wishing there'd been such a movement when her own children were small. 'In addition to lending you the space, please also let me make a large donation.'

'That's most kind and I'll happily accept on behalf of the board. I'm meeting my best friend Her Grace, the Duchess of Manchester next week when she travels over from England. We've known each other since she was simply Miss Yznaga. She's keen to be involved too. Perhaps you'd like to join us before the event? I'm sure there's more we could do if we all put our heads together. Why stop at one location when we could open more around the city? You're no stranger to finding and running premises yourself.' Mrs Vanderbilt eyed her shrewdly. 'I'm sure there's a lot we could learn from you,' she said finally, with an approving nod.

'I'd be delighted, but I think restaurants and childcare might be slightly different. My sister-in-law Mary, however, will be a great asset. Childcare is her passion. Can we involve her?'

'Absolutely. Bring her along too.'

'I will. Now let me show you to your table.' But as Grace said the words, a commotion sounded outside and both women turned to look out of the wide glass window, through the large gold hand-painted ornate sign that read *Lander's*. In the street, a horse had reared and was still rearing, its owner unable to get control, the carriage lurching wildly as the spooked horse attempted to bolt, hooves flying in the air.

Mrs Vanderbilt cried out, but Grace barely heard her. Blood whooshed into her own ears as she saw Arthur raise his arms to stop the inevitable, to stop the horse from trampling him, to try with all his might to get out of the way. But it was no use as the horse bolted into the street, dragging the carriage and sending Arthur crashing to the ground. Grace ran blindly, pushing people out of the way, screaming her husband's name over and over. But by the time she reached him, surrounded by shocked onlookers, Arthur was already dead.

Chapter 20

'Grace,' Mary whispered. 'Grace. You need to eat something.'

Grace was lying on her side in the bed she had shared with Arthur in their Fifth Avenue home. The opulent damask curtains that surrounded her four-poster bed were hardly ever pulled closed but this past week since Arthur had died, Grace had closed herself in and shut herself away. Night turned to day and back again, and Grace didn't know what hour it was – her eyes closed against the world, her curtains closed against her family. In her mind she drifted back to the early days of their marriage, seeing Arthur now as she'd not seen him then. He had been perfect. He had loved her. And she hadn't seen it. She'd had twenty-one years with him. But it hadn't been enough.

How had this happened? It wasn't supposed to be like this. They were supposed to rise together, their whispered promise to each other late at night as they worked for a future that had suddenly ended.

She ran through all the things she could have done differently to prevent his death. They should not have opened the restaurant. Then he wouldn't have been standing outside trying to greet and shepherd customers out of waiting carriages. No, she had to go further back. They should never have opened any of the restaurants and they could have remained as they had been, safe, with Grace cooking pasties for dockers and Arthur unloading cargo. His job there had been dangerous, their tenement rooms damp – more hardship than working in a rich house in the Cornish countryside. But he had done it all without complaint, tirelessly working to build their dream. And in the end it had been building a life of luxury that had killed him. A horse outside his own restaurant. Something so simple had ended the man she'd thought would live forever. He'd been so vibrant, so present. And now he was gone.

'Darling Grace,' Mary said again, smoothing her forehead. 'You have to eat.'

'I can't eat,' Grace said with a dry mouth. She wasn't sure she'd spoken today, or yesterday, or the day before.

'You'll waste away. Please, dear. Drink some soup if nothing else?'

Grace shook her head against the pillow, inhaling the faint scent of Arthur and choking on a sob.

'Oh, Grace, please. Your children need you.'

'I can't.'

'You have to, Grace. I know it hurts.' Mary's voice broke with tears as she sat beside her. 'It hurts all of us, and I can't imagine how *much* this must hurt you. But Rose and Daisy, they need you. They've just lost their father.'

Grace sobbed into her pillow. 'You think I don't know that? I don't want to be here anymore,' she cried. 'It's too hard.'

'I know,' Mary soothed. 'But we need to be together. Your daughters are as devastated as you. They need their mother. Please, please, get up and eat something, and let your children comfort you. Comfort them. I'll be downstairs with the girls if you need me. Please, think about them and come downstairs and hold them.'

Grace heard the click of the door as Mary closed it behind her. Mary had not left Rose and Daisy's side since Arthur had been killed, while Grace had pretended nothing about the last week was real – trying to shut out the reality that Arthur was gone. Every time she awoke from another abysmal slumber it took a few blissful seconds where she was entirely unaware of her surroundings before she remembered what had happened. But in those few seconds everything was alright, Arthur wasn't dead, and her world was perfect. And then she remembered. And despaired. How would she go on?

She had started her life alone, had gone to Trelenna alone, had allowed herself to fall for Laurie and he had left her alone. She had fallen for Arthur and now he had left her too. She was exactly where she'd been when she was barely a child, learning how to be a kitchen maid, so alone in a vast, new house. She had been better off then, before she had taught herself to let other people into her life. What did she have to show for it? Wealth beyond anything she'd ever known. But that had never been her dream. All she'd really wanted was to cook and to be happy, to give her family a little comfort and security. And yet, somehow on her rise to the top, she'd lost everything. She barely even cooked anymore and now Arthur was gone too.

After Mary's footsteps faded from the hall, Grace forced herself up on shaking arms and pulled the nearest bed curtain back. Sun was streaming through the windows but she had no clue if it was morning or afternoon. How could she do this? How could she carry on? How could she *live?* She didn't know *how* to anymore. Grace stood, pulling her aching limbs from her bed and walked into her adjoining bathroom. She ran the taps and let the bath fill with hot water, watching it emotionlessly until it reached a suitable depth. Shedding her clothes, finally removing the dress she had put on the day Arthur died, a week ago. She stared as it pooled around her on the bathroom floor. It would need to be donated; the deep purple crinoline would only ever be associated with his death. She never wanted to see it again. Then she slipped into the warm bathwater and, determined to begin again, if only for the sake of her children, Grace scrubbed herself clean, as if scouring away years of dirt, grime, love and hope – everything – until her skin was raw.

Chapter 21

Present Day

Zennor

It was the first time in months Zennor had need of a coat. But the weather was turning as the year moved through its seasons. Autumn was well and truly underway, arriving suddenly, bringing with it an abundance of apples, plums, damsons and pears for her to turn into bakes and tarte tatins, jams and chutneys. Produce-wise, it was her favourite time of year, but it also brought darker scudding clouds, rain and shorter days.

She left her hardy pink Quba jacket unzipped over her top and leggings, and walked through the gardens that were slowly coming alive bit by bit under Charlie's tender care.

The family had made the decision over the past few days to close to tourists on Mondays for the rest of the year, barring the upcoming half-term week and Christmas school holidays. They'd noticed the trickle of guests were condensed mainly to weekends. Today, this first Monday with no visitors, was the only time since they'd opened that Zennor hadn't been flat out in the kitchen or serving in the tearoom. She felt a bit lost, scratching around for things to fill her day once prep for tomorrow had been done.

Everything was so eerily quiet. Like those months when her parents had gone and Lamorna hadn't yet come back. She shook the reminder of that enforced solitude away, telling herself instead to enjoy the rest, it would be back to normal tomorrow.

Plans for the Halloween trail had been finalised and she was due to present the food and snacks offering shortly. She'd been sidetracked from what she called the Grace Project in order to focus on the Halloween Project. And shortly after that would follow Christmas plans. Grace had been bumped from priority number one to priority number eleven or twelve. Zennor felt she'd run the internet dry, following Grace's rise from a New York tenement block after her arrival to a grand house on Fifth Avenue.

At first Charlie and she had been confused, wondering if she'd been a servant in the house, but the restaurants and the society they'd moved in quickly proved that Grace's life had taken a dramatically different turn after the advent of the family's business, Lander's.

Grace, it appeared, had been a woman of note, and her husband respected – more than either of them had ever been here in this house when they were servants. At Trelenna, Arthur had absconded without notice. In New York he rose from dockworker to businessman, and Grace became an esteemed restaurateur. It was a meteoric rise. And then . . . nothing. The path to find out the next step in Grace's life went nowhere.

Zennor found Charlie on hands and knees in the children's play area. 'You missed your tea break,' she said.

'I wanted to give this a really good weeding before any kiddos arrive for Halloween next week.' Charlie stood, dirt on his face and forearms. He glanced at his watch. 'The morning's disappeared in a flash. Is that for me?'

'Service with a smile,' Zennor quipped. In a beeswax wrap she'd put a slice of apple and cinnamon cake, and she sat at one of the wooden picnic tables and benches she'd convinced Lamorna to invest in. Zennor had cut a slice for herself too and they shared Charlie's tea flask cup and ate cake, talking over the garden and where she could put stakes in the ground with illustrations of scary creatures and scarecrows that wouldn't damage any of his planting.

'When I thought of trying to keep Trelenna House alive, I didn't see much past cream teas and bunting,' Zennor admitted. 'I couldn't have imagined anything like Halloween trails and Christmas events. I'm not sure what I saw past summer . . . if anything.'

'You've created something wonderful. I might even come along to the Halloween trail. Will you hold my hand on the way around? Will I be frightened?'

'Probably by the cost of the cakes. Lamorna wants me to charge five pounds a slice for the extra-special seasonal bakes, which I think is a bit beyond most people. We don't need to charge that much to make money.'

'Tell her then,' Charlie suggested gently.

'Hmmm, I might. Sometimes you have to be delicate with Lamorna, make her think it was her idea in the first place for her to fully appreciate something.'

'Clever,' he said, tucking into his cake. 'You should be incredibly proud of yourself.'

'Oh, I make this cake practically every other week at this time of year.'

Charlie's eyes softened. 'I mean with the house. But the cake is awesome too. All this was your idea. And look at it.'

Zennor cringed at the compliment but felt a warm glow spark as she took in the house from here. It looked magical, alive. 'Yes, look at it. Trelenna has a life of its own now.'

'Which is how all good businesses go, right?'

'I wouldn't know,' she said shyly.

'Neither would I. But you ran a business before. Private events, right?'

She nodded. 'Although when I started my cookery business it was born out of someone else's idea,' she confessed.

'Whose?' Charlie asked between bites.

'A friend of my mum's, actually. When I graduated from catering college, she suggested I run a supper club. I couldn't think of anything worse than having a bunch of people I didn't know in my house and trying to entertain them at the same time as *feeding* them.'

'Which is exactly what you're doing now,' Charlie laughed.

Zennor thought for a moment and then laughed too. 'Yes, I suppose it is.' She looked into the distance thoughtfully. 'But a supper club feels . . . different, perhaps too intimate. But from that concept, the idea of being a private chef was born.'

'That was *your* idea though?' Charlie asked.

'In a way.'

'From little acorns grow mighty oaks,' he said. 'It's a bit like Grace and her restaurant empire.' Charlie rose and dusted crumbs from his muddy gardening trousers.

'Oh, Grace is very different to me. She was a servant. I'm only one in name, down in the dungeon cooking for the masses,' she joked. 'I might own this house. Along with the rest of them. But I do find it so thoroughly interesting that she made such a vast fortune from cooking at such a time. She must have been very brave.'

Charlie moved forward and planted a kiss on Zennor's lips. 'So are you.' He tasted of spice and sugar.

Zennor would not be put off, despite the lingering kiss. 'To go from nothing, being a servant, at someone else's mercy, to a doyenne of the gilded-age restaurant scene – I find that awe inspiring.'

'Mmm hmm,' he said, remaining close, trying to distract her into another kiss. She let herself be pulled gently into his embrace.

'I get it. You like me,' Zennor said playfully when they eventually let go of each other.

'Is it obvious?'

'A little bit. I like you too.'

Charlie grinned, picked up his gardening gloves and got back to work.

'Mind if I watch you for a bit?'

'*Watch* me?' His grin widened. 'Bit pervy.'

'You know it,' Zennor said unashamedly and resumed her position on the bench as she picked over the remaining crumbs.

After all these weeks together, the two of them hadn't gone beyond kissing. She wanted to be sure, not rush things. Although now it was nearly November – she wasn't sure if that was still classed as 'too soon'. Charlie hadn't spoken about it, or pushed. Ever the gentleman. But at some point, and likely soon, surely one thing was going to lead to another. And she trusted him enough to feel he was genuine and wouldn't trample on her heart.

Pulling her mind sharply away from that line of thought, she found it interesting how Charlie compared her to Grace, although there was only really the house and their shared love of food that connected them.

'I'm annoyed I can't find much about Grace in New York after the 1890s. Or anything, actually,' she said to him as he worked. 'And I haven't been able to do much more because of how busy we are and planning for everything. Then there's Halloween coming and almost the moment that's over, we switch to our festive offering. Christmas gets earlier and earlier. Pumpkins come down and tinsel goes up almost immediately. It's becoming more frantic than I imagined.' She could hear herself and made a point to check in on how lucky she was. 'I'm going to go through all the rest of the boxes,' she said determinedly. 'While I've got a tiny bit of time.'

Without pausing to consider, Charlie immediately said, 'I'll help. Just tell me when.'

She caught herself grinning; she liked that he seemed to enjoy researching Grace too, but she had to be honest, it was hard to find the right time. 'Don't know. Soon though.' She'd been dead tired by the time she got to the boxes still piled up in her room in the evenings, which was becoming her only free time these days. Maybe she could harness her energy and turn Mondays into her dedicated research day? But then there was the fact she and Charlie had only been dating for a few weeks and so far the majority of their romantic time together was spent in the garden or the kitchen. There had been no obvious opportunity to move things on, other than their beach dates at the end of summer. She wanted that to change, she just didn't know how. Glumly she scuffed the soft grass at her feet. 'I'm so tired when I finish each day I've only time for a guilty look at the boxes stacked in the corner of my room before I fall asleep. And the next day arrives and it all begins again. It's like *Groundhog Day*,' she said.

'That's an old film reference,' he laughed.

'There's nothing better than an old film reference. They're the best kind,' she countered, pulling her phone out of her pocket as it dinged. She leaped up. 'I'm late for our planning meeting but . . .' The note of determination was back in her voice. 'What time to do you finish your other work tomorrow?'

'I'll be done by about four-ish. Why?'

'Would you like to help me with the boxes?' The moment she asked she realised it was the most boring way to suggest a date. 'I mean—'

'Yes,' he cut in. 'I'd love to. But on one condition.'

'Which is?'

‘I want to take you on a proper date again. After the Halloween event week? When things calm down a bit, if you can spare the time.’

‘I can spare the time,’ she said happily.

‘Great. The beach was lovely, but I want to take you somewhere else if you’ll let me. I think the weather is still good enough for a picnic though, with jumpers. Until we’re confined indoors when winter properly arrives, let’s make the most of the light and the lack of rain.’

‘I’d love that.’

Her phone dinged again. ‘Okay, Lamorna is really annoying me now. I have to go.’

She stepped forward and kissed *him* this time, then, scooping up the beeswax wrap, she made her way back to the house, her mind full as she wondered just where Charlie might be planning to take her on their next date.

Chapter 22

'I've designed trail booklets so children can navigate their way and feel as if they're the ones accomplishing something,' Merry said, pushing a stack of leaflets towards his sisters. 'The printers were reasonably priced, I thought. And we've got loads so a lot of kids had better come.'

Lamorna made the usual face she pulled when anyone mentioned *any* financial outlay. 'I've been promoting it on social media for weeks,' she said. 'Which is free. And I've sourced some props, which are sadly not free.'

'Charlie's made a few not-quite-scarecrows,' Zennor said proudly.

'What's a not-quite-scarecrow?' Merry asked.

'A scarecrow that's not scary, obviously.'

'Obviously,' Merry laughed. 'Things are going well with you both?'

'That was a less than subtle way of segueing into that.' Lamorna inched forward to hear the gossip, curving her hand around a thick mug of tea to ward off the cold that, no matter how much they'd spent on renovations, always crept into the kitchen through the slight gap under the back door.

'Things are going well.' Zennor was unable to stop the dreamy smile spreading on her face. 'But it's still early. He's so easy, and lovely, and kind, and nice.'

'And fit,' Lamorna said.

'And fit,' Zennor echoed. 'Though don't let Zach hear you say that.'

'Oh, I won't,' Lamorna said darkly. 'Although Zach has seen Charlie's arms. He gets it.'

'Talking about me?' Zach asked as he entered through the back door.

'Always,' Lamorna said as Zach bent to kiss her hello and then greeted the others.

'How's it going?' he enquired, pulling up a chair and shuffling in close.

'We've just started,' Lamorna replied.

'Lamorna's bemoaning the fact everything has a cost attached,' Merry told him with a roll of his eyes.

'Oh, yeah, 'fraid so. Wait until you have to put the outlay in for Christmas lights. Hiring a specialist company doesn't come cheap.'

'I think we might be too late to book a company in for that, given how much advance notice these installation firms ask for,' Lamorna said thoughtfully. 'But we honestly didn't know how things were going to go, so booking anything big and fancy didn't feel like a priority. Still doesn't. We'll go big next year.'

Next year. It still struck Zennor as odd that all this had even happened *this* year. That her plan to save the house had taken shape so quickly and effectively. Going big on a Christmas event for next year sounded frightening. And thrilling.

'So what will you do then to take advantage of the festive season this year?' Zach asked.

The room fell silent.

'I think it's rather crept up on us,' Merry confessed. 'Just getting going for summer was task enough.'

Zennor scoffed and then tried to hide it – Merry had arrived merely days before opening, so he was hardly one to talk. But she thought better of it and asked, 'We don't have to go all-out for Christmas, do we? Just something to bring people here in what will probably be awful weather. What about an indoor Christmas market with some local suppliers? That would be festive and simple enough, I imagine. We could even host it over just one weekend, keep it neat and contained?'

'Great idea,' Merry said, his eyes lighting up. 'And what about dressing the house for Christmas too, so there's plenty to keep people entertained once they arrive? Amy and I went to one where every room had a decorated tree and ornaments, roaring fires and it was all decked out to cover different time periods.'

'Oh, I love that,' Zennor enthused dreamily, wondering if Merry wanted to talk more about Amy now he'd mentioned her, or if he would prefer it if his late wife *wasn't* talked about. It was so tricky to know the right thing to do. 'I can make festive sweet treats too, obviously, and we can offer pre-booked Christmas lunches for groups in the run-up to the big day, perhaps? I love decorating the house for Christmas, so I'll happily take on a few rooms.'

'We can offer mulled wine and ciders,' Merry said, smacking his lips together. 'I could go for a mulled cider right now. They're so good.'

'I'll take your word for it,' Lamorna replied, grimacing as she carried on scribbling down notes.

'And carol singers,' Zennor continued, getting into the festive spirit, despite the fact it was two months away. 'I bet Mum's choir will come along and support.'

'Yes, but will *Mum* come along and support?' Lamorna asked, fixing Zennor with a pointed look. 'Where are Mum and Dad now, anyway?'

'Australia?' Merry said with a questioning tone.

'I thought New Zealand,' Zennor said uncertainly.

'So over that side of the world then,' Lamorna mused. 'I'll call Dad and see if they intend to grace us with their presence for Christmas.'

Zennor's face fell. 'Oh,' she exclaimed. They all looked at her. 'Well . . .' she started. 'It didn't even occur to me they wouldn't return home for Christmas.'

Her siblings looked thoughtful.

'If so, it'll be the first Christmas *ever* where I haven't been with them,' Zennor continued a bit shakily.

Lamorna reached out and gave Zennor's hand a squeeze. 'I never thought of that,' she said. 'I've spent the last ten years being away from home, so when I have seen you all for Christmas it's usually been in a country close to me. Being here for Christmas after so long is going to be odd.'

'Remember that Christmas we met you in Thailand?' Zennor asked, squeezing Lamorna's hand gently in return, grateful for her sister, their bond that had seemed so stretched when Lamorna was half a world away. 'Massages on the beach. Pad thai for lunch. So strange. But at least we were together.'

'Some of you were,' Merry said, mock-gloomily. 'Some of us were freezing in Edinburgh.'

'We came to see you too,' Lamorna said exasperated. 'May I remind you I flew thirteen hours to come and see you one Christmas.'

Zennor and Merry chanted in unison, 'And a five-and-a-half-hour train ride from London to Edinburgh.' It was a phrase Lamorna had often reeled off to them.

'Yes, yes, alright,' Lamorna laughed, swatting her brother's arm. She turned to Zach. 'There are no direct flights from Singapore to Edinburgh,' she said with mock horror. 'It was a *nightmare* of a journey to do in December with only a thin leather jacket.'

'Not our fault you'd been away so long you'd forgotten a proper winter coat,' Merry teased.

'I didn't even own a proper winter coat,' Lamorna said. 'Left all mine here when I went. Nice to know they all still fit. Sort of.'

Zennor smiled, her eyes moving between Merry and Lamorna as they continued teasing each other. She loved this, this familial silliness, the gentle ribbing. It was off the chart when her parents were here too; Christmases of old that hadn't been replicated in any way since because they'd never been *all* together at Christmas since Lamorna left. There had always been someone missing, someone with other plans. More often than not it had been Lamorna, but in recent years it had been Veryan's turn too. Now, this year, it looked like it might be her parents.

Was Zennor eventually going to lose everyone bit by bit as they moved on while she stayed still? Everything was changing, again. While Lamorna was back and Merry too, it made her realise this might not be forever. They'd left once before, what was to stop them leaving again? She sighed. Why couldn't everything stay the same?

Her thoughts were disturbed by Merry's grumbling stomach.

'Shall we carry this on over lunch?' Merry suggested. 'I can make sandwiches quickly. Ham and cheese toasties are my specialty.'

'Your culinary skills really haven't moved on since university, have they?' Zennor teased, pushing the dark feelings away.

'No, they haven't,' he said proudly. 'You're the chef in the family so I don't need to learn. I'm merely the tortured novelist. But I can make a toastie and I'll even throw in crisps and salad, so you either want it or you don't.'

'Yes, please,' the room chorused and Merry stood up and got to work.

'A meal I don't have to make,' Zennor said. 'What a momentous day for me.'

'Are you okay?' Merry joked. 'Can you cope with me making toasties in your kitchen?'

'I'm sure it's a survivable incident,' she jibed in return.

'It's always fortuitous timing that I turn up for lunch.' Zach gave Zennor a wink. 'But I might not if Merry's taking over with toasties on a regular basis.'

'Who doesn't love a toastie?' Merry asked, assembling items and moving everything around in the fridge while hunting for the cheese, much to Zennor's silent annoyance. He wouldn't put it all back in the correct places either. She leaped up to help him find what he was looking for, so he didn't make too much mess. 'Anyway,' Merry continued, while Zennor rooted around in the fridge for him. 'Why are you here – right when we're having a strategy meeting? What a coincidence. Are you still helping or are you spying?'

'Zach doesn't need our amateur ideas.' Zennor looked round, defending their friend. 'He's got Port Carrack running like clockwork. Weddings and summer fayres and lights displays and all sorts. And he's done all that while still managing to make sense of his family archives *and* run tours. I don't even run tours.' Zennor piled up the fresh-cut butcher's ham and the Cornish Yarg cheese next to the artisan loaf she'd baked yesterday. 'And I haven't even got through the few boxes I've been given. So I've worked out Zach must be some kind of superhero to get through *everything*.'

'Want something doing, ask a busy person,' Lamorna trilled.

'I'm busy,' Zennor muttered, narrowing her eyes at her sister. 'How do you think the tearoom runs?'

Lamorna held her hands up defensively. 'That's not what I mean. I was just—'

Zach jumped in, presumably to prevent a sibling fracas. 'How many boxes do you have left? I assume you've not got much further with Grace given you're doing so much down here and managing the tearoom on top of it.'

Merry turned around from buttering bread and said to Zach, 'Don't suck up to her.'

Zach laughed. 'I'm curious, though. Any more news?'

'Yes, actually. I googled Grace in New York.'

She watched Zach's expression change. 'You googled?' His tone smacked of disapproval.

'I followed official resources,' Zennor defended. 'And found her first in Manhattan and then in Brooklyn and then she opens a restaurant and then another and before you know it, she's some sort of gilded-age entrepreneur with a mansion on Fifth Avenue. Well, not before you know it because the whole timeline seems to be about twenty years. But she made very good use of those twenty years.'

'Well done her,' Merry said, clamping down the toastie-maker.

'That's what I thought,' Zennor said. 'Have you buttered the top of the bread too? It crisps it up nicely.'

'No. Because *I'm* making it. Not you. Carry on.'

Zennor made an 'ugh' sound, then relayed as much as she could remember about the restaurants. 'Then I lose her in 1891. Charlie and I couldn't really find anything else after that.'

By the end of her tale, Zach was just as excited by all this too. 'That is quite rare. Back then the rise of the new monied was exponential between railroads and banking. So while America made faint promises of riches to everyone who immigrated, the harsh truth was that promise was hardly *ever* a reality. More failed than ever made it big. To go from a servant to a business owner even with all the hard work, it sounds like our Miss Pascoe got lucky.'

'And Arthur too. He and Grace seemed to have done it together, along with his cousin, I think it is. And wife. And all their children. The boys all played a role in the end but the girls didn't. Not from what we read.'

'She had children?' Zach asked.

'Two girls.'

'I wonder what happened to them,' Merry mused as Zennor tried not to go and rescue the now overly browned toastie.

'I've had enough trouble Grace-hunting without adding her two kids into the mix. I'm pretty happy just focusing my research on Grace.'

'She sounds interesting enough for all of them,' Lamorna said, tapping her chin thoughtfully as she took in the kitchen as if from a fresh perspective. 'Fancy Grace working here, becoming the cook and then she makes it big somewhere else. And Arthur too. From footman to restaurateur. I love that story. I love that happy ending for them. Well done, Grace.'

'Not quite so happy,' Zennor was loath to say. 'Grace is by herself at the end of my research. Arthur died. She was in her forties at the time the trail runs cold, but she appears to be a millionaire.'

'I would say that's young to be a millionaire.'

'You would,' Merry jibed. 'Being not far behind her.'

'Hey!' Lamorna protested. 'I'm only *thirty-one*! You're only a couple of years behind me, so you can talk.'

'Which is why I agree that it is very, very young,' he said, handing the first toastie to Zach. 'Guests first.'

'Thanks,' Zach said. 'I'm honoured. But I thought I was a spy?'

'Oh yeah. I forgot about that.' Merry took the plate back and gave it to Zennor, who picked up the toastie and gave Zach a smug look as she bit in. Her stomach immediately somersaulted unpleasantly and she put the toastie down. She couldn't stop it, the sudden inexplicable wave of nausea. Bile shot up from her stomach and she clamped her hand to her mouth, stood up hurriedly and panicked. She was going to throw up. Right here, right now. She couldn't. Surprise, horror, sickness and fear forced her into a blind run, and as Zennor tried to get to the downstairs toilet in time – she knocked her chair back so suddenly it crashed over behind her on to the flagstone floor.

◆ ◆ ◆

A knock came from the other side of the toilet door, followed by Lamorna's concerned voice. 'Are you alright?'

Zennor hadn't been sick. She'd simply heaved, over and over. And then, as quickly as it had come, the nausea had passed. She couldn't risk leaving the safety of the downstairs cloakroom quite yet. Just in case. 'Yes. False alarm,' she called through the door. 'It was the cheese. Don't eat it. I think it's off.'

'Oh no! I'll go and tell everyone.' Lamorna ran off back down the corridor.

Despite having not actually been sick, Zennor felt exhausted. She slumped down the wall and sat on the black and white tiled floor. She'd freshly repainted the walls with a new shade of dusky pink so visitors had a spruced-up space. At this level she could see a thin patch near the skirting board where she'd missed applying a second coat.

She thought back. When had she bought that batch of cheese? Only recently, from one of her favourite, most reliable suppliers. A week ago? Maybe two? *Cheese usually lasts for ages*, she thought, not quite able to pin down when exactly she'd bought that particular block for the family's fridge.

It wasn't even the taste of the cheese that had triggered the nausea. She hadn't got that far. It had simply been the smell that had got her retching. She pulled out her phone and scrolled back on her calendar, finding the date she'd been to the cheesemonger – about three weeks ago. Then she saw another date close by that was marked in her diary – a date that had passed by without notice; a date that had, until just now, completely slipped her mind. Zennor looked away from her phone, her eyes resting on the patch of wall that she'd missed with the paintbrush. She didn't see the significance of the date and what it meant for her.

And then, suddenly, awfully, she did.

Chapter 23

Fifth Avenue, New York City

1895

Grace

'Mama!' Rose called out from her room, and Grace sighed as she stood up from her dressing table and walked down the corridor of their Fifth Avenue mansion to tell her youngest daughter to stop shouting.

'What?' Rose asked innocently, glimpsing her mother in her mirror as she played with her blonde hair. 'Are you coming to tell me to stop hollering?'

Grace despaired. How Rose had grown up with such a vibrant American accent in an English household was beyond her, although Grace knew her own accent had changed remarkably in the nearly three decades of living so far from the place of her birth. 'The phrase is *stop shouting* and yes. I am. What is it you need?'

'Are my dresses from Worth here yet? It's been months since we ordered them.'

'No, darling. They've gone straight to the Newport house, as I told you yesterday.'

'Yes, you did. I remember now,' Rose said, offering her mother a winning smile. 'The day after tomorrow I'll get to see all my new dresses. I can't wait. I know the fashion is to keep them aside for a while so they don't look too new but I'm not going to. Connie Vanderbilt doesn't, so neither am I.'

Grace suppressed a smile at her youngest's penchant for flouting rules and expectations. 'People will see they're new. And they'll stare.'

'Let them,' Rose dismissed airily. 'They're too beautiful to keep under lock and key. And of all the excesses, of all the things people spend their money on, my dresses are hardly the worst. As you *constantly* remind me.'

'I do,' Grace said. Mrs Astor's annual January ball had cost upwards of a quarter of a million dollars, and Grace had made a point of telling both her daughters *exactly* where that kind of money could have been spent and what it could have done for thousands of poor families instead. Poor families like they had once been. She knew how easily all of them could still be struggling in a tiny two-room tenement on the Lower East Side, no hot running water, no money for dresses, no worrying about balls . . . It would have been public bath houses and one good dress for Sunday service, in the hopes of a tea dance every few months at most. The ever-increasing indulgences of her new world had shaken Grace – the wealth, the extravagance, when she knew just how far a little could go for those working hard to make a living. She made a mental note to increase her regular donation to the poor-relief charities. Her business may have given her the financial freedom she could never have envisaged, but she never forgot that long ago, she had needed help more than once too.

'As long as you appreciate it, I'll spend it,' Grace confirmed. 'But the moment you become a spoiled unappreciative madam is the moment it all ends.'

'I'm forever grateful,' Rose said, her eyes shining in the innocence of youth, something Grace wanted to always protect. 'You know that. I hope.'

'Every now and again you need reminding of where we came from.'

'Are you sending me into the restaurant kitchen again?' Rose asked, horrified. 'You know I'm terrible at cooking and I only get in the way.'

'It would do you some good to sweat out some humility every now and again. It's been a few months since I made you do anything at the restaurants.'

'You know I'm a laughing stock with the likes of the Astors when I'm caught there. They might dine at our restaurants, but they barely stomach us because they consider what you do "work". Let's not keep reminding them so visually where our money comes from.'

Grace sighed under her breath, the old conversation playing out much the same. Money could elevate your status but how you made it still mattered. 'Our name is above the door, darling. It's hard to hide the connection.'

'My name is a blessing and a curse.' Rose sighed, dramatically.

'One day, Rose, you, your sister and your cousins will inherit Lander's. If you want pretty dresses from Worth long after I'm dead, you're going to have to pay attention to what goes on. You can come with me today, learn something.'

'You're only forty-six,' Rose said dismissively, returning her focus to a new diamond hairpin. 'Most of my friends' mothers are so much older than you. I've got plenty of time before I need to worry about you passing on.'

'Your father died young,' Grace said without thinking, and then wished she hadn't. It still brought the same fresh wave of pain even years later.

Rose spun around on her chair. 'Of an accident!' she snapped, sounding more like a child than a young woman of twenty-one years. 'If a horse doesn't trample you to death too, then I won't have to go in the restaurant kitchen and pretend I'm happy about it!'

'I've yet to hear you say you're happy about it,' Grace retorted. 'Consider it a fractional payment for the thousands of dollars I've spent on your summer wardrobe.'

Rose stood, breathing heavy with energetic fire. 'Fine,' she acquiesced. 'But we're not telling anyone about it and I'm not making pastry again. Find me something else to do.'

Grace smiled, stepped forward and shook her spirited daughter's hand. 'It's a pleasure doing business with you.'

'Sure,' Rose said, rolling her eyes.

Grace returned to her room, adding the finishing touches to her Newport wardrobe, hoping she had the right amount of dresses for every eventuality, even if it mainly meant dresses to escort her daughters to events. The summer season in Newport was a *must* for her girls, 'so they could be seen in the right kind of society and marry the right kind of men'. These were her daughter Rose's words. Words that she'd uttered without a hint of irony and that Grace and her oldest daughter Daisy had laughed along with until they'd realised Rose had been deadly serious – the suffrage movement had clearly passed Rose by. So, for the second year, Grace was acquiescing, renting an outlandish mansion – comedically called a cottage – with sea views so Grace and Daisy could relax while Rose continued being choosy about the kind of men she'd let even so much as talk to her. At least she wasn't desperate. Quite the opposite.

If Rose was being choosy, Daisy was being even more fastidious than her sister, avoiding the opportunity to meet men, comfortable in her own company, drawing and painting or helping Grace make decisions about the restaurant. Daisy would never meet a man by locking herself in her own room so perhaps this summer season in Rhode Island might be the making of her eldest daughter.

Grace closed the lid of the trunk and then told Ruth, their relatively new lady's maid all three girls shared, that hers was ready to be sent on. 'Are the girls finished yet?'

'Miss Daisy is finished. Miss Rose is deliberating over jewellery.'

Two children. A happy world. A wonderful life. A home. But so much emptiness, her heart broken by losing the only man who'd ever loved her.

She put a brave smile on her face, reminding herself that there were so many things Grace had now that she'd never thought possible. Or perhaps, once upon a time in another place she had felt they were close by, that they were within her grasp. But it was so long ago. A different time, a different place. A different version of Grace.

Promises made by another man had been lies. Arthur had promised her nothing, and given her everything. The difference between the two men was so stark. And then Arthur had left her too. A love that had taken so long to blossom had been cut so short. But Grace never cried in front of the girls, knowing she needed to be as strong as two parents now. Stronger.

She was teaching her daughters to be resilient in a way she'd been forced into through circumstance. But there was only a certain amount of hardship she would force on *them*. Only Daisy vaguely remembered the old life they'd lived in the small set of tenement rooms, yet even now that memory was fading.

Daisy entered the room and tilted her head to the side. When the lady's maid left, she asked, 'What's wrong?'

'What makes you think anything is wrong?' Grace asked.

'Your expression. It's blank. You're thinking.'

'Just thinking about you. And your sister. And your father.'

'I miss him too,' Daisy said, twirling her dark hair around her finger. Daisy's long hair was brushed out, draped over her shoulders, ready for bed. Her deep, dark eyes and slim figure would be the undoing of many a man – if any caught sight of her. But that situation was rare if Daisy had anything to do with it. Her skin was tanned from walking in the sunshine and, as a result, a smattering of freckles dusted her nose all year round. While Rose gloried in her peaches-and-cream complexion, believing it far more becoming for her blonde hair and blue eyes. Both girls were striking in such different ways.

'Aren't you curling your hair for tomorrow?' Grace asked.

Daisy made a face. 'Not for a railway journey I'm not. I'm going to sleep in comfort for once.'

Grace laughed. 'Your sister will have something to say about that.'

'I'm sure she won't. She's the pretty one. She doesn't want me upstaging her.'

'You're both beautiful. It's a wonder I haven't had to fight fortune hunters away. Unless you're keeping secrets?'

'I'm not. I try not to meet fortune-hunting men. And Rose is fighting hers off on all our behalves,' Daisy said, toying with the lace trim on the bedspread. 'You don't need to worry about her. Ask her about Harry Dawes.'

'What about him?' Grace asked, sitting at her dressing table to let down her hair.

'He proposed. Last week.'

Grace's hand stilled for a second. 'She said no, I take it?'

'She did. Because she always does. Harry Dawes is nice to look at, though,' Daisy said idly as she began plaiting her own hair. Her daughter never did have the ability to sit still.

'But he talks nonsense and Rose doesn't want an idiot husband,' Grace said. 'This is the problem with you two. The embarrassment of riches means no man stands a chance with either of you. They'd have to be rich beyond our wildest dreams so I know they don't want you for your money. *And* they'd have to be so intelligent you could talk long into the night about any subject and not grow bored.'

Daisy sighed. 'It's a predicament,' she joked as she completed her plait and then shook her hair loose again down her back. 'At least you know I'll be with you forever. We're going to lose Rose one day soon though. She's ready to be lost.'

'This is what Newport is all about,' Grace sighed, as she removed her final hairpin. They really did need a second lady's maid, only Grace was too busy with the restaurant to give the staffing issue the attention it needed. There were already so many other things on her list to do.

'Perhaps this will be our second and final year in Newport,' Daisy offered hopefully. 'With any luck, Rose will find a man who fits all the criteria within minutes and we can come home early.'

'We can but hope,' Grace said.

Daisy remained in the room and Grace waited. When Daisy didn't continue, Grace turned from the dressing table and looked at her daughter. 'Something else is wrong. What is it?'

Daisy paused before replying. 'Mary Leiter is going away.'

Mary, the daughter of retail magnate Levi Leiter, was one of Daisy's closest friends. 'How long is she going for?'

'Forever. She's marrying George Curzon and is going to live somewhere called Kedleston Hall in Derbyshire but there's a chance she'll spend a lot of time in India too, because he's helping run the whole country.' Daisy threw her hands in the air at such a ludicrous set of circumstances. 'So I'll probably never see her *ever* again.'

'Oh, Daisy. I'm sorry.'

'She's not the only one either,' Daisy continued, her eyes stormy.

'I heard about Jay Gould's daughter, Anna,' Grace said softly.

'Well, I didn't know about *her,*' Daisy replied in despair. 'I was talking about Pauline Whitney marrying Almeric Paget. But there's at least a chance they'll stay in America. Where's Anna Gould going?'

'She's marrying a French nobleman.'

Daisy plucked at the coverlet. 'Of course she is.'

Grace coughed through a laugh to hide it. 'And how do you feel about that?'

'I feel like there's a transatlantic wedding trade going on where all my friends are being sold off to men on the other side of the world and I'm stuck here.'

From the dressing table, Grace smothered a laugh. She looked into her daughter's dark eyes and reached forward, taking Daisy's hands in hers. They were covered in oil paint. 'You don't want what those girls are about to have, do you?' she checked. 'You don't want fortune-hunting men. And they *are* fortune hunting. Their mothers are orchestrating all of this, exchanging daughters for titles. And then they must leave their families behind to live in far-flung places, in rundown, oversized, freezing, old houses that they'll have to save with their own money. Is that the dream you want?'

'No,' Daisy agreed. 'I do *not.* But I feel so angry that's what *they* want. Why do my friends want that? There's no benefit in any of it and they'll be in a cold, horrible, rainy country. I just don't understand it at all.'

Grace hid a smile.

'Father used to say England was awful. But I wouldn't know. I've never been, and everyone always asks where I'm from because I have this strange half-and-half accent and I end up confessing that I've lived in America my whole life and never once set foot in England.'

'But you *are* English,' Grace pointed out, unsure if it was the answer her daughter was looking for. 'Because your father and I are.'

'But I've never been,' Daisy reiterated. 'So I feel American. I think.'

'And you want to go? To the cold, horrible, rainy country you just spoke about?'

Daisy shrugged. 'Maybe,' she said in a voice that meant *yes*. 'But not because I want a man to take me there and never let me come home. I'd like to take myself. Perhaps. Just to see. I don't know. I want to see everywhere, without a man. Could I go and visit Mary Leiter when she's settled, before she goes to India? Oh, we could go together?'

Grace stilled, a chill running through her at the thought. 'I will never set foot on English soil again. And I will never get on board a boat again.'

Daisy sighed. 'So you've said. Even though I'm old enough to know better, if I cry, will that help you change your mind?'

'No,' Grace said staunchly. 'It won't.'

'Fine. I'll just have to wait to be invited. And Rose will have to chaperone me. And she'll fall in love on the boat with a kind-hearted, rich, intelligent Englishman – because she won't settle for anything less – and you'll be forced to follow anyway so you can see her and all the little English grandchildren she'll produce over there. So you saying no now will have all been for nothing.'

Grace paled, but tried to keep her voice light. 'Don't even say that in jest.'

Daisy smiled impishly. 'To be discussed.'

'We've just discussed it.'

'We'll discuss it again,' Daisy insisted.

Grace's pulse was skittering, but she refused to let her daughter see how much the idea had shaken her. She cleared her throat and laughed hollowly. 'Sometimes you are so different to your sister. And sometimes you are completely and utterly alike.'

'I know. Strange, isn't it?' Daisy leaned forward and kissed Grace on her cheek. 'We must get it from you.'

Chapter 24

'Would a Lander's work well here, Mother?' Daisy asked, linking her arm through Grace's as they finished their walk down Thames Street in downtown Newport.

They'd enjoyed the smattering of old shops and hotels, restaurants and coffee houses. Newport had the feel of old New York from years gone by, from when she'd first arrived fresh off the boat, before the tall buildings had fully taken shape around them. Shopping wasn't the luxury experience here it was on Ladies' Mile in Manhattan, but a few dressmakers and milliners gave the women something to look at as they walked. The street ran parallel to the waterfront, and Grace closed her eyes for a moment, inhaling the fresh salty air, pushing away the vision of Cornwall rearing up inside of her, where she'd last taken it for granted.

'I was asking myself the same question. I'm just not sure. I know your Uncle John has been thinking about expanding out of New York. We can't seem to settle on where. But off-season, I'm not sure there'd be enough trade here. We've done so well in the city, I think *another* city location might be the answer.'

'Boston, maybe?' Daisy suggested. 'It's close, so to speak.'

'Possibly.' Grace gave it some thought as they continued along the waterfront.

'London?' Daisy asked a moment later.

'Nice try.'

Daisy laughed. 'Every day is much the same,' she said, looking around her. 'Just today, I'm in a different state. I think I'm going to paint the sea and spend some time with Mary and Pauline in these few weeks before they leave me and let their husbands dictate the rest of their lives. I'll be back in time to get ready for the ball.'

Grace smiled kindly; she knew what it meant to leave everything you love behind. 'Would you like some company while you paint?'

'No, I'm fine. Thank you, though. I like being by myself.'

Her strong, independent daughter was so like Arthur it sometimes broke her heart. 'In that case, I'll go and find your sister at the tennis club.'

'Shall we take the carriage?' Daisy enquired. 'I could drop you off.'

'It's just one road. I think I might risk impropriety by walking alone. What do you think to that?'

'I think you're in danger of sounding like me,' Daisy said darkly, kissing her mother on the cheek. Grace watched the carriage pull away, and as she walked in the direction of the tennis club, wondered if she should do something to intervene to alter the direction Daisy's life had taken. Was a course correction needed? Daisy was twenty-five and when most of her friends were being snapped up and married in their early twenties, Daisy showed no interest, no sign of entering the marriage market. Was a little shove in the right direction needed? Or did everything happen for a reason and the right person would come along at the right time, embracing Daisy's independent mind and free spirit?

Grace was still weighing this up as she found her youngest daughter Rose drinking a mint julep and standing against the white balustrades, her focus half on a man she was speaking with and the other half on the tennis match playing out below her. But before

Grace could approach and greet her daughter, the young man said goodbye and walked away.

'Who was that?'

'No one important, sadly,' Rose replied in a bored voice. She looked beautiful as ever in a pale-yellow day dress, which emphasised her fair colouring.

'You want someone important?' Grace suggested.

'I want someone important enough to tell *you* about. And that one, sadly, probably wasn't. No one ever matches up.'

'To what?'

'To my standard of what a good man should be.'

'And what is that?'

'Someone like Father. Someone good, kind, clever, handsome.'

'Your father was all of those things,' Grace concurred, watching the players below.

'And you wouldn't want me to settle for anything less, would you?'

She could see both her daughters ending up travelling down the same path if she didn't do something to discreetly intervene. Perhaps she'd set *too* high a set of standards for her children. 'Don't dismiss every single person who comes your way, Rose. It's alright to get to know someone before allowing yourself to fall in love or to send them packing. You're not expecting to fall in love the *moment* you meet someone are you?'

'Why not?'

'Rose,' Grace said gently. 'You know your father didn't sweep me off my feet the moment I met him. You know I'd known him a while before I finally fell in love.'

'I know,' Rose replied. 'You found love your own way. Let me find love in my own way too.'

Grace squeezed Rose's hand softly.

'Would you like me to go and apologise to that man? I was very dismissive,' Rose confessed, looking guilty.

Grace gave her a disappointed look. 'Were you?'

'Yes, I'm sorry.'

'Well, don't tell me that, then. Tell him. I was friends with your father before we fell in love. While this young man might not be the one for you, you never know, you might make a friend.'

'Fine,' Rose said, sighing loudly. 'I'll go and make a friend.' She skulked off to where the young man was standing lost and alone, staring seemingly unseeing at the ongoing match.

Grace watched the man frown, puzzled by Rose's reappearance and then as she spoke, no doubt charming him with a dazzling smile and compliments, his features lifted into a warm smile. For the next twenty minutes Grace made conversation with acquaintances old and new while her daughter chatted with a group of friends that now included the dismissed young man – dismissed no longer.

'He's called Edward Easton and he's very lovely,' Rose told Grace and Daisy that evening. 'And, I hate to admit this, you might have been right telling me not to send him on his way so quickly.'

'Did you just say I was right?' Grace probed with a pretend look of surprise as she watched her daughter get ready for tonight's ball at Mrs Stuyvesant Fish's house.

'I did just say you were right. Revel in it all you like,' Rose said with a wicked smile. 'Because I shan't say it again. Edward will be there tonight too because he met Mrs Fish through the Vanderbilts, who he met in London. Or rather he *was* friends with the Vanderbilts, but now they're divorced it's complicated. Have you seen Alva Vanderbilt here this year?'

'Not yet.'

'Divorce is *not* for the faint-hearted,' Rose said knowledgeably, as if she was seventy-one and not twenty-one.

Alva Vanderbilt's divorce had been a shock to many but not to her friend Grace. Grace was under sworn secrecy that Alva and her long-time friend Oliver Belmont were soon to marry now she was free of her husband, so she said nothing. The scandal that would erupt if the situation were to get out . . . well, it didn't bear thinking about.

'Anyway,' Rose steamed on, 'Alva and Connie met him in London when they were trying to sell Connie to Sunny Marlborough, but I doubt that'll happen because we all know she's secretly engaged to Winthrop.'

'Rose!' Grace said sternly, aware of Ruth curling Rose's blonde hair into an elaborate twist. 'You can't say that. You can't say any of that!'

'Well, I just did,' Rose said unapologetically. 'And I said it to him too.'

'You did not!'

'I did.'

In the stunned silence Daisy asked, 'But is it true? Is she engaged to him?'

'You can't tell Alva! She'll ruin it,' Rose warned. 'She *really* wants Connie to marry the Duke of Marlborough but Connie doesn't want to. Anyway . . . Edward thought my gossip was interesting and fun. We talked about *all* the American girls being sold off to the highest bidder so they could be a lady or duchess or a countess, or . . . I don't know what else there is. I listed all the ones I could remember and all the titles they'd earned themselves over the years simply by crossing the ocean and pouring their cash into crumbling old mansions, and we giggled and giggled.'

'He thought it was funny?' Daisy asked, looking more than a little shocked. 'I don't think it's funny. I think it's sad. All my friends are leaving. But Edward wasn't incensed or . . . thought you were rude?'

'No. His humour seems quite aligned to mine,' Rose said as, behind her, Ruth placed the diamond hairgrips into her hair. 'Edward asked if he could dance with me tonight,' Rose continued. 'He looked so nervous when he asked. I've said yes. He also said' – and Rose turned around at this point and looked at her gathered family – 'that when he insinuated to Connie that he wasn't looking to get married for a few years because he's enjoying travelling, that most of his invitations dried up. We remarked how cut-throat it all is. And how *obvious.* People were inviting him so they could marry him off to their daughters.'

'He's not looking to get married?' Grace repeated.

'In which case you're safe,' Daisy said simply, with a wave of her hand like some visiting dignitary. 'You may carry on.'

Rose laughed. 'Oh, I don't mind. He's funny and friendly and perhaps talking with him and dancing with him tonight will deter the ones that keep getting under my feet. Oh, Mother, did I tell you about Harry Dawes proposing?'

Grace had sunk on to the chaise, her mind whirring to keep up with her daughter's ever-changing conversation. 'No. But your sister did.'

'That's alright then. I'm glad you know. Just in case his mother mentions it to you tonight, you know. But I can't imagine she would. The *humiliation.*'

'I really would rather *you* tell me when men propose to you.'

'Why? It's just another to add to the list of unworthy suitors I've turned down.'

Daisy shook her head in bafflement. 'Aren't they supposed to ask Mother first?'

'They're all scared of you,' Rose told Grace. 'I can't think why. They're all scared of me too but they're less scared of me it would seem. More . . . smitten. Anyway, we don't have to worry about Edward. He wants to see the *Wild West,* as he calls it. And New York and Boston and the Rockies and . . . I forget where else. So we'll make friends, and when the season's over he'll go off on his adventures and I'll keep turning men down until the right one comes along. Thank you, Mother.'

'What for?' Grace asked, still trying to take in her daughter's fast and confusing train of thought.

'For renting this cottage,' she said. 'So far, I'm having so much fun. Though shouldn't we leave for the ball soon? Edward says he's going to show me a book he found in Mrs Fish's library. It has drawings in it of some castles and homes he knows and has one of Blenheim Palace where Connie is being threatened with going. We can laugh about what a lucky escape she's getting by refusing to marry him.'

Grace blinked, trying to take it all in.

'Your new friend is bringing a book to a ball?' Daisy asked, re-puffing her sleeves lazily. 'I like him already.'

'Oh, you'll love him,' Rose said, standing up, smoothing the silk of her skirt and glowing in a way that made Grace feel a prick of concern that Daisy had been right: Rose was ready to be lost.

Chapter 25

Gilt-edged velvet-cushioned chairs were positioned at the sides of the ballroom, nestled between marble pillars and tall sculptures. Grace watched Rose as she danced with Edward, twirling to the orchestra, his hand on her back, just below the bare skin of her low-backed ballgown. Rose had a habit – when it suited her – of being totally unaware when a man was captivated. And it was clear from his expression he was indeed captivated.

'Has anyone asked you to dance?' Grace asked Daisy.

'Only people I don't want to dance with,' Daisy said as they stood near an oversized pot plant, its palm leaves spanning all directions. They were both watching Rose spin and be spun in time with the other dancers. The whole effect of fifty or so couples on the dance floor, waltzing together, was one of pure synchronicity as Rose whizzed past them once again on her way round the room.

'I'm sure someone will ask you,' Grace replied at the same moment as a man in his forties walked over to them, accompanied by one of society's most recognisable men, Harry Lehr. Harry was around Daisy's age and Grace couldn't put her finger on why, but she just didn't like him. He was a foppish social climber.

'Mrs Lander, may I introduce you to my dear friend Ogden Codman, the architect, who I was telling you about the other day at Sherry's restaurant. And this is Mrs Lander's daughter, Daisy Lander.'

'Pleasure,' Mr Codman said, directing his comment to both women equally. 'Harry has spoken about the Lander women all day. I just had to meet you.'

His face was handsome, his eyes were kind, earnest. But Grace had heard enough about Mr Codman to know that, like Lehr, he was best kept at arm's length.

'Well, now we've met,' Grace said, her tone just a fraction colder than usual, hoping they would get the hint.

'We have,' he replied, smiling on obliviously. 'Harry said not to be fooled by your steely English gaze. That I should persevere with conversation and ask you to dance.'

'Me?' Grace said, surprised at how forward he was. Among other things, he was far too young for her. 'I'm not really one for dancing.'

She felt Daisy's eyes on her.

'I didn't persevere for long enough, perhaps. Or at all,' he laughed. He turned his attention to Daisy and she could see his mouth open as if about to ask her to dance.

'Would you excuse me? I think my daughter is in need of some air.'

Daisy looked at her mother and immediately played along. 'Yes, I think a little air would do me the world of good. It was very nice to meet you, Mr Codman, Mr Lehr.' She nodded at them both and then took her mother's arm, a flush of embarrassment passing for illness rising on her cheeks.

When they were on the terrace Daisy hissed, 'Why did you do that?'

'I don't want you to dance with him. He'll *make* you fall in love with him and then marry him.'

'You got all that from what? And why is it a problem if I fall in love and marry him?'

'Ogden Codman, like Harry Lehr, is a *confirmed bachelor.*'

Daisy looked at her mother askance. 'So he *doesn't* want to marry me, then?'

Grace, unsure quite how much of the world Daisy understood, considered the cautious route, before deciding it was best to speak plainly. 'They don't like women.'

'Oh.' And then, 'Ohhhh,' Daisy said, catching on. 'They like each other?'

'I don't care enough to find out and I don't care what they do behind closed doors. What I do care about is that both of them are unmarried and not particularly rich.'

Daisy stared back into the room with a frown of confusion. 'I see.' And then, 'You are as bad as Rose for society gossip. How do you know all this?'

'I make a point of knowing all this. It's how I keep my daughters safe from dancing with fortune hunters.'

Daisy laughed. 'Well, it matters nothing to me. I don't care about dancing but it is a shame no one else has asked *you* to dance.'

Grace shook her head to dismiss her daughter's comment. 'I'm not interested.'

'Because you've had your great love?'

'Yes, your father was all I needed in my life. I'm only interested in making sure you and Rose are happy and that you have something to inherit.'

'So you keep saying,' Daisy said, still watching the dancers swirl in their satin and lace, a kaleidoscope of colour. 'If the path is clear, I'm going inside to observe that man Rose is dancing with fall in love with her. Do you think she'll introduce us to him before she casts him aside? I want to see the book he was talking about, with all the big English houses in it.'

◆ ◆ ◆

Grace didn't know if she was more surprised – when Rose introduced them finally to Edward Easton – on discovering he was English or that her daughter hadn't thought to mention it.

'Blenheim Palace is in Oxfordshire,' Edward informed them, pointing to the pages of a book of great houses of England as they sat around an unused card table.

'This is where Connie is going if her mother has her way,' Rose said enthusiastically.

'Keep your voice down,' Grace implored, casting around in the hopes that her daughter's impropriety wasn't noticed by the wrong sort, or especially the ones who enjoyed gossiping.

'She's only following in the footsteps of Jennie Jerome, that other American girl, who married into that family. Blenheim Palace will soon be full to the brim with American girls at this rate.'

Edward smiled warmly. 'Your daughter has been listing all the Americans who've travelled to England and telling me which houses they are now chatelaines of.'

'Has she now?' Grace commented. She wasn't sure the fact Edward was English made Rose's jesting about the English buying American girls better or worse.

'Actually, I used the term *sold off to all your friends*,' Rose said. 'It's alright. You can tell the truth. I already told them.'

'Not to any of *my* friends, I'm afraid. Your daughter had me in fits of laughter earlier today,' Edward confessed to them all congenially. 'She really is quite incredible.'

'Yes, she is,' Grace agreed, watching this man with interest. 'I hear you're going exploring soon.'

'Not exploring, really. More . . . sightseeing. I've travelled through Europe, and when I met the Vanderbilts and Mrs

Stuyvesant Fish in London they suggested I might like to visit America. I leaped at the chance. I may never get an invitation again. I know very few people on this side of the world. So I was delighted, *am* delighted, with everything I've found here.' He looked at Rose when he said this, Grace noted.

'And then what will you do, when you've seen the sights here?'

'I don't know.' Edward looked thoughtful. 'I'm expected to be a Member of Parliament but I'm not too sure it's for me. I need to decide if I'm going to be pushed into that path or not, because once I've said *yes* the wheel rather turns in an unstoppable direction.'

'What is a Member of Parliament?' Rose asked, and Edward happily regaled her with the history of the House of Commons and the House of Lords.

'And you can't sit in the House of Lords?' Rose asked. 'Because you're not a lord.'

'I am not. I am a nothing, I'm afraid.'

'Whoever sells their daughter to you is going to be *very* disappointed,' Rose said wickedly. 'A nothing. No title. What a shame.'

Grace widened her eyes at her daughter in warning, but Rose was too busy watching Edward laugh raucously instead.

'I was very nearly perfect for a moment, wasn't I?' Edward sighed dramatically. 'But no title. I appreciate that is a letdown for whoever ends up stumbling into my unfortunate path.'

'I'm sure no girl in her right mind would feel let down. But then you were very up front about it so I can't pretend to have been duped. Just make sure you're as upfront with them as you were with me. It's the mothers you've got to watch though,' she said darkly. 'They'll take you being *a nothing* so very badly.'

Grace coughed a loud warning, which Rose ignored. Daisy was trying not to laugh and Grace wished Daisy would help in some way.

'Edward, I know you're supposed to ask me to dance but would you mind if I asked you?'

Edward looked as if he'd just discovered it was Christmas Day. 'No, I don't mind at all,' he said, his dilated pupils betraying his attraction.

'Good,' Rose said, standing hurriedly and looking over his shoulder. 'Because Harry Dawes' brother is walking towards me. I turned his brother's proposal down only last week and I'm in no mood to have to turn down the brother too.'

Edward's eyes widened in surprise as he said, 'Please excuse me,' to Daisy and Grace before holding out his arm to Rose.

Daisy turned to her mother when the two were out of earshot, her voice overflowing with laughter. 'That young man is going to propose before the night is over.'

'I think he might,' Grace said. 'If I wasn't already sitting down I'd ask if you could find me a chair. I can't keep up with Rose. I don't know how anyone does.'

Daisy smiled at their retreating backs before they were swallowed up in the crush. '*He* keeps up. And he's very nice.'

'He is very taken with her, isn't he?' Grace admitted.

'I told you she'd find a nice Englishman,' Daisy pointed out.

Grace shot her a look. 'You said she'd find one on a boat.'

'Well, she found him in the tennis club instead and – Rose will remind you of this later, I'm sure – but it was you who encouraged her to go back and talk to him after she was so rude.'

'Hmm,' Grace murmured, exhausted. She'd never had this much energy when she was Rose's age. But then she'd been a servant, already been worn down through circumstance and heartache, whereas Rose had privilege and money. Neither of her daughters would experience anything like Grace's early life if she had her way.

◆ ◆ ◆

'So then he asked me to dance again,' Rose told her mother and sister in the early hours of the morning after they'd got back to their rented house.

'And you said yes,' Daisy prompted, eyes wide, hopeful for every morsel of development.

'Of course I said yes. I hate to admit this . . .' Her eyes travelled from her sister to her mother. 'But I rather like him.'

'Why do you hate to admit it?' Grace asked.

Rose stood up from the grand-piano stool and began pacing. 'Because I wasn't ready to like him. Or anyone, really. I was rather putting it off. Love, I mean. I was hoping to not have to worry about it for quite a while.'

'You've only known him a day,' Daisy pointed out, reclining on the sofa, her feet slipped from her shoes with a sigh.

'Oh, but what a day it's been,' Rose sighed dramatically, flouncing back down again on a different seat. 'He's asked me on a carriage ride tomorrow morning with Ogden Codman and his friend Edith Wharton. We're going out to Land's End, where the Whartons have their home and Mr Codman's been helping decorate it, so I said *alright.* Actually, I told Edward I'd think about it, and he was to ask me at the end of the evening, and I'd decide then.'

'You didn't?' Daisy asked, awed.

'I did. I want to know if he's serious. If he'd chase me if I made him.'

'That's playing games,' Daisy noted.

'Yes, it is,' Rose admitted. 'Needs must. Time is short. And, did you know it, he asked again so I'd best get my beauty sleep if I'm to go after breakfast as promised. Then after luncheon we're going to spend the afternoon at Bailey's Beach and you can see for yourself if he's serious or not. Then, when we talk about it later, I won't have to rehash everything. Also there'll be strawberries and champagne. So it's worth you coming for that alone.'

'We can have champagne here whenever we want,' Grace said stiffly.

'I know, but nothing tastes as good as someone *else's* bottle of champagne,' Rose trilled.

'You're incorrigible. I wish I had your confidence,' Daisy half laughed through a sigh.

'I'll happily give you some of mine. I've probably got too much. On the back of our Harry Dawes conversation he asked me how many men had proposed to me. I had to say six.'

'Why did you *have* to say six?' Grace asked, her eyes raised to the ceiling in despair.

'Because it's the truth,' Rose replied. 'And then he wanted to know all the reasons I'd turned them down.'

'What are they?' Daisy asked, settling even further into the settee.

'I didn't love them,' Rose said simply.

Both Grace and Daisy sat up in surprise.

'Don't look so shocked,' Rose retorted. 'What reasons did you think I had? It's the same reason for all six of them. I don't care how much money they have, or not. I don't care if their father was in trade or not, if their mother was a countess or not. I'm not even sure what one of those is, I'll have to ask Edward. The point is . . . if I love you, I'll do anything for you.'

'I can't even get you to work in the kitchen without grumbling,' Grace retorted.

'Ah.' Rose shot her a triumphant grin, as she said, 'I'll grumble. But I'll still do it.'

Grace laughed. 'You do have an answer for everything, don't you?'

'I really do. It's what makes me so lovable. It's a curse. And six times men have fallen in love with me and asked me to marry them. Edward won't ask though, I don't think.'

'I think he will,' Daisy said, sitting forward eagerly. 'I think he'll do it soon and he'll be talking himself out of it because he also thinks he's not known you long enough. He'll be wavering. You've spooked him.'

'How do you know that?' Rose enquired.

'Because that's what I'd be feeling in his situation. I think that's what any sane person would do.'

'Where does he live?' Grace chimed in. Because if her daughter was going to say yes to a proposal that hadn't even happened yet, she needed to know how far away Rose would be taken from her.

'England.'

'Where though? It's a big country,' Daisy asked.

'I don't think it is,' Rose pointed out, her face screwed up thoughtfully. 'Edward mentioned in passing you could get from his home to Scotland in a day – or was it two days? – on the railroads. He called it a rail*way* though. So sweet.'

'Have you asked him *anything* about himself or have you just talked about you, Rose?'

'A bit of both,' she said sheepishly. 'I know he likes a sport called cricket. I had to get him to explain that too. I still don't understand it. England is a completely different country to America.'

'Yes. It is,' Grace confirmed dully.

'And he loves reading,' Rose continued as if she'd never spoken. 'And doesn't like rain. And I know he loves to travel.'

'Do you know anything about his family?' Grace asked sharply.

'Yes,' Rose said proudly, overlooking or not noticing her mother's tone. And then pondering some more continued, 'Well, no, not really. I do know his mother died a few years ago.'

'Oh, how sad,' Daisy said.

'We both only have one parent and because we have that in common, we talked about it a lot. His mother wasn't very nice, by all accounts. He didn't really get along with her. Adores his father though. We talked about . . .'

'What?' Daisy prompted when Rose went silent.

Rose shook her head. 'Something he said, something he told me in confidence but it's not mine to share,' she said quietly.

'That's nice,' Daisy said in an uncharacteristically romantic way. 'Something between the two of you, so soon.'

'We talked for hours tonight. As if there was nobody else in the room with us.'

'I saw,' Grace said. She saw her daughter entranced by a man for the first time ever last night. And she could see her falling for him even now, when he wasn't here. 'Don't get your hopes up, darling. If he is going travelling . . .'

'I know,' Rose said, looking wistfully into the distance. 'We'll see what today brings. And then tomorrow and the next day. And then I think he's leaving. He doesn't want to outstay his welcome with the Fishes. Then he'll be gone. And anyway, no man proposes after that short a time, but I think we'll write to each other, maybe. Or perhaps we'll never hear from each other again.' Rose inhaled, filling her lungs and then spoke slowly, tired, as if she was running out of steam. 'Whatever it is, I've had a nice day today. And when he goes there will be more men, because there always are,' she concluded in a bored voice that Grace suspected she was affecting. And she hated herself for hoping that Edward would leave without confessing his affections, if only to save her the horror of ever having to return to England.

Chapter 26

After Edward and Rose had returned from the Whartons' and dined, they took a carriage ride to Bailey's Beach. It was only a few minutes from the Landers' rented home on Ochre Point Avenue. Edward and Rose's courtship had been whirlwind and there was hardly time to question Edward about his life. Grace had gleaned he had a house in London in a fashionable area where he'd been spending time getting to know the Vanderbilts prior to his arrival in America. Grace would have loved to know more about this man who had blown in from England and might be about to take her daughter with him if her suspicions were correct, but there never seemed time to pin him down. Rose dominated him.

When they arrived at Bailey's Beach, they walked past the watchman in his gold-laced uniform, ostensibly on guard to check no one undesirable entered the clubhouse.

It was moments like these when Grace always felt aware of where she'd come from. Although no one in the society they lived among now knew that Grace had once been a servant, she was always reminded of it at the strangest moments. In her old life, she'd never have been allowed here. In her old life, it wouldn't have occurred to her to have even tried. She thanked the watchman, although she wasn't quite sure what for, and they sat at tables under awnings by the beach near the private changing rooms, close to the shore.

It struck Grace that Edward and Rose both in bathing attire was a recipe for disaster. As if either of them would fail to be more attracted to each other. Edward was in a black and white striped short-sleeved shirt and shorts that stopped above the knee. Rose and Daisy, like Grace, were in pale flannel knee-length bathing dresses, nipped in at the waist with a belt. In any other circumstance this would be unthinkable attire but for bathing it was a must. Grace hated swimming in them though; the material dragged down with water made it impossible. On the rare occasions when she had found a moment to swim on her days off as a youngster, it had been stolen minutes in the Cornish sea in a rudimentary smock and bloomers. She'd never spared a thought to fashions for bathing, yet for her girls, it was of such importance not to get left behind those of their acquaintance.

Daisy had goaded Grace into bathing with them. The weather was too hot at this time of year to sit in full dress and they'd been hankering after a dip since they'd arrived. Grace watched as Rose and Daisy and Edward all entered the water gingerly. She sat quietly and watched her children, wondering when Daisy's turn would come for love. Wondering if, for Rose, this was truly it. Edward seemed serious enough and she watched his eyes focus fully on Rose as they talked and laughed in the water while they all tried to enter elegantly. When Daisy stumbled it was Edward who reached out first to grab her wrist, and she couldn't hear what they said afterwards but he seemed to be a genuinely pleasant man.

Was it enough for Rose, though? Did he sweep her off her feet, fill her with a feeling of deep intensity? Grace adjusted the belt on her still-small waist and breathed in the sea-salted air, closing her eyes, allowing herself to drift back in time to another country. She'd found herself thinking a lot more about Cornwall recently.

Edward's arrival into their world had brought with it thoughts of her homeland, even if it didn't feel like home anymore.

Grace opened her eyes to find Daisy had returned and was quietly sketching, her eyes flicking up every now and again to look at Grace.

'You fell asleep,' Daisy said.

'Did I?'

'Only for a few moments.' Daisy moved her hand, already smudged with graphite, over the page at speed.

'Are you drawing me?' Grace asked.

'Maybe,' Daisy answered coyly, her eyes not leaving the page. 'I've not seen you close your eyes and drift away in a while. You're always running around doing things, making plans. I thought I'd capture this serene moment, if only to prove it happened.' She finished sketching quickly, rubbed at the page to blend in and then turned it round to show her mother. 'You smile in your sleep.'

Grace smiled now as she took in the image. With her face in a relaxed pose, the frown line she saw in every mirror that ran vertically between her eyebrows, reminding her of every unticked item on her to-do list, had smoothed out. 'You've made me look pretty. And young.'

'You are pretty. And young.' Daisy turned the sketchbook back around.

Grace attempted to laugh. 'Being a mother is hard work. The worry. It makes me feel old.'

'You didn't look worried then,' Daisy said, and closed her book, her eyes drifting to her sister and Edward standing in the water at waist height, talking.

'I'm not usually very romantic,' Daisy started.

'You seem to be more and more these days.'

'Maybe,' Daisy replied. 'Perhaps it *is* a recent change. But even I can see that after only a short time, when Edward leaves, her heart will break. She pretends it won't. But it will. They appear to be very intense with each other.'

◆ ◆ ◆

The following days were a mix of society events and carriage rides, tennis matches and beach visits, balls and dinners. When Edward's last day arrived as swiftly as expected, returning from a final day on the shore, he walked them all from the carriage to the front door as if desperate to stretch out his final hours. His ferry left tomorrow afternoon, and while Grace and Daisy went upstairs to their rooms to bathe, they left the two lovers alone in the large entrance hall. But while the baths were being filled, Grace listened and watched discreetly from the banisters, out of sight, in what had to be the world's longest goodbye between two people who were clearly falling in love.

Rose's hands were clasped in Edward's. The footman, who opened and closed the front door to guests, had clearly gone back to the servants' hall, keeping out of the way.

'Might I call on you tomorrow to say goodbye properly?' Edward's voice echoed in the large marble-pillared entrance.

'I'd like that.' Rose's reply was soft, but still audible.

'Tomorrow morning?'

'Yes,' Rose said breathlessly, and Grace felt her own heart squeeze at the depth of feeling that seemed to echo in the space between them.

'Until then.' But neither made a move. Slowly Edward removed his hands from Rose's, turned and opened the front door without a backward glance.

When he was gone, Grace heard Rose sigh long and loud. 'Oh my *word*.'

She turned slowly, a wide smile on her face, and glanced up, catching sight of her mother peering from above. 'Oh, Mother,' she called, gathering her skirts and running up the stairs. 'He says he's coming to say goodbye, but I think he's coming to propose.'

'I think he is too.' Grace was thrilled for Rose, despite her concern that if they married Rose's new home would most likely be in England. She knew her daughter was happy and beginning to understand just how much that mattered. 'But how can he when he's leaving? Are you ready for it to happen if it does? I know you said before—'

'Yes. Oh, yes I am,' she breathed.

'You've not known each other long, my darling. Please be careful.' How she wanted to sweep her daughter up into her arms as she had when she was young, to protect her from the bumps and bruises that batter a heart so easily in this life.

'I know. Although my heart is lost to him. I'm completely lost to him. I don't know how it happened.' Rose's eyes were shining. 'You do like him, don't you?'

'I do, darling, but I'm not the one marrying him. You have to like him. You have to *know* him.'

'I think I do. That day at the beach we talked for so long in the ocean, I thought I would turn into a shrivelled piece of over-ripe fruit.'

'If he proposes I will have to speak to him. What does he expect from us financially? In lieu of your father not being here, I am going to have to ask some practical questions. And your Aunt Mary and Uncle John will want to involve themselves in this . . . deal.'

Rose shook her head passionately. 'It's not a deal. It's not a transaction. He's not buying me. We talked about that too.'

Grace baulked. 'Oh, Rose. Not again.'

'I wanted to be sure. I told him we don't have much money.'

Grace's mouth fell open.

'So what if I lied?' Rose exclaimed. 'It was a calculated risk. If he'd run away, I'd know he didn't really want *me*, that he just wanted another dollar princess to ship to England and save his palace or castle or wherever. I had to take that risk. I had to know. He knows we own restaurants, but he doesn't know much more than that. He doesn't know how well your investments have done.'

Grace paled a little at her daughter's tactics, but Rose continued. 'You want someone to love me but not to be a fortune hunter. How else was I going to discover this? You don't need to ask the practical questions. I already did! He said he doesn't care if I'm as poor as a church mouse or as rich as Croesus. He likes me for me. He has enough money, so he says. He has a house he doesn't even want to inherit and he'd rather watch it fall to the ground than spend every penny on the planet trying to save it. But it's not large. Or grand. Or rather, it's not so large and grand all *your* money will be spent fixing crumbling bits of it. So I got to the bottom of everything and his intentions are honourable. But if he doesn't propose and if he does just come to say goodbye tomorrow then none of this even matters. He'll go travelling and he'll either forget me or write to me and maybe, when he returns from getting shot at by lawless gunslingers in the west, he *might* propose to me then. But he might not and the thought he doesn't . . .' Her voice broke as she looked at her mother with eyes swimming with tears. 'It devastates me, Mother. It really does.'

Grace held her daughter as she collapsed into her on the stairs, letting her bury her face into her shoulder and stroking her hair as she had when Rose was five and had broken her favourite doll.

'You discussed our respective finances while standing in the ocean?' she asked, attempting to make Rose laugh.

'I did.' Rose pulled her face back and smiled through her tears. 'I had a good list of questions for him and I just worked through them all one after the other. *Bang bang bang*.'

Grace smoothed her daughter's cheek and smiled back. 'Just now he looked as if he didn't want to be parted from you.'

'I know,' Rose said happily, the rush of emotion quickly replaced with mirth. 'I was pretty taken aback how much more interested he was in me after that. Did you see the way he held my hands just now? I don't think there's anything I could say that would put him off. Only he's leaving.'

Knowing the words were pointless, Grace still spoke what was in her heart. 'Please don't be disappointed if it doesn't all turn out the way you want.'

'Oh, I won't be disappointed,' Rose said, as she began climbing the stairs for her bath and turning on the last step to fix her mother with an intense gaze. 'I will be distraught.'

Chapter 27

Edward arrived at the appointed time the following morning, ostensibly to say goodbye. Daisy and Grace had prearranged how they would gently extricate themselves from the room at certain moments so as not to make it too obvious, just in case his plan was to propose and not to bid them all farewell.

Grace reminded herself that long, long ago she had received a proposal from someone she'd loved when she'd least been expecting it. And Rose was expecting one that might not come. And if it did, what then? She would lose her daughter to England along with the hundred-odd other American girls who had gone before her, taking their wit and charm, independence and money with them.

Cornwall and Trelenna had held such painful memories that everything that happened at the end had overshadowed all the good that had come in the years before it. As her children had been born and the business boomed, Trelenna had been resigned to the past, to a life that was no longer part of them. And so Rose and Daisy knew very little about everything that had come before, just the essentials: how their parents had been friends in England before making a fresh start in America. To all intents and purposes, no one other than the older Landers knew the specifics of Arthur and Grace's reasons for leaving Cornwall or how they had lived in servitude there, or how their rise had started in the docks. No one in polite society needed to know *everything*. And that really was the way she'd hoped it would stay.

Edward sat in the drawing room, looking around at the high ceilings, white wood-panelled walls, and pale polished floors with Chinese rugs making it softer, homelier. The room was made all the brighter for oversized gilt-edged mirrors reflecting the sun around the space. In the distance, the sea swelled. The weather was changing. Edward's eyes roved, taking it all in. He perched on the edge of his chair as if he couldn't quite relax, couldn't quite commit himself to being in the room. Grace noticed but she wasn't sure if Rose had. He was half in, half out, which didn't bode well.

'Once the ferry deposits me in New York I'll be there for a day. And from there, a train will take me west. All the way to California. I'm fascinated by the Gold Rush. Fascinated. I want to see as much as I can because who knows if I'll ever be on this side of the world again.' He nodded jovially around at them all, emanating nervous anticipation, for his trip or to have a moment alone with Rose, Grace couldn't tell. But she noted Rose's expression dropped at the very mention of his journey.

'I think this is a once-in-a-lifetime trip. Although I've been talking myself in and out of it for days.'

'Have you?' Rose asked, her expression lifting marginally.

He nodded slowly, the sadness in his eyes easy to read.

'And where will you go after California?' Daisy enquired, filling the sad silence.

'Nevada, Wyoming and Utah. I'm going to take the new railways and stop where I can on the return from California.'

'Alone?' Grace asked, worried.

'Absolutely. I'll look after myself.'

'Do be careful,' Rose said softly. 'I should hate to think of anything happening to you.'

'I will,' he said, looking as deeply into her eyes as she was into his.

Grace took her opportunity. 'Do excuse me for a moment. I must talk to Cook about dinner.' She knew that Daisy would follow soon after and a few moments later she did.

'What was your excuse?' Grace asked, lingering in the entryway to the basement staircase down to the kitchen, out of sight, both of them languishing against opposite walls.

Daisy leaned back and looked up at the ceiling absent-mindedly. 'I said I needed to write an urgent letter, but he was to say goodbye before he left. I panicked. I should have had a better excuse but I don't think he noticed. He looked relieved I was leaving. I'll try not to take it personally.'

Grace was silent and Daisy coughed.

'Daisy, shhh.'

'There's no point. You can't hear anything from here. Want me to go listen at the door?'

Grace chuckled. 'No.' She closed her eyes, inhaled and exhaled nervously for Rose.

'What do you think he's saying?' Daisy asked.

Grace shrugged.

'He's either saying goodbye or I love you,' Daisy answered her own question. 'Or maybe both.'

Grace's face flushed hot, sick with nerves. 'How long do you think is too long to leave them alone? Propriety dictates we should probably go back soon—'

Just then the drawing-room door opened and – from their hidden position – the two women peered out as they heard Edward call out, 'I'm so sorry. Rose, please.'

'It's fine,' Rose dismissed, through tears. Her dress swished across the marble floor as she moved towards the front door.

'Let's not end it like this,' he pleaded, rushing after her.

'It's not ending. You said it yourself. You're asking me to wait for you, but you don't know when you'll ever be here again. A month. A year. You don't know.'

'That's not what I said.' Edward's voice was level and calm. 'Rose, please. Don't abandon me now.'

Rose's head flashed up, eyes hard and glittering. 'Who's abandoning who? You're the one leaving.'

'But you always knew I was going. I was clear with you from the start.'

'So then you have no right to ask me to wait for you for an unspecified amount of time.'

'Rose, you know I can't ask you to marry me and then leave you. What if I go and get shot, or whatever you think is going to happen to me?'

From their hiding place, Daisy and Grace exchanged a shocked look as the footman arrived on the stairs beneath them and paused in the stairwell at the sudden commotion. Grace shook her head at him, and he silently turned and retreated with an understanding nod.

'You said you wouldn't get shot,' Rose exclaimed.

'I won't. Rose, I won't. But if something happens to me and I've proposed to you . . . It's not fair.'

'On who?' Rose asked, her voice like ice. 'Because you're not even *asking* me to marry you. But you're still asking me to *wait*? And you're offering me nothing in return – less than nothing.'

'I see that. I do,' he continued to implore. 'But I don't know what else to do. I'm trying to be honest. I'm trying to do what's right.'

'But not honest enough. And not honest with yourself. I don't know what you really want at the end of all this. But if it isn't me, then now is the time to say. Because I am not going to wait on the off-chance you may or may not come back and that you *may* or *may not* propose *if* you do come back.'

'I don't know what else to say.' Edward sounded lost.

'You know exactly what to say. You just won't say it. And I don't want you to say it. Not if you don't mean it. I don't want you to sacrifice your adventure for me. And you don't want to either. But I wish, with all my heart, that you hadn't come here today. That you hadn't half promised me nothing. And that we'd left things where they were. Because nobody got hurt yesterday. And today, everybody's getting hurt.'

'Rose, I'm so sorry,' Edward said, his voice quivering with regret. 'I've gone about this all wrong.'

Rose didn't reply. And then she did, formally, stiffly. 'I wish you the very best, Edward. I really do. Please look after yourself.'

Edward's voice came thick and sorrowful. 'After all of this, you're offering me your hand to shake?'

'I'm being polite. I want us to depart as friends. Because if we ever happen to see each other again, we need to shake hands and part as friends now.'

'I see. Then I wish you the very best too, Rose. And I'm sorry.' There was a momentary silence. Edward's voice was strained. 'These last few days, in your company, have been the best of my life.'

Rose's voice was weighted with sorrow. 'I feel the same, Edward.' And then she prompted with a soft sob, 'You need to let go of my hand now. No good will come of you continuing to stand here like this. It's only causing pain for both of us.'

'Goodbye, then,' Edward said desperately.

The sound came of the front door being pulled back and Grace wiped tears from her own eyes, listening to her daughter's heart break even more with every inch she opened the door to let him go.

'Goodbye,' Rose said, and then the front door slowly closed in place.

In the entrance hall, Rose's sobs echoed as, in the distance, the low rumble of thunder began, the heavens suddenly opened, and the sky cried for Rose too.

Chapter 28

Rose didn't emerge from her room for the next two hours, despite both Daisy and Grace's entreaties. Outside, the gathering storm battered the windows.

'She won't let me in,' Daisy said forlornly as the morning turned to afternoon. She was sitting on the floor outside her sister's room helplessly. 'She asked me to go away. And I'm not sure if she's crying or not because it's gone very quiet.'

'Darling,' Grace said, knocking gently on Rose's door. 'I just want to know . . .' She didn't know what to ask. If she was alright? Of course her daughter wasn't alright.

Rose opened the door, eyes tinged red from crying. 'I'm still alive,' she said in a flat voice. 'And I can hear you talking about me. Won't you go away and leave me alone? I would like to sleep and I can't do that with you two twittering away out here like a pair of chattering birds.'

'Of course.' Grace wished she could do more. But what could she do? Her experience of heartbreak had only taught her one thing. 'Time is a great healer. You have to trust me on this.'

Even Daisy baulked at that one. 'Mother,' Daisy warned softly and shook her head.

'I don't know what to say.' Grace opted for honesty. 'Can we come in? Let me stroke your hair while you sleep.'

Rose's shoulders dropped and she sighed, short and sharp. 'Alright.'

She lay on the bed and Grace and Daisy sat either side of her, Grace stroking her hair, Daisy holding her sister's hand.

'I know what you're going to say,' Rose started, turning towards Daisy on the pillow. But she didn't wait for her family to speak. 'You're going to say it was the most unorthodox, most spur-of-the-moment way to start a romance. That it was bound to end so abruptly, because it started in much the same way.'

'I wasn't going to say that,' Daisy said.

'Neither was I,' Grace agreed. 'But I've thought about it . . .'

'I thought about it too,' Rose said. 'I worried about it, ever since he said he was leaving. I didn't want to like him. I wanted to feel . . . indifferent. But I couldn't help it. I couldn't help it, Mother, especially after you told me to go and speak to him at the tennis club after I was so rude.'

Daisy glanced over her sister's head and gave her mother a look that said, *I told you so.*

'It all felt so wrong,' Rose continued. 'Then so right. And then so wrong again. I knew I was right to dismiss him that day. I've only got myself to blame. It won't happen again. I'll be stronger next time.'

'Oh, Rose,' Grace said sadly.

'We know hardly anything about him.' Daisy tried to be helpful and it was Grace's turn to issue a pointed look. But Daisy missed it and continued on. 'He could have been *anyone.* He could have been a *smuggler*,' Daisy jested.

Rose's laugh was unexpected and full.

'Or,' Daisy continued, 'more realistically, what if he had a huge house with holes in the ceiling, after all? Even though he said he didn't. Or *no* house at all. What if he had *nowhere* for you to live?'

Rose smiled. 'Thank you for trying to make me feel better, but he wasn't a smuggler, and he had a home and it sounded idyllic – in the countryside but close to the sea. He told me that when we were standing in the sea. It's somewhere in Cornwall. I think I would have liked to live there.'

'Cornwall?' Grace asked in a sharper tone than she meant to, continuing to stroke Rose's hair. 'He mentioned London a lot.'

'He has a big house there too. All those old families do.'

'Two houses but not two dimes to rub together to save them,' Daisy thought aloud.

'I told him you'd grown up in Cornwall,' Rose said. 'You might know his house?'

'I doubt it,' she said. 'I didn't move in those circles back then,' Grace confessed, still slowly stroking Rose's soft blonde hair. 'But I do know Cornwall has a lot of beautiful manor houses.'

'Edward's home is only small,' Rose said drowsily. 'But it sounded perfect.' Her daughter was trailing into sleep.

'I suppose it depends on your definition of perfect.' Daisy tried to be helpful.

'I suppose it depends on your definition of *small*,' Grace said, readying herself to leave her youngest child to sleep. 'Does his house have a name?'

'Yes, it's called Trelenna.'

Chapter 29

The world seemed to stop for a moment, before her blood rushed in her ears. Grace stared at her daughter. 'What?' she whispered.

'You know it?' Rose's eyes opened.

Grace's breathing came thick and ragged. She couldn't hide it. 'What?' she asked again.

Daisy shot her a curious look. 'You've heard of it?'

Grace tried and failed to answer. Then her mind finally caught up to her. 'You told me his last name was Easton,' Grace accused. She couldn't stop her world spinning in circles. 'How does someone named Easton live at Trelenna?'

'It is Easton. But he's got three last names. Anyhow, what does it matter? He's gone.'

'Wh— What are the *three* last names? You said Easton,' Grace repeated pointlessly.

'Edward Easton-Thorpe-Trelenna,' Rose trilled.

'What?' Grace demanded again, standing up abruptly and pacing wildly. 'Trelenna? Why didn't you say that? Why didn't *he* say that?'

'He did say that to me but he introduced himself as Edward Easton when we first met. I didn't think it was an issue. And I was more wondering when he was going to propose than concerned about how many letters were in his last name. It's not important.' Rose shifted position and looked at Grace. '*Is* it important?'

'Why does he . . . ?' She tried to regain control of her breathing. 'Why is he a Trelenna? Why does he have three last names?' Grace's mouth was dry. She wasn't sure she was blinking anymore. Whatever Rose said, whatever her answer, it didn't matter. This man, this boy . . . he wasn't . . . he couldn't be . . . No, it was unthinkable. He just couldn't be one of them. He could not be Laurie's son. He could not be. She'd have seen some resemblance, wouldn't she? It would be such a significant moment, meeting Laurie's son, that she'd have just *known* if Edward had been one of them? Wouldn't she? She'd have sensed it within her blood, her soul, her heart. Despite what he'd done to her, she'd have known.

'His mother was an Easton-Thorpe,' Rose explained. 'I thought I told you about her. She's the one who brought all the money into the Trelenna family. She was one of two daughters and there were no sons, so *her* father asked as part of the agreement that she keep her name when she married and *her* children had to have her last name too or their line would die out. Same for her sister. Makes sense. Imagine if Daisy and I marry and drop Daddy's last name. Who else will carry it? Although I doubt I'll ever marry now,' Rose sobbed and then controlled herself again. 'But I like the idea of keeping my name, adding it on even if it will be an inconvenient mouthful, which is what Edward called it. He just goes by Edward Easton when he makes new acquaintances. It upset his father but made his mother happy. Or rather, it did, before she died.'

Grace faced the window; all energy had suddenly been drained from her. Outside the clouds rolled thick and black, rain pelting. 'Oh god,' she muttered under her breath. 'How has this happened?'

'How has what happened?' Daisy asked. 'Mother? What's wrong? Do you know the Trelennas?'

Grace stared out of the window, seeing but not seeing, her vision blurred. Downstairs the doorbell rang, loud and sonorous.

'Mother?' Rose asked, then when Grace made no move, she stood up and went towards her. 'Mother, sit down.' She pulled out her dressing-table chair and, as Grace looked as if she might faint, Rose ushered her mother into it. 'Are you alright? You're not, are you? I don't understand what's happened. *I'm* the one who just got hurt. What's happened to you? What have I said? Mother? Please tell me.'

'I'll be alright. I just feel a little unwell. I'm fine. It's nothing . . .'

'But you—' Daisy started and then stopped as a knock came at Rose's door. Instead of asking the servant to enter, Rose just leaped up and opened it.

'Mr Edward Easton is at the door,' the butler said. 'He doesn't have a card to present. Or rather, he does but – like him – it is soaking wet.'

Rose's eyes darted from Grace to the butler to Daisy, as if she was unable to comprehend what was happening.

'Edward is downstairs,' Daisy translated for her sister. 'Right now,' she said excitedly. 'He's come back. He's come back for you.'

Rose inhaled sharply. 'He's come back for me,' she repeated. And then her mother and sister were forgotten as Rose flew from the room and down the stairs. Daisy followed and hovered by the banisters. Grace inched her way forward until her hand hit the smooth wood of the rail to stand beside her daughter, every feeling in her body replaced by fear. In the hall downstairs, she watched her youngest fall into Edward's open arms as he dripped rainwater all over the tiled floor.

'I couldn't do it,' he cried, spilling over with emotion. 'I couldn't leave. I couldn't leave you. I can't ever leave you. I love you. I love you.' He pulled Rose tighter into his embrace and she let herself be kissed. Grace's hand reached out and gripped Daisy's arm tightly.

Daisy didn't seem to notice her mother's nails digging into her arm as she gasped in awe when Edward kissed Rose so passionately, in the middle of the entrance hall while he was soaked to the skin.

'I'm not going,' he said as he pulled back, his eyes searching Rose's. 'How could I go? How could I leave you? I love you.'

'Why did you change your mind?' Rose asked, as emotion took over and she too began crying.

'I got to the ferry and I didn't want to go.' Edward spoke fast. 'I wanted a sign – a sign I shouldn't get on the boat, a sign I shouldn't leave the woman I knew I'd fallen in love with. The rain kept falling and then the storm was rolling in, and the ferryman said he wouldn't sail today and we should come back tomorrow when the storm had passed and I knew . . . *I knew* I wasn't supposed to go. That was my sign. I got off the boat and came straight back. To you. Rose, I'm so sorry. Please forgive me. I didn't want to propose and leave you. But I'm not supposed to leave you at all. It took a storm to make me see it. But thank god it did. You and I are not supposed to be parted. You are supposed to be my wife. I know this with every part of my mind, every corner of my heart, every inch of my soul. Please forgive me, please say you'll marry me. I deserve to be told no, I know this. But I'm begging you not to. I love you and I'm begging you to marry me.'

'You don't need to beg me to marry you, Edward.' Rose laughed with happiness. 'Or course I will marry you. Of course I will.'

At the top of the stairs, Grace could take it no longer, her legs giving out in shock as she listened to Rose accept a proposal of marriage from Laurie Trelenna's son.

Chapter 30

Present Day

Zennor

Zennor was mistaken, surely. She had to be. As she sat slumped on the floor of the downstairs loo, she looked in horror at her phone calendar. She'd missed her period. By a lot. In fact, she was nearly due her next one. Zennor asked herself if it was the stress of opening the house that had caused her body to play havoc with itself, or if she was . . . in fact . . . No. She couldn't be. She refused to even think the word. She refused to think the unthinkable. Over the following days, she kept her head firmly in the sand, because if her world was about to turn upside down she wanted to put off knowing about it until the last possible moment.

She could feel herself withdrawing from her siblings. It was best to keep them at a distance so there would be no chance of finding cracks in conversation, moments of weakness when she might let her mouth and her fears run away with her. If she didn't speak, she couldn't tell them her worries. Then she wouldn't have to say them. Then they wouldn't be true. She was also careful with what she ate in front of them in case anything should trigger the sickness.

Zennor kept Charlie at arm's length too. At first she pretended to be too ill to take him up on his offer of helping look through the archive boxes. And then she pretended to be too busy, fobbing him off when he tried to make plans for another date. If she was *the-word-she-didn't-dare-think-or-say*, then there was absolutely no point at all in carrying on this fledgling romance with Charlie. He would not want . . . *this*. She agreed to swap rotas with Kayleigh, so Zennor was in the tearoom taking orders, making teas and coffees and serving food while Kayleigh was in the kitchen cooking and baking. She thought that might keep him away from her naturally. She just needed time to work out what was going on with her before she could turn her attention to what was going on between her and Charlie.

But Charlie had persistently come to find her each day, just for a few moments, popping his head in the tearoom at the end of his shift, not knowing anything was wrong. Each time he visited, Zennor gave him a wave and then made a face that she hoped conveyed how busy she was – although she'd always made time for him before, despite being run off her feet.

The Halloween half-term event was going strong and Zennor wanted to focus on this, make it a success and put off everything else until after it was over. Pumpkin spice lattes and white-chocolate meringue swirls in the shapes of ghosts were the most popular orders. She loved this time of year usually. But it was passing her by. She was on autopilot – here but not really here.

Zennor helped children claim their prize, a cute badge of their choosing for completing the Halloween trail and ticking off all the spooky things they'd seen in the house and garden. She loved watching their happy faces when she rewarded them, loved listening to them chatter about how funny Lamorna and Merry looked in their black cat and vampire outfits respectively, while they'd hosted the tours. Their effort and the little flickering lanterns they carried made the house feel especially atmospheric, but still child friendly. She loved catching snippets of their tours, especially when Lamorna or Merry were retelling Zennor's ghostly sightings of the young woman in the red dress in the attic, as well as various other local hauntings they'd researched in the run-up. The families had loved it, kids in particular. And this week, when thinking about children was the last thing she wanted to do, they were all over the estate, carving pumpkins and dressing up.

She was watching a toddler dressed in a princess costume by the back door of the tearoom. The child was waiting patiently for her mother to open the door so they could go in search of the children's play area. As they left, Charlie entered. Zennor felt guilt sweep her when she caught his uncertain face and she forced herself to make conversation as he approached, find a chair for him and offer him tea and cake. 'I can't stop though, but give me a wave when you go?' She'd never heard herself sound so falsely upbeat before.

'Oh, okay.' She heard the disappointment in his voice. He'd not tried to kiss her in public, remaining professional in front of visitors. But he clearly knew something was up. Each day Zennor waited. Because if she waited, her period might suddenly start and she could stop feeling this heightened tension that threatened to engulf her. And then just as swiftly as it had arrived, the Halloween week was over, and all the planning had paid off, Lamorna even popping a bottle of local fizz to celebrate that they were keeping the house's bills at bay, for now.

Then Monday arrived and enough was enough. Her period still hadn't appeared, so she left the house early and drove the few miles into Wadebridge, to a chemist where no one knew her or the Trelenna family.

Despite technically being closed, Mondays had, for the time being, become a strategy catch-up day, and today's was spilling over on to lunch. But she declined to eat, as Merry had insisted on making them cheese toasties again and she simply couldn't risk it.

Zennor bumbled her way through the meeting as best she could, staring out of the window or into the distance, distracting herself by wondering what Grace had looked like when she'd worked here, standing by the range, stirring sauces, rolling pastry. Had she had a neat little Victorian bun at the nape of her neck? Was she blonde, brunette, redhead? Was she tall? How had she changed when she'd come into money? Had she been proud of her roots or ashamed?

'So we're agreed then?' Merry asked. 'Zen?'

Zennor blinked herself back into the room. She nodded slowly, agreeing to whatever it was that had just been suggested.

'Great,' Merry replied. 'Christmas Fayre dates are confirmed. First Saturday and Sunday in December. And then up until December 23rd we'll have the house open to the public and dressed for Christmas. Then it's a well-earned festive break for all of us.'

'I'll sort social media posts today and then get on to the tourism events pages,' Lamorna said. 'Zen, you contact Mum's choir and see if they want to sing? Then talk to all your food suppliers and see if they want to rent stands, and I'll put together all the information such as costs and size of pitch available, you just have to sweet talk them. Merry, you're sorting a huge Christmas tree for the hall and smaller ones for each of the rooms on show. As for decorations . . .' Zennor zoned out as Lamorna and Merry continued talking enthusiastically. Her mind just wasn't in the room.

'Reconvene next Monday as usual and see where we're all at. Meeting closed,' Merry said, shutting the lid on his laptop. 'Unless anyone else has anything to say?'

Zennor shook her head, clamped her mouth shut. She had nothing to say – nothing anyone wanted to hear. Not until she knew for sure. And there was only one way to do that. She was already a bundle of nerves. She couldn't wait any longer. She had to know one way or another, although she didn't have a plan for either outcome. Zennor waited until her siblings had gone, leaving her alone once again in her kitchen. She took the pregnancy tests out of her hiding place, the very back of the messy kitchen drawer on the old Welsh dresser that no one ever opened, and shoved one into her jeans pocket.

Inside the downstairs loo, she shut the door behind her and stood with her back against it, closing her eyes for a moment and breathing deeply. Deep inhale. Deep exhale. Over and over, slowly psyching herself up to do something she thought she wouldn't be doing for a good few years yet. Then, hands shaking, she read the instructions. Two blue lines: pregnant. One blue line: not pregnant. *Easy enough to remember.* Then she immediately forgot and read it again, unwrapping the test carefully and binning the detritus. Even peeing on the stick became a nightmare, trying not to drop it in the loo. She'd never known her heart to race quite like this, her hands to shake so much. She put the cap back on and placed the test on the cistern while she washed her hands, zipped up her jeans and watched the timer on her phone. The test would accurately tell her in one minute if she was pregnant. But to be sure, five minutes was the maximum time.

'I am twenty-one. I cannot be pregnant. I am twenty-one. I cannot be pregnant,' she repeated over and over, as if saying it multiple times would make it true.

She picked up the test and waited. In less than five minutes, she would know if she was carrying a baby. Although if she was honest with herself, she already knew what the test was going to tell her. She watched one blue line develop and then . . . nothing else happened. She watched it closely. Still nothing more. Then she looked up in surprise as the toilet door opened and Charlie walked in.

'I didn't think anyone—' Charlie said in shock.

'I thought I'd locked it—' Zennor cried hastily.

'I'm sorry,' he said. Then Charlie's surprise turned to confusion when he glanced at her hands, noticing what she was holding. He looked carefully at the pregnancy test, for one second, two seconds, but didn't speak. Then his eyes raised slowly to connect with hers. 'I'm so sorry for barging in,' he muttered and backed away, closing the door behind him.

Zennor looked down to the test to see what he'd seen: two blue lines. Zennor was pregnant.

Chapter 31

New York

1895

Grace

Grace wasn't supposed to feel like this. Her youngest daughter was getting married and Grace was in despair.

She stood in famed dressmaker Mrs Catherine Donovan's brownstone on Madison and Fortieth being measured for a dress for Rose's wedding. Rose and Daisy too were being measured, shown swatches, champagne being poured for them. But while her daughters both touched and enthused over silks and lace, Grace could see only hopelessness. How could she stop this? How could she say anything that wouldn't give away everything she'd kept buried. The panic that thrummed through her was familiar; she had known panic like this before, long, long ago. Standing in the rainy night for a man who didn't arrive. The interview in the morning room where she'd lost her job. Then the unknown, long-term fright as she had drowned in misery; unemployment and homelessness. Thoughts that she'd never find a way out. Laurie. Betrayal. And now *his* son, marrying *her* precious daughter. Where was Arthur? Where was he when she needed him?

As the seamstress moved the tape measure along her arm, Grace relived her own private hell all over again. So young, believing the world was at her feet because she'd moved up to the position of cook. Nothing could touch her then. Nothing could have hurt her then because she had nothing left to lose – no family, no home. But she'd *had* a home, of sorts, at Trelenna, and Laurie Trelenna had been the one to hurt her, had been the one to take it all away despite promising her more. And she'd let him. It had all been her fault, believing his love was real, his proposal was real. And she'd been so careful for so long. Until she hadn't.

'You are his latest mistake.'

She dropped the glass of champagne she'd been holding, immediately apologising and bending to pick up the pieces, realising too late that the sharp shards were slicing her hand as she scooped them up.

'Mother, you're hurt. There's blood. Stop,' Daisy cried, rushing over.

'I'm so sorry,' Grace cried, although to who she wasn't sure.

The seamstress grabbed a piece of fabric and quickly tried to offer it as a bandage.

'It's alright. It's not much. It's not deep. I'll recover,' Grace reassured them all. But she wouldn't recover. Not from this, or from Laurie's actions, or from his son entering their world and taking her precious daughter with him to England. Because that's where they were going. It was important to Edward that both sides of his family watched him get married in England. Whereas Rose's family was so small and everyone was more than excited to travel overseas for a wedding. Everyone except Grace.

The seamstress bent to pick up the remaining glass. Once upon a time she'd been someone like the seamstress, fetching and scraping. Grace tried to help again.

'Mother!' Rose chastised and Grace knew she was embarrassing Rose, embarrassing Daisy, embarrassing herself. She stood up again and tried to control her breathing, control her mind, her agony. She looked at the blood, seeping through the cloth.

'Mother?' Rose asked from the other side of the room, watching, her face full of confusion and concern.

Grace avoided her daughter's gaze. Just nodded that she was fine. It was this that hurt more than anything – the lying. No, of course she wasn't alright. But she couldn't say. Laurie Trelenna had the power all these years later to wound, to cause damage within her family. *His* son was marrying *her* daughter, and she couldn't say, she couldn't tell anyone. Arthur was gone. She had no one to talk to, no one to share confidences with. It had taken her so long to trust again after Laurie. Her heart had been closed before him, and then again after him. He had been a lightning flash in an otherwise clear blue sky. And here he was again, decades after he'd broken her heart, breaking it all over again by taking her daughter from her. How could Rose marry Edward? How could Grace lose one of her precious daughters to a member of the *Trelenna* family, to Laurie's *son*? It haunted her daily, hourly. It was all the family talked about and she had to pretend. She had to *pretend* she wasn't in hell.

'Edward has written to his father to make a start with plans,' Rose called from the other side of the room. Rose was still eying Grace warily. The dressmaker waited patiently for Grace to resume her position, lifting her arm. The tape measure was lengthened out and everything was just as it had been a few moments ago. Except it wasn't.

'Has he?' Grace said, feigning disinterest. Mention of Laurie was unavoidable. When he wasn't in her mind he was in the air around her. 'That's nice.'

'Edward cabled him the moment I said yes. Or . . . shortly after, at any rate.'

'Oh,' Grace said, glancing over at Daisy, who was making a horrified face as a green silk was held up to her, washing her complexion out entirely.

'But we wondered when *you* would write to him,' Rose continued.

Grace's head snapped round towards Rose. 'Me? Write to him?'

Rose laughed. 'Your daughter,' she pointed to herself with good humour, 'is crossing an ocean to get married and is then going to live there. I assumed you'd want to get to know the man whose house I'll be living in, introduce yourself before the wedding . . . say *hello*, or at very least wrangle about what I'm worth.'

Grace smiled thinly at the joke. There was no one to tell. No one to talk to. No one to share this with. 'I suppose I could pen something. Suggest a dowry amount.' And now she was handing him money. What was this punishment for? What had she done for this to be how she lost Rose? She would hand her over to the Trelennas and then *give them money*. It didn't bear thinking about.

'After all, you'll be staying there for some time, won't you?' Rose continued.

'Staying?' The horror in Grace's voice betrayed her.

'Where *will* you be staying then? There are enough bedrooms, by all accounts.'

'I . . . Close by, perhaps. I'll rent a house. Yes, that might be for the best. I'll rent a house of my own.'

'I'm not sure there are that many nearby. And Edward's father will invite you to stay. It would be expected you'd stay. And Daisy too. There are no *hotels*. I don't think it's that kind of place. Why won't you just stay at Trelenna? It's going to be my home soon too.'

It was mine once. Grace tugged at her own dress, constricted and tight against her chest, her ribcage.

'Might I speak to my daughters for a moment, alone?' Grace surprised everyone in the room by asking. The seamstresses, obviously used to familial discontent, said nothing and collectively left the room.

'I don't want you to marry him,' Grace declared when they were alone.

'What!' Rose exploded. 'Why would you say that?' Tears gathered in her eyes. 'And why now?'

'He's not the right man for you.'

'Mothe—' Daisy attempted to inject but was silenced by a sharp look from Rose.

'Why?' Rose's voice was calm and measured, tears quickly replaced by a hard stare as she turned on her spot to fix her eyes on Grace.

'Because he's not. Because he's everything I don't want for you.'

'You like him,' Rose said. 'I know you do. You told me you did.'

'There are other things—'

'And . . .' Rose continued. 'He's not a fortune hunter. He's not like the other men. He didn't want a rich wife. He wanted an adventure. If anything I took that away from him. He's not going travelling now. He's taking me back to England and that's where I want to be, because *he* is there. He loves me. And I love him. Some of my friends haven't had any luck like this. They went into their marriages miserable and blind to the kind of man that awaited them. I don't have that. I won't have that. What more do you want for me? I won't throw him over. Not now. Not ever. And not because you ask me to. It's not a good enough reason.'

'Other girls would listen to their mother, do as they were told,' Grace snapped, drawing herself up. 'I regret the day I ever told you to have your own opinions. To be your own person. I regret it.' Grace felt rather than heard her voice crack and she fought back the burgeoning tears.

'No, you don't,' Rose replied, knowing she'd won. 'And I'll teach my children to be the same. Because I got it from you. Edward is the perfect man. I love him. He loves me. And he's going to be my husband. And I'm halfway through being fitted for a bridal gown. So now is not the time to ask that of me. Now drink your champagne, stop panicking and, Daisy, why don't you ask the seamstresses to come back and finish, so we can start working on my trousseau? After this we need to get to Cartier for my tiara appointment and I don't want to be late. It's the only time I'll probably wear one so it's got to be big.' Rose looked at her mother. 'I'm going to be alright. I'm going to be happy.'

Daisy moved towards the door, looking at Grace with concern, and Grace closed her eyes helplessly, the fight truly gone from her. 'Yes, I'm sure you will be,' she said weakly, and then under her breath, 'but I won't.'

Chapter 32

The letter had been started and stopped, started and stopped over and over again – the wastepaper basket by her writing desk brimming with first attempts in the following days. It was criminally wasteful how much expensive writing paper Grace was getting through. It took two days to be able to put aside her feelings and treat Laurie as if he was a stranger and eventually write the letter. In fact, once that idea entered her head, it was easy to write pretending he was indeed a stranger to her. Then in order to protect herself, she decided she would treat him not just as a stranger in this letter, but she would treat him as one when she inevitably encountered him in England.

While she was contemplating this, a knock at the morning room door brought the butler with a silver salver, on which was a letter.

'Thank you,' Grace said, and opened it when he was gone. The paper was thick, the handwriting broad and neat, and when Grace glanced to the end it said, *Yours warmly, Laurie Trelenna.*

She dropped the letter as if it was on fire and it sat on her dressing table face up, his words waiting for her, taunting her. But she couldn't touch it. She was still, perfectly still.

'Mother?' Rose asked, knocking at the door and then entering without an answer as usual. 'Oh good, you're here. I want to show you the Cartier designs, do you have a moment?'

'Yes,' Grace replied automatically.

'I've had a little play with them, do you think Monsieur Cartier will mind?'

'I couldn't say, darling.'

'I wanted it to look even bigger and with more diamonds than the Romanov Kokóshnik tiara Grand Duchess Elizabeth wore to her wedding. The pictures in the newspaper of that were gorgeous. But I worry about it actually staying on my head with such weight and all that height. I'll be wearing it all day but the society pages will have photographs of our wedding on both sides of the Atlantic so it's got to be grand. What do you think?' Rose thrust the sketch at her mother and then, spying the letter on the dressing table, she picked it up.

Grace went to snatch it back. 'Do you have any concept of privacy?'

'It's from Edward's father. Why is it private? Oh, is it about my dowry? Is it about what kind of *price* I'll fetch?' Rose laughed as she held the letter between her fingers. 'Like cattle at a market, am I going for a song or am I a prize heifer?'

'I haven't read it. I don't know what he's asking for,' Grace confessed. 'It just arrived.'

Rose lounged back on the sofa and began reading it dramatically aloud. 'Dear Mrs Lander . . .'

'I can read it myself,' Grace insisted, holding out her hand, but her daughter was engrossed.

'Oh, that's nice,' Rose said absently, skimming the words in her head. 'He sounds nice.'

'Hmm,' Grace murmured, her eyes fixed on the wallpaper as she waited for more. Rose began paraphrasing. 'He's asking for you to give instruction about the wedding. I'll do that. I'll write as he requests. But when it comes to money he's not asking for anything outright. Perhaps *you're* supposed to start the negotiations? Maybe you could get Uncle John to help you? Although a stonking great tiara dripping in Cartier's finest diamonds is about to enter the Trelenna vaults if you'll approve the design. So make sure you remind him of that.'

Grace looked at the sketch her daughter had brought in, then did a double take. 'Rose, it's huge!'

'We can afford it,' Rose said dismissively from her reclined position, 'especially if the Trelennas don't want a cash prize with their new bride. And think how it'll sparkle in photographs.'

'Oh my word,' Grace said, giving in. She didn't have the fight, didn't have the energy. She'd vowed never to let her daughters be ostentatious or spoiled. But in the face of everything else, she knew it wasn't worth the effort. Rose would have her way, and this was the last thing she could truly give her. 'Fine. If Cartier can make it, you can have it. It's your wedding day after all.'

'Oh, Mother, thank you, thank you. Think how jealous Mary Leiter will be. I've seen the design for hers and it isn't half this size. Alright,' Rose said determinedly with a gleam in her eye as she gestured to another sketch on the sheet of paper behind the first. 'Let's talk about this matching bracelet.'

When Rose had finally gone – Grace giving strict instructions her daughter was not to add a matching bracelet because it was frivolous and wouldn't be seen under the sleeves of her bridal gown anyway – Grace lifted up the letter. A letter from Laurie was the one thing when she was so much younger she would have been desperate for. Now it was the last thing she wanted, a letter from a man that she never thought she'd hear from again.

Dear Mrs Lander,

I wanted to write to you as soon as I heard the happy news about Edward and Rose. Edward tells me I will adore your daughter as much as he does and I'm sure I will. He speaks of Rose with such enthusiasm and adoration that his words tell me he is very much in love. In truth, it is all I ever wanted for him – a love match. And I cannot tell you how pleased I am he has found it in Rose, and a welcoming family in you and your eldest daughter.

He speaks with genuine warmth about you and his soon-to-be sister-in-law Daisy that I feel I know you both already. I look forward to meeting you all, welcoming Rose into our family, and hosting you at Trelenna House as wedding preparations begin.

And now for a confession: I do not have my late wife's ability to plan nuptials as she and her late mother planned ours and the only expectation from me was to turn up at the correct time. I would therefore be very much in your debt if you could direct my housekeeper and cook with regard to instructions ahead of time, while you make your transatlantic crossing.

I look forward to your reply as well as getting to know you as our children move forward with their wedding plans, and beyond.

Yours warmly,

Laurie Trelenna

The irony was not lost on her of being asked to direct Trelenna House's cook as to how to prepare a wedding breakfast for her own daughter after she'd married into the family. She stood up and fetched a cushion, put her face into it and screamed, letting out the years of rage and hatred for Laurie she'd been carrying for so long, in one lengthy muffled shriek.

Then, as if nothing had happened, she replaced the cushion on the sofa and sat back at her writing desk and re-read the letter again, as calmly as possible. She tried detaching the words from the man, wishing she didn't have to write back. But how could she not? Things had moved far beyond her control.

Grace closed her eyes, reminding herself how far she'd come – that she was Laurie's equal now – only to open her eyes to feel even more hollow and petrified than she had been before. She attempted to form rational thoughts to cut down the fear. The first being that it would be alright. When she saw him, it would be alright. Because Laurie would not remember or recognise her; she was Mrs Lander now. She had a different surname, a different life, a different social standing. She could not have been more removed from the young servant he'd hurt all those years ago.

'You are his latest mistake.'

'I'll bet he forgot me the moment I left,' she told herself, determined to finally put pen to paper and, in doing so, put this trauma to rest. For years she had worn him like a visible scar, whereas she was just a forgettable mistake to him.

The second rational thought was that her children knew nothing. They couldn't betray her even if they wanted to. The only person who had known the truth was Arthur. The pang for him was so deep even now, but he was gone too.

Then the third rational thought was that she wouldn't be in Trelenna House for long. That event at least was within her own control.

She was a different woman now. She was harder, her mind was sharper. She was more worldly wise, not as stupid now as she had been then. She sounded different, and at forty-six she looked very different to the young woman she'd been – little lines formed on her face, deepening furrows here and there. Sadness at Arthur's death had thinned her face through grief and she'd lost the plumpness of youth somewhere along the years, giving way to prominent cheekbones she didn't remember having when she'd been young. Her blonde hair was a few shades lighter now, and she sensed it was heading towards a tone of grey or even white that she hoped might blend unnoticed into the blonde. If she looked closer it was probably already there. There was no stopping the passing of time, the same way there was no undoing Rose's decision to marry Edward Easton-Thorpe-Trelenna.

Everything she'd ever done to protect her family – keep them safe from poverty and then fortune hunters – didn't *have* to come completely undone. For all his father's faults, Edward was not to blame.

And for herself, she could manage things, she could manage this awful turn of events. She could manage seeing Laurie again. She had to because she had no other choice. She clung on to her sanity with all her might as she wrote with shaky hands, making sure to sign off without use of her first name, wondering quite how this was happening, quite how she was writing *Laurie* a letter so many years later and feigning indifference or that she even knew him. This was madness. Total, absolute madness.

Dear Mr Trelenna,

I acknowledge receipt of your kind letter and second the contents with my own heartfelt congratulations to you in return. I believe we are both very lucky to have the kind of children we have and luckier still that they have found each other and wish to spend the rest of their lives together. I have no doubt they will be very happy.

Edward entered our world at speed but I delight in his company almost as much as Rose does, and I am confident two young people could not be more in love. To see them daily, in each other's confidences, making one another laugh, making plans, unable to see anyone else around them in a room but each other, gives me the greatest delight.

My daughter Daisy and I accept your kind offer to reside at Trelenna during the nuptials and details of our planned arrival will be with you in due course once our boat passage has been secured.

I would like now to turn to the subject of Rose's dowry. I propose offering the couple an allowance to live on of $75,000 per annum, in addition to a $1,000,000 one-off sum, a quarter of which will be comprised of railroad stock. I also propose to offer them a home in New York and in London, which they shall choose together so my daughter will always have a location that is hers to use in her lifetime. If the above is acceptable to you, please write by return and I shall instruct my lawyers.

With regard to the more aesthetic side of the wedding arrangements, I am happy to leave that to my daughter who has specific thoughts about this. I believe she will write to your housekeeper and cook directly.

I look forward to hearing from you in due course.

With regards,
Mrs Lander

Detached. Aloof. Factual. This was how Grace would be. This was how Grace *had* to be. This is how she would get through this whole, draining catastrophe. She wondered what he looked like now. If he looked the same or if age had been unkind to him. Then as quickly as those thoughts had come she banished them, sealing the letter and ringing the bell to summon the footman. In a few moments the letter would leave her hands, journey across the Atlantic and arrive in the hands of the last man in the world she ever wanted to speak to.

Chapter 33

Present Day

Zennor

It had been a week since Charlie had walked in on Zennor in the downstairs loo, a week since both he and she had found out simultaneously that she was pregnant. November had rolled in and the cold in the air sent the world around her into a crisp, wintery chill. The branches in the garden were bare and frosts were settling on the leaf-strewn ground, making everything look as if a blanket of shimmering diamonds had appeared overnight.

Zennor had done a lot of walking over the past week and with it, a lot of thinking. At first, denial had been her preserve. Then the waves crashed to shore and she had sat on the beach and cried. As the sun had arrived in the woodland, cutting through the trees, she had tried to come to terms with her lot – until moments later, when she ran the whole gamut of feelings all over again. There had been a *lot* of crying, coupled with frustrated panic, hopelessness and disappointment. She didn't want to tell her family until she knew herself what she was going to do. She didn't want them influencing her. It had to be her decision but she didn't know what to do. She was going to be twenty-two soon. That was too young to have a child. Sometimes she still felt like a child herself. But she'd always wanted to be a mother. She knew that right to her core. She just wasn't sure she wanted to be one *right now*.

And then there was the worry about what would happen to the house, to her siblings, if she had a baby to look after. How could she look after a baby and keep the house going? Saving Trelenna had been her only plan. She had wanted to keep it alive for future generations, her own children, her siblings' children. If she had to take her eyes off Trelenna House, would it mean her siblings might too? Might they grow bored of the endless breakages that needed fixing, the exhausting cleaning, the tours, the social media, the lack of tangible finances to reinvest without her there to remind them, to cajole or encourage? Would Merry help if Zennor had to step back? Who would run the kitchen? Kayleigh? She'd need help. How could they afford that?

There was so much to think about and, more than anything, there was a consistent ringing in her head, saying that she couldn't do any of this on her own. But that's exactly what was happening.

With shaking hands she booked a doctor's appointment. She wasn't sure why, but this seemed the most sensible next step. Zennor had never felt so immature in her life, seated across from her aged GP, talking about when she might have fallen pregnant (the date seared in her memory, the one and only time she'd slept with Reece). But it was the first date of her last period she'd not been able to work out. Who knew when that was? Her periods had always been erratic. Sometimes she came on for a few days, sometimes a whole week, sometimes she skipped a period entirely if she'd been too stressed. Her body was a strange wonder. And never more so than now because hers was growing a life.

She was unable to keep track of most of her *own* life, this house now too. How was she going to look after a baby?

'Letter for you,' Lamorna called out a few mornings later, popping it on to the Welsh dresser where leaflets, letters and local newspapers gathered into a wobbly pile before someone (usually her) dealt with them all.

'Thanks,' Zennor said absently, looking out of the window into the courtyard. Next to her the kettle had boiled and she'd left it so long that she had to boil it again for a morning cup of tea.

'Has Charlie changed his working hours?' Lamorna asked, sitting at the kitchen table and opening her laptop. 'I saw his car leaving at about ten a.m. so he must have started work here just when the sun was coming up.'

'Yes, I think he's been coming much earlier than usual at the moment,' Zennor said.

'He's keen,' Lamorna replied and then began tapping. He was keen. But not *that* keen. Zennor knew why he was coming early. He didn't want to see her. She was sure of it. Although he'd not actually said it. He'd not spoken to her since that day, not made any kind of contact. And now he'd changed his working hours presumably so he wouldn't have to run into her. He was up with the lark and keeping well away from the kitchen. Keeping well away from her.

It was this that added to her misery. After Charlie had walked in on her she hadn't known how she was going to look him in the eye, how she was going to talk about it all with him. This went beyond the realms of simply being 'awkward'. She was pregnant with another man's baby at the same time she and Charlie had been falling for each other. Well, that was over now, wasn't it? It had to be. What kind of man wanted to be with someone who was pregnant with another man's baby? There was so much to consider and it was *too* much, *too* big for her to think through all at once.

Zennor made two mugs of tea and put one in front of Lamorna, sipping the other while absently watching her sister work. Should she be drinking decaffeinated now? Wasn't that what pregnant women were supposed to do? She didn't own decaf tea. It was moments like this when she felt this tiny baby might really be taking up a space in her heart, the way it already was in her body. She was trying to make concessions for it, trying to weave thoughts of it being a more permanent fixture in her own mind – while telling herself she couldn't possibly have this baby, couldn't possibly keep it, but the alternative was what?

Zennor turned her back to Lamorna and pretended to look out of the window again but this time she touched her stomach and held her hand there, feeling, wondering. She'd not done this yet. Not dared to think about this little baby as being *real,* being hers. *She was growing a baby inside her.* She had been all this time and hadn't even known, hadn't felt the miracle of life taking shape. How could a miracle have gone unnoticed? She moved her hand gently around and couldn't fathom exactly *where* inside the baby was right now, couldn't fathom how big it was. What was the word slightly more grown-up people used? Showing. That was it. She wasn't *showing.* Her stomach was still relatively flat. It had all just completely passed her by – such a momentous occasion and she'd not known, so wrapped up in the house, presumably, to think about other things, bigger things arriving in her world. But this baby, although small, was huge enough to change everything.

Of all the times she'd paced the corridors, roamed the woods, stared out to sea or through the screen of her laptop into the middle distance thinking, thinking so hard – it was now, here in her kitchen that she'd come to the conclusion . . . no, she'd decided . . . she was going to have this baby.

Zennor laughed – a small bubble of excitement, laced with fear too, escaping from her lips.

Lamorna glanced up at her and, taking a cue from her sister's infectious laugh, smiled widely. 'What's funny?'

Zennor removed her hand from her stomach and faced her sister. 'I'll tell you over dinner when there's a bit more time.'

'Okay,' Lamorna said curiously, checking the kitchen clock. 'Oh, while I've got you, have the choir confirmed for the Christmas weekend? I know they were dawdling.'

'Yes,' Zennor replied, 'they have. They're going to come both days and sing carols, and asked if they could put out a collection bucket for the church roof?'

'It's the least we can do seeing as we're not paying them. We should probably give them something for the roof too.' Lamorna frowned as she glanced back at her screen. 'Much as it pains me to part with cash.'

'Okay. Great.'

Lamorna closed her laptop decidedly and stood to get ready for the 11 a.m. tour group. 'Don't forget your letter,' she called as she left, cradling her computer under her arm. 'And thank you for the tea.'

When she was alone, Zennor wandered over to the Welsh dresser and picked the letter up, opening it and preparing to put it straight in the bin, already consigning it to 'junk mail'.

But it wasn't junk. It was from the hospital. She'd been referred to the midwifery unit and had been given the date of her first scan.

Chapter 34

That evening Zennor took a deep breath. 'I need to talk to you both.'

'This sounds serious,' Merry commented, putting his cutlery together as they finished their dinner of salmon Wellington, a particularly complicated recipe Zennor remembered reading years before in an old cookbook in the library. Tonight she'd needed the distraction of cooking a multi-faceted dinner, focusing her energies on something traditionally fiddly and time consuming. She'd managed to put off thinking about what she was going to say while rolling pastry, then lining it with spinach, lemon and dill. And then during dinner she'd managed to put it off even further, by engaging her siblings in talk about Christmas event plans. But now, with their plates clean, Merry was eyeing the exit ready to disappear into a documentary hole once more, while Lamorna was already typing surreptitiously into her phone – Zach, no doubt. Zennor could see time running away from her. If she didn't tell them now, the moment would be lost. And she'd have to try again tomorrow.

'It *is* a little bit serious, yes,' she confirmed, turning from Merry to Lamorna. Her sister looked at her with deep concern.

'I'm not really sure how to say it.' Zennor laughed nervously as the silence in the room took the wind out of her sails. She paused, then tried again. 'I'm going . . . um . . .'

'You're going . . . where?' Merry prompted.

This wasn't working well. Perhaps she should have planned a speech. She cleared her throat and then thought, why mince her words? 'I'm going to have a baby.'

Silence.

'What?' snapped Lamorna a few seconds later, eyes narrowed to fine slits. 'What do you mean?'

'I mean . . . uh . . .' Zennor tried but failed to elaborate. So she repeated herself. 'I'm going to have a baby.'

There was more silence until – 'Shit,' Merry said slowly and indelicately, Zennor's words finally landing. 'You're going to have a *baby? Really?*'

Zennor nodded. 'I'm nearly three months pregnant.'

Lamorna's eyes had changed shape entirely, from fine slits to saucers. Her mouth dropped open.

'I know it's a bit of a shock,' Zennor said, trying to take hold of the conversation. 'I can promise you no one is more shocked than me. But I've had a while to think about it—'

'Three *months*?' Lamorna cut in, her facial features not quite returning to normal.

'Yes. Yes. I didn't know until last week and then I didn't know what I wanted to do about it.'

'Do?' Merry asked. 'What do you mean, *do*?'

'Well,' Zennor explained. 'You know. What my options were.'

'Oh. Oh, I see,' Merry said blankly as he reached for his glass of water, his hand a little shaky. 'And what did you decide?'

'I decided I'm going to have the baby. I'm going to be a mum.' She laughed. She'd not said those words out loud yet, not even to herself, and they sounded good – they sounded more than good. They sounded perfect. Perfect enough to say again. 'I'm going to be a mum.'

'Wow . . . I . . . don't . . .' Lamorna said and then stopped. She blinked and shook her head gently.

'It's not often you're speechless,' Zennor pointed out.

'I . . . can't . . .' Lamorna breathed in and then out, collecting herself. 'How are you going to do this? You're so . . .'

'I'm young. Yes, I know. I'm nearly twenty-two. I am going to be the first to admit this isn't ideal timing. It's not an ideal situation. But it is what it is. I have thought about all my options, trust me, in great detail. And what might be right for some women isn't right for me. I am very lucky I live where I live and that I live *how* I live. Bringing a baby up, here at Trelenna, will be wonderful.'

'It will be hard work,' Merry pointed out gently, his face still showing shock.

'Yes, it will. I know that.'

Silence descended again. She didn't miss the pointed look Merry and Lamorna gave each other. She felt like a child again. 'Don't do that,' she snapped.

'Do what?' Lamorna asked.

'Look at each other like that. If I was ten years older you'd be congratulating me.'

'But you're not ten years older,' Lamorna said. 'Do you want congratulations? I thought this was a situation, not a celebration.'

It took every ounce of strength Zennor had not to shout at her sister. Instead she spoke through gritted teeth. 'I can see where you're coming from. However, the baby is in there. It's happened. I'm pregnant and I'm going for a scan in a couple of weeks to see if it's healthy. If you can't be happy for me, while I work my way through this, the least you can do is be supportive.'

'I am supportive.' Lamorna blinked slowly, and continued. 'Or rather I will be once I've got over the shock.'

'Same,' Merry said quickly. 'I'll be right here if you need me. A baby . . . wow. Oh . . .' he said, as his face suddenly broke into wonder. 'I'm going to be an uncle!'

'You are,' Zennor confirmed, the buzz of excitement she'd barely let herself feel building up inside her. 'And you'll be an aunty,' she told Lamorna.

'Crikey.' Lamorna looked down at her empty plate and then back up. 'Oh . . . Mum and Dad . . . Have you told them they're going to be *grand*parents?'

'Not yet. I wanted to tell you two first because you're here. But I'll give them a call tomorrow, so please keep it to yourself for now.'

'And Veryan?' Merry asked, sounding excited now.

'I'll give her a ring, but it will probably go to voicemail.'

'Put it on the family WhatsApp and see if she even reads it,' Lamorna quipped snidely.

'She reads them. She replies every now and again,' Merry pointed out. 'Veryan's always there when you really need her.'

Zennor gave Merry a sad smile. When his wife had died they had all rallied round, coming from every corner of the globe to be with him. But ever since, Veryan had been very much living life on her own terms.

'If you're pleased,' Lamorna told Zennor, reaching for her hand across the table, 'then *I'm* pleased. Honestly, I mean it. I'll be here for you when you need me. You just have to say.'

'Thank you, both of you. I will. And I have been thinking about the house too and what we're trying to achieve here.'

'Oh, don't worry about that now,' Lamorna encouraged, but Zennor could sense her sister already mentally working out the unexpected costs.

'But I am worried about it,' Zennor insisted, as calmly as she could. 'Because we're a team and I'm about to ruin that.'

'No, you're not,' Merry pointed out. 'And look, we've got at least six months to worry about it. By which point we'll be in a much stronger position. But you can't run the tearoom while you're taking time to be with your baby. Dare I say it, but you might have to get some help. Let someone else cook in your kitchen . . .' He raised his eyebrows up and down.

'I don't want to,' Zennor said immediately, knowing she sounded like a child. 'But you're right.'

'Kayleigh?' Lamorna suggested.

'Maybe. I need to think about it. She's saving up to buy a van and convert it into a food truck, so she might not be around long-term.'

'Oh no. Really? But why on earth would she ever want to leave this level of stress and carnage?' Merry asked with a knowing grin.

'We don't need to worry about this today,' Lamorna chipped in quickly.

Merry's face scrunched up thoughtfully. 'Zen, can I ask a question?'

'Be my guest.'

'You and Charlie haven't been together very long.'

Zennor swallowed, knowing full well what Merry was asking without actually asking. 'No. I know. He's not the father.'

'Shit,' Lamorna spluttered. 'Not . . . ?'

Zennor nodded at her. 'It's Reece.'

'The *wine* guy?' Lamorna winced.

'The wine guy,' Zennor confirmed.

'But you're not . . .' Merry chimed in.

'We're not together, no. So . . . I'll have to deal with that too.' Zennor sighed deeply.

'Shit.' Merry echoed Lamorna, and Zennor almost laughed. She held up her hands as if there was nothing she could do about this turn of events, because . . . there wasn't. She looked Merry dead in the eye and said, 'Shit indeed.'

Chapter 35

Zennor walked across the crisp frost towards Charlie at the outhouses, feeling so conflicted and wishing she could just turn back and hide in the kitchen again. He closed the lid of the compost bin where he'd been adding the kitchen peelings she left out for him regularly and looked directly at her. His body language immediately changed. He looked defensive, wary, and it made Zennor's heart sink. But what did she expect?

'Hi,' she said simply, but it was a word laced with regret.

'Hi,' he echoed in the same tone.

What could either of them say to make this situation any better? Nothing. There was nothing. But it had been well over a week since they'd last seen each other, both staring at two blue lines. In that time she'd had to come to terms with so much. Her life was about to change. And his . . . he was avoiding disaster. And who could blame him. Having thought this through night after night when she was supposed to be researching Grace but had been catastrophising instead, Zennor had come to the sad conclusion that she couldn't bring Charlie into the mess that was her life. She was having another man's baby. And no one in their right mind would want to be dragged into that kind of situation, especially when their relationship had never really got off the ground. He'd probably be grateful, relieved. But he was at least owed an explanation before they went their separate ways.

'I brought you some cake,' she said, stepping forward to hand him a wrapped parcel of spiced fruit cake.

'Thanks,' he said, taking it from her. He kept his eyes on her the whole time, waiting.

Now she was here, nothing made sense in her own head. She should have written it out, but it was too late for that. Honesty had to be better than anything else. 'I didn't know I was pregnant,' she blurted.

Charlie's eyes widened and he laughed bitterly. 'Right.'

'I mean it,' she replied, a little desperate. 'Honestly. That moment you walked in on me . . . I wondered for a week or so before. I wondered, and panicked. But only because I felt sick and tired and . . .' She stopped, starting again. 'I'm sorry,' she said more calmly now. 'I didn't mean to dupe you. I didn't mean to like you as much as I did. As much as I do. And then to find out I was pregnant. I didn't mean for any of it to happen.'

She knew she needed to stop talking, needed to let it all sink in.

He shook his head, his gaze landing on the ground and then back to her. 'I don't really understand what's going on,' he replied. 'I need some help here.'

'Okay,' she said tentatively.

'I like you. And you like me. But you're pregnant with someone else's baby.'

'That about sums it up.' She realised as she said it that even a tiny hint of gallows humour was misplaced.

He refused to smile. 'How far along are you?'

'Three months, give or take.'

His eyebrows rose.

'I met you just after I slept with Reece. Terrible timing. I don't mean meeting you. That was the good bit. But the other bit, that was . . . not great, and now look what's happened.'

He smiled sadly. 'What are you going to do?'

'If you'd have asked me that question a couple of days ago, I'd have said *I don't know.* But I do now. I know what I'm going to do. I'm going to have the baby. And I'll have to tell Reece what's happened. And then . . . and then I don't know. I haven't thought that far ahead yet.' She took a deep breath. 'I realise that now ends anything you and I had together. And I'm *so, so* sorry.'

'Me too.' He looked as if he genuinely meant it.

'But . . . can we be friends? Even though we can't be anything else?'

Charlie nodded. His mouth made the shape of a reluctant 'okay', but no sound came out. 'I may . . .' he started, and then stopped.

'Go on,' she prompted, eager not to let the conversation die, eager to talk about something else, anything else with Charlie; she'd forgotten how much she missed his company. Or perhaps not forgotten, so much as willed herself to forget. Now they were going to have to be friends – forced to because they couldn't be anything else. She sighed quietly to herself.

'I may not come and help with the archive boxes now. If that's okay. Or come and see you for lunch. I might just see you around, at work. Here, I mean.' He gestured at the gardens.

Zennor hadn't thought it possible for her spirit to plummet even lower but now it had. 'Of course it's okay,' she replied with false bravado.

He nodded, short and clipped, while keeping his eyes on her. 'I'd better get on.' He was clearly waiting for her to take the hint and leave. 'Thanks for the cake.'

'Of course,' she repeated in the same false tone as before. And as Zennor turned and walked away, she knew she'd lost him forever, even as a friend.

Chapter 36

Over the coming weeks Zennor channelled her energies into the upcoming Christmas events. She needed something to take her mind off Charlie, to take her mind from the conversation she'd need to have with Reece. She knew she couldn't put it off but the more she *did,* the easier it became to keep doing so.

Merry had sorted Christmas trees for every one of the downstairs rooms and – with Lamorna's help – had tracked down and bought vintage decorations. Between them they'd settled on the theme of a late Victorian Christmas throughout the rooms. After all of Zennor's research into Grace's life, it seemed the most obvious choice. The rooms looked the part already and, until the trees came, the siblings had been busy organising other suitably festive arrangements. It took Zennor mentally back to school when she'd sat making Victorian pomanders – oranges studded with cloves. The scent was joyous, festive, sharp and instantly nostalgic.

Along with the house being decorated for visitors, Zennor wanted to make it special for the family too, and had decided she was going to make a floral display with poinsettias for the large dining room table, which sat twenty people. The family, even when all together, had only ever eaten there for special meals: birthdays, Easter, Christmas. So it felt right to dress it for the festive season. Who knew if they'd all be back on Christmas Day, but it would look pretty for those family members who were at Trelenna, as well as the guests taking part in the festive tours. They'd decided for the Christmas season they would let people wander freely between rooms, and they'd have some of Zennor's friends act as friendly hosts for anyone who had a question. Lamorna wasn't quite sure how they were going to keep an eye on anyone pinching the silverware otherwise, whereas Zennor had been concerned children might try to touch the lit fires, even with fireguards. A person in every room keeping an eye was the only way they could counteract potential disaster.

The Christmas market plans were running like clockwork. Zennor's suppliers were all consummate professionals who had attended many markets and fairs, meaning she only had to field the occasional email. They'd decided to hold the market in the ballroom to save on the cost of a marquee, and Zennor was off the hook for any proper sit-down catering with the usual tearoom space taken by suppliers. Although people would still be able to buy Zennor's various pasties and hot pulled turkey and applesauce rolls alongside her favourite festive sweet treats and gourmet hot-chocolate.

As another day came to a close, Zennor felt the happy glow of a successful day. Stretching after filling the industrial dishwasher for the last time – until tomorrow – she glanced at the clock. Zach was staying over so he and Lamorna had taken themselves off somewhere to either salivate over spreadsheets or each other, and Merry, as usual, had retreated to his room to watch documentaries. They each emerged every now and again to join her in the kitchen for a few minutes while they refreshed their mugs of tea or helped themselves to some of her test-batches of Victorian-inspired festive cookies. But more often than not, she sat alone each evening, practising recipes and avoiding thinking about the inevitable: that in around six months' time she wouldn't be sitting here alone. She'd be cradling a baby – her baby.

She touched her stomach. Tomorrow was her first scan.

Tomorrow she'd hear her baby's heartbeat for the first time, see her baby growing inside her for the first time. Tomorrow would be a day full of firsts. It was all beyond her control now. She was going to be a mother. A single mother, but a mother nonetheless. Everything would change. And as she sat in her kitchen she knew without a doubt that she was beyond petrified.

Breathing in and out slowly wasn't as calming as Zennor had been led to believe and the fear of what was coming – impending motherhood – threatened to send her into another spiral of emotional tears. She couldn't just sit here thinking about it. She had to do something productive, something that would distract her more than going over recipes was doing. It had been weeks since she'd last looked at the archive boxes, having given them up in favour of the more time-saving method of searching the internet for any clues about Grace. While there might not be anything in the boxes about Grace after her departure from Trelenna as a servant, she thought she'd look through some of the papers and documents, see if there were any festive snippets from Christmases gone by that might be useful in some way. She could put together a festive menu from the time, print it out in ornate handwriting and position it on the table so guests who were visiting over coming weeks would see what a real Victorian Christmas dinner had looked like, eaten at that *exact* dining table in Trelenna House by previous generations. Of course it would have most likely been cooked by Grace for a time, which made Zennor smile, but it would have been served to the rather unfriendly Mrs Georgiana Trelenna, and she tried not to focus on that.

Zennor trudged up the stairs, feeling that with all she now knew about Grace, she was more aligned with *her* than her own ancestor. She was fuelled with energy now, on the hunt for anything that might illustrate past Christmases at Trelenna House.

In her room, Zennor settled herself among the boxes and immediately remembered why she'd put it off for so long. There was just so *much* of it to go through, so many endless pieces of paper that seemed to relate to nothing else. What she wanted was menus, something in Grace's hand, ideally – not that she'd recognise it, but she'd hope for a date or signature to help her. But try as she might, she couldn't see anything in the first box, or in the second, that fitted. As she worked her way tirelessly through the third box of the four she'd earmarked, Zennor grew despondent.

Maybe she should change tack. Instead of a loose piece of paper, perhaps she should look for a recipe book. Issey Trelenna's diary from Singapore had wound its way into the archives, but maybe Lamorna had just been lucky. Why couldn't Grace's recipe books be here? That would give her so much more insight into who Grace really was. You could tell a lot about a cook based on their method, process . . . She couldn't have taken them *all* with her to New York, surely. Zennor put down the letter she'd been uselessly staring at, feeling hollow, and then sat up straight again. What if they'd been found and treated as just *books*? Zennor wasn't a great reader and while she'd been in every room in the house during the refurbishment and repaint, she couldn't remember the last time she'd paid attention to what was on the shelves in the library. Overcome with the urge – no, the visceral need – to find something else relating to Grace, Zennor went back downstairs and into the library.

She flicked the switch on the first of the table lamps, lighting her way into the rest of the room, navigating around the large wooden globe – more ornamental these days than useful – and towards the shelves. The library wasn't as hotchpotch as she'd imagined. All the more recent paperbacks the family had bought over the years had been consigned to their own shelves, making her quest a bit easier. Zennor found it funny that, in a room teeming with first editions and ancient copies of early Victorian novels, visitors were always drawn to the more modern shelves housing the family's dog-eared copies of Jilly Cooper novels and battered Agatha Christie mysteries. They'd discussed clearing these books out to make the room feel more historic, but Zach had suggested that it made the house feel lived-in, like they were part of living history.

Her father, many years ago, had made an effort to categorise the shelves but Zennor remembered him giving up, on finding himself surrounded by piles of books and not enough time (or inclination) to sort. She vaguely recollected helping him put items back on shelves. There had never been enough time to fully complete any chore at Trelenna. But then, if he'd put his mind to saving the house financially instead of simply rearranging books, the outlook for the house might have been different. They might never have opened the house to the public. Lamorna and Merry might never have felt the need to help and stay. Perhaps she should thank her parents and their errant ways. Perhaps it had done some good in the end.

'Time will tell,' she said aloud as she wrapped her oversized cardigan around her a little tighter and hugged herself against the cold. Zennor lit the fire easily, building the logs up and waiting for the match to take against the firelighter before standing back and admiring her efforts. The sound of the wood licking into flame was a comforting one as she walked along the shelves, her fingers touching volume after volume of leatherbound books, scanning their titles. Some looked as if they'd never even been opened: pristine from a hundred years ago until now. Some were truly worn, the bindings falling apart, the spines in need of repair. She worked her way along the shelves meticulously, not quite having the confidence in her pregnant condition to climb the rolling wooden ladder to the very top. She stared up at the spines and wondered.

She'd worked her way to the end of the room and with only the more modern volumes left to look at, she stared pointlessly at their shiny spines. She could tell which books had been bought by who. Most of Zennor's cookbooks were in the kitchen on various shelves and a few of her older, worn-around-the-edges recipe books that had inspired her all those years ago were stored in clear plastic boxes in her pantry, out of reach of anyone who might have a clear-out. She never needed to even look at them now. The recipes were so much a part of her she could likely recite them all from memory.

Zennor trailed her fingers over the novels and noticed there was hardly anything here of Veryan's. She hadn't read much. She'd been more of a glance-at-a-magazine kind of reader, devouring books about ponies as a child and then nothing else after that. Their mother was responsible for the Jilly Coopers, Lamorna's contribution was mainly travel guides to Asia and other exotic locations far, far away, and Merry – being a writer – had addictively bought more books than the library at Trelenna could ever hold about all sorts of subjects and – other than a few well-loved volumes – must have taken most of them with him to Edinburgh. Their father, she reasoned, was responsible for the non-fiction books about estate and land management. She wondered if he'd even read them.

'At least he tried,' Zennor muttered to herself half-heartedly as her eyes roamed. Biographies and autobiographies were her father's speciality, and a few about Churchill met her gaze. A few titles looked interesting – not interesting enough to read in full, but she dutifully pulled some down to read the blurb on the back. The most exciting title she read was *The 450.* The spine gave nothing else away. Intrigued, she pulled the book out and read the cover: *Dollar Princesses: The 450 Gilded Age Heiresses Who Traded New Money for Old Titles.*

Zennor opened the first page and read the introduction.

> *By 1915, over four hundred and fifty American heiresses had left America, leaving behind their families and taking vast amounts of wealth with them on their voyage across the Atlantic. Their goal? To marry titled European aristocrats.*

'Good for them,' Zennor muttered, flicking through the book. Each of the four hundred and fifty women had at least a paragraph dedicated to them; some had more depending on how interesting they were.

Zennor's tired eyes followed names on pages. Jennie Jerome: daughter of financier Leonard Jerome married Lord Randolph Churchill and later gave birth to Winston Churchill. She wondered if her father's love of Churchill had prompted him to buy this book.

Consuelo Yznaga, daughter of a Cuban-American diplomat, married George Montagu and she became the Duchess of Manchester.

Mary Leiter married George Curzon who later became Viceroy of India. Nancy Langhorne became Viscountess Astor. Mary Goelet married the Duke of Roxburghe. Alberta Sturges married the Earl of Sandwich . . . and so on and so forth. It read like a who's who of British aristocracy and the American women who'd married and bankrolled them. Clearly being an aristocrat was an expensive fate to be born into back then, Zennor reasoned. And all these American women, over four hundred and fifty of them, had offered themselves and pots of cash to men who, presumably, they hardly knew.

She flicked through the book, reading a few lines here and there about each of the dizzying number of women who'd left everything they'd ever known to move thousands of miles across the Atlantic, taking much of their vast fortune with them. Not every marriage was happy. Most weren't, if her quick flick through was anything to go by. Not only were some women forced to put up with their husband's well-known infidelity, but Consuelo Vanderbilt '*who was essentially forced down the aisle by her own mother and whose face was tear stained underneath her wedding veil*' and the ninth Duke of Marlborough had eventually divorced due to reciprocal unhappiness, which was near-scandalous for the time.

There was no alphabetical listing system, and indeed the book wasn't even covering the women by year of marriage. The book seemed to be front loaded with the prominent, more famous women first. She put her thumb in the book to mark her place and popped the fireguard back in situ, leaving the fire to burn itself out to embers. Zennor turned the lamps out one by one and then began climbing the stairs, opening the book to glance at it as she climbed. Then she stopped dead still on the stairs as her eyes landed on a name she recognised; a name she hadn't been expecting to see at all.

Chapter 37

Cornwall

1895

Grace

The crossing was dreadful. Weeks of rolling swell had obliterated Grace's stomach and she had felt every tumble, every rise and fall the steamship made. The first time she'd crossed the Atlantic she was in third class and sick as a pig.

Now she was in first class and unable to enjoy the comfortable cabin due to throwing up so often. She thought she'd have got over seasickness, despite never having set foot on a boat of this size from that day to this. She thought age might have eradicated the affliction. She'd been unable to eat, unable to drink much more than a few sips of water, and she'd forced herself to sleep so much she thought she need never sleep again. She remembered Arthur convincing her to look at the horizon all those years ago and she'd forced herself on deck, clutching the railings for dear life as if she might be flung overboard. Now, the other first-class passengers seemed to be walking or enjoying games set out across the deck by the stewards or embarking on entertaining discussion to pass the time. It was a far cry from her own state, and after a futile few minutes, she decided to spend the remaining time in her cabin. The moment her feet touched the ground in Southampton she breathed more than just a sigh of relief, although being back in England was categorically not where she wanted to be. She didn't know how she would be able to make the return journey again in a few weeks' time. She'd been weakened by the voyage, whereas her two children had been bolstered by it.

'I cannot believe we're really in England,' Daisy said as they prepared to board the passenger train at the docks. She looked around, pleased by the industrial might of the docks as if she'd never seen anything like it, despite being raised near to one in New York. 'I am so excited. Everything is so exciting.'

'I know, darling,' Grace said as they settled into the comfortable first-class train carriage with polished wood-panelled walls and sumptuous chairs. 'You've told me a hundred times today alone.'

'Are you still feeling queasy? It'll pass soon. It has to. You're not on the boat anymore,' Rose said.

'Mmm.' Grace was non-committal, wondering if the sick feeling in the bottom of her stomach would ever truly leave her. The closer they got to Trelenna, the worse she felt.

'I swear a glass of beer might make you feel right as rain,' Edward suggested. 'Shall we make ourselves known in the dining carriage?'

Grace felt even more nauseous at that suggestion and closed her eyes.

'Sorry, am I making things worse? It always works for me,' he continued on jovially.

'Mother, you'll miss everything if you close your eyes,' Daisy said as the steam bellowed past their windows and down the platform and the train began noisily moving forward. Daisy leaned over and squeezed her mother's leg gently, but Grace didn't move.

'I plan to look at everything,' Rose declared, turning towards the window. 'I'm not going to miss a thing about England.'

'You'll be seeing it *all* for the rest of your life,' Daisy pointed out. 'I've only got a few weeks. I want to *do* everything and *see* everything.'

'And so you shall. We'll make a plan.' Edward's energy was infectious. 'All the things you should see and do. We'll visit London and—'

'The Royal Academy?' Daisy enthused. 'I've longed to see it. Can we go?'

'After the wedding, we'll all go,' Edward said. 'We'll go anywhere you want.'

'Edward, I think you're about to become my favourite brother-in-law,' Daisy joked.

'After the wedding you'll want to go on honeymoon, surely?' Grace said, eyes still closed for fear of throwing up.

'Oh, there'll be plenty of time for that,' Rose replied airily. 'I don't want to lose you both so soon. I want to spend as much time together, here, as possible. And if I can convince you to stay on for longer, then it's all the better.'

The idea of staying on longer than the allotted two weeks filled Grace with dread. But London, away from Trelenna, away from Laurie and whatever kind of man he'd turned into . . . London might work better. Yes, perhaps as soon as the wedding was over, perhaps they'd go to London then. She intended to gift the married couple a house there and wanted to be nowhere near Laurie Trelenna.

'You must have been to London a hundred times before though,' Edward said, turning to Grace, now settled enough into the rhythm of the steam engine to open her eyes.

Grace smiled enigmatically. How would she ever begin to explain herself if she said no, she'd never set foot in the capital.

Edward knew nothing about her, and her daughters knew only what she and Arthur had told them, which was precious little. She would pretend she'd never set foot in Trelenna before. With so many houses in Cornwall it wouldn't be unheard of, regardless of which section of society they assumed she had been born into.

'Remind me which bit of Cornwall you're from?' Edward asked, his interest piqued.

'Redruth,' Grace replied honestly.

'Don't you agree, Mrs Lander, that Cornwall is the most beautiful place on earth?' Edward asked, excited to be on home ground. 'Rose, you're going to love it.'

'So you've said.' Rose gave a joyful smile and nestled into him a little closer, her arm looped through his. 'I can't wait to be Mrs Trelenna.'

Mrs Trelenna, thought Grace. A hot, sick feeling took hold of her again.

'I can't wait to be your wife, and I can't wait to see your home,' Rose carried on.

'Your home also, soon,' Edward said. 'Now, Rose and Daisy, tell me again how many of your friends are already here and if we can expect them all at the wedding. And what ship are your aunt and uncle on board? We must send a carriage to greet them from the station when they arrive.'

Grace let their chatter about the upcoming wedding fade into the background as her stomach churned once more and she allowed her eyes to flutter closed. Because it was far, far too late now to stop Edward and Rose being together.

Chapter 38

It was as if she'd never left. Grace remembered the turn of the drive from the lane and the cut of the road through the parkland, the sweep of the drive round the woodland and that first glimpse of the house that had the power to render the viewer breathless. It rendered Rose and Daisy breathless. But to Grace, it brought a fresh wave of distress. *My god, we're here.*

The house loomed over its surroundings. After all these years, there it was, exactly as it always had been. Trelenna. Its pale Portland stone brick a stark contrast to its granite counterparts that made up almost every other house of standing in Cornwall. Next to Grace, Rose breathed in audibly and Daisy gasped in wonder. If Grace hadn't been gripped by unbridled fear, she'd have wondered if her children had never seen large houses before. In Newport it was all they saw, New York too. But for some reason her children were enamoured here, first with Cornwall and now with Trelenna.

'Oh, it's beautiful,' Rose said dreamily as the horse and carriage brought them closer.

'You like it?' Edward's happiness was palpable as he stared lovingly at his wife-to-be, taking in every expression.

'I love it,' she said joyously.

'It looks so delicate,' Daisy chipped in.

'Delicate?' Edward laughed.

'Like a real-life doll's house,' Daisy explained.

'It does.' Rose nodded her agreement, reaching for her sister's hand.

'I'm pleased you like it. What do you think, Mrs Lander? Is it what you imagined?'

But Grace couldn't reply, her lips fixed together, her gaze never leaving the house. It was exactly the same as it had always been. Exactly the same. As if time had stood still, as if the moment she'd left, shrouded in shame, the house had preserved itself in aspic.

'Mrs Lander?' Edward prompted.

'It's beautiful,' she breathed out in one go. And then her eyes left the house as the horse-drawn carriage continued towards it. She swept her gaze to the side as they passed the woodland. The last time she'd been in those woods she'd had her heart shattered into pieces by Edward's father. She blinked, feeling all of twenty-one and the first flush of betrayal, and looked down at her lap. How was she going to do this? How was she going to get through this? How was she going to bear the next few weeks? This was a nightmare made real. And now it was happening it was even worse than she'd anticipated.

Somewhere in the recesses of her mind she told herself it was nearly three decades since she'd been here as they drove into the sweeping circular drive. The staff were walking out of the front door as neatly as she remembered, lining themselves up to greet Rose and her family. Directly after the wedding, Rose would be their new mistress.

Grace's eyes quickly swept the staff as the carriage pulled up by the front steps. She recognised no one. Nearly sagging in relief, she found herself caught by the number of staff – slightly depleted from when she'd worked there, but she didn't have time to ponder more. For her eyes were drawn up the steps to where Laurie Trelenna was standing to greet them.

Grace inhaled sharply, the sound drowned out by the footman opening the carriage door to let them out. Edward jumped out eagerly, offering his hand to each of the women in turn, welcoming them to his home. Grace took his hand willingly to steady herself, not daring to look up at Laurie, but knowing all the same he was there, *feeling* that he was there.

The butler stepped forward to greet them and Grace kept her eyes down, refusing to raise them, refusing to allow her gaze to be drawn up the steps to look at Laurie. If she could put this off for even a minute longer she would. She listened while Edward introduced all the staff one by one and Rose spoke to them individually to say hello. Rose gave them her brightest smile and said how much she was looking forward to getting to know them all over the coming days, and working with the housekeeper and cook with regard to last-minute wedding preparations.

And then Edward led Rose up the stone steps. Out of her peripheral vision, Grace saw Laurie extend his hand to Rose as she reached the top step. But still she couldn't look at him.

'I am delighted to meet the woman who is about to make my son the happiest man in the world. My dear, you are every inch as radiant as Edward has described you in his letters. Welcome to Trelenna. Welcome to your new home.'

'Thank you so much.' Rose clasped his hand in return. 'What a warm welcome all round. I can't tell you how delighted I am to be here, how enchanted I am by what I've seen of Cornwall and of Trelenna so far. The park is so pretty. May I introduce you to my mother and sister?'

'Please,' Laurie said. Grace stood tall and proud. She was wearing a black hat with a plume of dark feathers, to match her chocolate-brown dress. Foregoing all colour and trying to blend into the background was her main objective and she raised her eyes from the ground at the last minute, forcing a smile she didn't mean on to her face. Every single move she made now was a challenge to herself and she barely heard Rose say, 'Mr Trelenna, allow me to introduce you to my mother, Mrs Lander. And this is my sister, Miss Daisy Lander.'

'Mrs Lander,' Laurie said genially, extending his hand. It was as if time stood still as after all these years the palm of Laurie Trelenna's hand met hers and she slowly dragged her gaze up to his face, looking at him for the first time in so long. His eyes were the same deep-brown shade she used to fantasise about, but much like hers were now lined around the edges when he smiled. There were flecks of grey sprinkled through his otherwise sandy hair. His face was still as handsome and it hurt Grace so much, too much, to see him smile so affably. That false smile hid all the damage he'd done to her. An anger she did not know still lived within her sparked. For time had been kind to Laurie Trelenna, because he lived a life unburdened by strife or regret, and for that she could not forgive.

Grace pulled her hand away and encouraged the smile to remain on her face. He had not recognised her. How insignificant she had been to him. She thanked god for that fact.

'A pleasure to meet you,' she forced out emotionlessly.

Laurie's attention turned to Daisy. 'Miss Lander,' he said. 'You are most welcome at Trelenna. I hope we have enough to keep you entertained while you're here.'

'Well, Edward tells me you have horses and so if I get bored, I'm sure I can make myself useful in the stables.'

Laurie paused and then laughed. 'I can't tell if you're serious.'

Daisy nodded vigorously. 'Oh I am, most assuredly. I adore horses.'

'Can you ride?'

'A little,' Daisy replied unabashed. 'Not much call for it in the city though.'

'In that case I've got a wonderful little mare that you should ride while you're here. She's very gentle, very docile. I'll take you out there and show you her myself later on, if you like?'

'I would *love* that.'

'Now would you all like some tea or to rest first?' Laurie addressed them as they walked up the steps towards the doors she had never walked through. Mrs Day's voice suddenly rang in her eleven-year-old ears that servants were only to use the kitchen entrance. The front door was for those privileged enough to be counted as guests of the Trelennas.

'We'll have something a little stronger than tea, I think,' Edward suggested and Grace heard Laurie laugh as, for the first time in nearly three decades, she braced herself to enter Trelenna House.

Chapter 39

Grace's heart hammered so hard she was sure she could feel it reverberate around her entire body, her pulse thickening in her skin to the point of explosion. What was this? What was happening? Her mind was in turmoil. She must get a better hold of her feelings. But what were her feelings? She didn't know.

It didn't feel real. After all this time she was back – in Cornwall, in Trelenna, back in the company of *Laurie.* At her request, she'd been shown to a water closet off the main hall. It hadn't been there twenty-five years ago. Before, they'd all relied on chamber pots. Laurie must have had this installed. What had been there before? She tried to remember, tried to distract herself. What had it been? Part of a cupboard? If she continued on down the hallway towards the end, down a few steps, she'd find the kitchen – her kitchen. But she dare not go there. Not now.

She felt transported back to her youth. She'd spent her formative years in that set of rooms at the end of the house. She could picture the kitchen and the servants' hall, the range she'd used, the scrubbed worktable on which she'd spent years preparing food. Suddenly she was gripped with an urgency to see it, an urgency to spend time anywhere but in Laurie's company, an urgency to find familiar ground. She clenched her hands in the hopes of alleviating the need, hating that after so long she was still more at home in a servants' hall than she was in a drawing room.

Grace brushed down her dress, tried to make herself a little taller, and then closed her eyes to prepare herself. She sprung her eyes open with a sense of renewal, a sense of purpose. She just had to get through these next few weeks. She opened the door, left the water closet, and moved back towards the drawing room. A footman had been positioned nearby to show her the way. She passed the small morning room in which her world had been turned so horribly upside down by Laurie's mother.

'You are his latest mistake.'

She glanced in, anger rising within her – with no outlet. The décor in the morning room had changed to a mix of pale-blue wallpaper and a yellow chaise longue. But other than that, she could not say if anything else was different. That was the only room above stairs she'd ever seen. And now – now – she was *only* seeing rooms above stairs. She had been for quite some time. She had risen, succeeded, and had brought her daughters back with her. Now she was as good as the rest of them, if not better because she would *never* have treated someone the way Laurie and his mother had treated her. Never.

Anger and a sense of righteousness threatened to burst from within her as the footman escorted her into the drawing room. She immediately thought of Arthur and how this had been his job in this house so long ago. She had returned to Trelenna, but his chance to prove his worth here would never come. She felt herself practically shaking as the butler stood with a tray of champagne, offering it to her. Grace took a glass purposefully, resisting the urge to drink the entire contents in one big gulp. She tried so hard not to look at Laurie as he talked with her daughters.

Edward moved over to her. 'Are you feeling better now?' he asked softly.

'Yes, thank you. I think a large glass of water and I'll be on the mend.'

'I'm pleased to hear it.'

Edward nodded at the butler, who in turn nodded at a footman to fetch Grace some water.

'I want you to be as at home here as you've made me feel in Newport. If there's anything you need, please don't hesitate to ask.'

'Edward, you're really very kind. Rose is lucky to have found you.'

'I'm the lucky one. Not long and then I'll be her husband. I only hope I can make her as happy as she deserves to be.'

'You already make her as happy as can be,' Grace said distractedly, but meaning it.

Edward smiled bashfully.

'Mother, I hope you're not over there talking Edward out of it,' Rose teased from the other side of the room.

'Quite the opposite,' Edward said, moving towards his fiancée.

'Good, because Edward's father has just agreed to walk me down the aisle.'

'Call me Laurie, please,' he said.

'That's wonderful news,' Grace said flatly. Hating how Laurie would be carrying out a precious task that Arthur should have been doing on Rose's wedding day, Grace tipped the rest of the contents of the champagne saucer straight into her mouth.

'You've barely said a word,' Rose chastised Grace that evening as they dressed for dinner.

'I'm tired.'

'And she's unwell. That seasickness has made you pale, Mother,' Daisy pointed out as she entered Rose's room, her elegant lilac skirts rustling as she walked. Her bodice was a swathe of golden silk draped in tight ruffles, which made for a striking two-toned effect. 'Is this going to be your room always, Rose? It's beautiful. There's so much . . . gold.'

'It is very gold, yes,' Rose said, looking around as Ruth finished her hair. The lady's maid would be staying with Rose to help ease her transition into her new life with some familiarity, meaning Grace would have to hire a new one on her return to New York. 'I like it. But I honestly cannot believe there's no plumbing upstairs. It's so *backwards*. The housemaids and footmen have been up and down those stairs fetching buckets of water for my bath. Can you believe that? In this day and age? I almost felt guilty for putting them to such work.'

'Almost?' Grace asked.

'Mother, why are you being snappish?' Rose spun in her seat to face Grace, momentarily forcing her lady's maid to pause with a diamond pin mid-air.

Grace shook her head and said nothing, wandering over to the window and looking out at the parkland. Deer were grazing on the grass and the late summer sun was setting in the distance. Out of sight was the sea, and to the right was the woodland. It should have been beautiful. But Grace hated this house with every part of her soul.

Laurie was at the head of the table and Grace seated directly to his right in order of precedence. She'd hardly said a word to him since her arrival. After champagne in the library had been swiftly dealt with, she'd retired upstairs to 'recover' from the journey. Then over cocktails, where Daisy was full of talk about the little mare Laurie had shown her, Grace had the perfect excuse to avoid conversing with him at all. But when the butler announced dinner, Laurie was suddenly offering his arm and, despite wishing she had any reason to refuse, found decorum forcing her to place her hand as lightly as possible on his sleeve, as he led her into the dining room.

The only solace to this hell was that clearly he did not remember her. That, for him, what they had done together so long ago was utterly unmemorable. His mother had been right. Grace had been just another error, a blip in his life quickly erased from his house and memory. How she hated her younger self now for allowing that to happen with him, for believing all the well-told lies. Seeing him now, all those old feelings had resurfaced. Hatred ran through her as fresh as the day he'd left her standing, waiting for him in the woods, in the torrential rain.

Conversation flowed over her, the young people talked of weddings and gowns, jewellery and travel, as she concentrated on her plate.

'My son puts me to shame.' Laurie leaned forward and said conspiratorially to Grace, 'He's very well-travelled. I found myself green with envy that he took himself off to America. Worried sick, of course. It's just the two of us these days and I'm not sure if he relies on me or if I rely on him. I suspect it's the latter.'

'I suspect you're right,' Grace said in a distant voice, embracing fully any shred of an American accent she'd garnered over the years. 'I suspect I need my children more than they need me now.'

'Rose is in safe hands here with us, you know. You don't need to worry about her being so far away from home once they're wed. Anything she wants or needs, Edward will move heaven and earth to get it for her.'

'That's perhaps what I'm worried about,' Grace replied in a neutral tone.

Laurie chuckled. 'They seem very much in love.'

Grace looked across at Rose, who was smiling with delight at something Edward was saying. It made Grace's happy words flow without the reserve she was trying to uphold. 'I believe they are. I witnessed Edward run into my home to find Rose hours after saying what we all assumed was a final goodbye. Soaked to the skin and desperate to find her. I know he loves her. It's beyond doubt.'

Laurie looked at Grace and smiled, then glanced at Rose, Edward and Daisy.

'You're lucky to have two children. We were only blessed with Edward.'

Surprising herself that she could maintain a conversation with her blood at full boil, Grace smiled as she continued to converse calmly with the man who had nearly destroyed her life. 'I didn't think I would be fortunate to have another, but Rose surprised us all happily and she's been surprising us ever since.'

'Edward is my pride and joy. My late wife instilled into me the need to protect him as much as possible. I'm pleased he's broken free though, and become his own person, found his own way in life.'

It was Grace's turn to look away. She watched the grown-up children talk and laugh, ignoring Grace and Laurie entirely.

'Daisy doesn't mind that her younger sister has married before her?' Laurie continued.

'Oh no,' Grace confirmed. 'She's overjoyed. Rose marrying an Englishman gave Daisy the chance to leave America.'

The footmen stepped forward to clear their first-course plates and Grace sat back while the changes were made.

'She's not happy in America?'

'She wants to travel.' Grace looked on at her eldest daughter, her adventurer. 'One day I feel I'm going to lose her to the big wide world. And I think she's ready to be lost too, in her own way.'

'I hope Daisy feels as welcome here as her sister is. The sisters are welcome to be here together as long as they choose. And of course you also.'

She heard Laurie's reply, but couldn't bear to look at him. Why had she been so open? Grace swallowed. She had to remember they were strangers. 'Thank you,' she said. 'That's very kind. But I think Rose and Edward will want to begin their married life without all of us around. And we intend to visit London after the wedding.' She paused, this congenial tone taking all her energy. 'What will *you* do?'

'I've been wondering the same thing,' Laurie confessed. 'I believe I'm quickly going to be surplus to requirement. I imagine Rose and Edward will want to start a family and the next generation will be among us before we know it. I may take myself off and travel the world, leave Edward to manage the estate. He's more than capable. I'll let them enjoy an extended honeymoon and then on their return they can tell me what my destiny is to be,' he said with mock seriousness.

'That's very generous of you,' Grace replied. She sipped her wine as she surveyed him over the rim of her glass. Grace didn't know what to make of this version of Laurie. The one she knew had been just like this. Until he hadn't. She didn't care enough to find out if Laurie now was older and wiser. If he was, it didn't undo the hurt he'd caused her. In a few days she'd be gone to London with Daisy, leaving Trelenna – and the traumatic nightmare of once again being so close to Laurie – far behind her.

Chapter 40

Rose stood in front of her mother in her wedding gown; a highly structured, tight-bodice silhouette showed off her figure and small waist. The floor-length cream gown was studded with tiny pearls that shimmered in the light. The effect was mesmerising.

The gilded mirror caught the full effect of Rose in that moment, her long lace veil moving delicately over her shoulders as she turned in a slow circle. Positioned within her elegant high-curled chignon was the Cartier tiara that Rose had so desperately wanted. It was indeed bigger than any Grace had seen before.

'I feel like a princess,' Rose said with the widest smile on her face.

'You look like one,' Daisy said in awe. 'But with a very heavy tiara on your head. Oh, Rose, you look so beautiful. Mother, doesn't she look beautiful?'

Grace could hardly speak for pride. She could hardly even see through the tears that blurred her vision.

'Mother?' Rose queried and then she laughed. 'Oh, don't cry.'

'I never dreamed,' Grace started, taking Rose's hands, 'that I would ever have children who would grow up to be this beautiful, who would make me so proud.' She took Daisy's hands too. 'You both make me so happy.'

'We know,' Daisy said. 'You love us.'

'I do. Never forget that.'

Rose breathed in and then out, and looked at herself in the mirror again. 'I'm getting married today,' she said in disbelief.

'You are.' Daisy pulled Rose's veil slowly into place over her sister's shoulders.

'*You* look like a princess too,' Rose said. 'You both do. That blue is just your colour, Mother, and I am so glad you chose the pink, Daisy, it really does flatter you.'

'We're going to be late for the church, so if you think we look presentable enough—' Grace teased.

'Oh, you do, you do,' Rose said. 'Daisy, I wonder if any of Edward's friends might be suitable for you, and in that dress too . . . There's one Edward told me about who sounds like he might be just the thing. Remind me to—'

'How can you think about finding me a husband on *your* wedding day,' Daisy scoffed.

'I'm not *totally* self-absorbed.' Rose laughed, then took her sister's hand. 'I want to see you happy too.'

'I am happy.' Daisy beamed, giving her sister a kiss on the cheek. 'Now go and get to the church, but not before us, please. Mother?'

'I'm coming,' Grace said. She stood and looked at her daughter one last time before Rose walked down the aisle and became a wife. 'I love and adore you.'

'I know, Mother,' Rose replied and looked at Grace with meaning. 'I love and adore you too. Both of you. Funny that for a little while, since Father died, it's just been us girls. And now, it's not going to be. I'm breaking that up.'

'You're doing no such thing,' Grace admonished. 'You're starting a new life with someone you love deeply and who loves you in return. I just wish it wasn't in England.'

'Mother,' Daisy warned.

Grace waved her concern away. 'I'm being silly. My one real wish is that I would give anything for your father to have been here to see it.'

'I always feel him near me,' Rose said solemnly. 'He can see me today, I know he can. Because he's always with me.'

Grace battled an overwhelming need to cry. 'I know,' she said, forcing back her sobs. 'I feel the same. And if you have one tiny moment of the happiness I felt with your father, you will be the luckiest woman on earth.'

'I'm already the luckiest woman on earth,' Rose said. 'And you made it that way. I'll never forget everything you and Father did for me, what you worked for, what you gave me. You made all this possible. You put me on this solid path. I'm forever grateful. I've just got to do the rest from here.'

Grace held back her tears of joy and gave her daughter a delicate squeeze, careful not to put any of Rose's adornments out of place. 'I will see you in the church shortly.'

'I'll see you there,' Rose said, and Grace was sure she could see happy tears behind Rose's eyes too.

As Grace and Daisy descended the stairs to their waiting carriage, Laurie was standing at the bottom.

'Is Rose ready?' he asked agreeably. 'I'm not sure who is more nervous at having to walk down the aisle in front of all those people, her or me.'

'Oh, it's you,' Daisy said with a laugh. 'Rose is always ready for anything and she looks a picture. You wait. No one will be looking at you.'

Grace shook her head. Why were both her children so impertinent?

'I'm pleased to hear it,' Laurie said, glancing at Grace and smiling in return. 'But the two of you, however, look absolutely delightful.'

'Thank you,' Daisy said. 'You look very charming too.'

Grace nodded and her gaze fell to the floor because Daisy was right. He did look wonderful. It pained her beyond anything to see that Laurie had turned out this handsome. Why hadn't he aged *badly*? She breathed and took control of herself. They were only staying a few more days and then she'd be gone. To London. To anywhere away from Laurie Trelenna. She just had to hold her nerve a few days longer. She could do it, she could.

Grace watched her daughter walk down the aisle arm in arm with Laurie. In another world it would have been Arthur, and she felt a pang deep within her chest. Nothing about today made sense. It was as if Grace had fallen into a strange existence, one that no longer felt real. Rose had said she was on a solid path, and thank heavens one of them was. Because Grace's path now was so uneven she felt unable to stay upright, in constant danger of stumbling. The church was beautiful and just as Grace had remembered it from Sundays long ago. In all those years, she'd never been to a wedding here, and the cascades of white flowers studded with fragrant orange blossoms draped at the end of each pew and adorning every spare surface in the old stone church took Grace's breath away.

She watched her daughter now stand next to the man she loved, and felt as if she'd gone back in time. The familiarity of the wooden pew, the stained-glass window still with a slight crack in the top right corner. It was as if time hadn't passed at all, as if nothing had changed in all the years since she'd expected to stand here marrying a man who would break her heart. Grace couldn't fathom how this had happened.

'If anyone knows of any just cause or impediment . . .' the vicar asked.

If only everyone knew. She looked away at the pockmarked flagstones on the floor, under which were crypts housing generations of Trelennas.

Edward and Rose exchanged rings, said *I do,* and Grace tried not to think that Rose was lost to her. Instead Edward had been gained. It was not his fault that Laurie was his father.

And after, Rose and Edward looked at each other as if there was no one else in the ballroom at Trelenna House, as if there weren't at least a hundred people watching them dance into their first day as man and wife. A smattering of American heiresses, married and carrying newly gained ancient titles had travelled from their various estates inherited by their English husbands – and the women's reunion squeals could be heard across the ballroom.

Rose's aunt and uncle and her two cousins had arrived this morning on the overnight sleeper train from London. There had been no time for socialising, but Grace had shared a brief moment with her sister-in-law when their gaze had connected across the crowded library. Few would understand the mix of emotions Grace was experiencing, but Mary did. Grace was lucky to have her, they didn't need to say the words aloud, their secret beginnings had led them here. Raising her glass in a silent toast, Mary joined her before being laughingly swept away into a dance by her husband John, who was glowing with pride. A Lander marrying into the British gentry; it was a thing none of them could have dreamed of. Grace only wished she could be so happy.

As she moved through the room, shaking hands and exchanging nods with their few American guests and those connected to the Trelennas and Edward, she overheard one young woman ask her mother if *all* the eligible bachelors were going to be married off to monied Americans. Grace had smiled congenially; it seemed that even English society was concerned with these marriages of financial and societal gain. But she didn't care enough to be offended. Rose was happy and loved, and that was all that mattered.

Finding herself in a corner, Grace swayed in time to the music, a glass of champagne in her hand. This was her second and it lightened her mood a little, unstiffened her. It was becoming easier being here with every passing hour, although only marginally. Couples waltzed together and she listened to the orchestra play. Grace sighed happily, sipped her champagne and cast her eyes around for Daisy. She had probably escaped out to the stables with the horses.

A voice surprised her. 'Might I have this dance?'

Grace looked to her left to see Laurie standing next to her. How long had he been there?

'You haven't danced once,' he said, implying he'd been watching her for a while. She wasn't sure what to think of that. 'And neither have I. Shall we show them how it's done?'

'I don't . . . I haven't danced in a very long time.'

'Neither have I,' he repeated. 'There hasn't been much call for it. But today, I think we might go unnoticed if we get a few steps wrong.' He extended his hand and Grace felt her throat constrict so tightly she might stop breathing.

He looked at her expectantly, as if afraid she would say no. His hand was still outstretched. She couldn't seem to breath, let alone speak, so instead she found herself taking his hand, not wishing to look rude and show herself up at Rose's wedding. Just one dance and then she could move away from him forever. Touching his hand again after all these years stirred her in a way she'd never thought possible. Her mind went back to the woods, back to the night when she'd been so young, had been undressed, had been made love to, had believed false promises, then, ultimately, abandoned. She wanted to run, to fight, to flee. But all she felt was trapped.

Laurie escorted her towards the dancers. Rose caught her eye and beamed at her, the freshly married glow radiating from her beautiful daughter, but Grace couldn't smile back. The effects of the champagne were wearing off and she stiffened again as Laurie placed his other hand on her waist. He looked down at her and Grace glanced up, immediately wishing she hadn't, immediately regretting her decision to dance with him, immediately hating herself for all the mixed emotions coursing through her body.

She felt young again as he spun her into a waltz. It had been so long since she'd done this with Arthur she wasn't sure she remembered how. But Grace felt Laurie's body move towards hers with every spin they made and she went through the motions of the dance. She counted steps, counted time and looked anywhere but at him. Her pulse raced and she fought the light-headed feeling overwhelming her with everything she had. Until eventually, mercifully, it was over.

Grace breathed an audible sigh of relief and now there was no choice but to look up at him. His expression was unreadable, his face gave nothing away.

'Thank you,' he said softly. 'You have made my day.'

She nodded, issued a small smile, still unable to speak, still hating herself for feeling anything *other* than hate for him. When she couldn't work out what to do, there seemed nothing else for it but to walk away.

Reasoning that one daughter had no use for her, for the moment at least – she knew as soon as Rose fell pregnant she'd be once again in high demand – Grace made her escape and went in search of Daisy. Moving through the ballroom and out into the grounds, she turned to take in Trelenna House behind her. It was beautiful, each of its sash windows showcasing flickering candles in glass lamps, lit up to show the house in the best light for anyone walking the grounds or talking idly on the steps or the terrace. Music followed her outdoors and the sound of joyful chatter buzzed in the still night air. In the distance the woodland loomed, shadowy and sinister. Funny that now she viewed it that way – to be avoided – when so long ago it had held such happiness. She would never go in there again if she could help it – the memories were too awful. Turning away, she walked along the length of the house only to see her daughter alone, coming from the stables.

'There you are,' Grace called out happily.

'I've been with the horses,' Daisy replied, looking tired.

Grace looped her arm through her daughter's in comfort, not sure if it was for herself or Daisy. 'I thought you might have been but you've been gone so long. Have you been avoiding people?'

'A little,' Daisy confessed, leaning into her. 'I think I had my fill of talking and dancing.'

'Did Rose force any of Edward's friends on you as she promised?'

'As she threatened, you mean. Yes, she did. A painter. He was nice enough.'

'A painter?' Grace prompted, hoping for more. 'Well, that's something you have in common. What was his name?'

'Mr Rutherford. Nice. Not nice enough, though. Hence why I ended up escaping discreetly to the stables.'

Grace nodded. 'Understood. Has anyone else caught your eye?'

'Mother,' Daisy warned. 'You'll be the first to know if anyone does. Don't worry.'

'I'm not worried.'

'Good. Neither am I,' Daisy challenged. 'I promise I'll try to marry someone before the decade is out. Is that a compromise?'

'No, it's not,' Grace said forcefully, turning to clasp her daughter's hands and fixing her with a concerned look. 'I don't want you to marry for the sake of it. You must know that?'

'Of course,' Daisy said, her pale pink dress rustling in the light evening breeze as she looked sadly into the distance. 'I'm happy, you know. With you. And with Rose. But now she's leaving us. So that leaves you and me. And . . . I just wish I had Rose's looks. I'm so much older than her and I've not been proposed to once.'

Grace's heart squeezed for her daughter; she knew what it felt to wonder. 'It's because you escape to the stables or to a secret nook in a library to read or draw every time you meet a man.'

'They all bore me.' She sighed.

'They all bored your sister too. You're both very choosy. And that's not a bad thing. Was Mr Rutherford keen?'

'He seemed to be.'

'But you weren't?'

Daisy shrugged. 'Not really.'

'So now perhaps the sad, dejected Mr Rutherford is standing with his mother, lamenting his luck with women the way you are with me.'

Daisy snorted, her eyes clearing a little. 'I doubt it.'

'The evening is wearing down,' Grace said, turning back towards the glow of the house. 'Shall we attempt to sneak in a few more glasses of champagne before stocks run dry?'

'How many have you had?' Daisy looked at her mother through narrowed eyes. 'You're swaying a little.'

'I've probably had too much,' Grace confessed, hoping another glass or two might diminish the memory of Laurie's lingering touch as they'd danced. 'How many have you had?'

Daisy hooked her arm through her mother's again and said darkly, 'Me? Oh, I've had nowhere *near* enough.'

Chapter 41

Too much champagne and celebrating had worn a hole in Grace's mind. Unable to sleep, unable to think coherently, unable to stop the tide of emotions that refused to retreat, she sat up and fumbled for the gas lamp at the side of her bed.

She sighed deeply with pure frustration at not being able to drift off. She'd wrongly assumed that tonight of all nights she'd sleep like a log. Today had been the most wonderful day – in the end. Rose was happily married and looking forward to her new life as mistress of this house. The day after tomorrow, she and Daisy would leave for London to spend time with their American family, seeing the sights, and then they would all go back to New York to continue expanding their restaurant empire. Everything was as it should be. Except it wasn't. Everything felt all wrong. Too much excitement. Too much champagne. She knew she shouldn't have drunk two more with Daisy, ensconced in the corner and trying to let go of everything weighing her down.

Grace got out of bed and went to the window. She'd forgotten how cold this house could be, even in summer. She'd always assumed it was just the servants' quarters in the attic rooms that were freezing but, no, it was the entire house.

Rose would be the one to put this right. Rose would install plumbing and central heating. There was no way her daughter would put up with this. And, of course, it would be Grace's money that Rose would use to do it. Her dowry would go on upgrades to Trelenna House. She sighed deeply from the back of her throat. There was no point lamenting it all. What was done was done and what would be would be. The house that had brought her such unhappiness would soon receive a financial injection with her own money. Suddenly she laughed, unable to stop the ridiculousness of her situation – her daughter becoming Mrs Trelenna; the very same dream she'd harboured at twenty-one, her daughter had fulfilled. It all just seemed so very funny now it was all done. Oh, she needed to sleep. Her mind was ruined and busy and she was too jittery, too cold to attempt to sleep again. The clock read five o'clock and the party had finished only hours ago. The family would sleep in, but the servants would be moving soon, readying themselves to light fires, blacken the range, begin the breakfasts.

Grace smiled, remembering those days. She had been happy for most of it, for nearly all of her time here, in fact. All those years, they hadn't been terrible, when she'd been below stairs. That kitchen had been the happiest place in the world to her. It was where the impossible had become possible, where she had made soufflés rise and learned how to cook complicated dinners for visiting dukes and duchesses, where she had met the man who'd become her best friend, her husband, who she would go on to raise two beautiful daughters with.

No, it hadn't been all so terrible back then. She shouldn't conflate so many happy years with two terrible final days. That kitchen had held such happiness for such a long time. She glanced at the clock again. If she was quick, she could go down to the kitchen where she'd been so full of joy and see what it looked like now, see what had changed, see what new contraptions the Trelennas had invested in for their staff – although she doubted any. She could spend a few moments in there reclaiming the happier years of her life and still be back in bed by the time a housemaid came to light the fires and the kitchen maid appeared to begin her chores. *Yes*, she thought determinedly, as she pulled her silk dressing gown around her and put her feet into her slippers. Yes, she could be quick. This was her only chance, surely. She was awake at this ungodly hour. She might as well. It was now or probably never.

Grace opened her bedroom door and peered into the corridor, the only light coming from her own lamp as she let her eyes adjust slowly to the darkness before closing the door behind her with a quiet click. Grace began walking along the corridor, the squeak of warped floorboards sounding beneath her with every tread. Yet another thing her money would probably be used to fix. Grace belted her dressing gown tightly around her, although it was so pointlessly thin it did barely anything to ward off the cold. She'd not imagined she'd need a warmer one for her voyage to England. How quickly she'd forgotten. How short her memory was of being in this house.

The polished wooden banister was cold to the touch but light from the moon shone its way through the downstairs sash windows, guiding her so she had no need to grip the handrail. And yet she did, through exhaustion or through excitement, she didn't know which.

The closer she got to the kitchen along the flagstone floor, the more her excitement grew. Would it be like stepping back in time, or would everything have changed and all that awaited her down the approaching few stone steps be disappointment?

She would find out in a matter of seconds and she looked at the steps and smiled, doing all she could not to leap down them and open the door inwards at the bottom. Only in Newport had she been in bigger houses than this and never 'downstairs'. Suddenly it dawned on her that this house was laid out with the servants' hall and kitchen in close proximity to the 'upstairs' part of the house. In her mind's eye, the 'downstairs' had been a basement, but no, the servants' area was just a few steps away, as if it had been added as an afterthought. She wondered if it had, and then about all those people who had come before her: the cooks and footmen, the kitchen maids and butlers.

Slowly she turned the handle, hoping beyond all hope that no servants would be awake at this hour, reassuring herself that it was far too early for even the servants to be working. The door creaked lightly on its hinges and Grace entered the dark room. Again she had to pause to let her eyes adjust, the moon on its descent streaming through the windows going some way to light her path.

'Ohhh,' she said slowly, drawing out the word. 'Oh, it's just as I remember.' She took in the large room. The scrubbed wooden worktable was in the middle, just as it had always been. The range had not been replaced because, presumably, the old stalwart was still as strong and as useful as it had ever been. The two dozen or so copper pans gleamed from their hooks on high. They were the same ones, she was sure of it, and Grace stood on tiptoe to reach for one of her favourite saucepans with a wide base and short sides.

She looked at it, touching it fondly, remembering dishes she'd made and happier times, and then cleaned it up on her dressing gown, removing her fingerprints before rehanging it. Grace stood back to take in the entire room, then moved over to the window to look at the courtyard. She'd stood out there many times, drinking tea and soaking up the sun in the summer or with a thick shawl wrapped around her in the winter, while Arthur smoked or the hall boy regaled them with stories of his naughty siblings while waiting for an instruction to be barked or for a bell to ring. What had his name been? She closed her eyes trying to remember. But try as she might she couldn't. Then there was the dog. What had the dog been named? She screwed her eyes up tighter, thinking. Gladstone. That was it. After the prime minister. That dog. It was the dog that had started everything.

Turning, Grace moved into the adjoining servants' hall. Everything in here was the same too. The large dining table, clean and ready for the next meal. A stack of newspapers on top of the upright piano, which drew her in with copies of *The Cornishman*. It was a newspaper that hadn't existed in her time here and she flicked one open to read local news. *Four youths performed public penance in Blisland, near Bodmin, for assaulting a servant girl named Eva Neil.*

Good, thought Grace. Young men shouldn't be able to go around thinking they could do whatever they wanted to servant girls and that there'd be no comeuppance.

Next she picked up a discarded copy of *The Times,* which had been folded over on a page highlighting the upcoming wedding of Mr Edward Easton-Thorpe-Trelenna to American restaurant heiress Miss Rose Lander. The article made her smile and she put it back down on the piano and then turned, inhaling the room, letting it all come back to her, letting her insomnia-addled mind remember the years of friendship, joy, progress and work she'd enjoyed before it had all been taken away from her. But then, look at her now. What might have happened if she hadn't lost herself to Laurie? Not this life, surely. Not the life she led now. Would she go back in time and do it differently? Would she have avoided Laurie Trelenna, been stronger than she had been, withstood his advances? If so, would she have married Arthur eventually anyway? Would it have been the natural conclusion to the only two servants of similar age working in such close proximity? Would they have gone to America? Would her life have turned in this direction? She couldn't have said. She'd never know what the alternative would have been. And perhaps, it had all worked out for the best. The folly of youth had brought her a marvellous life with a lot of hard work, although back then Grace would never have expected that to have been the outcome.

She yawned, tiredness finally finding her. She was glad she'd done this. Pleased she'd snuck down here, reminded herself of what once was and what might have been. Everything was as it was supposed to be. She had to accept this now, had to overcome her anger at Laurie and how he had treated her, had to be happy for Rose, happy for *herself.* She had to move on from the past, embrace this new present and look forward to a future for herself and her two daughters – whatever that might look like. *Yes*, she thought, as unlikely as it sounded, perhaps everything had happened for a reason and it was all just as it should be.

She'd done what she'd wanted to do, seen what she'd wanted to see, achieved what she'd wanted to achieve and she was ready to go back upstairs, back to her life. The life she had built from the ashes of her old one. She stepped forward to leave and then stopped, sucking in a sharp breath.

Laurie Trelenna was standing in the doorway dividing the servants' hall from the kitchen.

Grace was caught entirely off-guard by his presence. If anything she'd expected to be disturbed by a kitchen maid, not by *him*. Still no words came, her voice lost. How could she explain herself? There was no rational explanation for . . . anything.

'I . . .' she started. What could she have come here for? 'I was hoping to fetch a glass of . . .' What? *What* could she be here for? 'Milk,' she finished.

Laurie nodded thoughtfully, his gaze sweeping the room. There was no sign of a glass of milk and just when she was trying to rationalise how to explain why she didn't have the very thing she'd just lied about being here for, she found herself feeling panicked, light-headed, like a bird in flight with nowhere to go. And that feeling only intensified when Laurie Trelenna returned his gaze to her and said, 'Grace, did you really think I wouldn't recognise you?'

Chapter 42

Present Day

Zennor

Zennor stood over the kitchen table and took the lids off the plastic boxes holding all her old cookery books. With a bit of stolen time off she could have been in her room diligently working through the archive boxes. Instead, she was looking over her own memories and attempting to find interesting Christmas recipes.

A mug of decaffeinated tea was going cold on the kitchen table while she pulled books out at random and remembered the first recipes she'd cooked from each of them. It had been such a long time since she'd looked them over. They had informed her cooking from an early age. They'd served their purpose. But even so she'd been unable to send them to the charity shop. Perhaps hoarding – or 'archiving', she thought with a grin – was a family trait, because when it came to Zennor's cookbooks, they were too sentimentally precious to say goodbye to.

There were four large tubs, housing what must be well over a hundred cookery books from various stages of her early years of learning to cook. She picked some up and looked at the spines. Marco Pierre White, Nigella Lawson, Nigel Slater, Rick Stein,

Delia Smith. Most of these she'd picked up in charity shops. Some she'd coveted and paid the full price for. Collected essays about food were her particular weakness. Knowing other people were out there being as fussy about food as she was made her feel like she was part of a secret group, before finding her crowd at catering college. A precious copy of *Kitchen Confidential* by Anthony Bourdain sat on top of *Salt, Fat, Acid, Heat* by Samin Nosrat. Underneath the ever-joyful Gizzi Erskine were books by Grace Dent and Ella Risbridger. Sandwiched among them all was a beaten black leather-bound book, its spine torn, the front leather worn away at the corners. Zennor opened the cover to the title page: *Modern Cookery for Private Families* by Eliza Acton. Memories flooded back to Zennor of reading this – or attempting to read it – when she'd found it in the house's library. How old had she been? She had no idea. Six? Seven? Maybe older. She didn't recall but she *did* remember taking it and squirrelling it away. It was the only cookbook she'd ever seen in the house at the time and it had brought a whole new world to her. The book fell open on a recipe for white chestnut sauce and, given the book was early Victorian, the dish sounded as delicious to her now as it must have done back then. Some dishes sounded vile. Boiled pike, for example, was something Zennor knew she'd never cook.

Zennor had taken this book as hers, claimed her right to it as no one else was going to, and now felt a bit guilty for taking something from the house's library and keeping it for herself, locking it in a box for the past few years. She would look through this later for some festive recipes and see if anything leaped out at her for inspiration. Time was against her, as always, and she put the book to one side as Lamorna entered the kitchen, packing away most of the others but keeping *Nigella Christmas* out too. She knew those recipes off by heart but Nigella was always good comfort reading. In reality she should have been planning so many things for Christmas long before now but she'd been diverted, diligently reading through as much of the non-fiction book she'd found in the library as she could. A few pages before bed and then she'd fallen asleep. The Gilded Age heiresses made for fascinating reading and she'd read the page about Rose Lander over and over, hoping a previously unread fact would leap out the page at her. But it never did.

Yet while the few facts about Rose marrying into Zennor's own family were written as plain as day, Zennor was still struggling to work out quite how it had happened. How had Rose Lander married a member of the *Trelenna* family?

'Edward Easton-Thorpe-Trelenna.' Zennor pondered the name aloud as she sipped the rest of her tea.

'Still no closer to working it all out?' Lamorna asked, as she went through her usual routine of setting up her laptop in the vicinity of the kettle.

'No. What I find intriguing is—'

'All of it?' Lamorna stated as she walked over to the mugs and flicked the kettle on.

'Ha. Yes,' Zennor confessed, screwing up her eyes at the text again. 'For one thing, why does *he* have three surnames, but we don't?'

'Because it was a mouthful of a name and, cleverly, someone ditched most of them before we were all born.'

'Possibly,' Zennor acquiesced.

Lamorna picked up the book while the kettle boiled noisily in the background and looked at the accompanying photograph of Rose Lander. It was the first and only image they'd found in the house of any of their ancestors. In it she was in her bridal gown and wearing an enormous tiara.

'Where did that tiara go? That's what I want to know,' Lamorna said. 'That would buy us a new roof.'

'That would buy us a new house,' Zennor joked back.

'No, thank you.' Lamorna laughed. 'One failing house is quite enough to put up with. We don't want another.'

Zennor sighed and sipped her tea. 'I keep reading it and waiting for something I've missed to appear to me but no matter how many times I look at the page, nothing new ever does.'

Lamorna read the page out loud.

'*Restaurant heiress Rose Lander from Manhattan, New York City, New York. Daughter of restaurateur Arthur Lander, who founded the chain of eponymous restaurants across New York City. At age twenty-one, Rose married Edward Easton-Thorpe-Trelenna, of Trelenna House, Cornwall, England.*'

'It says so much but also so little,' Lamorna said, putting the book back down. 'Although now we know what Rose looks like.'

'But I want to know what *Grace* looks like,' Zennor bemoaned, feeling childish and wondering if it was the hormones. 'And she's not even mentioned. But in one of the articles I read online she was instrumental in setting up the Lander restaurants. *And* she was originally the cook *here*. And that's not mentioned at all.'

'I find that really intriguing,' Lamorna said, making her cup of tea and sitting down next to Zennor. 'I wonder if Grace hid her background. She rose through society enough that her daughter became an *heiress*. Maybe Rose and Edward met each other because of the shared Cornish connection?'

'Or maybe they met despite it.'

Lamorna laughed. 'Maybe we'll never know.'

'One thing is clear though: Grace's daughter, Rose, is one of our ancestors. Which means that *Grace* is one of our ancestors.' Zennor beamed. 'Grace's daughter married Edward Trelenna. I think that's incredible. The Gilded Age was the dawn of a new era if a servant could become rich and her daughter married off to landed gentry.'

'All those men from humble beginnings making bank and then sending their daughters off to re-populate Europe with new money,' Lamorna said in awe.

'And women making money. Grace was important too. Because she could cook, she was the one making bank, as you say.'

'But it looks as if her story has been downplayed. What was it Zach told me when I was researching Issey? The women sometimes just look as if they're bit parts to the men's stories. For the women it sometimes all boils down to three certificates: birth, marriage, death.'

'I think Zach might be right,' Zennor said glumly, glancing at the book. Her alarm sounded on her phone, making her jump. 'Oh god, I've got to go. It's my first scan.'

Lamorna's excited face looked hopeful. 'I've got a phone call scheduled but I will happily move it if you want someone to come with you?'

Ever since the dinner when she'd told her siblings about her pregnancy, she'd worried that maybe Lamorna didn't approve, that she was . . . upset at how Zennor's life was playing out. But looking at Lamorna, hearing the anticipation in her sister's voice, made her feel as if she was coming round to the idea now the initial shock of the situation had passed.

'Um . . . it's okay, because Merry already asked if he could come with me.'

'Merry?' Lamorna asked in surprise. 'Oh. Okay, then. That's fine.'

'You could come too?' Zennor offered.

'No, it's fine.' Lamorna bowed out gracefully. 'There'll probably be some rule about only one person being in the room at a time, and it won't go down well if Merry and I have to fight to the death just so one of us can be the winner. You both go and promise me you'll bring me one of those little black and white pictures home. I want to see my niece or nephew the moment you get back.'

'I promise.'

Merry and Zennor sat on plastic chairs in the waiting room watching other pregnant women being called in for scans.

'I told you we were too early.' Zennor's knee jostled up and down.

'Stop it. You're shaking the whole bank of chairs. And we're not too early. We're perfectly on time.'

Zennor's nerves were getting the better of her. 'What if the baby's not okay? What if—'

'You can stop *that* too,' Merry instructed. 'You can't fear the worst all the time.'

'I'm not,' Zennor said. 'I'm just worried. It's normal to be worried, right?'

Merry shrugged. 'I don't know. I guess so.'

'You're no help. I should have brought Lamorna.'

'Hey!' Merry made an offended face.

'I don't know what I'm doing. I don't know what's meant to feel normal. I've never done this before.'

'I don't know either. This is why we're here. You can ask all your questions in a few moments when—'

'Zennor Trelenna?' A smiling midwife in a blue uniform called from a doorway. She looked to be in her thirties, which felt oddly reassuring as she ushered Zennor and Merry into a small room with a clinical bed, computer and scanning equipment. She ran through a set of questions while Zennor settled herself back in the bed, lifting up her sweatshirt and inching down her chocolate-brown gym leggings as instructed.

'They're lovely maternity leggings, where'd you get those?' the midwife asked conversationally.

Zennor cringed. 'They're just my normal leggings. I haven't bought any maternity clothes yet.'

'She's just sort of stretching out the things she already owns,' Merry chipped in with a grin.

'You'll have to move on to his t-shirts as you get bigger then,' the midwife joked with Zennor.

'Over my dead body,' Merry said seriously, making the midwife do a surprised double take.

'Sorry. He's not the baby's father. He's my brother,' Zennor said, answering the question the midwife wasn't quite daring to ask. 'He's here for support.' Zennor glanced at Merry and made a face. 'Of sorts.'

Merry made a face back.

'Oh, I see,' the midwife said.

Zennor glanced at the midwife's name badge: Julie. Zennor didn't miss Julie's discreet look at Merry's ring finger and she definitely didn't miss the look of disappointment on Julie's face when she spotted the gold band.

'Alright, Zennor, are you ready to see your baby?'

'Yes, please,' Zennor said and automatically grabbed hold of Merry's hand for comfort. Merry leaned forward in the chair to see the screen. Zennor tipped her head to the side to do the same as Julie put cold gel on her tummy and moved the transducer around.

A whomping whooshing sound emanated from the machine on repeat and Zennor breathed in, in wonder. 'Is that . . . ?'

Julie was silent and then . . . 'That's baby's heartbeat. All sounds fine.'

'Oh, Merry,' Zennor exclaimed and then she stared at the screen as a black and white grainy image moved in and out of focus as Julie moved the wand and clicked the mouse to save images.

Over the next few minutes the midwife clicked and dragged, taking measurements while Zennor and Merry watched in amazement. On the screen was her baby. *Her baby.* Zennor couldn't quite believe it. That little black and white grainy object was her baby and she was growing it inside her.

'Does it look okay?' Zennor asked nervously.

'Everything looks lovely,' Julie replied calmly.

'Can you tell what it is?' Merry asked.

'I can,' Julie replied and looked at Zennor for permission. 'Would you like to know?'

'Oh . . .' Zennor said uncertainly. Up until this moment absolutely none of this had felt real. She'd been so concerned there might be something wrong with the baby that she hadn't thought much past today. 'I'm not sure.'

'Oh go on,' Merry burst out excitedly, eliciting a laugh from Julie.

'I didn't think you could tell until the second scan. How can you tell what it is so early?' Zennor asked.

'Experience,' Julie said, bringing a sense of calm to the room. She pointed at the screen in various places. 'We look at the angle of the spine and the angle of the nub in-between baby's legs. And, over twelve weeks, which you are . . . we can tell.'

Zennor hesitated. She didn't want to be told it was one thing only to be told at the next scan it was another, although she didn't mind what she had. Boy, girl, she just wanted them to be healthy. 'Have you ever been wrong?'

Julie smiled knowingly. 'Not yet.'

Zennor looked at Merry's face, full of excitement. His energy was infectious and Zennor laughed, squeezing Merry's hand tighter.

She nodded at Julie. 'Okay.'

'Congratulations,' Julie told Zennor. 'You're having a girl.'

Chapter 43

'I can't believe you cried,' Merry said an hour later as they were sitting in the café at the Lost Gardens of Heligan. Seeing as it was Monday, they'd decided to skive off for the rest of the day and treat themselves to an afternoon out. They were badly in need of one after the months of non-stop work at the house, and hadn't been to the gardens in years.

'You cried too,' Zennor countered.

Merry sat back, looking mortally wounded. 'No, I didn't.'

'Yes, you did. I saw your eyes go all wet.'

'You're having a baby *girl*,' Merry said. 'What's an uncle to do if not cry?'

'Would you have cried if Julie had said I was having a boy?'

'Who's Julie?'

'The hot midwife.'

'Oh, yeah probably,' Merry confessed with a slanted smile.

'I can't believe you didn't spot the midwife really fancied you.' Zennor knew this was going to be a dangerous conversation.

'No, she didn't,' Merry scoffed. But Zennor noticed he'd picked up his fork and was scraping around distractedly at his cake crumbs.

'I think she did. When I said you were my brother, the first thing she did was look at your ring finger.'

Merry glanced at his wedding ring but his face was unreadable. 'Oh.' A pause and then, 'You were very observant for someone worried and distracted by her first baby scan.'

'I *was* observant, wasn't I?' Zennor confirmed. She felt easier now, lighter. Thank god the scan was over and everything was alright. It didn't ease any of her other problems – namely that she was still putting off telling Reece he was going to be a father. That interaction would bring another level of predictable awfulness. And then there was Charlie, who had taken himself firmly out of her life. He smiled politely whenever he saw Zennor, but it was over between them. They were less than friends now. It was like nothing had ever happened between them. In a way she wished nothing *had*. Then they'd at least be on speaking terms and not . . . whatever this was. Or wasn't. She missed him – his conversation, his kisses, his arms around her.

'Just because I'm sad, single and lonely doesn't mean you have to be too,' she pointed out, immediately realising she'd said the wrong thing.

'I'm not single. I'm widowed. There's a massive difference.'

'Sorry,' Zennor said. 'I know but . . .'

'But what?' he asked, his gaze challenging.

Zennor decided to use the fact Merry wouldn't shout at a pregnant person in public. 'You can talk about it with me if you want.'

'But I don't want. Why do you want me to talk about my feelings?'

'Because—'

'Do you want me to tell you that I'm sad, that I miss Amy every single day? Because I do. Do you want me to tell you that in addition to crying about you having a girl, a few nights ago I also cried myself to sleep?'

'Oh, Merry.' Zennor reached out and took his hand across the table.

'I'm not telling you this to make you uncomfortable—'

'I'm not uncomfortable,' she insisted.

'Oh. Good.' He smiled, sadly. 'It's only been two years. I'm not ready to flirt with any hot midwives called Julie. I'm not ready to hook up with anyone. I'm just not ready.'

Zennor gave him a sympathetic smile.

'I know that losing Amy hurt everyone,' Merry continued. 'I know you looked at her as if she was another sister because you'd known her nearly ten years. You were a child when you met her, so I get it, I do. If you want to talk to me about her and all the things you used to talk about, you can.'

'Will it hurt you if we do?'

'Yes, of course,' Merry confessed. 'Lamorna said she was hurting too and I'm sorry because I know I'm being selfish, but Amy was my wife so it's my grief. And I'm sorry you've got your own grief, but I can't handle yours too. I can only handle *mine.* And if there's a manual on how to handle it then buy it for me. Because I'm obviously doing it all wrong.'

Merry looked pained, and Zennor wondered if she'd pushed too hard. 'I don't think you are, but I understand. Grief is personal and you're not ready to meet hot midwives. Or anyone. I get it. I won't mention it again.'

'I just need a bit more time.'

'I hear you,' Zennor said. She squeezed his hand. 'Shall we go for a walk around the gardens now?'

'Why not?' Merry rose, looked away for a moment and zipped up his coat, before looking back at her. 'I'm going first on the rope bridge though.' And racing away, he left his sister laughing at him as he ran.

Chapter 44

Zennor's phone call went unanswered yet again. This was the third time she'd tried to get hold of Reece over the last twenty-four hours, and it pained her that in leaving all these missed calls on his phone she might look a bit desperate. She sort of was, though. But not for the reasons he'd probably assume. She just needed to get this done, get him told and take it from there. It was frustrating and Zennor looked at her phone as she hung up, noticing the time and wondering, if she rang Veryan, if she'd decline to pick up too. She'd messaged an upbeat-sounding 'Can you call me when you get this?' to her sister when she'd come to terms with being pregnant. But there had been no call back.

Veryan was now officially the only member of the family who didn't know Zennor was pregnant. She wanted to share her news, share her joy, share the fact she was having a baby. She wanted to post her grainy black and white scan photo and show the world her little baby girl.

She stood in the kitchen and messaged her one more time. 'It's important, Veryan. Please call me.' If she didn't phone back today she'd just have to tell her in a text message. She switched tack and called her mum.

The dial tone was long and sporadic.

'Hello, darling. How are you? How's baby?'

'Hi, Mum. I'm okay. We're okay. Where are you now?'

'Egypt. We've just got back to the hotel. We've been to see the pyramids.'

'Sounds like you're having the best time. The pyramids are on my bucket list,' Zennor confessed, wondering if her bucket list was ever something she would actually complete now.

'You'll have to go with baby when they're older. Take the little one to see all the things the world has to offer.'

'I will. Mum, I wanted to tell you I'm having a girl,' she blurted.

'Oh, Zennor, that's lovely.' Jennifer, Zennor's mum, called out to her husband. 'Michael, Zennor's having a baby girl.'

She could hear her dad's excitement from the other end of the phoneline.

'I'll send you the scan picture. But I'm not putting it on the group chat yet because I can't get hold of Veryan and I don't want her to find out like that. I want to tell her over the phone. She still doesn't know she's going to be an aunty. Do you know where she is?'

'I thought she was in Dubai. Isn't she being put up in some gloriously outlandish hotels for free and just has to post pictures about them every now and again to justify her stay?'

'Dubai? That's only a few hours ahead. I'll try her again in a moment.' There was a brief pause, then Zennor asked the question she'd been dreading. 'Are you and Dad coming home for Christmas? It's less than a month away.'

Zennor wished her parents would be a bit more forthcoming with their plans. She wished Veryan would be too. Keeping cards close to their chests clearly ran in the family. Although it hadn't filtered down to Zennor, who was aware and proud of the fact she wore her heart on her sleeve.

'Yes, we are home for Christmas. We don't intend to be apart from you at such a special time,' Jennifer said as if Zennor was mad for suggesting such a thing.

'Well, I wasn't sure because . . . I just wasn't sure. It'll be so lovely with nearly everyone here. It's been years. The house looks so different, you won't recognise it. And we've dressed every room on the tour in a Victorian festive style. We've been making paper chains until our fingers are sore.'

'How is the Christmas market taking shape?' Jennifer asked. 'I'm very proud of you all, you know. I'm very proud of *you*, Zennor.'

Zennor blushed. 'Oh well . . . had to be done,' she said self-deprecatingly.

'Yes, I know. You're very clever. Your father and I just didn't have it in us. Wouldn't even have occurred to us to do all that. But you kids . . . Well done, all round. We'll try to help as much as we can when we're home, but we won't interfere if you don't want us to. The three of you clearly know what you're doing and we don't want to rock the boat.'

Zennor sighed happily, looking out of the kitchen window towards the growing vegetable patch. 'We're sort of learning on the job to be honest.'

'Best way,' Jennifer comforted and even though the silence stretched, Zennor felt closer to her mum than she had in a while, almost like she was in the next room. 'Sorry, darling, I've got to go. We've got a dinner reservation and I need to shower this dust off me. I'll see if I can get hold of Veryan too, nudge her in your direction.'

'Thanks, Mum. Love you. Love to Dad.'

'We love you too.'

'Love you!' her dad called out.

When Zennor had hung up, she tried Veryan one more time and when there was no answer, in pure frustration she made a decision.

Bringing up her Instagram account, she posted the picture of her baby scan and captioned it: *A new arrival at Trelenna House next summer. I'm going to be a mum!*

And then one by one all her friends started excitedly texting, reacting and ringing her.

Chapter 45

A week later the Christmas Fayre was busier than the family had expected, with entry tickets to the decorated rooms and a festive children's trail of things to spot inside the house being more popular than they could have hoped.

'I was worried it wouldn't be enough to lure them,' Merry confessed as he met Zennor coming from the opposite direction on the first-floor landing. 'I was just so worried we'd be outgunned by all the stuff National Trust has going on and the light trail at Heligan.'

'I think people are doing a load of festive things, not just choosing one. Someone buying a sausage roll from Kayleigh told her this was their *third* Christmas market in as many weeks. They started back mid-November,' Zennor said.

'One's enough for me. Have you seen Lamorna?'

'She's in the gardens. Someone in the children's play area fell over and she's gone out with the first-aid kit.'

'I'll await the impending lawsuit.'

Zennor tutted at him. 'It's just a child with a cut knee. I'm pretty sure we won't need to inform the insurers. It's my turn to stand guard in the dining room and keep the fire going, so I must dash down there. Where are you next?'

Merry looked at his time sheet, showing the locations of everyone working that day. 'Entry hall for the next hour. Welcoming committee. Zach's just taken my place in Veryan's bedroom. I've had to stop two people touching the Rutherford portrait. Why do people feel the need to touch? Look with your eyes. Not with your hands. Baffling. Do you think there might be a bit of time to sneak into the fayre so I can buy you all some presents?'

'You're going to buy all our gifts from our *own* Christmas Fayre?'

'Yeah?' Merry said uncertainly. 'Is that not alright?'

Zennor rolled her eyes. 'Bit lazy.'

'Shopping local, I thought,' Merry reasoned.

'Shopping *very* local,' Zennor said, laughing to herself.

'You handpicked all the suppliers in there so it'll be nice gifts under the tree for you.'

'Yes, yes,' she said, still laughing at her brother. He really could be quite clueless sometimes. 'See you later.'

Zennor made her way down to the dining room, greeting one of her many catering college friends who were happy to be paid for a couple of hours' work in-between their various other jobs.

'How's it been?' Zennor asked her friend Nicole.

'Fine. No one's tried to nick anything but I'm no good at keeping this fire going. I think I've let it go down to embers and the new log won't light. Do you need me anywhere else?'

'I think Kayleigh might like a hand serving hot drinks? Maybe clearing some of the tables if the rubbish is building up?'

'I'm on it,' Nicole said. 'Catch you later.'

This was all going so much better than she'd envisioned. Actually, she hadn't envisioned anything much except perhaps a trickle of customers. She knew Christmas Fayres were big business, she'd just not anticipated so many regulars she recognised from the summer would be happy touring Trelenna House again now it was dressed for Christmas.

On the long dining table was the family's china and best crystal that hardly ever came out of the cupboard, showing places set for twenty. Zennor had painstakingly copied out a Victorian Christmas Day menu on thick white card in her best calligraphy-style handwriting and propped it up so guests could have a feel for what Christmas food at Trelenna might have looked like in that period.

She bent to start rebuilding the fire from scratch, stacking the kindling and a firelighter. Then when it had caught, she put another log on, watching it crackle and spit.

'That's better.' She stood over it, warming her fingers.

'Hi,' a voice came from behind her. 'Do you have a minute?'

She turned to see Reece.

'Oh,' she said in surprise. He hadn't returned any of her calls and now he was here. She knew she needed to talk to him but not here, not now. Not like this. She hadn't known how she was going to feel seeing him again, but the main feeling she was fighting off was confusion. Why had he just turned up?

'I can't talk in here,' she said quietly, her eyes darting to a group of guests who'd wandered in, admiring the high ceilings, the handcrafted garlands Lamorna had made from foliage on the estate, the poinsettia displays that ran the length of the table. In the space towards the window, far away from the fireplace, was one of Merry's historically accurate and intricately dressed twelve-foot trees. This one was lit with electric Victorian-style candles casting an authentic flickering glow to the room. 'But in an hour I'll be in the Christmas Fayre serving on our food stand. Wait for me there?' She could hear the pleading in her voice.

Reece looked solemn. He nodded. 'Yeah, okay.' He turned and left but not without glancing quickly at her stomach, well hidden beneath her new thick maternity gilet.

So he knew, then. Perhaps that Instagram post had worked better than she could have imagined. Fixing a smile on to her face, she greeted the next set of guests as they worked their way slowly round the room, stopping to ask Zennor questions about the house and family history. This was the bit Zennor had been dreading – family history wasn't really her forte. Lamorna had coached her with some snippets, and a list of important dates and various names was folded in her pocket, but it felt unprofessional to hook it out and read from it, although when they asked about Victorian Christmases at Trelenna House she didn't need the notes.

She talked about the food that would have been eaten and they'd all done a bit of research about Victorian country house traditions: church in the morning, followed by gifts and games. Not too different from today, Zennor reasoned. She talked more about the Christmas lunch of turkey or goose, sometimes both, with roast hams and beef often on the Victorian Christmas table in a house such as this. She explained exactly what oyster soup and figgy pudding were and that at Trelenna there were three family members living here who would have enjoyed Christmas dinner in this room: Herbert, Georgiana and their only son, Laurie Trelenna. That, for now, appeased the guests but Zennor knew they'd be given much better information if Lamorna was here instead.

Was it wrong that Zennor's interest in her family's history was only really piqued by Grace and not by anyone else on the family tree? As the guests moved through and out into the hall, Zennor wondered where Grace sat on the tree. Was it possible that she herself was descended from Grace by way of Rose? Only if Rose had had children, she guessed. Zennor would have liked to know. But there was still the second day of the Christmas Fayre to go, and in a few moments she had to find Reece and have a very awkward conversation. Zennor felt this year had just been one long string of awkward conversations. And now this baby was zapping all her energy and there was Christmas still to come and presents to source and the family Christmas food to buy and . . . so many things were taking up her time and resources.

Grace had been benched, for now.

◆ ◆ ◆

The ballroom offered no place for a quiet conversation, so when Zennor found Reece nursing a coffee by himself at one of the small tables put up in the corner of the orangery, away from the Christmas Fayre stands, Zennor gestured for him to follow her.

'Shall we go for a walk?' she asked, and without waiting for an answer Zennor opened the French doors and stepped out on to the terrace, into the biting cold.

He didn't speak but he looked glum and Zennor realised that she hardly knew this man. They'd met at a Cornish vineyard event and dated for a few weeks. She'd liked him and he seemed to like her. She'd enjoyed the dates they'd been on, had felt they'd had shared interests, loved how knowledgeable he'd been about wine and had sensed a fellow foodie. Sleeping with him had been spur of the moment. She just hadn't been clever enough to realise it was a one-and-done deal for him. And, as she zipped her gilet higher over her not-very-present bump, she knew the repercussions of that night were going to last forever.

'It's going to get dark soon,' Reece observed, probably to fill the silence.

Zennor nodded. 'It's dark by five, now. But we've got some stringed white lights that will come on automatically in the garden soon. We put them in especially for our Christmas tours.' She could hear herself rambling. They stopped round the side entrance to the kitchen before the vegetable garden.

'I saw your Instagram post,' he said.

Zennor crossed her arms over her chest. 'But not my three missed calls and messages asking you to ring me?'

He looked taken aback by her frankness. 'Yeah, I saw those too,' he said. At least he was being honest.

'Why didn't you ring me then?'

'I . . .' He exhaled loudly. 'I don't know. I didn't think it would be about . . .' He glanced at her stomach and trailed off. 'Is the baby mine? Is that what the calls were for?'

Oh, she could have *screamed.* What kind of woman did he think she was? 'Yes, Reece,' she said through gritted teeth. 'The baby is yours but you're more than welcome to do a paternity test at some point if you like.'

'Christ. I . . . I wasn't even thinking about . . .' He recovered himself. 'And you're keeping it?'

'Yes.' Her voice was tight now. 'Yes, I'm keeping it. Yes, it's yours. It's a girl, by the way. I'm having a girl.'

He looked shocked, then smiled and then looked into the distance. 'Okay,' was his non-committal response.

Zennor had run this all through in her head, so she carried on. 'I don't expect anything of you—'

'You'll expect money though, right?' he cut in.

His words threw her immediately off course and her mouth gaped open, but no words came.

'I don't know how it works,' she said when she'd gulped down enough oxygen to continue functioning. 'I haven't thought that far. But here's the thing. You're the father but only if you want to be. I think it would be a shame for the baby not to know her father. But I don't expect anything of you. I think you should be involved but it doesn't have to be . . . daily.'

If she never had to see him again it would be a blessing, but the world didn't work like that. The world was complicated, messy. She'd made her life difficult and now she was reaping what she'd sown.

'I see,' he said. 'Do you have another copy of the scan picture?'

'Just the one, sorry.'

'Okay, I'll try to download that one you put on Instagram.'

She felt sorry for *him* now. How had he done this? 'I'll see if I can make a copy. I think Zach's got a scanning app.'

'Who's Zach?' he asked quickly.

'My sister's boyfriend.'

'Oh. Okay.'

What was this? What was he feeling?

'Zennor, I saw your post yesterday and I've been dwelling on it all night and all day today. I assumed you were ringing because the baby was . . . is . . . mine. I know I went quiet after we . . .' He shrugged. 'But I'm here now. If you want me.'

'If I want you?' she queried, not quite understanding. 'You mean . . . No, sorry, what do you mean?'

'I think, if the baby is mine—'

'She is,' Zennor cut in. 'I don't sleep around. You were the only person I'd slept with in a *year.*'

His eyebrows shot up as if that was a foreign concept to him.

'Okay,' he said. 'Then, I mean it. I've given it some thought. I don't think it would be a good idea for our child to grow up without both parents if we can help it. And we can help it. You and I, we should give it another shot. We should try to be together. I think we can make it work because I think we don't really have much choice.'

'Oh,' Zennor said. 'Oh . . . I . . . I don't know. I wasn't expecting you to say that.'

He smiled – that devastating smile that had got her into bed in the first place. 'I'll be different. This baby changes everything. We're going to be a family. Can I?' he asked, his hand outstretched towards her tummy.

She nodded, watching him as he rested his hand on her stomach in awe, although there was not a lot to feel through the padding of her gilet.

'My baby is in there,' he said.

A whole mix of emotions she couldn't fathom ran through her. 'She is.'

'Do you have any names yet?'

'I hadn't got that far.'

'Maybe we can think of some names together? See what we like?'

She smiled. 'I'd like that.' He wanted to be a part of the baby's life from the start. She couldn't have hoped for more, so why did it all feel so strange? He'd totally surprised her.

'Zennor, I'm so sorry about what I did to you.'

'It's okay,' she said automatically. Although it wasn't. She just didn't want to fight.

'Can you forgive me?'

She nodded slowly. She'd have to forgive him if they were going to move on with their lives. Even if they weren't together, they were going to be parents.

His eyes searched hers and she looked back into his. She just wanted everything to be easy. Zennor wondered if he was about to kiss her. And if he did, was she about to let him? She didn't know what her reaction was going to be. But as Reece moved closer to her, letting his lips brush hers gently, she made the decision to let him. She wasn't sure what she felt while he kissed her, but she kissed him back as if on autopilot, going through the motions, before settling in, allowing herself to enjoy it, to feel desire again and to feel *desired*. If they did this, if they were together, then this little baby would have two parents who were trying to be together. That was better than two parents who'd never tried at all. At least trying . . . that had to be better. And given everything seemed to be so hard at the moment, she just wanted *something* to be easy.

Chapter 46

On Monday morning, Zennor was in the kitchen as usual, enjoying the much-needed quiet now the Christmas Fayre weekend was over. Until the school Christmas holidays began, midweek trade was limited. Although they had a Women's Institute group coming in for a special Christmas lunch, so Zennor needed to nudge them on their pre-order form at some point today. Merry was doing the rounds of the house, filling up the Christmas tree buckets with water, and Lamorna was hoovering with a special focus on hunting down every last dropped pine needle. At least being pregnant got Zennor off heavy cleaning duties. Light dusting anything eye level was the absolute maximum of what her siblings would allow her to do now. Bliss. She had other things to do anyway and was sitting at the table, making plans for the family's Christmas dinner.

Zennor felt well and truly in the Victorian Christmas spirit now and put a playlist on. The soundtrack to *The Muppet Christmas Carol* resounded around the kitchen in all its classic and whimsical glory. She moved along to the joyful sound of the Ghost of Christmas Present's upbeat lyrics while reading through Eliza Acton's recipe for hot punch dessert sauce, which was so alcoholic Zennor wouldn't be able to have any. The recipe called for rum, brandy and sherry and someone had scribbled the quantities out and had upped them considerably in pencil, which made Zennor laugh. She'd overlooked this book for so long.

Revelling in the inspiration, she scribbled down thoughts for the most sumptuous and traditional feast she could imagine, featuring her own take on prawn cocktail and a smoked salmon platter to start, followed by every single trimming she could think of to accompany the roast turkey. She didn't want to reinvent the wheel, but she did want to have fun with the menu. She chewed on the end of her pen, wondering if she should also cook a goose. Grace probably used to roast one, if not two, in that old range, and she was just wondering how much would be too much when a knock sounded and the back kitchen door creaked ajar.

Charlie. Her heartbeat was suddenly keeping double time. He still had the same effect on her now as he had all those months ago when she'd first met him.

'Hi,' she said earnestly. 'How are you?'

He nodded stiffly. 'Yeah. Fine. How are you?'

'I'm good.'

'How's the baby?' Charlie asked. Whenever anyone asked that their eyes were always drawn to her stomach.

'She's fine too.'

'She?' Charlie asked softly, entering the room fully. 'You're having a girl?'

'I am. Another little Zennor running around the house.'

'Lucky house,' he commented and then glanced away. 'Shall I close the door? Keep the cold out?'

'Yes, please.' She took it as a good sign. He wanted to talk to her. It was the first time in a long time she'd seen him properly. 'Do you want a cup of tea? Some cake?'

'Tea would be lovely. No thanks to cake, though.'

She felt a fluttering in her stomach at his presence. It wasn't the baby. It was him doing this to her. She didn't want to scare him away but she did want to know why he suddenly wanted to be near her when before he'd been so studiously avoiding her.

'The Christmas Fayre looked like it was a success. Busy.'

She turned around from making tea. 'Were you there? I didn't see you.'

'Yeah. Saturday. My mum came down for the weekend. She wanted to see where I'd been working.'

'That's lovely. You brought her to Trelenna. What did she think?'

'She fell in love with the house.'

'I'm pleased. The Christmas decorations probably help,' Zennor said. 'What did she think of your efforts in the garden? I hope she's as proud of you as I am.'

He tilted his head to the side and gave her a curious look but chose not to address what she'd just said. 'I suppose it's hard to measure real progress in December, other than the evergreens are looking healthy at this time of year and the kitchen garden has a good selection of kale, Brussels, cabbage and parsnips. I've got some polytunnels protecting the crop now.'

'I've seen. Clever.'

'Seeing as the greenhouse is missing nearly every single pane of glass, it's a bit unusable for much at the moment.'

'It's on the list, don't worry,' Zennor said. 'And all those veggies are going to come in very handy for Christmas dinner. Where will you be at Christmas?' She handed him a mug of tea and automatically went to cut a slice of sticky ginger cake he'd already refused. She didn't care. She just wanted to keep him here as long as possible.

'I'm not sure where I'll be,' he said.

'Will you be with your mum?'

He shook his head. 'No, that's why she came down to see me, to spend some festive time together. They're going to Thailand on Christmas Eve.'

'And you're not invited?' Zennor asked, appalled.

He shrugged.

'What about your dad?'

'I'm not sure yet. Waiting to hear back.'

'Oh, Charlie,' she said mournfully. 'Well . . . I'm planning the world's largest Christmas dinner at the world's largest dining table so . . . please come.'

His eyebrows raised but he didn't speak.

'I can't see you on your own. It would kill me to think you're on your own at Christmas.'

He shook his head. 'I'll find something to do. And that's not why I came in, to beg an invite to gatecrash your Christmas.'

She stepped forward. 'You're not begging, I'm asking you. I'm asking you to join us for Christmas. It'll be fun. It'll be carnage, actually. There's always games. I'm notorious for losing at charades. So you could help me and I might even win for once. We'll all be here, other than Veryan, we assume. My mum and dad will be back for the first time in months and—'

'Thanks,' he cut in. 'Can I think about it?'

Immediately deflated she replied, 'Of course.'

He stood looking at her for a moment and she looked back at him, and then it was as if he'd remembered why he was here. 'Um . . . after tomorrow I'm not going to be here for the rest of the week.'

'Oh,' she said sadly. 'Why's that?'

'I've got a few days' temporary work with the Carr-Lyons at Pencallick House. It's just seasonal. I'm on car park duty for their Christmas event but I need the extra money. So I just jumped in here to let you know I'm going to do all my hours for the week today and tomorrow. If that's okay?'

'Of course, that's fine.'

'The agency will need you to authorise my time sheet, so I didn't want you to think I was cheating you out of money and not turning up.'

'I would never think that about you. I haven't seen you much anyway recently,' she hinted.

'Great,' he said, ignoring her point. 'I wanted to talk to you about something else too.'

She looked at him hopefully although she didn't know what she hoped he'd say. She wanted to be his friend, if he'd let her. Perhaps this was just the start of rebuilding that friendship.

'After Christmas I thought we'd bring the goats in to tackle the brambles before spring comes. It'll be quieter and less chance of tourists getting nibbled by hungry goats if we do it on days you're closed.'

'Goats. Yes. Fine,' she said, heart sinking. 'Good idea.'

He put his mug of tea down, undrunk. 'I'd best get back to it.'

'Take the tea with you,' Zennor said desperately. 'And the cake. Look, I'll wrap it.'

'Uh, okay, thanks.'

'My pleasure.'

'I'll bring the mug back when I leave this afternoon.'

'Why don't you pop in for lunch with me? Bring it back then?' she asked hopefully.

He looked away, swallowed. 'No, I won't. I'm just going to keep going all day. Get my hours in.'

Zennor nodded and tried to put a bright expression on her face.

'I'll see you when I see you, then,' he said, doing his best not to look at her.

'See you when I see you,' she repeated with false enthusiasm, as behind her eyes she felt tears forming.

She shouldn't feel this way. She and Reece were going to try to have a relationship together. They were doing it for the baby.

But she was doing it for herself too. He'd had his momentary lapse of judgement, he said. He wanted to make it work. This should be everything Zennor wanted. They were going to be a family. So why, when she'd said goodbye to Charlie just now, had her heart hurt so, so much?

Chapter 47

Zach joined Zennor on the sofa in the sitting room one evening later that week while he waited for Lamorna. Zennor had the book with Rose Lander's picture open over one knee and on the other was her scan picture.

'She has kind eyes,' he said.

'Who? The baby or Rose Lander?'

'Both.' Zach grinned. 'The baby more so, obviously.'

'Obviously,' Zennor agreed.

'Don't tell me you're trying to find a family resemblance between Rose and your baby scan.'

'Of course not. Although now you mention it.' She laughed. 'I've just been thinking about her. She fascinates me. American. Monied. We probably owe her our deepest gratitude for bringing electric lighting and central heating, and I reckon it was her who installed the en-suites.'

'Most probably. It would have been quite the financial outlay. And she did it with Grace's restaurant money too, I'd imagine.'

'I think that's pretty cool,' Zennor said, proud of Grace.

'Have you worked out who Rose is to you yet?' Zach asked.

Zennor screwed up her face, thoughtfully. 'No. I was going to draw it all out, but I had arrows going all over the page of my mocked-up family tree and I got confused and gave up.'

'May I?' he asked, taking her notepad from the table in front of her.

'Please,' she encouraged.

Near the bottom of the page, he wrote *Zennor* and then above that an arrow extending up from her name where he wrote *Michael,* Zennor's dad. Above him he wrote Zennor's grandfather *Richard* and then above that, *Antony Trelenna.*

Next to Antony he wrote the name *Issey Trelenna*, which made both of them smile. Issey was their aunt many times back, but she belonged on the tree too.

Next Zach extended an arrow up from Antony and Issey Trelenna and left the space for their parents blank, current unknowns. Then in the space above *that* one he wrote *Rose Lander and Edward Trelenna.* 'We know from records that Edward was an only child, so it stands to reason that . . .' But he didn't finish his sentence.

Zennor felt immediate chills shoot across her arms. Zach held the page out to her and she took in all the names in a row of her ancestors while she worked it out.

Rose Lander & Edward Trelenna

Antony Trelenna and Issey Trelenna

Richard Trelenna

Michael Trelenna

Zennor

'Rose Lander is Antony and Issey Trelenna's grandmother?' Zennor asked.

'And so Grace must be' – Zach extended the arrow up from Rose and wrote in Grace's name at the top – 'your great-great-great-great-grandmother.'

Zennor put her hand over her mouth, smothering her excitement, but it burst from her regardless and she laughed happily. She'd not been able to work out where they sat in relation to her but to hear that Grace was her four-times-great-grandmother, it stirred emotions. She'd followed as much of her journey as she could. From the kitchen at Trelenna to Fifth Avenue, New York. From Grace's departure from here, for some reason Zennor couldn't fathom, to her rise to riches. And then she'd found Grace's daughter Rose in the pages of the book on her lap, marrying into the very family her mother Grace and her father Arthur had once worked for. 'Oh no, why am I crying? Being pregnant makes me so emotional.'

'You're crying because she did so well and it's a happy ending,' Zach said. 'And that's always worth a cry.'

'Is it a happy ending? I still don't know what happened to Grace. But I do love that she's Issey's great-grandmother – two women generations apart who both left Cornwall to find adventure and make something of themselves.'

'Where's Lamorna? You've got to show her this. She'd love to see the connection.'

'I will,' Zennor confirmed. 'I so desperately want to know what happened to Grace, though. Her daughter marries a Trelenna and then . . . nothing.'

Zach looked thoughtfully down at the hand-drawn family tree he'd made as if it held secret answers. 'Sorry, that's the best I've got for you today.' He handed her the notebook and Zennor looked at it with happiness in her soul. Grace and Rose were part of her family. She might not have inherited Grace's adventurous spirit, but maybe that was where the cooking gene came from? She smiled to herself, wanting to share the news with Lamorna, with Merry, and with Charlie. He'd been part of this journey too. Until he wasn't. But she wouldn't see him until next week. She wondered if she messaged him if that might seem a bit out of the blue? She glanced at the scan picture containing another man's baby. No, maybe she should just let her friendship with Charlie be on his terms.

'Oh, while I've got you, can you do me a favour and scan something with that app you've got? I'm too tight to buy it for the only thing I'll ever need to scan in my life,' Zennor said dryly.

'Course. The picture of Rose?'

'The picture of the baby, please. I've got to send it to Reece. He wants a proper copy.'

'Sure.' Zach got to work scanning it and then handed it back to her. Her phone dinged with the copy seconds later.

'How's it going with him? Lamorna tells me it's back on again.'

'Yeah,' she said, giving nothing away. 'I think it is.'

Zach watched her, waiting for more.

'I feel strange about it all,' she confessed. 'Has Lamorna told you that too?'

'She has. Strange how, though?'

'It should be everything, shouldn't it? It should be everything I want – Reece wanting to be with me so we can be a family. On paper it sounds like the most sensible plan for everyone. But somehow . . .'

'It feels really wrong?'

Zennor nodded. 'And I don't know why.'

'Because you don't love him?' Zach pointed out simply.

Zennor took a deep breath. 'I know. But I think I could.'

'Does he love you?'

She shook her head. 'I doubt it. This isn't about being in love now, though. It's about the *possibility* of love forming, one day. We have to try, don't we? We're going to have a baby together.'

'You might be asking the wrong person,' Zach admitted. 'I know this from experience, though: you can't force love to come. You can't force it to come because you *want* it to. And when you do fall in love, it should be . . .' He thought for a word. 'It should be the most glorious feeling ever. Lamorna swept me away like a wave. I just couldn't stop myself falling in love with your sister.'

Zennor smiled. There were those tears in her eyes again.

'I would love to see that for you. I know your sister would too. And, I hope I'm not speaking out of turn, but Reece . . . he treated you so badly and I worry that he'll do it again when things get hard. He did it before when things weren't even remotely complicated,' Zach continued gently. 'I had a bit of a shitty relationship before your sister came along. And I broke up with my ex knowing the alternative was to be alone for a while. Sometimes being alone isn't a bad thing. It's better to be alone than be with the wrong person.'

Now she really *was* crying.

Zach pulled her in for a hug. 'Oh, Zennor I'm so sorry, I didn't mean to make you cry. God, Lamorna's going to kill me.'

Zennor laughed at that. 'You didn't make me cry. You made me think. Though my gut instinct is to try with Reece, to find out for myself. But if it's not working between us . . .'

'Nothing ventured, nothing gained?'

'Something like that,' she said.

'I'm here if you need me or if you just want to sound off. And whatever you decide going forward, I'll respect your decision,' Zach said. 'So you don't need to worry about me judging you.'

'Will Lamorna respect my decision?'

'Absolutely not,' Zach joked. 'She is going to be on at you about this every five minutes until you change your mind. But you know she just wants you to be happy.'

Zennor gave a tearful laugh. 'I'll consider myself warned.'

'Are you going to be okay?' he asked softly.

'Yeah.' Zennor smiled wanly. 'I will be. I just need to think.'

Zach gave her a sad smile and stood up, ready to go and find Lamorna. 'I'll leave you to your thoughts, then. Oh . . . and . . . I know I've just made you cry so is now a terrible time to ask for a favour . . .'

'Go for it,' Zennor offered, wiping her tears away.

'Would you mind if I joined you all for Christmas dinner?'

'Of *course* you can – we'd be disappointed if you weren't with us. Where are your dad and sister?'

'My sister's boyfriend is hosting with his family this year and my dad's going along to enjoy the fun. I was invited too but I really want to spend Christmas with Lamorna. It'll be our first one so . . .' He looked shy.

'Absolutely you can come. You'll meet our parents for the first time too!'

'I know. I'm petrified about that.'

'Oh, don't be. I've invited Charlie so perhaps he can take the edge off, although I'm not sure if he's going to come or not.'

'Charlie?' Zach asked. 'Was that a slip of the tongue? Do you mean Reece?'

Zennor sat upright a bit. 'No. I'm not sure if I want to invite Reece for Christmas. Feels a bit soon. A bit odd? I'll think about it. But Charlie's on his own so . . .'

'Oh, that's sad. Well, I like Charlie. And yes, maybe I can hide behind him when meeting your parents. He's got no skin in the game after all, now you two are just friends.'

'Yes.' Zennor nodded. 'Charlie is just my friend.' She looked down at the picture of her scan, the picture of her and Reece's baby, and said under her breath, 'Because he can't be anything else.'

Chapter 48

The doorbell resonated through the ground floor on Christmas Eve while Zennor was in the kitchen with Merry, working out her turkey timings on a notepad. The bell was a sound Zennor wasn't too used to hearing these days. Friends and family usually used the back door into the kitchen, and when they ran tours, the front door was always open, ready to welcome guests into their home.

'Courier?' Merry suggested, getting himself in a bother scraping price tags off the back of his gifts. 'Better get it in case it's a last-minute present for someone.'

'The pregnant woman will get up and go then, yes?' Zennor asked, rising.

'Yeah, thanks,' he replied distractedly, attacking a persistent label with his nail. 'Are you going to roll that line out every time the bell sounds from now until summer?'

'Yes, I rather thought I would,' Zennor called airily as she went up the stone steps and into the entrance hall. Pulling open the heavy front door she stood back, ready to accept a parcel, only to find Reece with a wide smile on his face. *That* smile. Her heart should have lifted – she remembered it distinctly from their second date – but it sank the other way.

'Hi,' he said, well-dressed as usual in an evening suit and tie.

'You look nice,' she said, accepting the kiss he offered on her cheek. 'Going somewhere glamorous?'

'Cocktail party at a friend's. Can I come in?'

'Of course.'

If this was supposed to be so right, why did it still feel so weird? They'd seen each other a few times since the heart-to-heart at the Christmas event. He'd tried so hard, cooking her dinner in his flat. The flat where they'd both thrown responsible behaviour to the wind and got themselves in this mess. This time she hadn't slept with him though, and he hadn't made any of his previous moves. And this had just perplexed her even more. Did he not fancy her anymore? Was he as confused as she was? Was he being a gentleman *now* when it was a bit too late for that? And if he was, was it better late than never? She'd tried to push aside Zach's words, and her own feelings. But she felt as lost as ever.

'I wanted to give you your Christmas present,' he said.

'Oh, that's so kind. I . . . um . . . haven't . . .'

'You haven't got me anything?' He chuckled. 'It's okay, Zennor, I've got a lot of making up to do, so I wasn't expecting anything.'

'I'm sorry,' she said genuinely.

She showed him into the sitting room and they sat on the sofa. He gave her a gift bag emblazoned with the name of a local jeweller.

'Open it now,' he said. 'I want to see if you like it.'

She did, opening the heavy-lidded, hinged box, revealing a diamond tennis bracelet with matching earrings. 'Oh, Reece,' she breathed, entranced by the way the reflection of the flames in the fire lit up the pieces in all their glory. Then she found herself saying, 'I can't accept these.'

He looked surprised. 'Of course you can. You deserve it.'

'It's too much.'

'It's not. Not by a long shot. I can afford it. I want you to have the best. If you and I are going to do this . . . if we're going to try to make this work, you'd better get used to expensive gifts for you and everything money can buy for our daughter.'

'Oh my word,' she said, blinking at him slowly. 'You really mean it?'

'I do, and I've been thinking . . . I'll sell my flat and buy us a house, somewhere our baby can grow up. Where we can all be together.' There was a beat, and then he asked, 'Move in with me?'

She was too astonished to speak. 'Oh,' she said slowly. A heavy pressure arrived in her chest from out of nowhere. Leaving Trelenna? Moving in with him? Everything felt wrong. So wrong. Her knee started jerking up and down nervously. Everything was happening too fast.

'Zennor?' he prompted.

'I don't know,' she said.

'You don't *know?* I thought you'd be delighted.'

'I thought I'd be delighted too,' she whispered so quietly he asked her to repeat herself.

'Have you been seeing anyone, after me?' she startled him by asking.

He looked trapped. It was a question she'd never even considered. Until now.

'I was. But I'm not now. I called it off so I could focus on you. Focus on our baby. On us.'

'Okay,' she said processing this, her leg still jiggling. But she didn't know how to process it.

She looked at the present in her hands. She didn't want expensive gifts. She just wanted to be loved, and to love in return, for her daughter to have parents who loved each other, not merely tolerated each other.

'Do you love me?' she asked.

That trapped look again.

'Zennor,' he said in a tone she couldn't place. A warning tone?

'Be honest,' she pleaded. 'Do you love me?'

He exhaled.

'Say it,' she asked.

He shook his head. A sad expression on his face. 'No. Do you love me?'

'I want to,' she said quietly, tears back in her eyes.

'I want to love you too,' he replied.

'But you don't.'

He closed his eyes. 'But you don't love me either.'

'This is quite a situation,' she conceded.

He put his head back against the sofa cushion and looked up at the intricate plasterwork on the ceiling. He looked as deflated as she felt. 'Is it a situation?' he asked. 'Or is it really simple? We try *really hard* to love each other.'

Zach's words filled her head. *You can't force love to come because you* want *it to.*

'For our baby,' Reece said. 'We try really hard.' He looked at her hopefully.

She thought. This was her future, her daughter's future. 'Can I make another suggestion?' Zennor asked. She couldn't believe she was going to ask Reece the exact same question she'd asked Charlie all those weeks ago. 'Can we . . . can we just be friends?'

His eyebrows lifted in surprise.

'I think we might be better at it,' Zennor finished nervously.

'You want to just be friends?' he asked disbelievingly. 'Who raise a child together?'

She nodded. 'It's unconventional. But it feels like the right thing to do. Trying to be together, just for the sake of our baby . . . while it *should* be the right thing, feels wrong to me. Doesn't it feel like the wrong thing for you too?'

He sighed. 'A bit. I suppose.'

'We'll end up hating each other. I can feel it. And if you don't love me and if you're waiting for love to happen, and it doesn't . . . Then if you meet someone you *do* fall in love with and you're stuck with me . . . a whole world of hurt is going to destroy you, me *and* our daughter. Somewhere down the line. And you and I, we'll have wasted our lives living a lie. This way . . . it feels right.'

He didn't speak. He was watching her sadly. 'You might be right. And what if we don't meet anyone we want to be with?'

'Then so be it. But at least you and I will be friends, and our daughter will have parents who don't *love* each other, but who don't *hate* each other. We might actually be quite good parents if we're not trying to force love into the equation.'

'You really want that?'

'Yes,' she said. 'I think it's the only solution that makes sense.'

He was silent.

'What do you think?' she prompted.

He exhaled air out of his cheeks. 'I suppose it seems sensible.'

'I do too.'

'I want to do this right. And if this is the way . . . then okay. Let's do it.'

Pure relief fell over her.

'Can I tell you something then, as a friend?' Reece asked.

'Please,' she invited.

'Zennor, I'm shit-scared of being a father.'

'I'm shit-scared too. But at least now we're doing it together.'

'But apart,' he said with a sad smile. 'Together but apart. Friends who parent.'

'Friends who parent.'

'Okay,' he said, with a bit more confidence than before. 'Let's give it a try. Can I hug you? Or can you hug me and tell me it's all going to be okay?'

She laughed. 'Reece, it's all going to be okay.' She held him, not quite sure who was comforting who. Her world felt lighter, pressure lifting from her shoulders, as if her future, with Reece as a friend, didn't look quite so bleak and joyless now. It would be complicated and strange, but it would be more manageable than the alternative.

'What do we do now?' he asked, pulling back.

'You go and have your Christmas and I'll have mine and we'll talk after. I'll keep you updated with what's happening and when the next appointment is, if you want to come?'

'Okay,' he said, his spirits clearly lifting. 'And then what?'

'And then . . .' she said, laughing. 'And then . . . we're winging it because I've got *absolutely no idea*.'

Chapter 49

Later that evening the string festoon lights came on automatically in the garden, much to Lamorna's angst about the electricity bill – as darkness descended on the grounds of Trelenna House. Zennor loved looking out of the windows and seeing the garden lit up, the branches bare, the canes staked among the rose bushes, the poly-tunnels protecting future harvests.

Now the festive tours were over, the house was just theirs again for a while. January would involve a deep clean and the occasional weekend opening, including plans for a special ticketed Burns Night supper she was devising to bolster what was probably going to be a quiet January turnover-wise. And then would come a Valentine's supper, followed by the February half-term holidays, and before she knew it, the year would fill with tours and events again.

She'd put on a Spotify playlist in the dining room and was busy getting ahead for the big day, laying the table for tomorrow, setting out places for all her family – minus Veryan, who she still hadn't heard back from. Spaces were set for Zach and Charlie. She had no idea if Charlie was joining them, since he was sticking very steadily to his new regime of being uncommunicative with her.

With King's College Choir singing carols beautifully from the mini speaker on the side and the fire crackling away in the hearth, Zennor didn't think she could be happier. Even with her romantic life in tatters, she was carrying a healthy baby and nearly everyone she loved would be in this room tomorrow. She counted place settings, cutlery, glasses and, wondering if 'baby brain' was a real thing, she counted the settings again, deciding for the second time that seven people *was* the right number.

Outside, the sound of crunching gravel came, accompanied by car headlights.

'Mum and Dad are home!' Zennor bellowed to her siblings as she dashed to the wide, heavy front door and pulled it open, descending the steps to greet her parents who climbed out of the taxi and immediately rushed towards their youngest child.

'Let me look at you,' Jennifer said. 'Oh, you've got a tiny little bump now under that jumper.'

'I know,' Zennor replied, beaming. 'It's finally happened. A bit of proof she's in there.'

'Hello, darling,' her father Michael said, coming in for a hug. The taxi driver was pulling hold-alls and suitcases out of the boot, and Merry appeared behind her, taking the stone steps two at a time to greet his parents and help with the luggage.

'You're here!' Lamorna cried, jogging behind her brother and embracing her parents.

'Aren't you a sight for sore eyes?' her father said, holding her back so he could look at her. 'Lamorna is back on British soil and at Trelenna no less. I never thought I'd see the day.'

Lamorna grinned. 'That's old news. I've been back months.'

'We've missed so much,' Michael said.

'You're here now. In time for Christmas.'

'And a proper catch-up. I am very much looking forward to meeting Zach,' Jennifer said meaningfully.

'I'm very much looking forward to giving him the third degree,' Michael joked, rubbing his hands together.

'For god's sake don't do that,' Lamorna begged. 'He's already petrified.'

'As he should be,' Michael replied with a wicked laugh.

'How many are we for dinner tomorrow?' Merry asked as they walked towards the house to get out of the cold, everyone other than Zennor and her mum laden with luggage.

'Seven, I think,' Zennor said and then added everyone up again in her head, still worried she'd counted wrong.

'Zennor's cooking turkey *and* goose,' Merry said.

'Goose? Are we Victorians now?' Michael asked.

'We might as well be. Wait until you see all the decorations. It's like going back in time,' Zennor enthused.

'I'm such an idiot. I forgot to tell you!' Lamorna turned to Zennor. 'Charlie *is* going to join us for Christmas. I saw him in the garden when I was trying to fix one of the festoon bulbs that had gone out. He said to tell you.'

'When was that?'

Lamorna made a face. 'Yesterday. Sorry. Do you have enough? I should have said earlier. It slipped my mind. You can always give me a tiny portion if there's not enough.'

'No, no. That's great news,' Zennor said, her spirits lifting. 'And yes, I've always got enough food. You know me.'

'Enough champagne though?' her father asked with concern, when they were all in the entrance hall.

'Yes, and port for Boxing Day, don't worry.'

'Well done. Clever girl. And everyone's got their Christmas jumpers, I hope,' Michael said, slamming the front door behind him.

As everyone moved towards the sitting room, carols playing merrily away and the fire roaring, Zennor felt the happiest she'd been in ages. In her world, things were almost perfect. And as she climbed into bed later that night she felt nearly at peace. All her presents were wrapped and under the tree. Her leftover wrapping paper had been donated to a panicked Merry an hour ago when he realised he'd got nothing in which to wrap his. The vegetables were washed and scrubbed of soil, and she'd set her alarm to get the turkey and goose going in time for a 1 p.m. lunch. Absolutely nobody was allowed to help (not that they really wanted to). It threw her out of sync and she wanted everything to be just perfect and hassle free. And everything nearly was. She was as ready as she could be at this time of night but, instead of being exhausted as she normally was, tonight she was wired and buzzing. Just like the night after their first day of opening. Unable to sleep, Zennor gave up pretending and got out of bed to pace, waiting for tiredness to find her.

What was she worrying about? Charlie was on her mind, but she would see him tomorrow and they could start rebuilding their friendship. No, it was something else bothering her. She cast her gaze around the room. In around five months a tiny person would be in a little cot in here with her, right where those archive boxes were currently sitting, gathering dust in the corner. She hadn't forgotten them, far from it. But having exhausted them in search of Grace, she was struck by an idea – perhaps *Rose* would be in these boxes somewhere? These boxes were her relations, her family from a different era calling to her from a space in the room where a new generation would need to go.

Gripped by a sudden determination to nest, to clear the space, to finally get to grips with the remaining archives, Zennor put her dressing gown on for warmth, turned the dial up on the radiator and sat cross-legged on the floor. Buoyed by a newfound, restless energy, she put her laptop next to her and waited for it to whir into life. Tonight she was going to throw every resource she had at this. She was going to find everything out about Rose and Grace that she could. Zach's enemy – internet research – would be mixed in with cross-referencing any documents she could find. She'd use his log-ins for the various heritage websites and before the night was out, Zennor would know once and for all what had happened to Grace Lander after her daughter Rose had arrived at Trelenna House.

Chapter 50

1895

Grace

Next to her the small grandfather clock struck six as Grace stood in the servants' hall, Laurie Trelenna blocking her exit.

'Grace, did you really think I wouldn't recognise you?' he asked.

Like her, he was in a dressing gown but his was thicker, trimmed with ermine.

Grace stared at him in panic, her mouth open in abject surprise as she felt a horrid whooshing sensation in her ears that threatened to unbalance her. She'd felt feeble since the weeks after Arthur's death, but now, staring at Laurie Trelenna, everything had unravelled and she pulled out a chair at the servants' dining table and slumped into it.

Grace could feel his eyes on her as he entered the room. She didn't have the confidence to speak, to look up. She put her head into her hands and closed her eyes, shutting it all out, shutting him out. Across the table, she heard the scrape of a chair being pulled out as Laurie sat down. Still she didn't look at him.

It was Laurie who began. 'I didn't recognise Rose's surname at first. Lander. Because . . . why would I? Why would I *ever* link a footman from so long ago to the woman my son met and proposed to on the other side of the Atlantic? Until I saw you climb out of the carriage. Then, everything made sense. Only . . . *nothing* made sense. Nothing made sense at all. You. *You* were *here*.'

He waited but she couldn't speak, wouldn't speak. She lifted her head out of her hands and observed him warily. He had hurt her once before. So deeply. There was nothing he could do now that would ever hurt her again, unless he tried to hurt Rose in some way. And to protect her children, she would do anything.

'You married him,' Laurie said in disbelief. 'You married the *footman*.'

'Yes,' she said, looking him dead in the eye. 'I married Arthur. I had two beautiful children. I made something of myself. And it was no thanks to you.'

He sat back, face expressionless. 'What do you mean?'

'Don't,' she warned. 'Just tell me what you want from me, now that you know.'

Laurie looked dazed at her reply. 'What do I want? I want to know why you did it.'

She blinked at him.

'I want to know why you pushed your daughter into the path of my son. Why you forced them together. Was it to hurt me in some way? Some sort of sick game?'

'How dare you!' she cried. 'That's a terrible thing to say.'

'Then why?'

'I didn't push Rose and Edward together. They met in Newport and fell in love. I had nothing to do with it. And when I found out he was your son I tried to talk Rose out of it. But it didn't work because I could hardly tell Rose who you were to me. How could I explain that? Rose loves him and he loves her, and I cannot tell you how much I hate it. I hate it because he's your son and there was nothing I could do. Do you have any idea how much I hate leaving Rose here? How much *I* hate being here?'

The surprise never left his face. 'Why did you come back then? Why didn't you stay in New York?'

'Because my daughter was getting married. I'm losing her forever.'

'So you thought . . . what? That you'd arrive and stay in my house and that . . .' He sounded incredulous. 'That I wouldn't recognise you? And then we'd live the rest of our lives just pretending what happened between us *didn't happen*? You'll be here again, you know. A birth? A christening? What were you going to do each time you came back to visit Rose – pretend nothing had ever happened between us? Pretend we didn't do what we did? Pretend we didn't say what we said to each other? And hope every time I saw you that I *wouldn't recognise you?'* He was standing again, his voice raised.

'Why would you?' she cried back, the chair scraping against the flagstone as she stood. 'Why would *you* ever recognise *me*?'

'Because I loved you.'

She stopped, breathing heavily, her heart playing out a dangerous tune in her chest. Then she shook her head. 'No, you didn't. Don't do that. Don't lie like that. You lied before to me when I was young and naive. Don't do it now when I am neither.'

'After everything you did to me, you dare tell me *I'm* the one lying?' he said, his voice icy.

'After what *I* did to *you?* You lied to me. You seduced me. You promised me the world and you took everything away from me.'

'I promised you the world and I meant it. *You* left *me*.'

'I left because you told your mother about me and you lost me my position.'

He stared at her, his eyes wide, accusing. 'I did no such thing. You and the footman ran away together.'

'We ran away together because I had no job, no home, and Arthur intended to sail to America. He took me with him, out of *pity.* I was supposed to be leaving with *you.* I was supposed to be marrying *you*. You told me you loved me but all I hear in my head, every time I think about you, are your mother's words, that you made mistakes and I was simply your *latest,*' she hurled back at him. 'How many others had you done that to? Made those promises to? Lied to? A housemaid left the year before I did – was that you? Did you do that to her too?'

He sat back down in the chair again, too shocked to speak. His eyes searched hers. 'What?' he whispered. 'I didn't do any of those things. I loved you.'

'I don't believe you,' she said flatly.

'Then we've reached an impasse,' he replied. 'Neither of us believes the other.'

'It would seem so,' she said shakily.

Grace looked up as she saw movement in the adjoining kitchen. The kitchen maid had arrived to begin her chores. Grace moved slowly, so as not to drag her chair against the flagstones, but she failed and an inevitable scrape sounded. She needed to get out unseen. She couldn't be found in here, with him, in the state of undress they were both in. The kitchen maid jumped at the sound and stared in through the doorway.

'Oh, my apologies, sir,' she said when Laurie turned around.

'No apologies necessary.' His voice was calm. 'It is us who must apologise for startling you. We met in the hall, Mrs Lander and I, both feeling peckish and unable to sleep after last night's festivities. We'll leave you to your duties.'

'Very good, sir.' The kitchen maid bobbed a curtsey and turned back to her chores. If she was surprised at what she'd seen, she pretended not to be.

Laurie and Grace left one after the other, Laurie walking in front, his back stiff, his strides purposeful, and she followed him upstairs in silence, the fast beat of her heart the only sound. She was eager to be back in the relative safety of her bedroom where she would pack and leave as soon as possible.

A housemaid was just exiting Laurie's room, carrying a charcoal bucket for lighting fires. 'I'm sorry,' she said, apologising for simply having encountered them.

'Good morning, Dora,' Laurie said as the housemaid scuttled past and along to the corridor on the other side of the staircase.

Grace had been so stupid coming here. Laurie was right about that. Leaving Trelenna couldn't come soon enough. She didn't know what she'd do when it came to seeing Rose, but she could never visit Trelenna House ever again.

'Goodbye, Laurie,' Grace said finally, turning one last time to look at him and leaving him at his door.

Chapter 51

Present Day

Zennor

In the early hours of the morning, Zennor held the letter in her hands from a young Laurie Trelenna to his father. Buried in among newspaper cuttings, receipts for portraits and theatrical programmes, she had missed it the first time. She re-read it again.

Dearest Father,

I have slipped this under your door while you sleep. By the time you wake and read this I will be long gone and so will Grace Pascoe. Please don't be angry with me when I tell you we have fallen in love and intend to marry. Indeed, by the time you read this we will have been married some hours and be bound to Italy where we intend to reside until the dust settles on our elopement. Believe me when I tell you these are not sudden decisions, or ones taken lightly because I have wronged her and must put it right. Nothing could be further from the truth. I am her husband in body and soul, if not yet in the eyes of God. But today, that will change.

I only want love from a marriage, trust and mutual respect. With Grace I have found all three. I consider myself the luckiest man in England that she loves me in return and I cannot bear the thought of life without her. I know you will support me, over time, and I ask only this: please keep my news to yourself for now. The house will awaken soon and the fact we have gone will reveal itself naturally. I am sorry to leave you to manage that news.

Love is a great divider. But it is a great uniter too and I hope my family will choose to support us and not disown us. I want my life to be different from the future Mother planned for me. Please tell her I love her, as I do you. My only hope now is that, in time, when you have understood my reasons for doing this, Grace and I may be welcomed back to Trelenna House as man and wife.

Until then, I remain as always, your loving son,

Laurie

This made no sense. Grace and *Laurie Trelenna*? If this letter was to be believed, they had been in a relationship before Grace had taken flight, before she had run away to the other side of the world with Arthur Lander. Laurie had been in love with Grace? Zennor sat back against the wall, stunned, her legs stretched out in front of her as she rested her head back.

If Grace and Laurie had been together in 1869, then they had spent nearly three decades apart when Rose married Edward. Why had Grace gone with Arthur if it was Laurie she should have been leaving with? Nothing in this letter gave it away. Perhaps the letter had been found by Herbert Trelenna too early, slipped under a door as it was. Perhaps Laurie's father had gone into overdrive and stopped his son? Perhaps the mother had? Zennor wasn't sure she'd ever know.

She read it again. Laurie had clearly loved Grace. If she'd found a man who said these kinds of things about her, Zennor would have been more than happy. Her eyes landed on one passage: *I am her husband in body and soul, if not yet in the eyes of God.* What did *that* mean? Did that mean what she thought it meant? Or was she misunderstanding? She wished the Victorians would just say what they meant sometimes.

Zennor felt a tiny swish inside her, akin to a fluttering, and her hand immediately went to her stomach. It was the first time she'd felt the baby move.

'Oh,' she cried excitedly, looking down. 'Hello, you. How's it going in there?' She laughed at herself for talking aloud like this. 'Are you awake as well? It's Christmas tomorrow.' She looked at the time on the top right of her laptop screen. 4 a.m. 'It's Christmas *today*,' she corrected herself. 'Happy Christmas, little one. Your dad won't be popping in today but he's going to come to your next scan appointment so he can see you properly. And Mummy gets the impression he's going to be a generous father. He seems very keen.'

Mummy. She was going to be a mummy. The feeling didn't grow old. She smiled, closing her eyes, lulling herself to an upright sitting form of sleep. She was going to be a mum. And she wasn't having to go it alone. She was pleased she and Reece were able to be adult about this, pleased he'd be a part of her daughter's life, pleased she'd told him about the baby.

'I'm sorry Mummy and Daddy aren't together though,' she apologised to the baby. 'For a while Daddy wasn't involved at all. But he's on board now. Mainly because he finally knows and—' Her eyes pinged open while she thought about something.

Zennor had been making notes, of sorts, with every discovery she had made and she reached for her notebook and pen, turning back from the list of timings she'd made for today's food, back from the family tree Zach had drawn, back, back, back until she found the dates associated with Grace, her arrival in New York, her marriage to Arthur. And then she looked at another set of dates entirely.

She wanted to know what had happened to Grace after her daughter Rose had married into the Trelenna family, so what *had* happened? Using Zach's logins, she'd looked previously at US historical records and had found nothing for Grace after she'd made a success of her restaurant empire in the 1890s. But with Rose in Cornwall, was it wholly unlikely Grace might have returned to England every now and again?

Maybe there were later passenger lists that showed her returning here. Or maybe she even bought a *house* and moved here to be closer to Rose? Surely Grace would have seen her own grandchildren, which would have put her back in front of Laurie at multiple points, if not at least once? At some point throughout all of this, Grace would *have* to have seen Laurie again. It made no sense that she wouldn't.

This time, Zennor didn't type *Grace Pasco*e into the search bar of the British records. This time, she typed *Grace Lander*.

And instead of finding very little to go on, Zennor watched as the screen filled with results and wondered if everything she thought she knew about Grace's time at Trelenna House might be completely wrong.

Chapter 52

1895

Grace

In the upstairs hallway, Grace looked back at Laurie one final time. She'd said goodbye and there was nothing now for it other than to wait for Rose and Daisy to wake up so she could explain that she was going to London. She had to leave. She had to leave now.

'No, you don't,' Laurie said, striding forward and taking hold of her wrist with a firm grip. 'I haven't waited this long to find you, just for you to leave again.' He pushed open his bedroom door and pulled her in after him.

'What are you going to do? Keep me captive?' she hissed, as she skittered across the room, her chest heaving. He closed the door with a quiet click and leaned back against it.

'If I have to,' he said sternly, his eyes molten. 'And keep your voice down.'

'What do you want me to do, tell you what I've already said but differently?' she challenged, raising herself up. She commanded an empire now, she dined with the richest Americans in the world, counted the Vanderbilts as close friends. This man couldn't touch her now.

But as he stalked towards her, Grace's resolve faltered.

'No, but *I* will. The night before you and I were due to leave, I wrote my father a letter. In it I told him my plan, that I loved you, that I was marrying you, and if Mother wanted to disinherit me then so be it, because I would never find a love like yours again. I trusted my father. He never loved my mother. Theirs was a marriage grounded in money and hate. And I was the product of it. Then, just as I was leaving my room, bags packed, my mother found me. She told me you had run away, that you had been gone hours, that the talk in the servants' hall was that I had been made an utter fool. My father validated what my mother said. I was an embarrassment. I had to leave.'

'I . . . didn't do any of that,' Grace stuttered. '*You* were the one who didn't come to the woods. You promised and you weren't there,' she accused, feeling the two decades of fury finally being let out.

He was only inches away now. '*I* wasn't there because you had already gone.'

Grace refused to flinch. 'I hadn't. I was waiting. I waited so long. I was soaked through when I finally gave up, when I finally knew what you'd done.'

Laurie frowned, taking a step back. 'No . . .' He shook his head. 'No . . . that can't be right. My father said . . .' He stopped speaking, running through a past he had believed so wholeheartedly. 'No . . .'

'Your trust in him was misplaced,' Grace said flatly, as the truth hit her.

Laurie didn't speak, his frown deepening, eyes roving the floor slowly as he worked his way back in time.

'He was weak,' Grace said into the silence, knowing she should be kind, but unable to be. 'He told your mother.'

'He hated my mother.'

'He told her all the same.' She pulled her hair away from her face, loose around her shoulders, trying to settle her racing heart. 'You left? You went to London?'

'Yes. I was destroyed. I was . . . beyond broken. I loved you and . . .'

'And you allowed your mother to put you in a carriage and send you far, far away. And all the while I was standing in the woods as arranged, drenched, carrying everything I owned, waiting for you.'

Laurie inhaled shakily.

'You were in a carriage to London. And I was let go.'

'No . . .' Laurie stared in disbelief.

'You believed them? You believed I'd run away. And all the time, I was still here and then in an instant, I was let go, told to leave that day.'

Laurie sank on to the ottoman at the end of his bed and looked at Grace through sunken eyes. He shook his head sadly, his expression was hollow.

'But . . . you and the footman. You went *together*,' he said uncomprehendingly.

'Because you weren't *there*,' Grace cried. 'I waited and waited for you. And Arthur . . . he was there. And you *weren't*.' Tears soaked through the sleeve of her dressing gown as she wiped her face. She turned to the door.

'Don't leave,' Laurie begged, standing up and rushing towards her, reaching out a hand to stop her. 'Please. Not yet.'

She sighed, desperate for this to end. She moved back from the door, took a chair away from his shaving stand and turned it to face him. She sank into it and put her head in her hands. 'What an awful thing they did to us,' she exclaimed, and let her tears fall.

Laurie sat back down on the ottoman. 'Yes,' he said. 'Because they wanted me to marry someone with money, they ruined my life.'

'They nearly ruined mine,' Grace said and then looked up. 'Your life has hardly been ruined by what they did,' she said calmly, honestly. 'Look at you. Perhaps they saved you. What would have happened to us if we *had* run away together? It was idealistic.'

'It wasn't. It was love. On my part. Wasn't it on yours too? Didn't you love me too?'

She nodded, refused to look at him. 'It was so long ago, it doesn't matter now.'

'Doesn't it?' he asked.

She didn't speak.

'We'd have lived in Italy,' he reminded her.

She issued a short, sharp laugh. 'You remember.'

'Of course I remember. You wanted to go there. I had it all planned. You were my world. And I let you slip through my fingers because I was talked into believing a lie. A lie I thought was true until this very moment.'

Grace wiped relentless tears away again and dared look at him. He had tears in his eyes too and did as she did, wiping his away with his sleeve.

'I married a woman I hated because of that lie. I was so lost, so angry with you, so beholden to my mother and her need for me to marry someone with money. Love was a myth, she said. No one married for love. Everyone married for money. I believed her about that too. The estate needed saving. My father had lost everything and they needed me to marry well.'

'And you did,' Grace said. 'You saved the house.'

'And it cost me *everything*,' Laurie cried. 'Their greed cost me you. I've spent every year since, miserable and alone, believing the only woman I'd ever loved had never loved me in the first place.'

'How could you believe that?' Grace sobbed. 'You knew I loved you. I let you make love to me. I said yes when you asked me to marry you, yes to running away with you. I lost everything. I lost everything by being with you.'

'We both did,' he said.

'No,' Grace replied emphatically. 'You didn't lose what I did. You didn't face ruin the way I did.'

'You married the footman.' Laurie raised his voice.

'I had to!' She raised hers in return. 'I had to let him save me. Otherwise I'd have been ruined.'

'Why would you have been ruined?'

'Because when I left,' she shouted, 'I was carrying your child!'

Laurie stood up at speed. 'What?' he whispered, walking towards her.

'No,' Grace cried into her hands. 'No, no, no.' How could she have said that? How could she have told him that? She had worked her entire life to protect that secret. No one knew. No one other than Arthur had ever known. No one.

Laurie's eyes darted across the room as he tried and clearly failed to comprehend her words. He knelt in front of her, his face frowning in consternation, panic, confusion. He took hold of her hands, pulling them gently away from her face. 'Say it again,' he whispered. He was so close, too close, treacherously close.

'No,' she said.

He cupped her chin in his hand and tenderly lifted her head so her gaze was forced to meet his. 'Say it again, please.'

'I can't. I can't ever say it again,' she cried.

He was silent, his hand touching her face, the other holding hers within his. His eyes searched hers uncomprehendingly. And then he suddenly understood as he whispered the one name she'd been dreading he would say. 'Daisy.'

'No,' she snapped. 'You can't say it. You can't ever say it.'

'Daisy is mine.'

'No,' she wailed. 'No.'

'Yes,' he said calmly, challengingly. 'Daisy is my child, isn't she? *I'm* her father.'

'Laurie,' Grace pleaded, her voice dropping in desperation. 'Please.'

'Please what? What are you asking me to do?'

'You can't tell her. You can't tell anyone.'

'Oh my god, it's true. Daisy is mine. Daisy is *mine.* Does she know?'

'Of course not.' Grace almost laughed out the reply as her life seemed to fold in on itself. 'Of course she doesn't know. She idolised her father.'

'I'm her father.' Laurie's face was streaked with tears.

'No,' she said sternly, ripping her hand free of his. 'Arthur was her father. You were the man who left me with no other choice.'

'I didn't do it,' Laurie said. 'I loved you. I still do.'

Grace looked at him.

'I still love you,' he repeated. 'I always have. Even though I thought you'd left me. I still loved you. I remembered every interaction, every time I went into the kitchens just to be near you. I remembered all of it. When I made love to you, I'd never . . . I'd never known anything like it. That love, with you. Nothing else mattered. No one else mattered. You were everything to me.'

She shook her head, the panic drying up as the sadness took over again. 'Laurie.' She sobbed his name pointlessly.

'And now you tell me that we made Daisy. Our love made Daisy.'

'No,' she said, taking charge. 'No. We can't talk about this. We can't talk about her like this ever again.'

Laurie looked at her beseechingly. 'Then what do you want me to do? You want me to go the rest of my life never acknowledging her as my daughter?'

'Yes,' Grace said relieved. 'That is exactly what I want you to do.'

Tears rolled down Laurie's face. 'Why?' he begged.

'Because you'll ruin her life.'

'I don't see how.'

'How can I ever tell her everything she thought was true was a lie?' Grace wailed.

'Look at us. We were dragged apart because of a series of lies and look what it's done to us,' Laurie cried. 'We have to tell her the *truth.*'

'No,' she said emphatically. 'The truth will kill her. The lie keeps her safe. Don't you see? Arthur was the only father she's ever known. Don't take that from her. I'm begging you not to take that from her.'

Laurie was still. So still. The morning light was streaming through the windows. Night had gone and now the noise of servants and guests in the house seemed to rush at her all at once.

'Grace, this changes everything.'

'No, it doesn't,' she whispered. 'Please. Please, Laurie, if you mean what you say. If you love me, you won't tell her. Do this for me. Do this for her. Your family hurt us, don't let them be the cause of hurting Daisy too.'

'Grace,' he cried. 'You don't know what you're asking of me.'

In the hallway a door opened and closed, and both Laurie and Grace turned to look in the direction of the noise. Grace could have sworn her heart had stopped.

'I have to go,' she whispered. 'I can't be in here.'

Laurie rushed towards her. 'Don't leave Trelenna. Not yet. We have to talk.'

Grace breathed in and out desperately. 'I have to get back to my room. I can't be caught here like this.'

He grabbed her wrist again, then thought better of it and let go. 'Please,' he begged. 'Meet me after breakfast. In the woods, where we used to meet. We have to talk.'

She went to open the door.

'Wait,' he said. 'Stop. Let me . . . But first promise me you'll meet me.'

'Fine,' she said quickly, anything to get away.

'*Promise* me you'll come,' he whispered desperately.

She met his searching eyes. 'I promise,' she said and meant it. Laurie opened the door and looked up and down the hallway. 'It's fine. There's no one there. Go.'

Grace dashed from Laurie's room as fast as she could for fear of being seen. She found her own door, opening it quickly and darting inside. But before she closed it, she looked back at the man she'd once loved standing by his door looking after her.

Chapter 53

At the breakfast table Daisy had loaded her plate with eggs and buttered toast, and was clearly feeling worse for wear, wincing every time someone moved a chair or clanged cutlery against their plate. Rose and Edward talked excitedly through every moment they'd experienced of their wedding day and, with a level of joyful deliriousness, Edward couldn't stop calling Rose *Mrs Trelenna.*

Grace had expected to feel relieved by now that the worst was over, that soon she'd be leaving. But she was in the middle of the worst part of being here. She needed to get this over, needed to finish breakfast and talk with Laurie and then end her association with this house, despite the fact her daughter now lived here and it was Grace's money that would be used to keep the house on the straight and narrow. Suddenly, unexpectedly, Grace found herself laughing at the absurdity of it all. Laurie looked up at her sharply and she stared back at him, her laughter stopping as abruptly at his confused expression. This was all such madness and she was in the grip of a mania, surely, right here at the breakfast table where her kedgeree sat untouched on her plate.

'I was just thinking you were being unusually quiet,' Rose told her mother. 'And then you laughed. What are you laughing at?'

'It's awful of me,' Grace grasped for a quick, suitable lie. 'But I've just caught sight of your sister's plate.'

'I know. So much food,' Daisy said, a sickly look on her face. 'I'll never eat all this but I just feel so dreadful. I need to eat something.'

'Eggs?' Rose asked. 'You drank too much champagne and think eggs are the solution. Don't eat those, Daisy. It'll end so badly. Possibly for all of us if we have to watch you.'

'I think you're right,' Daisy said, her head in her hands, then she remembered where she was and put her hands in her lap and tried to fix a normal expression on her face.

Grace glanced at Laurie, who was watching Daisy – *her* daughter. *His* daughter too. No. She had fought for so long to keep that secret safe only to blurt it out in the heat of the moment. Too many things had happened with Laurie in the heat of the moment, but this one topped the list. She glanced at Daisy and felt nothing but love, as ever. Maybe *one* thing that had happened with Laurie had been good in the end, even if it had been Grace's undoing at the time.

Laurie put his napkin down and stood. 'Excuse me, everyone. I intend to walk off my breakfast before it rains.'

'But you've hardly eaten anything to walk off,' Edward pointed out. 'And I think it's going to rain before you get the chance to leave the house.'

'Then I'll have to be quick about it,' Laurie said affably.

When he'd gone, Grace felt the pressure mount. She had to go. She had to speak to him. She had agreed she would. This time they would be meeting not to determine her fate, but the course of Daisy's. Whatever happened, Grace would not allow him to tell Daisy what he knew. Even though he would inevitably see Daisy without Grace being there to stop him over the course of the following years. Daisy would visit Rose for extended stays. How could she stop two sisters from seeing each other just because Laurie would ruin everything? How dare he do this to her? Spurred on, she too rose slowly from the table. 'I think a walk before it pours sounds ideal if we're to be trapped indoors due to rain for the rest of the day.'

'I can't think of anything worse,' Daisy grumbled, sinking into her chair now that Laurie had gone and the need to be polite was over.

'Hear, hear,' cheered Rose, looking more tired now than she had done before. 'Maybe we all need a restorative cocktail . . .'

And Grace took this as her cue to go, taking her long coat and hat from the butler as he opened the front door for her. Grace looked at the gunmetal sky as she stood at the threshold, black clouds rolling in ominously. She only hoped she would say what it was she needed to say to Laurie before the heavens opened.

When Grace found Laurie he was where he had said he would be, in their usual spot, deep into the woods, hidden from the prying eyes of the house. The fern still covered the ground much the same as it had when they'd made love here so long ago, bracken still crunched underfoot as she walked. Slowly she came to a stop a few feet from him; he had watched her the whole way into the glade. He was standing with his hands in his pockets, and on seeing her he pulled them out and then looked as if he didn't know what to do, eventually letting them hang limply at his sides.

He spoke first, clearly desperate to finish their conversation. 'Last night . . .' He shook his head. 'This morning, I told you I loved you. You told me Daisy is my daughter.'

Fresh hurt rolled in again at the same speed as the blackening clouds. 'I'm sorry,' Grace said flatly. She just wanted this over. They could never see each other again. It was the only option she could foresee leading to any good for everyone.

'I'm sorry too,' Laurie confessed. 'I'm sorry we were both lied to. I'm sorry I spent the rest of my life wondering where you'd gone. Love turned to hate. I hated you. And I loved you.'

She nodded but couldn't speak, despite the fact she wanted to. Where would this end? She had loved Laurie. Then she had loved Arthur. Anything else now felt like a betrayal of the man who'd given her everything.

As if he could hear her thoughts Laurie said, 'It wasn't my fault. I need you to believe me. Even if we never see each other again, I need you to know I was honest with you. I wanted to be your husband.'

Grace tried not to cry; her gloved hand flew to her face, covering her mouth. Somehow hearing that here hit her in a way she had not expected. She couldn't look at him. Her eyes scanned the ground, then stuttered as they fixed on the place she'd lain with Laurie twenty-six years ago, the very spot where they'd conceived Daisy. Tears flooded her eyes and she gave up. What was she supposed to do with this information now, after all this time?

'You loved me then as I loved you,' Laurie pointed out.

'Yes, of course I loved you. I'd never . . . I'd never have been with you if I didn't.'

He nodded slowly, thoughtfully. 'Do you love me still?'

'It's been so long. I loved the man you were.'

'I'm still the same man, Grace. And you're still the same woman.'

'Are we?' she asked doubtfully. 'I'm not sure we are. I'm not sure I am. Too much has happened.'

'I love you,' he repeated.

She narrowed her eyes. 'What do you want me to say?'

'I want you to tell me you love me, that we can start again in some way.'

'Are you mad?' Grace asked. 'How can we? I thought I was the one gripped in lunacy this morning, but *you* are.'

'Perhaps we both are,' Laurie pointed out sombrely. The rain began falling and in the distance the low roll of thunder reverberated across the sky. They both looked in the direction of it. The foliage above was outmatched by the sudden downpour, but while Grace's hat shielded her from the worst of it, Laurie's fair hair became soaked.

'There is too much to conceal for us to be anything to each other now,' Grace said sadly. 'I loved you. Perhaps I love you still. But I love Daisy more. And I can't let you hurt her by telling her Arthur isn't her father. You'll destroy her. You'll destroy the relationship I have with her. And you will never have a relationship with her if you tell her. It won't work the way in which you want it to. She'll hate you for it.'

'I did wonder that,' Laurie confessed. He tipped his head up into the rain as it continued falling on them both, his eyes closed. Eventually he looked back at her, wiping his face. 'It may not surprise you to know I couldn't sleep after you left.'

'Neither could I.'

'I thought about what you said. I thought about what price I would give to be with you again. What price I would give to keep Daisy near to me, to be a father to her without ever saying so.'

Grace's lips parted.

'I would give up everything I have for both of those things. To have you again, properly. To have Daisy and to love her and to keep her safe throughout her life, but to never tell her. I would pay that price. I don't want her to hate me or you. I want her to love me as a father but perhaps just not realise she does. It is a price I am willing to pay to keep her close. It is a price I will pay to keep you close, to love you the way I always did.'

Grace's coat was drenched. The sound of thunder rolled closer. 'You mean it?' she asked over the deafening sound of the rain hitting the ground, the trees all around them. There was no escape from it.

'I won't tell her. And it comes with no obligation. You can choose to leave me again. If you don't love me, you can leave safe in the knowledge that Daisy will remain ignorant of the fact I am her father. Whenever you are home in New York and Daisy is here at Trelenna visiting Rose, you can rely on me to keep my word. I promise to protect Rose as if she was my own and I will protect Daisy too, because she is. And while I will not tell her, you realise you can't stop me loving her as my daughter, not now that I know.'

'I know. I know that.'

'You're going to return to New York with her soon,' he pointed out. 'So the time I have with her now is precious.'

Grace watched Laurie's face, full of sadness. He had always been so happy, so full of energy and life when she'd known him. Her heart broke into so many pieces watching the man she'd loved and tried to hate. His heart was breaking too.

'Come under the tree,' he said, and together the two of them moved and stood under a canopy of leaves, shielding them from hardly any of the torrent.

'Edward is Daisy's half-brother,' Laurie said when they were stood together.

'I know,' Grace replied softly, 'And I'm sorry for it that he can't know either.' She'd had so much time to consider it. But for Laurie the news was only hours old. 'The entire time he was with us in New York after I found out who Edward was, I thought it. I thought how utterly awful it was. Daisy and Edward. Half-siblings. They can't know. It will hurt Edward too. It's our fault, our cross to bear. And not theirs.'

There was so much sadness in his expression. She reached out and touched his face – an uncontrollable motion she didn't want to have control of. Almost three decades later Laurie Trelenna still had the power to take hold of her heart, especially like this when he was so open, so honest, so vulnerable. How could she hate him?

He closed his eyes at her touch. 'There are more people than just us involved, Grace.'

'I know. But I don't know what else to do.'

'It's alright,' he said. 'It's alright.'

'It's not.'

He laughed, short and bitter. 'No, perhaps it's not,' he said honestly. 'But perhaps in time it will be. And we don't have to know all the answers at this moment in time.'

She looked at him and tried to stop the strands of love from pulling her back towards him. She had been by herself for five years. She thought she'd been fine, determined to face the world alone for her daughters. But now, here, with Laurie, the thought of turning away from him hurt her too much to bear. But what could they do? What could they reasonably do? In her mind was Arthur. Arthur who'd saved her, who'd loved her, who she'd loved so deeply in return.

'We can find a way to navigate this. But I promise I won't tell her.'

'Thank you,' she said.

'May I hold you? One final time?' Laurie asked.

Her gut told her that she shouldn't allow this, that it was a terrible idea, that she'd be lost if she held him, if he held her. But she couldn't stop herself. She wanted it. 'Yes,' she said, so quietly she barely heard her own voice over the roar of rain.

She allowed herself to be pulled gently against him, her face against his shoulder, his heart beating strong and fast through his wet clothes. She looked up at him and felt an urge deep within her, an urge to hold him forever, to kiss him forever, to be loved by him forever. But instead he pulled back and looked at her, his eyes damp from withheld tears. 'You're going to leave me again, aren't you?'

'I don't know what to do.'

'Neither do I. I still love you,' he told her.

She couldn't stop the tears gathering in her own eyes. 'I thought I hated you. But I don't.'

'You love me,' he prompted.

'Laurie,' she despaired.

'You love me,' he said again. 'Look at me and tell me you don't.'

Her face was wet with rain and tears, the two mixed together streaking her face. 'I love you,' she said quietly.

He held her shoulders and pleaded with her. 'Please don't leave me again.'

'What do I do if *not* leave?'

'Stay,' he said simply. 'Stay with me.'

'How?' she cried as thunder cracked in the skies directly above. Were they safe here under this tree? She didn't care. If they were killed together in this moment, she just didn't care. 'How can we possibly be together now after everything we've just said to each other?'

'How can we *not* be together now?' Laurie reasoned.

'Because of Daisy and Rose. And Edward.'

'None of them need to know what we were to each other,' he said desperately, reasoning it aloud. 'Edward, Rose, Daisy, none of them need to know about us . . . before. None of them need to know anything. It could simply be a case that you and I have been thrown together and were swept up in the joys of their wedding and readily fell in love after being alone for so long. That's the story we'll tell them.'

'We've only known each other here, because of the wedding, a matter of *days*. They'll never believe us.'

'They will. Because the alternative doesn't bear thinking about.'

There was so much at risk for Daisy if she and Laurie acted on their love. But that risk remained even if they didn't. 'I don't know what to do,' she said.

'You do.' The light had returned to his eyes while all around them felt dark. 'You know we're supposed to be together. You know we are. You're meant to be here now. And so am I. We'll tell them what we want to tell them and everything else is ours. And will remain just ours forever.'

She was torn. She'd hated him. She'd loved him. She'd always loved him, always carried a piece of him in her heart. She needed to let the hate be a distant memory. But she couldn't let Laurie be a memory. She couldn't. 'And then what?' she asked, her mind unable to untangle what was being said.

'Marry me,' he said and his words catapulted her back to so long ago – back to a time when he'd asked her the same question, suggesting her world could be different, suggesting he'd love her forever, suggesting she and Laurie Trelenna would be together until their dying days.

'Marry me,' he repeated as a flash of lightning lit the sky on the other side of the wood, casting them in a momentary glow. The storm was passing but the rain continued. 'I meant it then and I mean it now. Grace, I am as in love with you now as I was then.'

'Laurie.' She reached forward and gripped his sodden jacket with a desperate need to hold on to something, to right herself. 'This is madness.'

'It is. Yes. But love is madness.'

She shook her head, hoping for common sense to prevail. 'I can't see how we do this. We can't do this.'

'We can,' he said decidedly. 'Of course we can. Do you want us to live out the rest of our lives without each other? We are neither of us yet fifty. We might have a long and miserable life, forcing ourselves not to be together if we do that. We've already spent so much time apart. If you truly love me why *would* you do that to me? To you? To us? Because I don't want to live the rest of my life without you now I've found you.'

She couldn't believe she was hearing these words.

'Say yes,' he said. 'Tell me we can be together after all this time. Say yes.'

'Laurie.' She said his name, knowing she wanted to say yes, knowing she wanted to be happy, knowing she'd be happy with him because she had been before. Their circumstances were complex and wrong before and they were even more so now. And then Laurie kissed her, urgently, frantically, and she kissed him back, holding him so tightly and never wanting to let go. This time she would never let go of him. She felt herself thrown back to a time when he had loved her and she had loved him. She felt she might drown in his love the way she had before. Being in love with Laurie Trelenna swarmed through her as though it had never left. 'Laurie,' she whispered, pulling back from his kiss to look at him.

'Don't say my name,' he begged. 'Say yes.'

'Laurie.' She was crying, despairing now. She wanted to, she wanted to say yes so much.

'Say yes.' He was desperate, all hope almost gone.

'Yes,' she said, equally as desperate as her lips touched his. 'Yes.'

Chapter 54

Present Day

Zennor

Zennor stared at the marriage certificate she had unearthed in the local parish records. Reunited after so long apart, Grace Lander had married Laurie Trelenna in 1896.

They were always supposed to be together. Laurie had certainly believed it, according to the note he'd written his father. But then why had Grace 'fled' so suddenly according to the letter Laurie's mother had written to the housekeeper – the letter that had started Zennor off on this path months ago? Had Laurie and Grace been forced in different directions, a destiny out of their control?

Zennor now understood her sister's hesitation when it came to displaying the most personal information about Issey Trelenna. Lamorna had chosen to tell the love story of Issey and Alex on her tours, but had only displayed the most factual early pages of Issey's diary showcasing life in Singapore before the Japanese had invaded in the Second World War. Some parts of her story were too personal to show. Zennor knew she wanted to have Grace's story told to visitors, but how to do it in a way that didn't *betray* Grace? She could show the census records, create a display about the staff downstairs during the time. Perhaps she could even put the display along the corridor that led to the kitchen and large store pantry – what had once been the servants' hall. She also had the photograph of Rose Lander on her wedding day to help illustrate Grace's social rise from downstairs to upstairs within this very house. It needed thinking about but as she stared at the evidence of a love that had survived decades and oceans, she wanted Grace's story told in an honest, true and honourable way. Grace deserved nothing less.

Zennor wondered if she might even feel confident enough to take on tours herself at some point so she could initially tell Grace's story how she wanted. Perhaps she could use one of those baby carriers and carry the little one around with her, experiment with a sleeping baby and a tour group. Might that be taking too much on? She would like to give it a try.

Zennor looked at her stomach as the fluttering continued. The baby was still awake and kicking, at this hour.

She plucked up her notebook and looked again at when Grace and Arthur had married in New York, and then at when Grace's first child, Daisy, had been born. They were not nine months apart. They were not even eight. Taking into account the time taken to cross the Atlantic, it struck Zennor that Grace had already been carrying a baby when she'd left Trelenna and had been in a relationship with Laurie. Had Laurie been Daisy's father? Had Arthur married her to save her, giving her a new life in a new country? And then they had gone on to have another child together, to rise from the very bottom of society to financial security, Grace returning with her head held high before becoming mistress of Trelenna.

Zennor put her hand on her own stomach. Both she and Grace had fallen pregnant while living in this house, but at that time being unmarried and pregnant meant being an outcast from society, a fallen woman. While for Zennor, no such fate awaited her.

If Arthur hadn't married Grace, she might have become destitute. If Rose hadn't met Edward it seemed unlikely Grace would have ever ended up back at Trelenna. And then Zennor wouldn't be descended from Grace, from Rose and all those who followed after.

Grace had been brave to start a new life with her child and with a man who was not her baby's father, given all the complexities that might have brought. Zennor's mind jolted towards Charlie – a man she couldn't have because it wouldn't be fair on him to re-enter her world in any capacity other than friendship. But she pushed it all away again.

She tidied up her notes and placed them back orderly in the archive box, closing the lid, fully satisfied she now knew what had happened to Grace and the kind of woman she was. Zennor looked at the scan picture by the side of her bed as she climbed under the duvet for a few precious hours' rest. Grace had been a fighter. And Zennor knew she would have to become one too.

Chapter 55

'Wake up, sleepyhead.' Merry jostled Zennor gently.

Her eyes opened drowsily and she blinked up at him. 'What's going on?'

'Happy Christmas!'

'What time is it?' Zennor cried, scrambling up and staring around for her phone.

'Relax. It's seven.'

'No! I can't relax. I need to pre-heat the ovens.'

Merry smiled. 'I've already done that. Even though you said I wasn't allowed to help. I didn't think even *I* could mess up an oven pre-heat. I also brought you a cup of tea.' He smiled as he picked up the mug he'd placed on her bedside table.

'Is it—'

'Yes, it's decaf.'

She sank back against the pillow and took a restorative sip. 'You're being very helpful all of a sudden. What's going on?'

He shrugged. 'Brother's prerogative. You've been doing too much. Got to keep you stress free, apparently.'

'In this house?'

'Yeah, I know. Tricky. So I'm here volunteering myself as some sort of kitchen slave. If I let you sleep in any longer, you'd probably kill me. So, set me a task.'

'Thank you,' Zennor said after a pause. 'Peeling and chopping alright?'

'Yes, Chef.'

'But carrots and parsnips have to be in elegant thin sticks, not those horrid chunky rounds you do.'

Merry sighed. 'Oh, it's going to be like that, is it?'

'Yes, it is.' But she was smiling.

'Want me to clear up that lot over there?' He nodded his head in the direction of the archive boxes. Her laptop was still open on the floor and the boxes were haphazardly placed like oversized stepping stones.

'No, it's fine, there's a sort of method to it, would you believe? I've finally been through everything and I think I've pieced together the story of Grace and what happened to her,' Zennor said excitedly.

'Brilliant! Tell me all about it downstairs? And when you're done, we can put these boxes away, can't we? Or I can. Just don't you lift them, will you?'

'I think Lamorna wants the boxes sorted through and everything categorised so she can put things on display and rearrange the archive room properly. I've got a few fabulous letters we can put on display, and the newspaper clippings and—'

'She wants the boxes sorted *and* categorised?' Merry baulked. 'She's lost the plot if she thinks I'm doing that with the ones she shoved in my room. Who's got time for that?'

Zennor slid a glance over to him as he continued to stare askance at the pile of boxes. 'Have you looked in any of yours yet?'

'No. I've put them on top of the wardrobe. Out of sight, out of mind.'

Zennor poked him in the side like they were children again. 'You're the ones running the tours. Don't you want new discoveries? Fresh stories to tell?'

'Not at the detriment of my free time, thank you very much. I'm already giving this house every hour of my life.'

'You're giving those Netflix documentaries a lot of hours too,' she pointed out.

'They're useful, for work. For book research.'

'The boxes might be useful too,' Zennor said doubtfully as Merry rose to leave her to get dressed. She wondered why he was up so early. He was already dressed. Perhaps he'd been unable to sleep too. This must be a terrible time of year for him, grieving his wife on Christmas Day.

'Merry,' she called to her brother.

He turned back from the door. 'Yeah?'

'Happy Christmas.'

'Happy Christmas, Zen.'

Merry and Zennor worked in harmony in the kitchen, although it was a challenge to stop micro-managing.

'What do I do now?' Merry asked eagerly when she'd been unusually silent for more than two minutes.

'Herbs and spices into the stuffing mix?' she suggested. 'It's fun. You can get your hands in and squidge.'

'Squidge? Is that a professional chef's term?'

'It's a try-to-make-it-sound-fun term.'

'You're a good teacher. You should do this professionally.'

'Ha, ha,' Zennor deadpanned.

'Hey, I'm being serious! You should teach. You make it enjoyable, once you've realised the kitchen won't catch fire if you let go of a bit of control.'

'Teach?' she echoed. 'Teach cooking?'

Merry shrugged. 'Why not? You know what you're doing. It could help the house make some extra money too. I'm sure I could be persuaded to babysit my little niece for a few hours a week if you wanted to show other people how to cook, pass on your skills. It's just a thought. You have this amazing talent. You're using it to keep the tearoom well stocked but if you wanted to host events or supper clubs or whatever . . . If it would make you happy to do something new with your skills, then the babysitting offer is there. And it's not like we don't have the room.'

She thought about it for a moment. It was entirely out of her comfort zone. But perhaps that would be a good thing. If anything, Grace's story had taught her sometimes taking a risk could pay off. Of course it wasn't quite the same as travelling halfway across the globe to the new world, but her kitchen made her happy. Perhaps it could make other people happy too. The kitchen table seated eight comfortably with space to work. It would be a lovely, intimate way to teach a class. Excitement rose inside her. She would love to do that, love to pass her skills on to others. What a good idea.

'Merry?'

He looked back at her, his hands messy, a cheerful expression on his face. 'Yeah?'

'Thank you.'

'What for?'

'Just for being a good brother.'

He laughed. 'You're welcome. You're a pretty good sister as well.'

The landline rang, making Zennor and Merry jump. 'Who rings the landline these days?' Merry asked, his hands in the stuffing mix.

'Always someone trying to flog facias and soffits,' Zennor trilled, happy in her position blitzing breadcrumbs for the bread sauce. 'Ringing on Christmas Day is a bit much, though.' She wiped her hands on her apron and moved over to the wall by the dresser and picked up the phone. 'Hello?'

There was nothing but a sound of clicking and hissing, and just when Zennor was ready to hang up on the prank caller she heard a woman's voice say faintly, 'Hiiiii.'

'Who's this?'

Another delay and then, 'It's me, Veryan. Happy Christmas!'

'Veryan?' Zennor cried excitedly. 'How are you? Where are you?'

Merry joined her, hands in mid-air like a surgeon, covered in stuffing. He pressed his ear against the edge of the phone, trying to share with Zennor.

The delay each time Veryan answered was beyond frustrating. 'You'd never believe me if I told you but let's just say I was invited on the opportunity of a lifetime, and I've gone from desert heat to biblically cold. You'll see it on my socials if I can ever connect to them again.'

'Are you coming home soon?' Merry asked.

'Merry!' Veryan called. 'You're there too! It's so hard to hear. They've let me borrow a satellite phone. I'm so sorry I haven't been in touch. It's mad at—'

The line clicked and popped and Zennor said, 'Veryan?'

Veryan was still talking, unaware the line had temporarily cut out her news. '. . . so I wanted to say Happy Christmas before we practically disappear off the edge of the world. And I wanted to say I'm so happy I'm going to be an aunty. I'm so sorry I haven't replied. I wanted to ring and talk through your news properly but there hasn't been time. But I had to ring on Christmas, even though it's chaos here!'

'I'm having a girl!' Zennor cried.

There was no reply as the satellites carried their voices to and from wherever Veryan was. 'I'm really struggling to hear you both. A girl? I can't wait to meet her!'

'You'll be home before that though, won't you?' Merry asked. 'That's months away.'

'I love you all! Tell everyone, Happy Christmas!' Veryan called.

'Happy Christmas,' they both cried back. Then Veryan was gone.

Zennor beamed and replaced the phone back on the receiver. 'She called!' she said happily.

'She's alive, then.'

'Never in doubt. She sounds busy.'

'She sounds far away,' Merry said, going to the sink to wash his hands. 'A satellite phone? Mad. She avoided my question about when she'd be back.'

'I noticed that.'

Merry dried his hands as a knock at the back door sounded and then someone opened it.

'Hi,' Charlie said, laden with bags and wrapped up in a thick coat and scarf. He put his gifts down and shut the door behind him against the cold.

'Hiya,' Merry called, moving over to shake Charlie's hand.

'Happy Christmas,' Charlie replied, shaking Merry's hand in return then passing him a carrier bag containing two bottles of red wine.

'Happy Christmas indeed,' Merry said, peering inside the bag.

'You could go and put them in the dining room,' Zennor hinted, knowing that the beat her heart was making didn't deserve even the slightest bit of attention. But god, Charlie looked good.

Merry took the hint and left them to it.

'Is it still okay that I'm here?' Charlie asked once Merry had climbed the stone steps and turned out of earshot.

'Absolutely. I'm *so* pleased you're here.'

'Thanks. Me too,' he said, still a little nervous, a slow smile making her forget what she'd been doing before he arrived. 'Can I do anything to help?'

'You can just keep me company, if you like. I think everyone else is milling around playing games already though, if you'd like to join them.'

He stood awkwardly and then, 'You look lovely.'

'Do I?' she asked bashfully. 'Thanks. I've bought some maternity clothes finally.' She was wearing a black stretchy wool dress covered in sequins. 'Sparkly dress for Christmas,' she reasoned. 'You look lovely too. I've not seen you in anything other than your work clothes or jeans and a t-shirt.' She heard herself rambling, but Charlie was already so attractive, and now he was ruining her by wearing a suit with a white shirt unbuttoned at the collar.

He smiled, shrugging off her compliment.

Feeling slightly lost in her own kitchen, Zennor turned back to survey the line of food on the countertop, trying to remember what she should be doing. Potatoes then Yorkshire pudding mix, that was it.

'I bought something for you,' he said, reaching into a gift bag. 'It must be miserable not being able to drink when everyone else is, especially at Christmas, so . . .' He presented her with a cold bottle of something fizzy and some non-alcoholic mulled wine.

'My step-mum recommended the mulled wine. She said this one tastes like the real deal. And I made the elderflower fizz for you from dried elderflowers.'

'You *made* it for me?'

He nodded, that shy expression again.

'Charlie, you're so thoughtful. Can I open it now?'

'Of course. It's not your present. It's just something to drink today.'

'You . . . you bought me something else as well?' she asked.

'To say thank you. For having me. For cooking and, er, rescuing me on Christmas Day.'

'I couldn't see you be on your own. I would have felt dismal today knowing you were alone. I'm so pleased you came. We usually do presents after lunch if you're happy to wait until then. I got you something too.'

'Thanks. You didn't have to. I wasn't expecting anything. You've got enough going on, I'm sure, with the baby.' Zennor didn't get the chance to reply as Charlie steamed on while opening the fizz for her. 'I love that you have a set time for present giving. A Christmas tradition. I never really had that. Glasses?'

'Up there.' She pointed to a cupboard and he fetched some. 'You never had Christmas traditions?' She felt so sad for him. 'Even before, when your parents were together?'

He shook his head. 'I suppose Father Christmas brought all my gifts.' He gave her a knowing smile. 'So I'd rip them open in the morning and spend the day playing with them while my parents spent the day arguing about . . . whatever it was they used to argue about.'

'Oh, Charlie,' she said despondently.

'Shh, it's fine. I'll just be a part of your traditions today and learn how it's done. What else do you do?'

'Games and lunch, presents and then a big walk around the estate. Leftovers tomorrow go into big pies. Non-stop snacking for two days straight. Christmas Day is basically our one dressy day of the year. And then tomorrow it's Christmas jumpers. My dad cracks open a new bottle of port on Boxing Day and we play competitive card games. Then he never touches the stuff for the rest of the year so I use it up in recipes. And champagne all day today. It's ridiculously decadent but mandatory. Not for me this year though, sadly.'

He handed her a glass. 'That sounds like a *lot.* I'm ready for it. Cheers.' They clinked glasses and he sipped his, giving her a nervous glance. 'Is it okay?'

'It's delicious. You're very talented. Did you grow the elder-flower too?'

He nodded. 'I've planted some in the garden here for you too. It'll bloom around May and you can make your own then. Or I can make it for you.'

'You'd make it for me?'

'Of course.'

'I love the thought of you being here in summer,' she said. The thought of him not being here hurt her heart. If she couldn't be with him, she could at least talk to him for a bit while he was working. It was better than nothing.

'Summer's when the garden will look its best. You can come outside and see me when you push the baby around the garden in her pram.'

'I'd like that.' It was a mediocre alternative for what she wanted, what should have been but now couldn't be. She put her hand on her stomach. She'd gained something wonderful. But losing Charlie because of it hurt more than it should.

Chapter 56

'Are you off travelling again?' Zach asked Jennifer and Michael as they served themselves from heaped platters of turkey, goose and all the trimmings. Zennor had purposefully made too much, because then she had enough pie filling for tomorrow's lunch. She stared at her parents in trepidation. The thought they might leave again had never occurred to her. They couldn't do that to her *again* could they? Although the damage had been done, really. Their departure had forced Zennor's hand into saving the house. The worst had to be over, even if they did take off yet another time.

'No, that's us very much done,' Jennifer said. 'We're here to be with our loved ones.'

'Good,' Zennor replied immediately, passing her home-made cranberry sauce over to her mother. 'You were missed. I don't want you to go again, especially now I'm having a baby. I need my mum.'

'And you've got me,' Jennifer confirmed, giving Zennor a loving look. 'I'm here now. We both are. You've done very well holding the fort. You wanted to save the house and you did it. I hope you are very proud of yourself. As we both are of you.'

'Thank you, I am.' At her heart Zennor knew her parents had given her the choice, to take on the task of saving the house from sinking into irredeemable debt or to sell it and be done with it as they were. It still saddened Zennor that her parents hadn't cared enough to save it. And that if left up to them, they wouldn't be here now, enjoying another Christmas in their ancestral home. 'You were gone far too long,' was all she could say.

'We weren't gone *that* long for two retired people with grown-up children,' Jennifer pointed out.

'You've been gone half the year!' Lamorna cried.

'*You* were gone for the best part of ten years, young lady, so don't you try that one on,' her dad countered.

Lamorna widened her eyes and Merry sniggered.

'You can talk,' Lamorna directed at Merry.

'I went to uni, that's different.'

'And stayed in Scotland for six years after you graduated!'

Zennor glanced over at Charlie, whose eyes roved between everyone as if he was watching a tennis match. Zennor leaned into him. 'Are you okay? I told you it would be loud.'

'I think it's brilliant. Your family are fun. Thank you for inviting me.'

'I'm pleased you're here. It means a lot to me.'

'It means a lot to me too,' he said, holding her gaze for two seconds, three seconds.

'Charlie, I hear you're to thank for the garden looking beautiful,' Jennifer called over to him. 'I doubt you can see much evidence of my efforts out there now. I tried my best but it's too much for one person. Too much for me, should I say. But I did love having a go.'

'I found some evidence – some gorgeous David Austin roses with their tags still on. Was that you?'

'It was! I was at a garden centre and had a massive spend-up.'

'As usual,' Lamorna mouthed to Zennor, who promptly hid a smirk with her hand.

Charlie continued. 'And I've uncovered what will be glorious white hydrangeas. Some ivy and weeds got to them, so I've hacked it all back. They didn't look their best this summer but hopefully next year . . .'

'I don't know how you're doing it,' Jennifer said.

'Bit by bit, every day. It's quite a job. I nearly said "no" when I came to look around.'

'What convinced you to say yes?'

Charlie glanced at Zennor and then away. 'Saying yes felt like the right decision.'

'Well, it looks fantastic so far,' Jennifer confirmed.

'Just wait. I've planted so many bulbs and . . .'

Zennor listened to Charlie talk enthusiastically about the estate she loved so much. Her mother seemed as charmed by him as she was herself. 'And in summer,' Charlie finished, 'you won't recognise it.'

'Yes . . .' Jennifer said wistfully. 'Summer seems a long way away.'

'It'll be here before you know it.'

'And the parkland will need mowing again,' Michael said gleefully.

'That's my job now,' Merry said possessively. 'Bloody good fun going up and down in that sit-on mower.'

'It *is* great fun. That's why we can share that job. Good investment, that mower. One of my best.'

Zennor wondered how her parents could have completely lost their grip on the estate's finances but thought an eleven-thousand-pound sit-on tractor-mower was a solid investment.

'Weren't there sheep on the estate at one point, keeping the grass trim?' Charlie asked.

'Yes, there were. I'd love to work with a farmer again to keep a flock here.'

The conversation drifted on loudly and happily over dinner, crackers were pulled and plates were cleared, Zennor's Christmas pudding was served and she watched Charlie close his eyes and say 'Mmmm' as he ate the first mouthful. The effect was too much for her and she nearly knocked her water glass over as she reached for it.

'Why is this so good?' he enthused. 'Why is this so . . . soft? What do you *do* to this?'

'She'll never tell you,' Merry declared from across the table. 'It's the one secret she says she'll take to her grave.'

Charlie gave her a dubious look. 'Really?'

Zennor nodded. 'Really.'

'What's the time limit for each go?' Charlie asked as he and Zennor settled on the sofas in the sitting room, ready for charades. Zennor's parents took an armchair each, and Lamorna and Zach were on the other sofa. Merry sat cross-legged on the floor and declared he would float between teams depending on who was winning.

'You get one minute per go,' Lamorna trilled, loving rules.

'That's not long,' Charlie said.

'Want to go first?' Michael offered.

'Alright.' Charlie took a card from the suggestion pack and read it. 'Oh, easy.'

Zennor sat up expectantly.

Charlie stood up, and when the timer had started, made the universal sign for a video camera.

'Um, film,' Zennor said, and following Charlie's hand gestures said, 'Two words. Oh . . . one word.'

'No, that's two words and then first word.'

'Right. Yes,' Zennor said.

'No talking, Charlie!' Lamorna cried.

'Lamorna gets very competitive,' Zennor muttered.

Charlie stomped around like a dinosaur, making Zennor smother her mouth with her hand as she snort-laughed her way through his performance.

'Dinosaur . . . dinosaur something,' she said.

'Time's up!' Lamorna cried.

'Oh, come on, Zennor, it's *Jurassic Park,*' Merry cried.

'It is,' Charlie said, sitting back down next to her.

'Sorry . . .' Zennor said. 'I'm really bad at this.'

'You really *are*, aren't you?'

'Hey,' she drawled, 'I can't be good at everything.'

'That's true,' he said quietly. 'That Christmas pudding redeems you, so we can lose at charades.'

We. Zennor leaned in closer to Charlie and said quietly, 'The Christmas pudding is Nigella's.'

He turned and looked at her, a stunned smile on his face. 'And you've been passing it off as your own for how long?'

'Oh, years. But everything else you've eaten is my own. I promise. Nigella was the first cook I watched on TV when I was a kid. What can I say? The woman knows what she's doing with a Christmas pud.'

'Do I have to take this to *my* grave too?' His wide smile made her laugh.

'Afraid so. It's our shared dirty little secret now. Don't tell Merry.'

'Don't tell Merry what?' Her brother's ears pricked up.

'That I am going off to make everyone coffee and am sacrificing my place in the game,' Zennor said, getting up and heading towards the kitchen. 'Back in a mo.'

She was half tempted to go into the orangery so she could use the tearoom's powerful coffee machine, but instead settled on the filter machine in the family's kitchen for ease. She just couldn't be bothered to clean the big coffee machine out today. Zennor waited in the kitchen while the aged filter machine dripped into the pot slowly and the comfortingly deep, warm smell of coffee filled the room. A shame she couldn't drink the good stuff. She flicked the kettle on to make herself a decaf, glanced at her crossed-off food timings in her notebook, and then pulled the page out and threw it away. That was *that* all done for another year. How quickly time passed, how quickly her world had changed. What would next year bring? A baby. Everything was changing.

Zennor leafed through her notes on Grace, feeling that she knew her so well now, even without having met her. It was such a strange feeling. Part of her wondered what had happened to Daisy. Had Daisy ever found out the man she'd thought was her father might *not* have been? Did any of the boxes upstairs hold the answer to *that* particular question? She didn't know enough about Daisy to feel the connection to her. That story would be there for someone else to discover. It was Grace, her counterpart in this very kitchen, who had drawn Zennor into her story, into her life, her departure from this house, her rise to greatness. She smiled. Grace had gone from downstairs to upstairs, had lost her love and then found it again with Laurie after it had looked so utterly hopeless.

Charlie appeared at the door. 'I thought you might like a hand.'

'Thanks. It's a bit of a wait, though. The machine takes *quite* a while. How's charades going?'

'Lamorna and Merry are having a . . . discussion, shall we say. About time limits. So I've snuck out.'

'Wise.' She laughed. 'The kitchen is always the best place to be.'

'I remember you told me something similar, the first time I met you. That this was your happiest place.'

'It's still true. Everything good happens in the kitchen.'

'I'll try to remember that.'

Zennor wondered if he was readying himself to say something but was stalling for time. She wanted so much to tell him about her situation, how it had all changed again, but an awkward silence settled between them now as she too stalled for time, not knowing how to start, not knowing what even saying it would bring.

'What's that?' Charlie asked, pointing at the tatty, faded cookery book on the kitchen table.

'Eliza Acton. One of the original Victorian cookery writers. I used some of her recipes to recreate the Christmas menu plan for the dinner table display. And I might have had a little help with the goose today too.'

'Help?' he prompted as he gently turned the delicate, wafer-thin pages teeming with tiny print. 'Another secret I need to take to my grave?' he joked.

Zennor laughed. 'Eliza recommends flouring the top of the goose to get it to brown toward the end of cooking.'

'Does it work?'

'Seems to.'

'It was delicious,' Charlie said as he continued turning the pages back. 'Today was the first time I've ever had goose.'

'And what did you think?'

'Sort of like duck . . . ? Or beef? Maybe? But milder? Does that make sense?'

'It does. I still think I prefer turkey, though.'

'Your turkey was the best I've ever had. Honestly. Buttery. Soft. Moreish.'

'Thanks.'

'Did Nigella have a helping hand there too?' He looked up from the book with a knowing grin.

'Shh.' She laughed. 'Don't say it too loud.'

Charlie's eyes returned to the nearly see-through pages of the cookery book. He was definitely stalling. Until this month, Zennor hadn't looked fully through the book since she'd found it as a child. But this cookbook had been the first book she'd read that spoke to her; it had set her on her path to her career, she realised now.

Charlie frowned as he reached one of the front pages and he looked up sharply. 'Zennor, I take it you've seen this?'

She moved over to him and followed his gaze to where tiny, soft, thin, slanted pencil strokes in the top right-hand corner said, *G.P., 1865.*

Zennor inhaled sharply in surprise. She stared at the page as if it couldn't be true, as if it couldn't be there. Grace. These were Grace's initials, surely. Who else's could they be? The date was when Grace had been here, in this very room. And her initials in this book of Zennor's . . . had been there all the time. The link to the past, *her* link to Grace, had been there the entire time within this book. She had never noticed it, too wrapped up in reading ingredients and method to wonder who had made the gentle annotations in the margins and amendments to cooking time or temperature that never failed her.

Grace Pascoe had owned this very book, had held this book, had written in this book. Her four-times-great-grandmother had left this book behind and it had been swallowed up into the jumble of books on the shelves. Zennor wondered who had found it and when, if anyone else had used this book over the years, how it had come to have a place in the family's library, put on a random shelf among other leather-bound volumes of similar colour, forgotten about . . . for how long? Until Zennor had found it as a child, squirrelled it away, taken it for her own. This book had changed the way Zennor saw her world. This book had started something magical for her, and it had been Grace's.

Charlie gave her the book and she held it in her hands, looking at the print, running her finger over the initials in disbelief and then in happiness. A bit of Grace had been here all along. Not just in the archives, but in this room. Grace had always been with her.

As Zennor looked up at him, she saw Charlie was looking at her as if he knew what she was thinking and her eyes connected with his. They didn't need to say it. They didn't need to say anything. Their expressions said it all. Charlie understood her. She understood him. He smiled and so did she, shaking her head a little in disbelief.

Behind them the coffee machine puttered and continued its endless, slow, rhythmic drip into the pot. Zennor stepped back, reluctantly pulling herself away from Charlie, the man she'd found herself falling for, the man she'd had to say goodbye to so he could be spared from her chosen messy single mother life. Life was so confusing. *Her* life was so confusing. And it was only going to get more confusing, more chaotic when her baby was born.

Charlie coughed, clearing his throat. 'Can I ask . . .'

Zennor waited, curious to know what he was going to say.

His position changed and he stood taller, bracing himself. 'I did wonder where Reece was today,' he asked softly. 'And if he would be here.'

'No,' Zennor replied gently. 'He wasn't . . . he wasn't coming today. He's with his parents.'

Charlie nodded. 'I wasn't sure if I should come or not because it might have been too odd, too hard.'

'Too hard?'

'For me, I mean. Too hard for me to see you and him together and then *I'm* here too . . . the man you dated for a bit. Awkward, you know. I panicked, today. I wondered if I should stay at home, just in case.'

Zennor stepped towards him again, an earnest expression on her face. 'No. I want you here. I'm pleased you came.'

He looked at the floor and she could tell he wanted to say something else.

'I'm happy for you, you know. The three of you. I'm pleased you and Reece got back together. It's how it should be. The baby will have both her parents. You'll be a family.'

'Yes,' she said somewhat vaguely. Zennor wasn't quite sure what to do now, what to say. She stepped away, turned towards the coffee machine, counting the coffee cups on to the tray. 'We are going to be a family,' she said, turning to him. 'A weird, strange one.'

Charlie's face took on a half-smile, half-frown.

Then Zennor wondered aloud. 'How did you know Reece and I got back together? Did someone tell you?'

He looked sheepish. 'I saw you both together at the Christmas Fayre, when I was with my mum in the gardens. I was coming over to say hello, but I stopped because I saw him kiss you. I saw you kiss him back and it just . . . I know we agreed we weren't going to see each other anymore but it still hurt. For incredibly selfish reasons, it hurt, because we said we'd be friends but we weren't even that, really. So I had no real right to be pissed off but I still was. And I realise saying all that makes this conversation even more awkward now. But I just wanted to tell you—'

'Charlie,' she cut in.

'I just want to say, that I'm happy for you. That's what I'm trying to say. So . . . there it is. I'm happy for you.'

'Thank you,' she said. 'That can't have been easy.'

He smiled a half-smile.

'I'm not with Reece,' she said with no preamble.

'Sorry?'

'We aren't together. I gave it a go. But we didn't even last a few weeks. It just didn't feel right. For him, or for me. We wanted it to be right. I was forcing it, for the baby. I think he was forcing it too. I wanted her to have two parents who loved each other and . . . we don't. And I'm not sure we would. Nothing about being together felt right. But everything about being apart did. Our baby will have two parents. Reece wants to be involved. But he'll live at his flat and I'll live here, and we're neither of us sure how it's going to work but it's going to work better apart than us trying to force something that isn't real.'

Charlie's face was pure confusion. 'You're not . . .'

Zennor shook her head. 'We're not.'

He was silent. So was she. She was pregnant, with Reece's child. She'd broken it off with Charlie the first moment she could in order to spare him. After all of that, what she was about to say was so wrong on so many levels. So why did it feel so right?

'I don't expect you to feel the way I feel,' she started.

'What do you feel?' He stepped forward automatically but whether or not he knew he'd done it she didn't know.

'I was falling in love with you,' she braved. 'I was . . . I was *really* falling in love with you. And . . . then . . .' She looked at her stomach. 'And I didn't want you to be any part of that.' She started crying. 'I'm going to have a baby and you can't . . . I can't expect you—'

'You can't expect me to love you? To want to be with you?'

'Yes,' she confessed.

'I fell in love with you too,' he said, and his expression changed to one of deep sadness. 'And *then* you told me I couldn't be with you, and you really thought I would stop? How can you expect me to just *stop* being in love with you. Like it's something I can turn on and off because you *told* me to.'

She looked at him through her tears. 'You love me?'

'Of course I love you.'

'Charlie . . .' she wailed hopelessly and tears filled her eyes. 'I love you too. But I don't want to drag you into this mess. My mess. I can't do that to you. I love you too much to do that to you. It's not fair.'

He rushed towards her and took her hands in his. There were tears in his own eyes. 'Zennor, for god's sake. Please stop pushing me away.'

'I don't know what else to do. It doesn't feel right, making you be a part of this. But it feels so wrong when I'm not with you.'

'It feels so wrong when I'm not with you too. It's torture.'

'I don't know what to do,' she said.

'You do. You do know what to do. You know what you want and so do I.'

'It's going to be awful, for you. It's going to be so hard.'

'Why is it going to be awful? Zen, are you and Reece going to get back together?'

'God, no. Absolutely not,' she said emphatically.

'Then it's already so much better than it was five minutes ago.'

She laughed and then she cried again. 'Why do I keep crying so much all the time?' she wailed.

He rubbed his own damp cheeks. 'I don't know but I'm doing it too now.'

'I love you,' she said. Everything she wanted was here, right now. Charlie, her baby. Her world had always been here at Trelenna and now, if he wanted it, Charlie's might be too.

'I love you,' he replied and he kissed her, changing her world again entirely for the better. His hands pulled her closer, enveloping her in his arms, in his love and his strength. Only happy thoughts swirled around her.

'Oh,' she said suddenly as she pulled back, touching her stomach. 'The baby's moving.'

'Can I feel?'

She nodded, taking his hand and putting it in the right place. She held her hand over his and it just reinforced how much she'd missed him, his touch, his love. 'Do you feel that?'

'I'm not sure.' He tilted his head towards hers, waiting to feel the baby kick. Nothing happened but she held his hand in place a little longer, enjoying the sensation of being able to be near him again, of having him touch her again. She laced her fingers through his and he smiled. 'Everything good does happen in the kitchen,' he said.

She laughed. 'See, I told you. Charlie?'

'Yes?'

'This is all going to be so weird.'

'Yes, it probably will be.'

'And anytime you want to leave you can.'

'You already pushed me away. And I came back. I love you. And I'm going to love this little person too, if you'll let me. A tiny version of you. I can't think of anything better.'

'I thought it was going to be the worst way to bring up a child,' Zennor confessed. 'But now I think she is going to be the luckiest little baby in the world with so many people to love her.'

'She's already lucky, with you as her mum. Zennor, I love you so much,' he repeated, almost as if he couldn't believe they were saying this to each other.

'I love you,' she whispered again as he moved in to kiss her, deep and meaningful, making up for lost months. She sighed with happiness as he pulled back and she already missed his kiss as he placed his hand back on her tummy again.

Zennor wondered how lucky she was that she'd failed to keep Charlie at arm's reach, failed to keep him out of her chaotic life because he'd wanted to be a part of it. She was beyond relieved that she had failed. She couldn't predict the future, couldn't predict what would happen when the baby arrived, but somehow, she knew it was all going to work out, the way it had done when she'd decided to try to save the house. She was carrying a future generation now. It was now more important than ever she carried on saving Trelenna House for all the Trelennas that came after her.

Zennor felt the baby's hand or a leg push her stomach this time, rather than a swift kick, exactly where Charlie's hand was resting.

Charlie's eyes widened with excitement. 'Oh, was that . . . ?'

'I think that's her saying hi to you.'

'Hi in there, little baby,' Charlie said, awed. He looked up at her. 'Does she have a name yet?'

'Yes.' Zennor smiled knowingly. 'I thought I might call her Grace.'

Epilogue

It was two in the morning when Merry finally climbed the stairs to bed. The day had brought him such happiness but such pain. This was his second Christmas without Amy and he didn't know how he was doing it, how he was coping, how he was even upright each day. Was it getting easier with every week, each day? The grief counsellor had said it would. But he had yet to feel it, his face permanently adopting a brave expression he didn't recognise.

Zennor had taken him at face value and hadn't mentioned Amy to him again. And the word had obviously spread around the family because no one else had mentioned her today either. But he regretted asking that of Zennor now. Sometimes he just wanted to hear someone *other* than himself say her name out loud, even if it hurt.

He slumped back on top of his bed, still fully clothed and feeling slightly worse for wear. Between the red wine Charlie had brought and all the champagne he'd manage to sink, alongside Zennor's triumph of a boozy Christmas pudding, it was a wonder he could move at all.

He'd watched Charlie and Zennor this evening and sensed something had changed between them, something they weren't sharing just yet. That look of love that passed between them when they were talking by the fire over coffee was unmistakable. He remembered he'd looked at Amy that way and she'd looked at him the same. It was real. It was forever. And then it had all been taken away.

As messy and as complicated as it all sounded with a baby arriving, Merry loved that his sister was on her way to finding some happiness. He just wanted it to last for her and not go the way it had for him.

Merry had had his great love with Amy. It was Zennor's turn to know what real love felt like. And soon, he'd be an uncle and Trelenna House would be a riot of noise and colour again when for the last two years his life had been so . . . grey. Perhaps Zennor was giving them all a gift they didn't know they needed by bringing new life into the world, into this house.

He folded his arms behind his head. The light was still on above the bed and he stared into the bulb mindlessly. He had no intention of turning it off, no intention of sinking into darkness, literally or figuratively. Each sleepless night was the same now. His own thoughts haunting him. He couldn't fight them off, couldn't fall asleep until pure exhaustion took over. He knew tonight would be no different, only he couldn't face another documentary. He'd worked his way through most of them, if not all, and was pretty sure he was currently in the middle of something he'd watched last month. They merged into one. He usually took nothing in, just let his mind and body fall asleep to sounds that weren't his own thoughts. He hated that Zennor clearly suspected why he spent his nights staring mindlessly at his screen, hated that she'd called him on it, hated her suggestion that something else might take his mind from his thoughts.

His gaze drifted to the boxes he'd thrown on top of his wardrobe, Zennor's words hanging over him that they might give him ideas for books he no longer felt able to write. He was so far away from sleep he could wear his mind out sorting through his family history or he could lie awake all night.

Reluctantly he opted for the former and swung his legs round, standing up. Still cursing Zennor for putting this thought into his head, Merry went over to the wardrobe, reached up and pulled the first box down, settled back against his pillows, took out the first pile of documents and started to read.

ACKNOWLEDGEMENTS

The most heartfelt thanks to superstars Victoria Pepe and Victoria Oundjian for your editing excellence. I'm so lucky to have the both of you on this journey with me, telling me some of the things I already know and lots of things I don't! There's a reason authors need editors. Thanks for steering me in the best of directions. Victoria Pepe, thanks for believing in the series so wholeheartedly and making it fly from the get-go. Thanks to Melissa Hyder for gentle and also forensic copy-editing and to Nicole Wagner and all the team at Lake Union for doing all the behind-the-scenes things I don't see but which get this series into readers' hands.

Thanks to the best agents in the business, Becky Ritchie and Oli Munson, for all you do, and to the rights team, Alexandra McNicoll, Jack Sargeant and Milla Hamm French, for finding such wonderful publishing homes across the globe for my writing. Thanks to Gosia Jezierska for sending the best emails ever.

My lovely husband Steve and my girls, Emily and Alice, are my everything and I'm lucky I get to do what I love around people that I love. Thanks for all the support from Mum, Dad, Luke, Cassie, Natalie, Sarah and Nicky.

To all my writing friends both near and far. We are a band of brothers and no one knows our pain like we do. Super thanks to all the Savvies, Chelmsford RNA, Rayleigh Writers, Write Club and authorly bestie Mandy Robotham.

And, finally, so many thanks to you, lovely reader, for buying a copy of this novel, or borrowing it from your library, and continuing your Trelenna House journey. There is more to come so stay tuned for the next book. The biggest thanks ever go to you if you're one of those amazing readers who preorders my novels. And if you leave reviews too, then my heart is full!

Keep in touch on social media or join my (very occasional) newsletter for lots of book club chat: http://lornacookauthor.substack.com.

And get in touch through my website as I love hearing from readers and will always reply and share your pics. I can't get enough of your photos reading my words in paperbacks, or on Kindles, or with headphones on as you blitz through an audiobook. It all spurs me on even faster when I'm at my desk, gunning it towards a deadline.

Lorna x

ABOUT THE AUTHOR

Lorna Cook is the author of bestselling historical novels including *The Dressmaker's Secret* – which was nominated for the Romantic Novelists' Association Best Historical Novel Award – The Girl from the Island and the Kindle Number 1 Bestseller *The Forgotten Village*, which was her debut novel, sitting in the Kindle Top 100 for four months. It sold over 150,000 copies and won the Romantic Novelists' Association Katie Fforde Debut Romantic Novel of the Year Award and the RNA Joan Hessayon Award for New Writers.

Lorna also writes contemporary love stories under the name Elle Cook.

Keep up with all her news and bookish chat at:
www.lornacookauthor.com
www.facebook.com/LornaCookWriter
www.instagram.com/lornacookauthor
TikTok: LornaCookAuthor

Follow the Author on Amazon

If you enjoyed this book, follow Lorna Cook on Amazon to be notified when the author releases a new book!
To do this, please follow these instructions:

Desktop:

1) Search for the author's name on Amazon or in the Amazon App.
2) Click on the author's name to arrive on their Amazon page.
3) Click the 'Follow' button.

Mobile and Tablet:

1) Search for the author's name on Amazon or in the Amazon App.
2) Click on one of the author's books.
3) Click on the author's name to arrive on their Amazon page.
4) Click the 'Follow' button.

Kindle eReader and Kindle App:

If you enjoyed this book on a Kindle eReader or in the Kindle App, you will find the author 'Follow' button after the last page.

PRAISE FOR LORNA COOK

'Entrancing, evocative and romantic.'

– *Woman's Weekly*

'Gathered me up and swept me away. A beautiful, uplifting tale of life's many types of love, and how the truest are never forgotten.'

– Amanda Geard

'A beautiful, emotional story of love and strength.'

– Liz Fenwick

'Lorna Cook has had me utterly captivated . . . I adored every sumptuous, atmospheric page, and can't recommend it highly enough.'

– Jenny Ashcroft

'Kept me turning the pages eagerly.'

– Tracy Rees

'Kept me guessing right up to the last poignant page, I found it difficult to put down and impossible to stop thinking about when I did.'

– Iona Grey

'I was so absorbed I read it in a single day.'

– Kate Riordan

'A beautiful, evocative story of love and coping with loss that kept me turning the pages late into the night. A triumph!'

– Rachel Burton

'Had me turning the pages late into the night . . . The historical detail is astounding.'

– Louise Douglas

'Evocative, gripping and emotional. I absolutely loved it.'

– Eleanor Ray

'An insightful, gripping and poignant depiction of the perils and heartbreak of war. A deftly told story of love, legacy and loss, this is one novel you won't want to miss.'

– Holly Miller